COMANCHERIA

Also by Reavis Z. Wortham

The Tucker Snow Thrillers:
Hard Country
Broken Truth

Texas Red River Mysteries:
The Rock Hole
Burrows
The Right Side of Wrong
Vengeance is Mine
Dark Places
Unraveled
Gold Dust
Laying Bones

The Sonny Hawke Thrillers:
Hawke's Prey
Hawke's War
Hawke's Target
Hawke's Fury

The Cap Whitlatch Westerns:
The Journey South
The Only Saloon in Town

Standalones:
The Texas Job

PRAISE FOR REAVIS Z. WORTHAM & *COMANCHERIA*

"Horror goes hat-in-hand with grisly tales of the Old West, and Reavis Z. Wortham knows how to keep you turning the pages and having bad dreams."

—C. J. BOX,
#1 *New York Times* Bestselling Author of *Battle Mountain*

---

*"...A brilliant and unique new take on the Western myth....
No pressure, Reavis, but I want more. Now. Bravo!"*

—JEFFERY DEAVER
#1 *New York Times* Bestselling Author of the Colter Shaw Novels,
the basis for CBS's Prime Time Show, *Tracker*

"I'll read anything Reavis Z. Wortham writes!"

—MARC CAMERON
#1 *New York Times* Bestselling Author of
the Arliss Cutter Novels

"... A hard ride into very dark territory to spin a yarn about a deeply weird west! Action-packed, twisty, and intensely enjoyable!"

—JONATHAN MABERRY
New York Times Bestselling Author of *NecroTek: Cold War*

"If legends are the bones of the West, then this book is its restless soul, that rare Western that honors its ghosts without taming them, beautiful and brutal, shot through with buckshot, mysticism and unvarnished dread."

—BARON BIRTCHER
Award-Winning Author of *Knife River*

"Wortham delivers yet again, showcasing his in-depth knowledge on Texas history and lore in Comancheria, *a chilling horror twist on the classic Western novel that will leave readers of both genres craving the next one."*

—TAYLOR MOORE
Author of *Cold Trail*

PRAISE FOR REAVIS Z. WORTHAM & *COMANCHERIA*

"Complete with curses, mystics, and non-stop action, Comancheria is a western gothic odyssey sure to please fans of Joe Lansdale or S. Craig Zahler."

—JAMES WADE

Two-Time Spur Award-Winning Author of *Narrow the Road*

"Dead or Alive, cursed Texas Ranger Buck Dallas is one relentless badass. Jump on board for a wild ride!"

—DP LYLE

Author of the Jake Longly & Cain/Harper Thriller Series
and Co-Creator of the Outliers Writing University

"A modern classic is born. Comancheria is that good! ...Reavis Z. Wortham has become the new master of Western Supernatural Suspense."

—W. MICHAEL GEAR & KATHLEEN O'NEAL GEAR

New York Times Bestselling Authors of *Buffalo Justice*

"There's a term we use in the west, the genuine article, and those words fit Reavis Z. Wortham to a Texas T."

—CRAIG JOHNSON

#1 *New York Times* Bestselling Author
of the Walt Longmire Mystery Series

"Clear a space on your bookshelves, folks, because the real deal has arrived."

—JOHN GILSTRAP

New York Times Bestselling Author
of *Threat Warning* and *Damage Control*

COMANCHERIA

REAVIS Z. WORTHAM

HAT CREEK

HAT CREEK

An Imprint of Roan & Weatherford Publishing Associates, LLC
Bentonville, Arkansas
www.roanweatherford.com

Library of Congress Cataloging-in-Publication Data
Names: Wortham, Reavis Z., author
Title: Comancheria/Reavis Z. Wortham | The Hollow Frontier #1
Description: First Edition | Bentonville: Hat Creek, 2025.
Identifiers: LCCN: 2025943383 | ISBN: 979-8-89299-062-2 (hardcover)
ISBN: 979-8-89299-063-9 (trade paperback) | ISBN: 979-8-89299-064-6 (eBook)
Subjects: BISAC: FICTION/Westerns/Weird West | FICTION/Horror |
FICTION/Westerns/General
LC record available at: https://lccn.loc.gov/2025943383

Hat Creek trade paperback edition April, 2026

Cover Design by Casey W. Cowan
Interior Design by Natalie Brianne
Editing by Anthony Wood & Rachel Santino

This one is for David Morrell, who sent me on this journey way back in 1972, when I beheld the wonder of his novel, First Blood.

AUTHOR'S NOTE

I'VE EXPLORED THE WEST IN both contemporary and traditional novels. This one came as a dream during the Covid lockdown, complete with plot, characters, dialogue, and virtually every detail included in this volume. All I had to do was write it down, as if I'd watched a movie. I hope you can see this strange world as I did that night.

ACKNOWLEDGEMENTS

I OFFER THANKS TO THOSE WHO influenced my writing through the books I absorbed as a youngster, and eventually an adult who is still addicted to books. Here's a posthumous thanks to those authors I never met, including Robert C. Ruark, Louis L'Amour, Max Brand, Clay Fischer, Donald Hamilton, and Donald E. Westlake, to name only a few.

ONE

MISS HATTIE LONG'S HUSBAND DIED on her fifty-fifth anniversary and she lost much of her mind not long after. Despite friends and family who desperately wanted to help, she walked away from their little Ohio farm and embarked a strange, ambling trip west.

Not alone, of course. She rode with a westbound wagon train for a while, unhappy with the chaos of traveling with so many people. Shouts, dogs, kids, arguments, all too frequent stops for water and meals, and especially the dust from big wheels and hooves, all drove her away to walk alone.

A week later, she joined an old mountain man named Cephus Black, heading back to Santa Fe after visiting family one last time in St. Louis. Old, bent, and knowing his days were numbered, he traveled alone and that suited her just fine.

He'd first encountered her on a wagon road southwest of Springfield, Missouri. Cephus followed Miss Hattie on his horse for more than half a day before the old woman with long gray hair tied back with a piece of faded ribbon realized he was behind her. She kept to the trail, arguing with unseen travelers, and repeatedly uttering the words *duty* and *baby*.

She occasionally stopped, gathering berries in the tail of her skirt that was frayed and dirty from dragging the ground and tough grass. A tattered patchwork quilt roll over one shoulder was her only possession. Her odd conversation ceased when she turned suddenly to find Cephus riding a jack and leading two other pack mules.

"You gonna shoot me with that there rifle?"

He glanced down at the Sharps rifle across his cantle. "I don't expect to."

"I'm a-travelin' to a place that's waiting for me. Where you going?"

"Well, I intend to take my time traveling back to Santa Fe, where I plan to die when I see fit. Until then I'll see new country and enjoy a world without them who irritate me and clutter the land."

"Uh, huh. Like I said, I'm going somewhere that's waitin' for me."

He nodded. "We probably all are."

She studied his mount. "You seem like you have some sense. Mules are smarter'n horses and won't lay down and die on you as fast. Some of 'em got more sense than their owners. What's your name?"

"Cephus Black. Folks call me Cephus."

"I'm Miss Hattie, Cephus Black. You may call me Miss Hattie. You're gonna go with me for a while, I reckon."

"What makes you say that?"

"The dreams. The dreams tell me lots, like you got some jerky in a sack on one of them mules. I could eat a bite. The dreams say I need to be at the water when they come."

"Who's coming, and what water?"

"Them that are headed east, and I'll know the water when I see it . . . 'cause it's a-callin' to me."

"You intend to walk all that way to wherever you're going?"

"Mostly, unless I need to ride from time to time on one of them mules."

Knowing she had no chance on the open plains, Cephus followed her lead for several weeks, listening to her stories about strange dreams that came each night and sometimes during the day.

Miss Hattie was entertaining at least, and for that, he taught her how to survive the spring blizzard that caught them in the mountains not far from Fort Smith. In the weeks that followed, they squatted at the edge of the Indian Territory as he taught her how to avoid starving to death by foraging in a land full of food, for them that know.

When they reached the Red River Fork of the Arkansas River, he expected her to proclaim that was where she was going, but instead, she insisted on crossing as soon as possible. They waded muddy streams, clearwater creeks, and stopped at cold springs rising from the ground sweet and fresh.

They reached the Cimarron River one hot afternoon and that's when she stopped still as a statue on the western bank, the tail of her dress soaked from the knees down. "You go on now, Cephus, and thanks for your help. The good Lord'll see you safe to Santa Fe, and I'ma gonna follow that there deer trail to where I'm going."

He studied the narrow trail splitting off from the wagon road winding through a grove of quaking cottonwood trees. "Miss Hattie, that trail leads southwest down into Comancheria. They're some tough customers, and don't tolerate white people in their country."

"I'm not afraid of Comanches, nor any other tribe. I'll be just fine, 'cause that's the way I'm pulled."

"Well, you go ahead on, then. I'll see you on the other side." Urging his jack on, the pack mules followed and, he headed west without looking back, to finish his own life in a place that was free of settlers and crowds.

Miss Hattie struck off down the deer trail afoot, feeling an almost magnetic pull drawing her deep into Comancheria, a huge expanse of land extending from the Rockies down through the Texas North Central Plains, all the way down to San Antonio.

Five days after they separated, she came upon a sweet-water spring in a wooded sanctuary in the High Plains. Seeming to boil up from deep in the ground, the powerful spring was shaded by willows and cottonwoods. It left the natural pool, forming a wide, shallow stream that meandered from the woods and crossed the rocky landscape.

The old woman found a crumbling sod house beside the chuckling stream and proclaimed it her own. This oasis on the plains provided a constant supply of water for a wide variety of hardwoods and wildlife that was drawn by its purity. She spent the first night watching deer and turkey come in at dusk for a drink. They were joined by quail, dove, and meadowlarks that came and went without fear.

"I do believe I done found the Garden of Eden." She spoke to no one but herself and the stars flickering overhead. She made her bed that first night beside a log outside of the one-room house and slept as still as the dead beneath her thin quilt.

She spent the next two days cleaning and repairing the house, though she owned nothing more than the quilt, a butcher knife, and a cap-and-ball pistol Cephus had pressed upon her during their travels.

"Sorry, mice, but y'all need to find somewhere else to live. This is my place now."

On the third, while looking for wild onions, she found the remains of the person she suspected lived there before her. Nothing more than scattered bones in the grass, she couldn't tell if he died from violence or natural causes. She buried the remains and decided she liked the open prairie around her refuge, capped by a bowl of blue during the day and lit by billions of stars at night.

ON THE MORNING OF THE FOURTH DAY, she ducked under the sagging, sloped lintel above the door and stepped outside the soddy to find a band of painted Comanche sitting on their horses. Face full of fury, one angry, arrogant young man swung down and approached, shouting in a language she didn't understand. When Hattie simply stood there with the pistol hidden in the folds of her long skirt, two other warriors dismounted and joined his aggressive posture.

"I don't understand a thing y'all are saying. I know you don't want me here, but here I am and this is where I'll stay." She flicked a hand to dismiss them. "Get gone and go bother somebody else."

Though they apparently didn't understand the words, the warriors felt her dismissive sentiment. Another young man dismounted and postured in front of the old white woman who simply watched without expression.

Tension mounted for several minutes until the first enraged warrior yanked a knife from his belt. He shouted and slashed the air between them. When she refused to back away, or even show fear, he lunged forward and thrust the razor-sharp blade at her, then wagged it in her face.

He apparently saw a change in her eyes and with the knife still raised between them, turned to laugh back at the men in a semicircle behind him.

She'd had enough. Raising the .36-caliber revolver, Miss Hattie thumb-cocked the hammer and pulled the trigger. The ball struck the warrior's knife edge and split. The force of the bullet knocked the weapon backward in his hand and the long blade penetrated the man's chest, just below the ribcage, killing him instantly.

The two halves of the bullet continued past his body. One hit the dismounted warrior in his bare stomach. Shouting, he fell, holding the small, ragged hole with one bloody hand and pointed at her with the other.

The other chunk of soft lead caught the warrior on her right in the cheek, tearing through his jaw and splitting the tissue so wide his white teeth were exposed. He staggered back, then fell under his own horse who almost stomped him into a greasy spot before the others could react and get the surprised mount under control.

Stunned by the events, the remainder of the band looked to their leader who sat bolt upright, shocked at what he'd just seen. Eyes wide, he glanced around at the three men on the ground, then back to Hattie. Fear filled his face, and he spread both arms, speaking loudly in their language. The others nodded, and pulled their horses back a couple of feet, as if that short distance provided more safety from the witch woman who could shoot three men with one bullet.

When he was finished, they loaded the wounded and dead, walking their horses slowly away to prove they weren't truly panicked, but looking back over their shoulders in what she realized was barely restrained terror.

Miss Hattie woke up the next morning to find a dozen lances buried around her soddy and the spring. It took her a while to figure out that she was staked inside the rough circle almost a hundred yards in diameter, or the Comanche were staked *out*.

After that, war parties and traveling bands of Comanche passed the crumbling house from time to time, shouting at her in anger, but staying beyond the lances and avoiding the watering hole that was once theirs.

Protected by spirits neither the Comanche nor Hattie Long understood, she waited beside the spring that had drawn her from Ohio. In a dream one night, a prairie rattler crawled up to her while she was planting squash and told her that she had to stay right where she was.

The snake said she was there for a reason, and to be patient, because the reason would be revealed someday.

A YEAR LATER, TWO BUFFALO HUNTERS STOPPED by to water their horses and were surprised to find rumors they'd heard while trading with Indians to the west that the place was inhabited by an old white witch woman were true.

Smoke rose from the soddy's rock chimney as they rode in, calling from a distance lest someone inside mistake them for Comanche and open fire. At her invitation, they stayed for the night and told her the spring had been a traditional watering place for Indians on their raids as long as anyone could remember.

The Comanche were angry that she was there, but no one could touch her because she'd cast a spell around the area and they could no longer drink. Their leaders said she was a witch woman, and it was a dangerous place for the People, which is what the Comanche called themselves.

They also brought more news about how Hattie had impacted the Comanche nation. The man who'd been wounded in the mouth by the bullet half was named Tahayti, their rising holy man. The chunk of lead damaged nerves in his neck before coming to rest somewhere inside his skull. Adding to the injury, the horse's hooves caused even more damage to Tahayti's brain, eventually causing his left side to wither and twist.

Seeing he was going to live, the Comanche changed his name to

Twisted Root, who lost a wife and daughter soon after to cavalry soldiers, leaving him with only one grown son. Twisted Root was an apt name because his abnormal mind warped into one goal, the slaughter of any white man and woman he encountered.

The hide hunters helped Miss Hattie shore the soddy back up, installing a new, stronger ridgepole to hold up the roof. They spent considerable time rebuilding the structure until it was in no danger of collapsing on the old woman, and left a month later, promising to bring back several pounds of buffalo tongue.

She never saw them again, assuming the friendly men had been slaughtered by Indians. So she lived there alone, tending her little garden, talking to herself and the occasional passerby who was lucky, or tough enough, to traverse Indian country all alone.

One morning she woke up and realized that every morning for the past few weeks, something different hurt. She was losing her wind, and the stamina she once had was depleting at an alarming rate. Holding the one cup of chicory coffee she allowed herself each day, she stepped outside her house to see a coyote loping past, a limp rabbit dangling from its jaws.

No matter what was happening inside her magic circle of lances, life went on.

But she was still concerned. "I wish that the reason I'm here in the first place would hurry up and come like the snake said. I'm runnin' out of time."

TWO

A GENTLE BREEZE BRUSHED THE OCEAN of buffalo grass at the top of a slight ridge in the North Central Plains where two young Texas Rangers reined up to study a line of tall cottonwood trees fringing a small creek below. The hot sun directly overhead beat down on the prairie, baking the two lawmen in unusual heat.

To the west, dark thunderheads rose thousands of feet into the air. It was the third day they'd built, only to collapse in on themselves when the cap of heat over most of the plains refused to budge. Once, massive herds of bison grazed across the ocean of grass that evolved to rely on urine and droppings of the grazing beasts that took days to pass. Now, the great southern herd was fragmented, but still big enough to attract buffalo hunters.

Captain Buck Dallas tilted his felt hat back and wiped sweat from his forehead. He was born in Nacogdoches, the oldest town in Texas. Brown hair curled over his collar. Ice-blue eyes and the deep dimples chiseled in his cheeks usually sent the ladies to fanning.

One particularly fetching Southern woman who spotted him standing in front of a saloon in Austin told her close friend in a soft Southern drawl, "Why, when I saw him and those eyes, I had to press my pearls."

Buck reset his hat. "Let's get out of this heat for a little bit. These horses could use some rest."

"That's the smartest thing you've said all day." Captain Lane Newsome attracted female attention not from good looks, but his pleasant nature and a personal foundation of right and wrong that was as solid as bedrock. Born not far from Buck's family farm, he could have been a farmer, rancher, or sheriff. Instead, his sense of adventure led him to become a Ranger when he was barely twenty years of age.

He took a sip of water from the canteen looped onto his saddle horn and wiped his sagebrush-colored mustache. Now a veteran of the plains, he was always eager to see what lay across the next horizon. Lane pushed up in the stirrups and swiveled to scan the empty, rolling country around them. An unseen covey of bobwhite quail called, likely scattered by a coyote or bobcat.

"I say a lot of smart things." Buck Dallas wasn't much on giving up on an argument.

"You say a lot of things you *think* is smart." Lane shook his head. Experienced law officers and Indian fighters, they were on the trail of a young white child taken by a band of Quahadi Comanche led by a homicidal, *puha*, or medicine man named Twisted Root, who was unnaturally gnarled by an old injury.

"I read a lot. I know more'n you." Applying slight pressure with his heels, Buck urged his roan toward the skinny, winding band of green fringing a glistening stream down below. The horse didn't need much encouragement to head for the shade and water they all needed.

"There you go again. I read, too, and I know quite a bit myself. You might have book smarts, and you're a fine Ranger when it comes to outlaws and bandits, and maybe women, except for that harlot over in Natchitoches who I will admit was particularly comely, but sometimes I question your common sense when it comes to little things, especially about Louisiana women."

"Like what?"

Humor pulled at the corners of Lane's mouth. He purely enjoyed ribbing Buck. "Like the time when we was nineteen and you killed that big buck down in South Texas. I told you it was too heavy to carry on your shoulders, but you were so hardheaded you didn't listen. Remember what happened?"

"I do."

"When a man asks such a question, he usually expects a full answer."

Lips tight, Buck stared straight ahead. "You didn't ask for a whole explanation. Besides, you know as well as I do what happened."

"Say it, then."

Buck frowned, reluctant to answer in order to avoid old embarrassments. Such events always aggravated him because once a traveling preacher standing under an arbor shelter said he was destined for great things that would forever change the course of history.

When he became a Ranger, Buck figured he'd bring law and order to a savage land, but there were times when he questioned that was all he was supposed to do. Maybe he was meant to do something else. No matter, he always tried to ride off from anything that didn't offer to further his destiny.

"All right I'll say it for you. You were trying to prove something to that gal in Goliad who thought you hung the moon. You wanted to show how strong you were, and instead of gutting the damned thing, you decided to carry it back to town on your shoulders. When that buck's muscles finally relaxed, he wet all down your neck." Lane laughed loud and long. "Lordy, did that deer piss stink!"

Uncomfortable with the conversation, Buck changed the subject. "Well, I was young and foolish, but right now we're running low on supplies. I doubt we have more'n three days' worth of food right now." Buck shook his head in dismay. He loved to eat, though no matter how much the slender man consumed, his weight never changed. "I reckon that'll get us to Adobe Walls."

Lane sighed. "I hate buffalo camps. Come to think of it, I dislike hide hunters too. The last time we were there the whole blamed place was full of fleas and flies." He scratched a phantom itch on the back of his neck.

"We can rest, though, and it'll be safe with all those big guns around." Buck twisted to look back over his shoulder.

Traveling through Comancheria was always tense. Neither man ever let down their guard for even a minute because the Comanche were the fiercest warriors in the world. In fact, Mexico urged Stephen

F. Austin to settle in Texas to act as a buffer between the Comanche nation and themselves.

"It'll stink to high heaven too." Lane shivered, despite the heat. "I'll allow we'll leave with a crop of those blamed fleas or bed bugs."

"No, we won't."

"How do you know that?"

"I've already thought about it." Buck waved a hand as if the rough town was right in front of them. "We'll camp well outside of town."

The horses smelled the water ahead, on the other side of the rise. Ears forward, they could barely contain their eagerness to get a long, cool drink. Their pace ate up the distance.

Buck bit the inside of his lip, thinking. "Maybe somebody there'll have some information on that little girl."

"Her name's River Dawes. You always call her a little girl. Why don't you use her name?"

"'Cause I'd rather think of her without a name, in case something happens. I'm not like you. I don't get all balled up inside calling her by name as if I knew her."

Lane adjusted himself in the saddle with a familiar creak of leather that neither of them noticed. He was ready to get off for a while and maybe take a nap. He'd been almost dozing in the saddle ten minutes earlier, a dangerous thing to do in Comanche country. "I just might strip down nekkid as a jaybird and have me a bath when we get down there, if there's a deep hole in that creek."

Buck sighed. "That'll be about the time Quanah Parker and his boys'll come by and I'll have to fight 'em alongside a nekkid man. I don't favor that idea one little bit neither."

The horses stopped when the ground in front of them sheared off in a twenty-foot drop. Lane's gray gelding snorted and shook his head. Had they been running their mounts, or even loping, they might have gone off the sudden drop, but instead, the horses paused, uncomfortable with the drop-off.

Thousands of years of erosion cut a wide swath through the countryside, like the creases of worry already forming along Lane's brow.

The wide creek bottom extended for a mile on their side of the life-giving stream and continued on into the same distance beyond.

"Damn! That was close." Buck pulled the reins, backing the roan away from the edge. He pointed. "I see a game trail. I think we can pick our way down over there."

A wet thud cut him off and Buck grunted and hunched forward over the saddle horn. A moment later, a gunshot behind them echoed over the prairie.

Lane twisted in the saddle to find a band of more than a dozen Comanche warriors charging through the waving grass. Without thought, the Colt came to his right hand from the holster on his offside.

Though it was too far, he fired a shot, hoping to slow them down. A second slug slapped the pommel of Buck's saddle and whined away a heartbeat before the sound reached them. "I'm hit." Buck's voice was a gasp. "Bad."

"Hang on!" A feeling of dread washed over Lane at the sight of a large exit hole in the front left pocket on Buck's shirt. A hole that large meant only one thing. Someone had a big Sharps behind them, a buffalo gun, and he knew how to use it.

Leaning forward, Lane snatched the reins out of Buck's hands and spurred his horse forward. The only option was to pitch off the sharp drop. The gray resisted for a moment, but feeling Buck's roan gathering himself, they both plunged over the edge.

If given their heads, and without interference from their riders, horses can maneuver down steep inclines if necessary, and they did. The Rangers did nothing but drop their heels forward in the stirrups and lean back in their knee-high boots for balance against the violent, dusty drop. Small avalanches of dirt under the horses' hooves met and widened, following them to the bottom of the decline, releasing a cloud of dust that rose behind them.

Briefly out of sight from the war party, Lane concentrated on keeping himself and Buck in their saddles. "We'll take a stand in the trees! Hang on!"

Centuries of erosion had washed the grass away, providing a solid base for the horses' hooves that dug in once they reached level ground. Spurring their mounts, they raced toward the cover of the cottonwoods that were their only chance of survival in such wide-open country.

Seconds later, Buck grunted again, deep and wet. A second hole appeared in his shoulder. The wound was just as nasty as the first, and a glimpse of white, splintered bone protruding from the sun-faded material of his shirt told the story of a destroyed joint. Thunder from the shot reached them a heartbeat later.

"Son of a bitch! Somebody back there can *shoot!*" Lane let go of Buck's reins and grabbed a handful of material to hold the gravely wounded Ranger in the saddle. "Grab that horn!"

The well-fed horses pounded side by side as a fourth heavy slug whistled past Lane's head. He glanced back in terror to see a huge man with a red beard and hair down to his shoulders kneeling on one knee at the edge of the drop, steadying the rifle on a pair of shooting sticks. He had to have been a white buffalo hunter who'd joined the Comanche. Known as Comancheros, the men who turned against their own people were as dangerous as rattlesnakes.

The distance increased, and Lane threw one last fearful glance over his shoulder. Relief flooded through him. They were going to make it. What he *didn't* see was the muzzle flash as he turned forward. The Sharps belched lead again, and this time Buck's horse took the big slug, going down in a complete forward roll and smashing the Ranger's limp body face first onto the hard earth before landing on top of him.

Lane instinctively reined up, but the moment he looked down to see his partner's blank eyes full of dirt, he knew sure as shooting that Buck was gone. No one could survive two .50-caliber slugs and then have a thousand-pound horse fall directly on him. Still, Lane couldn't leave his partner for the Indians. Experience had shown they mutilated most of the men they killed.

Yanking his Henry rifle from the saddle scabbard, he threw it to his shoulder. Quickly estimating the distance, he thumbed up the rear dovetail sight, tilted the rifle's muzzle high, and squeezed the trigger. Shooting at an elevated target at such a distance was tricky business, but he had to try. The round fell short of the redheaded murderer, striking the top edge of the ridge just below the man's feet and careening off a rock, but the Comanchero fell back in surprise.

Kicking free of his horse in an instant, Lane wrapped the reins around his left hand and dropped to the ground. He grabbed Buck under his shoulders and gave a heave, but the roan lay across both legs, anchoring the limp body as solid as a mountain. There was no way to get the lifeless body out from under the carcass, and staying there was suicide. The only cover on the open ground would be the horses, and it would be easy for the Comanche to surround him.

A ragged volley of gunfire echoed from the ridge, and slugs tore into the ground far short, kicking up dirt and tufts of grass. He looked up to see a line of heavily armed warriors, shouting and shooting in glee. Like water over the lip of a pitcher, they poured over the edge in a steady stream, following the game trail that lead to the bottom.

"Sorry, pard." Lane swung back into the saddle and spurred his horse toward the shelter of ancient cottonwoods that had been there for a hundred years or more. A different grass, tall and green, grew in the shade of the old trees, softening the edges of the narrow creek and making it feel cooler than it actually was.

He'd already seen that the greenbelt stretched for miles each way, and he had an idea. Instead of fighting it out there on the banks against maybe fifteen times his number, he'd cross the creek and keep going, using the timber for cover. It wasn't that far to Adobe Walls, and he figured he could make it with a little luck if he pushed hard.

As his horse waded a shallow crossing, more gunshots echoed through the trees, slugs clipping limbs and leaves. The guns fell silent once he was on the other side, and several minutes later, they crackled again behind him, this time at a murderous level.

As Lane let the gray have his head, he wondered if they were celebrating the death of his friend, or if some unknown group had encountered the war party. Cavalry? Buffalo hunters? A family of dumb farmers looking for somewhere to set down roots. It didn't matter, for the first time in his life, terror had hold of him and Lane fled for his life.

Miles later, he reined the lathered horse up and paused to listen. Lungs billowing, the gray hung his head and sucked in great drafts of air. There was no sign of the Comanche, and he figured they'd changed their minds about killing him.

Maybe they *had* run into a much larger bunch of fighters who ran them off.

Still under the cover of the cottonwoods, he dismounted and rifle in hand, he walked the horse to cool him down. A still pool of water sheltered by a downed cottonwood gave him the opportunity and enough cover to stop for a moment.

The gray lowered his head to drink and the adrenaline wore off. With it gone, a wave of grief and guilt washed over Lane. His knees buckled and the man who seldom showed any kind of sorrow dropped to the ground, sobbing. He'd killed men before, many men shot down because they were either Indians on the warpath, or outlaws he and Buck ventilated, or hung with a short rope from a tall tree.

In most cases, they'd intended to kill him or Buck first, or had murdered others. He'd also lost friends and men in his company, but losing someone closer than his real brother who lived in a fine house back East was almost overwhelming.

Neither he nor Buck had ever left a fellow Ranger or friend behind. They'd promised each other several times in the past that if one was killed, the other would take him back to Austin for burial. But they would in no circumstance leave the other behind if they were wounded. Everyone knew what the Comanche or Apache did to captives.

But he'd left his friend's body to save himself. Something he never imagined he'd do. Alone and unseen, grief rose like a spring and Lane wept into his hands until he could get hold of himself. Finally wiping his face with the scarf around his neck, he regained control as the gray finished drinking.

Wrung out both physically and emotionally, he finally dipped his kerchief into the water and spent the next half hour wiping the horse with water to cool him down even more.

Despite his desire to get moving, he allowed the gray to graze on the soft green grass growing under the willow and cottonwoods. Soon the horse perked up and it was time to move on. Remounting, Lane came to a decision, though it might be folly. Allowing the horse to walk at his own pace, he reined him back toward where they were ambushed.

Twilight gathered, and long shadows fell over the land. He kicked the gray into an easy lope that ate up the miles in a wide loop back to where he came from. Eventually it was the sun's turn to lose the last battle of the day. Darkness smothered the land, and he continued at a slower pace. When it was full dark, stars appeared. There was no hurry, the gray took his time and they traveled quietly, Lane watching for any telltale flicker of a fire that would signal danger.

He was going back to bury his friend.

When Lane felt he was near the place where Buck had fallen, he looked upward for the sharp cut in the land. It took nearly an hour before he arrived at the steep ridge defined by the stars. Exhausted, he dismounted, sat with his back against the crumbling bank, and laid the Henry across his lap.

As was his habit, he wrapped the reins loosely around his fingers so he'd feel it if the horse tried to pull free. A huge bubble of pain rose in his chest, and he held back his sorrow before finally dozing off.

THREE

VIBRATION IN THE GROUND CUT through Buck Dallas's consciousness. Coming awake, he couldn't see for the dirt in his eyes. It took a few seconds to realize he was still alive, but barely. War whoops reached his ringing ears, and a great pressure on his legs caused as much pain as the bullet wounds in his chest and shoulder.

Wiping the dirt from his face, he blinked his eyes clear. The blue sky came into view, along with waving grass and the band of green willows and cottonwoods nearby. Groaning from the pain, he realized the roan was laying on both legs. Hoping Lane could keep the war party at bay until he could get out from under the heavy carcass, Buck gritted his teeth and set about pulling free.

A bullet slapped the dead horse. Groaning with pain, he raised up on his good elbow to glance over the huge body to find the charging Comanche were getting close. Another slug puffed the dirt to his right and whined off toward the creek.

Weak as a kitten, he felt for his Henry rifle and was relieved to find the horse had fallen so the worn leather scabbard was on top. He yanked it free and using only his good arm, jacked the lever to chamber a shell, and fired from the awkward angle. The whooping warriors split their charge at the return fire, giving him a moment.

In weakening desperation, he twisted sideways and felt his right leg move. Encouraged, he pulled as hard as possible, losing his tall boot, but freeing that leg in the process. More rounds buzzed overhead. More than a few impacted the horse's corpse.

Near dead and half crushed, Buck folded himself closer to the horse's still body and laid the rifle across the saddle. The war party was over a hundred yards away. The renegade buffalo hunter was nowhere to be seen. Worried that he might be trying to work his way around to shoot from the side, Buck scanned the surrounding area and found nothing.

Seeing his head peek over the horse, the Comanche set up a howl and fired again. Buck was astounded by how well armed they were and laid the blame on the Comanchero. Seconds later, the warriors organized themselves and charged. At that same moment the big buffalo rifle boomed again. The slug tore through the horse and buried itself in the ground behind the Ranger.

He dropped flat, cursing himself for the action, because by the time he hit the ground, the slug was underground. The party split when they reached the horse, but one excited brave came straight ahead and leaped completely over the Ranger, who instinctively raised the Henry's muzzle and pulled the trigger.

The round caught the horse directly in the heart and it collapsed the moment both forefeet landed. It cut a flip, throwing the warrior headfirst onto the ground. Rolling onto his knees in agony, the Comanche could do little to fight. Buck drew his pistol and fired twice at a distance of only fifteen feet, killing the man.

Twisting back around and gasping in pain, he looked for Lane, hoping he was somewhere close, but his partner was nowhere to be seen. A pang of heartache rose. His friend was down, likely dead close by.

The will to survive kicked in, and despite his grievous wounds, Buck somehow summoned enough strength to fight back a little longer. Dust from the horses' hooves filled the air, giving him some cover. An odd flicker of color caught his attention. It was a redheaded Comanchero, the man with the big rifle. He'd reined up and with the Sharps to his shoulder, the man was drawing a bead on the desperate Ranger.

Buck shucked another round into the Henry, laid the rifle barrel across the horse, and shot the man's mount, the biggest target he had. It went down in a flurry of kicking legs, throwing the Comanchero to the ground. When the stunned man rose, Buck shot him in the chest. Howls of fury rose from the attackers.

Horses are big targets, easier to hit than a slender man. Instead of trying to aim at the Comanche from his awkward position, he simply shot every horse he could see. Buck levered round after round into the Henry, dropping one after another, while bullets and arrows sought his own flesh.

An arrow caught him in the thigh bringing another jolt of sharp pain. A whooping warrior rushed in from the side, bow in one hand and a butcher knife in the other. Buck shot him at ten yards, and then the rifle was empty.

Knowing the superiority of numbers, they closed in from all sides as Buck drew the pistol. A tall warrior rose from the ground only a few yards away. The twin booms from a shotgun roared and a dozen large pellets impacted the desperate Ranger at the same time. One penetrated his hand and the pistol fell.

Down to the sheath knife on his belt, the dying Ranger drew the razor-sharp weapon at the same time someone landed on his chest. A war club caught him in the side of the head and neck. Something inside snapped and all feeling in the Ranger's body went away as blackness closed in like the jaws of a vise. The echoes of victorious war whoops followed him down.

FOUR

THE MORNING SUN WAS MAKING its way into a deep blue sky when Lane Newsome jerked awake. He'd fallen asleep with his back against the steep slope to make sure no one could get behind him during the night. From his position, the golden shortgrass prairie stretched unbroken to the tree-lined creek.

It took a moment to realize where he was, and memories flooded back. He marveled at the distance he and Buck crossed the previous day in such a short time, all the while in the sights of an expert marksman firing a Sharps .50 rifle. Experienced buffalo hunters regularly took 500-yard shots with stunning accuracy, and the fact that the man was making hits on a running target told Lane he'd been extremely lucky to survive.

Now empty of all emotion, he rose and stomped the stiffness out of his legs. Ears pricked, the horse watched. He gathered up the reins. "Let's go bury our friend."

He slid the Henry into the scabbard and swung into the saddle, heading away from the rising yellow of the ball that would soon become unbearably hot. To his surprise, the horse seemed to know where they were going. It followed the bottom of the ridge until they came to deep scuff marks that showed where he and Buck had dropped over the edge in their race for the creek.

It was easy to follow their trail through the grass and a mass of black wings circling in the distance. Before long, he saw the body of an Indian pony, already stiff-legged in the hot morning air. Then another. And a third. He allowed the gray to walk at his own pace, dreading what he might find and worrying about what had happened while he ran like a scalded cat.

Who'd killed them? What kind of battle had occurred? A familiar nagging in the back of his mind said this was Buck's work because he always shot at the horses in a battle, preferring to put their antagonists on foot where it was easier to deal with them.

But when he neared the spot where Buck fell, it was much worse than he could have imagined. The first body was the redheaded buffalo hunter. He lay sprawled on his back, a hole in his heart and flies buzzing around the wound. His mount lay nearby.

"Good God." Lane frowned at the sight. "This is Buck's work." He choked back a cry and turned away.

Buck always said shoot the horse, and then when the man was on the ground, he was an easier target and less likely to get much closer.

The clash he heard wasn't between cavalry, or buffalo hunters, or a strong trading party heading for Santa Fe. It was his friend, fighting for his life . . . alone.

Not far away was Buck's roan. Not yet wanting to see his friend's body that would likely be close by, Lane drifted across the battlefield. His elevated position in the saddle revealed another body. This time it was a painted Comanche warrior. Bare from the waist up, except for a porcupine quill breastplate and paint, he lay face down.

A huge exit wound between his shoulder blades finally confirmed what Lane didn't want to believe. *My God. I left him alive.*

Only one person consistently shot like that, at what he called the pump room. Buck always took dead aim at an assailant's chest, the biggest target on the human body, and he seldom missed.

"Aw, hell. *Buck.*" He urged the horse closer.

Still keeping watch, just in case the Comanche were still nearby, Lane reined toward another horse and a Comanche, center shot.

Why didn't they take their dead? Indians seldom left their people behind. Something's wrong.

Lane circled the corpses, studying the tracks and torn up ground that told a story he couldn't untangle. He still hadn't approached Buck's roan. He needed to understand what had happened here first. What happened in the fight?

"Why the hell are these braves still here? Comanches don't do this." Lane didn't realize he was talking out loud, repeating himself. "Did he kill 'em all without any help?"

He was dead! I saw his eyes, half lidded and full of dirt. He was limp as a dishrag when I tried to pick him up.

His face reddened with embarrassment and pain. He'd run from a fight that took his friend's life. He wondered what the buffalo hunters, or cavalrymen, would say when he finally rode into Adobe Walls and they recognized him as a coward by the expression on his face.

By the time he was through counting bodies, there were nine Comanche corpses swelling in the morning sun.

He'd never made such a mistake in all his years as a Ranger, and he attributed it to the fog of thinking he'd lost his best friend. From force of habit, he examined the trees not far away, then surveyed the surrounding area to be sure he was alone.

Sensing his intent, the gray walked slowly toward the roan's body. The horse stopped and pawed the ground, snorting. When Lane finally found the courage to look, Buck's body wasn't there. A wide stain of drying blood and spent brass marked the spot where the Ranger fell. His rifle was gone. His pistol, too, along with the cartridges in the belt.

Good God. Buck woke up and managed to get himself out from under that horse and take on those Comancheros all by himself. I always knew he was much of a man, but now I'm sure of it.

Another wave of guilt washed over Lane like a flash flood. He dismounted and picked up the leather gun belt. The Henry was nowhere to be found.

Lane stepped back into the saddle, squeezed his legs, and the gray stud walked toward the trees. They circled the scene once again, trying to piece together a story that made sense. Standing in the stirrups to gain a little more advantage, he watched a tiny wisp of smoke rising from inside the cottonwoods.

The Indians were gone, and he was confident they weren't hiding and waiting for him. The closer he came to the burned-out fire, the more he realized something terrible had occurred there that night after he fled.

No, worse than terrible. It was something horrible. Unthinkable.

Shocked into numbness, Lane reined up at the sight of Buck's scalped and mutilated body that was staked out on the ground, bound by rawhide thongs. They'd kindled a fire on his lower abdomen and it burned through, down deep inside.

A hoarse sob broke the stillness. "Oh, no." Unaware he was speaking out loud, Lane tried to understand what he was seeing. He fought the contents of his stomach that rose, heavy and burning. "He was alive. Comanches don't stake out *dead* white people."

He dismounted and knelt next to Buck's body. His once-handsome face that caused the girls to swoon was slack and gray, slitted eyes dull and unseeing. The rawhide thongs around the Ranger's wrists had cut deeply into the flesh. His shirt was gone. Crusty blood from deep knife wounds slashed across his chest and arms trailed down his sides into a coagulated pool on the dry ground.

So I was right. He did make a fight of it, and there weren't no others here shooting at them Indians like I first thought. He wasn't dead when I left him. They only stake out folks so they can torture them to death, and I left him to it.

His stomach again rolled at the sight and it was all he could do not to make public once again the stale cornbread dodgers he'd consumed for breakfast.

Horror upon horror piled up that morning. Something was in Buck's mouth, and Lane was terrified of what it could be. Indians were known to cut off a man's privates and stick them down their throat, the most dishonorable thing they could do to the corpse, but Buck's lower body was so horribly burned he couldn't tell if he'd been mutilated.

What looked like a small feather protruded from between his lips. Lane reached out to touch Buck's ashen cheek and jumped to his feet when he felt not cold flesh, but slight warmth. He gasped, then sobbed again. He waved his hand over his friend's abdomen, feeling faint heat from the dying coals.

Buck hadn't been dead long enough to cool. The Comanche had been here only minutes before he rode in.

Lane snatched his Walker Colt from the cross-draw holster at his waist, crouching and cocking the weapon at the same time. He scanned the area, waiting for the first war whoop, or the whizzing of an incoming arrow, but there was nothing but a loud blue jay and the distant gobble of a turkey brought to him on a slight breeze.

He looked toward the stud that cropped at the grass, completely unconcerned, telling Lane they were alone and in no danger. Holstering the pistol, he knelt again beside Buck's corpse.

Tears rolled down his cheeks. "I'm so sorry, buddy. I surely thought you'd gone under, or I wouldn't have left you."

Using the tips of his fingers and hating what he had to do, Lane gently spread Buck's lips apart. At the same time, he pushed down on the man's chin to open his mouth. The corpse was still so fresh that rigor mortis hadn't yet set in, and the jaw opened easily.

Choking down a gag, he withdrew a dried blue bird, the feathers still bright as when it was alive. He studied the talisman, knowing immediately that some Comanche had worn it as a great medicine in his long hair. They'd do that. One warrior he'd heard about was known to wear an entire hawk woven in his hair so that it hung behind his right ear. The preserved shell of that huge bird must have been light, nothing more than skin, head, feet, and feathers.

There was something else. With shaking fingers, Lane reached in and withdrew a small piece of fresh, bright red flesh. It wasn't anything like he'd ever seen before, and he studied it for a long while. Red, tough, and oddly shaped, he couldn't figure out what it was.

His tongue? Now used to touching his partner's face, Lane pulled his chin down to find Buck's tongue was still there. He turned the piece of flesh in his hand and was stunned to see the stump of a large artery on the back side. It was part of a human heart. But though Buck's upper torso was slashed more than a dozen times, the knife hadn't invaded his chest cavity. Wondering at the significance of the flesh and bird, Lane cut the bindings with a pocketknife and crossed Buck's arms over his chest.

"You rest easy there, hoss. It's all over now. I'll go dig you a grave in the shade right there."

He rose and wiped his eyes, once again scanning the horizon to find nothing but waving grass and the bodies scattered across the prairie that were already swelling in the summer sun. By the next day, the stench would be overwhelming.

By midafternoon, a cloud of buzzards circled the bodies scattered across the prairie and Buck rested under three feet of soil. The ground was so hard Lane could dig no farther with the big knife he carried under his belt, but he collected enough good-size rocks to cover the fresh grave and keep the animals from tugging his friend back up to the surface.

Using two cottonwood branches for a crude cross, he tied them with a rawhide thong from his saddlebags.

"*Adios,* my good buddy."

Finding nothing else but a gathering swarm of flies, he finally turned west toward Adobe Walls, again following the line of trees growing in the moist soil along the small stream. Though it was up in the day, a darkness weighed upon him as he rode away from Buck's grave and soon Lane's head was too heavy to hold upright. Exhaustion and grief overwhelmed him, though he was all cried out. He stopped after only a few miles.

One place is good as another.

Making a cold camp in the thickest part of the trees, Lane hobbled his horse and studied Buck's empty gun belt hanging over the saddle horn. For no reason other than it was something to do, he opened his saddlebag and dug down to the bottom where he kept a spare pistol and shells.

The second well-oiled Colt was already loaded, but he thumbed shells into the belt's loops, just in case he needed an extra gun in a hurry now that Buck was gone. It was dangerous territory, and running into another band of fighters was a distinct possibility. There were also outlaws, both white and black, that lived in the no-man's-land, robbing travelers of whatever took their fancy. They usually left their victim's bodies for the scavengers.

Finished, he used the saddle as his pillow and leaned back, hoping he could rest. He was asleep as soon as he closed his eyes.

FIVE

THE SUN WAS UP, AND birds flitted and chirped in the trees overhead. It was another bright, warm day on the North Central Plains, or as many people called the high prairie owned by the Comanche—Comancheria. Beyond the tree-lined creek where Lane made a cold camp, there was nothing but shortgrass prairie stretching from horizon to horizon under a vaulted blue sky.

One man camping alone in such hostile country was a dangerous thing, and Lane slept fitfully through the night until he finally sank into unconsciousness at the same time the sky began to gray in the east.

"You gonna lay there all day?"

The familiar voice cut through Lane's sleep, and he roused up to answer with his eyes still closed. "I was sleeping pretty good, and that's a fact. Yesterday was hard . . ."

His breath caught. He must have been dreaming, but Buck's voice sounded as real as it did when he was still alive. Naw, he was hearing things, maybe the tail end of a dream that wouldn't let go. Lane opened his eyes, expecting to see nothing but big cottonwood leaves against the sky.

Instead, it was Buck grinning at him.

Shocked, Lane whirled on his butt and raised up on the balls of his feet to see his old friend standing astride his saddle with that big, dopey grin of his.

Lane ground both fists into his eyes. "It was a nightmare. Oh, my

God, what a dream." Mouth dust dry, he tried to swallow and couldn't. He tried again and gagged on spit thick and white as cotton.

When he lowered his hands, Buck was still standing there but dressed in Lane's spare shirt and pants. He hadn't yet buttoned the shirt, and his chest and abdomen were smooth and unmarred, except by pale, ropy skin outlining the horrible wounds that killed him.

It hadn't been a nightmare. What happened was as real as the unconcerned deer drinking from the creek behind Buck. The blisters on Lane's hands were proof that he'd buried his friend the day before.

Buck's finger fluttered one at a time on the buttons, hiding the healed wounds from sight. "What's wrong with you, Lane?"

Some apparition was speaking to him. Lane slapped the side of his head, hoping to jar something loose. "What's wrong with *me*? What kind of question is *that*?"

"I think it's a damned good question. Why'd you bury me like I was dead, and then ride off like you had good sense? You had no call to do that. And you buried me without a stitch on. There I was after the sun come up, nekkid as a jaybird with nothing but my hat and boots, and I had to reach in and dig *them* out as well. What'n hell come over you, son?"

Lane backed away from the apparition, lowering his hand onto the butt of his pistol.

Maybe I'm dreaming. Wait, I dreamed the whole thing. That's it. The whole thing was a nightmare.

"Lordy mercy. What a nightmare." He worked up enough spit to wet his lips. "It's good to see you standing here. I had a bad dream that you had holes in your chest, and your stomach was burned through and you were sliced up like a squirrel ready for the frying pan."

Buck's hat was a little dirtier, and his boots were filthy. Dirt flaked from his hair and landed on the shoulders of Lane's clean shirt like dandruff. "Look, I don't know what's got into you, but what happened yesterday? My mind's a blank after we had breakfast yesterday."

Unable to explain, Lane stared, his mouth opening and closing like a fish.

Buck coughed, and a single blue feather flew out of his mouth and drifted slowly to the ground. "I'd expect to be hungry, but you know, I'm not." He walked around Lane to pick up the gun belt hanging over the saddle horn. "This ain't *my* pistol. It's your spare. I don't understand any of this."

He buckled it over his hips and waited for an answer. When it didn't come, he tried again, rambling like a man addled by a hard blow to the head. "None of this makes any sense, you riding off, and camping way out here." He narrowed his eyes, apparently confused. "And why'd you have my gun belt?" His voice took on a lighter pitched accusatory tone. "Hey! Why'd you *bury* me?"

Lane blinked at the little blue feather at their feet and the realization that it was real yanked Lane back into reality. "Stop yakking for a second. I need to think."

It wasn't a dream. Buck's corpse was standing right in front of him, someplace he shouldn't be, because he ought to be resting still and quiet under the dirt where a good corpse ought to.

Shaking like a leaf, Lane drew his Colt and thumbed back the hammer. "Get your hand away from that pistol and stop talking for a minute." He gasped at what he said. "You're *talking*."

"A-course I'm talking, but not good." He ran out of air and had to take a deep breath. "That's how people communicate." Buck paused, frowning. He bit his lip in thought, just as he always did. "Except for that horny toad that told me which way you went." He paused. "You know, that did seem a little strange, now that I think of it."

"Horny toad? Buck you're talking and not making one damn bit of sense . . . and y'ain't *supposed* to be doing either one of them things. You died day before yesterday. You get what I'm saying? You're *dead*."

"Ain't neither." Buck's brow furrowed. "How could I be standing here talking to you if I was a corpse? Anyhow, something's coming back to me, but I can't get a handle on it. It's like a little bird is flittering around in my head, you know? No, wait. Maybe the fluttering's in my chest." Buck placed the palm of his hand over his heart. "Christ almighty, I could use a good drink of whiskey."

I need a bottle, Lane thought.

"Buck. You can't *be* here." Lane looked down at the pistol in his hand and as if moving in a dream. "I buried you yesterday and spoke some words. You ought not be standing out here in the open like this. You need to go back and lay down like you're supposed to. Furthermore and all that, I'll thank you to take that gun belt off and put it back where it was for a minute."

His partner tilted his head, apparently trying to figure out what was happening.

"Your neck was broke." Lane demonstrated with a finger. "You can't turn your head like that."

Buck reached up and rubbed the back of his neck. "Well, it kinda grinds in there this morning like there's gravel between the bones. I must have slept wrong or something." He staggered for a moment and leaned his weight on the rough bark of a nearby tree. "I've been walking since sunup through Comanche country, following your tracks. And without nary a gun too." He lowered his head, thinking. "And the next thing I remember, I'm putting on your shirt and pants. That don't make no sense. Everything is kinda jumbled up in my head right now, but when I get here, you pull a *gun* on me? What's *wrong* with *you*?"

Retreating another step, Lane held out his free hand. He had to say it again for validation, to hear the words come out of his mouth. "Buck, you're dead. I buried you."

"No I *ain't*. I'm standing right here." The argumentative corpse rested his hand on the butt of the pistol. "You need to put that hogleg down and explain what's going on."

"Don't you raise that hand!"

"Quit pointin' that *gun* at me, Lane!" Buck's hand closed on the butt of his pistol, thumb on the hammer to cock it once the revolver was free of the leather.

It was halfway out of the holster when Lane, who was wound tight as a pocket watch, pulled the trigger on his revolver. The sharp blast cracked loud in the creek bottom and Buck's right ear flicked as if someone had thumped it. Shocked that his partner'd fired, Buck could do nothing more than reach a hand up to feel the hole through the cartilage. "You *shot* me!"

"I told you to lower that gun. I don't know what's going on around here, but I don't aim to be shot by no walking corpse."

"I'm not *dead*, you damned fool! And why'n hell would I shoot *you?*"

Lane's mouth fell open in awe as he watched Buck's ear slowly fill in with flesh and skin to cover the hole. He pointed with his free hand. "It's gone."

"What's gone? My ear?" Buck reached up to see if it'd really been shot off.

"That hole I just shot in it." He spoke softly, with wonder in his voice. "The damned thing's done filled in and healed up while I watched."

"No it ain't." Buck reached up to find his ear intact. "What'n hell?" He examined those fingers for blood.

Finding none, he took his hat off to scratch his head, and instead of running fingers through thick brown hair, he found nothing but a wide strip of bare skull. The discovery startled him, and forgetting they'd been squared off with one another, Buck walked over to the slow-moving creek and leaned over to check his reflection.

"Goddlemighty! Lane, them Indians lifted my hair!"

"That's the least they did to you." He could see understanding in Buck's eyes, or as much as either of them could grasp in that moment.

The recently deceased Ranger's hand moved back and forth between the wound that was still there, and the ear that was inexplicably healed. "I reckon the scalpin' took better'n that slug you put through my ear. For some reason it didn't heal up, if what you say is the truth." He paused. "Now what I just said don't make no difference neither. I'm not talking right."

"You understand you're saying things that ain't possible." Lane kept the pistol more or less aimed at his old friend. "Good lord, you standing there talking ain't possible neither." He rubbed his face with one hand. "This must be a dream. That's it. I'm having a dream."

Buck looked down at his dusty boots as Lane's eyes rolled in his head, and he fell flat on his back.

SIX

THEY RODE ACROSS THE TEXAS prairie that hot afternoon, with Buck secure in the saddle and Lane riding double behind him. Buck had insisted on being in front because as he said, he'd been sick.

Emerging from the creek bottom, they found the rolling countryside empty of everything except an occasional hawk, birds, and jackrabbits kicked into flight by their passing.

"It's coming back to me in little bits and pieces, but it's all hazy, like in a dream."

Lane couldn't help himself. He'd been thinking about it for the last two miles and finally could stand it no more. He leaned forward to sniff the back of Buck's dirty neck. "You don't *smell* like a corpse. I'd figured you'd stink to high heaven by this time."

"Well, you don't smell so good yourself. You need a bath."

"You can still smell?"

"Not really, but I think I can taste the dust on my lips, that by the way, you put there last night." He tapped his front teeth together. "There's still grit in my teeth."

"I had to bury you. Dead, you know?"

"You keep saying that."

"It's the truth."

"I don't know what the truth is anymore."

"Well, hell. Neither do I."

The truth was neither of them knew what to think when Lane woke up after his fainting spell. Buck was by the creek, staring at the water flowing past. Each time he reached his hand down to dip below the surface to cup a drink of water, it recoiled and refused to let him touch it. No matter where he moved it, there was a big hole of nothing around his fingers.

When he grew frustrated and jumped in, the water parted like Moses' staff had driven itself into the creek bed, leaving Buck standing up to his neck in a hole in the water, with nothing but mud underfoot.

Thinking about what he'd witnessed, Lane twisted around to watch their back trail. There was nothing but waving grass and buzzards riding the thermals above what he figured was the place where Buck died. "None of this makes any sense."

"Look. If I was dead, do you think I'd be sitting up here talking to you? Look at this horse. He'd be sunfishing all over this country if things weren't right. I just can't remember what happened yesterday is all, or where my own horse could be."

"It's laying back there under them buzzards, and I've noticed you haven't had food or a sip of water since we made that dry camp two *days* ago, and that was before you died."

"I haven't?"

"Nope, not a bite and . . . you're not thinking about biting *me* or nothing, are you?"

"Why would you say that? Why would I want to *bite* you?"

"Well, I don't know, but I had a crazy dream last night about dead people wanting to eat me."

"That's the most ridiculous thing I've ever heard."

"Like I said. It was a dream, and I'm probably dreaming right now because we still haven't reached Adobe Walls and it feels like we've been riding double for days."

"Nah, it's just up ahead." Buck pointed to the west. "Likely just over that rise."

"I can't wait to get there. I need a bottle of whiskey and a bath. And I need to work all this out away from you. Maybe with a woman."

Buck barked a laugh. "Well, you won't be finding one of them at the Walls, not the kind you're looking for."

They rode in silence for a while until Lane had to ask another question. "Hey, speaking of women. Since you're dead, I was wondering . . . can you get your, uh, your thing up . . . you know what I'm trying to say. Does your business still work?"

"Dammit! I'm not dea—" Buck straightened with concern. "I haven't thought of that." He looked down, pondering. "I haven't peed, have I?"

"I haven't been watching all that close, but I don't reckon." Riding right up against him, Lane felt Buck twitch and flex his hips. "What are you doing now?"

"Seeing if I can work anything up."

"Well, stop it. I'm right here behind you and I don't want to think about any of that right now."

"You asked me." Buck sounded petulant.

"Now I'm *un*-asking you. I don't know why I brought it up in the first place, except that I was hoping there might be a harlot or two once we get there."

"You'll have to knock the ticks off of 'em first."

They rode for several minutes before another realization hit Lane after he drew a long, deep breath. In an uncomfortably strange situation, he reached around and rested his hand on Buck's chest. "Buck, you're not breathing." He gasped. "And your heart ain't beating either."

With that declaration, Buck inhaled. "I am too."

"No, you weren't. Your chest didn't move until you needed to talk."

The gray plodded on for several minutes while Buck considered the implications of Lane's announcement. "I reckon you may be right. I need air to push the words out, but breathing don't come natural anymore."

Lane thought about it. "Breathing is something we don't think about, but once it gets in your head, you're aware of it. Now I'm feeling like I have to think every breath in and out."

Buck held a hand against his own chest. "I don't inhale until I need to say something. I'm like a damned squeeze-box."

Lane shivered, and they rode on in silence.

The sun settled toward the golden grass that lined out the bare horizon. Behind them, their shadows stretched toward the east. But when Lane glanced back once again, the long shadow cast across the grass contained only one figure sitting far too back on the horse.

With a gasp, Lane shoved off and hit the ground with both feet. He backed away as Buck reined their mount around and frowned. "What'n *hell* are you doing now?"

"I have another question."

"Fire away."

"Why don't you cast a shadow?"

Buck reined the horse sideways to the sun that barely hung above the grass. The only shadow they could see was that of the horse bearing an empty saddle. He studied the situation as he always had when he didn't understand something. "I *have* to. I'm right here, as real as this horse."

Lane watched and waited as the sun settled lower, melting into the horizon.

When Buck swung his leg over the saddle and dismounted, the horse still stood as if ground tied, his being the only shadow that dimmed as they watched. He kicked the grass as if trying to scare his recalcitrant shadow back to the surface where it belonged.

Suddenly wary again, Lane circled around his partner until the sun was at his back, remembering the blue bird stuffed in there, and the little feather that floated out that morning. "Open your mouth."

"How come?"

"Because I'm still trying to make sense of all this. Just open your mouth for me and stick out your tongue."

Frowning, Buck opened his mouth and the last rays of sunlight filled the void. He stuck his tongue as far out as possible, and something else moved in there.

Horrified, Lane gasped. "You're a damned devil now." He drew fast as lightning and pulled the trigger. He was never a great shot, and that was evidenced when the big .45 slug missed Buck completely. Lane thumb-cocked and fired again, this time blowing off Buck's right index finger when he went for his own gun.

Buck dropped the revolver and grabbed his wounded hand. "Con-

found it, Lane! Dammit, that stings." He held up the damaged append-age, staring at the stump where his index finger used to be. "You done shot off my trigger finger! Why do you keep shooting off pieces of me all of a sudden?"

"I wasn't trying to shoot off any kind of digit or protrusion. I intended to kill you." Lane looked down at the pistol in his hand, as if wanting to blame it for his trouble. "I missed is all."

Forgetting he was absent a right trigger finger, Buck made a fist, intending to emphasize his anger by pointing in accusation. They gasped when the stump produced a skinny sprout that swelled like a carrot in the ground.

They were staring at the reconstructed digit when that last little piece of the sun melted into the grass and was gone. The instant the yellow vanished, Buck collapsed where he stood and was as dead as the still air around them.

SEVEN

TWISTED ROOT SQUATTED ACROSS A fire from Quanah Parker and Isa-tai, two Comanche warriors who every person in Texas had heard of and feared. They met in a shallow coulee, which was enough to break the stiff wind. Between the two war parties, their men numbered nearly two hundred, a terrifying army to all who lived and traveled the Llano Estacado or Staked Plain.

Quanah was the half-white son of Cynthia Ann Parker, child captive and grown wife of Peta Nocona, a Comanche war chief who terrorized Texans and Mexicans all the way down to Mexico City.

The warriors gathered nearby, some squatting, others standing. A south wind blew their long hair, creating waves that matched the rippling grass around them. A few of the younger warriors guarded the huge herd of horses grazing not too far away, and within sight of the men.

Two youngsters with Twisted Root's band watched the gathering from a distance as they kept an eye on their horses. Nine Toes and Shouts His Name were too young to be full warriors, but they'd proven themselves in other ways.

Always thinking and analyzing their situation, Nine Toes swept an arm across the camp. "We are many *Numunuh,* but my grandfather says the white men are as many as the stars in the night sky."

"We have lost a lot of warriors, but Isa-tai's visions will come true and we can push the white devils away." Shouts His Name crossed his arms, as if putting a period at the end of his statement.

"I don't think so. We have made peace with the Apache to the west. Maybe we can do the same with the *taibos*."

"They aren't peaceful."

"Not the ones we've seen, but I would like sons and daughters. I would like to die an old man in a lodge."

Shouts His Name studied his friend's face. "Are you afraid?"

"You know I am not. But our people have built our world for more summers than we can count. We should try and understand the white man, so we can defeat him in other ways."

"I understand them. They want our land. They kill our buffalo. They kill women and children. Now, we should kill them all, and with this many warriors, we will win."

"It is the way of the world. Our grandfathers took this land from the Apache and the Kiowa, but they took it from the Old People who were here first. Now the white men are trying to do the same. It is like the seasons. They come and go and someday the whites will be pushed out by another tribe."

Shouts His Name sighed. "I hope you're right."

"I am always right."

"I am right most of the time." Shouts His Name crossed his arms, a habit he'd picked up when he wanted to show strength.

"You weren't right about playing Push Him Back last year."

Nine Toes was named Runs Far before he and several of the other youngsters were playing Push Him Back. The game required two opponents to separate several feet and throw knives as close to their opponent's feet as possible, hoping to make them back or jump away from the blade that thumped into the ground.

He was playing with Rides a Strange Horse, who was good enough to throw his knife only a hair from the other's foot. But that day, he missed, and confident in the youngster's ability, Runs Far didn't flinch. The razor-sharp butcher knife hit the ground in a thud, cutting off the little toe on his right foot, and giving him a new name not long after.

"It isn't funny." Nine Toes gave Shouts His Name's shoulder a shove. "I walk different now."

"It was a good joke on you."

They both laughed, receiving a glare from some of the warriors gathered around the campfire. The boys quieted and listened. Shouts His Name was hoping to learn something that would help save his nation.

★ ★ ✭ ★ ★

AT THE FIRE, QUANAH SWEPT A HAND in the air. "Go with us. We're going to wipe out all the whites that are in our country. Isa-tai is a great holy man who says his magic can turn bullets."

Twisted Root studied the men around them. Quanah and Isa-tai had convinced the leaders of almost every tribe in the area to join them. He was surprised to see Penatekas, a usually peaceful branch of the Comanche nation, were there and painted for war. His own small band, reduced by the terrible fight against one lone Texas Ranger, were now all Comanche. It was annoying to him that Quanah now fancied himself a great chief and wouldn't quit talking.

"We have danced the Sun Dance, and now Kiowas, Cheyenne, and Arapaho have all joined us. See Yellow Horse there. He believes in Isa-tai's medicine. We will slaughter the white-eyes like they have slaughtered our buffalo, and their scalps will hang on our lances and in lodges."

Quanah threw back his shoulders and thumped his chest. "Every lodge will have scalps from this, even those of the old people who can't fight any longer. It will be a great victory for us all."

"I have to kill a witch, first, then a Mexican woman who dares to poison this land with her presence." Twisted Root pointed first to the east, then west. "Once that is done, my own medicine will be strong and we can all exterminate the *taibos* with you."

Isa-tai shook his large head. Broad face reddening with anger, he made a sign with his fingers. "My medicine is stronger than yours. I have belched up a wagon load of cartridges and flown beyond the sun to sleep next to the Great Spirit. Our People have seen this. It is true. Help us kill the hide hunters. After that, we can wipe out the Tonkawas who have allied against us and the *taibos* will see the power of the Comanche."

"That is a pleasant thought. I never did like Tonks, but that old woman is in our way. Many times I want to drink in that spring, but she has strong medicine too." Twisted Root pointed at his face, then his withered left arm. "She did this to me with her magic bullet that killed two others before resting in my head. Every now and then she awakens the bullet and it poisons me again."

Quanah pursed his lips, thinking. "I have heard that story. I would like to have some of her magic bullets. You and Isa-tai can blend your powers and that should be enough to block hers. We can go kill her after we are finished with the hide hunters."

Isa-tai calmed somewhat. "I will paint myself ochre. Your colors and mine will blind her. It is a good thought."

"But we will not go with you to the hide hunters camp." Twisted Root stood. "I feel it is time to find the traveling woman I have heard about. Go do your business. I will do mine."

"We will meet you at the Boiling Springs, then." Quanah also stood, forcing Isa-tai to do the same.

Twisted Root scowled. He didn't want to rise because his withered side stiffened after sitting for so long. But at the same time, the *puha* refused to look up to his competitor. He stood, willing himself not to grunt in pain and show weakness. "You will miss a great fight."

"There will be others." Quanah's eyes swept the band of fighters who accompanied Twisted Root. "You have enough warriors to do the job."

Twisted Root flicked his fingers. "My magic is great. I have more than what I need."

Without looking back, Quanah strode to his horse and leaped onto its back. His men followed.

The two bands separated without looking back.

EIGHT

IT WAS AFTER MIDNIGHT AND the moon was high when Lane finished burying his partner for the second time in twenty-four hours. This time he wasn't in as much of a hurry, and the digging was a little easier. Dropping one last rock on the still-damp earth, he reached into his saddlebag for a worn Bible bearing only the back half of the cover. Much of Genesis was gone, torn off somewhere in the past, but he opened the thin pages to the New Testament.

Squatting beside the fresh grave, he struck a match inside his hat to hide the flame and read John 5:24 aloud, finding a different meaning since the last time he'd read that passage over a fallen comrade down near the Canadian River. "Verily, verily, I say unto you, He that heareth my word, and believeth on Him that sent me, hath everlasting life, and shall not come into condemnation, but is passed from death to life." The howl of a distant wolf raised the hair on his arms as Lane considered those words. *Were you dead, or alive all day today? Maybe the words I said the first time weren't enough. I hope that passage works for us both.*

He studied on what had happened, wondering if he'd lost his mind and rode all this way with Buck's corpse hanging across his cantle. Maybe he had. That would explain the events of the day and why he was burying his friend so far from where he fell.

He dropped Buck's hat onto the rocks, as a marker.

Refusing to sleep beside a fresh grave on the open prairie, he swung into the saddle and rode a short distance from the same death he'd already left behind once before.

Buck had been right. Adobe Walls was just over the next soft ridge. Squatting in a wide, shallow bowl, the camp was nothing more than a scattering of melting mud and grass buildings suffering the persecutions of wind and rain. Scoured to the color of the landscape from which it grew, the camp was constructed of sod and adobe structures sitting silent in the darkness along a single street, if that's what one called the two paths leading from the plains to widen in front of the buildings that all faced the same direction in one strip.

Leading away on the other side of the settlement, the two-lane track again met its master in the Llano and gave up its enthusiasm to be a road when it narrowed to nothing more grand than a wide game trail.

There was enough silver moonlight to make out several empty wagons, an adobe corral, and a number of horses and mules both in the corral and hobbled nearby. The glow from a single small window was the only sign of habitation.

He knew better than to go riding into a dark buffalo hunter's camp in the middle of the night. Men like that tended to sleep with their fingers on their triggers and were apt to shoot the first thing that moved in the darkness, so he sat there for a while, studying the stars and surrounding ghostly landscape. His thoughts went to Buck and the odd circumstances he'd experienced within the past several hours.

Finally deciding that he wouldn't try to tell anyone about what had happened since the Comanche attack, he nodded, as if someone else made the suggestion. He'd simply explain to anyone who asked that his partner, Captain Buck Dallas of the Texas Rangers, had been killed by a particularly lucky band of Quahadi warriors.

It was the simple truth. No one would believe the rest.

Along about three in the morning, the sultry temperature robbed him of the sleep he desperately needed. Hobbling his horse, he unsaddled the gray. Leaning back on the saddle, he breathed in the sweet smell of fresh grass and ever-present horse sweat.

Pulling his hat over his eyes, Lane rested the Henry across his lap in its usual position and dozed in and out, dreaming about Buck's shirtless body staked out on the ground. Guilt for leaving him behind was a tidal wave of dark emotion that rose again and again in his mind. In one particularly vivid nightmare, he was standing over his friend with a knife in one hand and Buck's bloody scalp in the other and mumbling strange prayers in an unknown language.

The throbbing flush of sage hens startled Lane awake. The sun was up, already heating the air. Thinking the birds rose because Indians were putting the sneak on him from behind, Lane spun and cocked the rifle. He stopped with a sharp cry of horror.

Buck approached not thirty yards away, and he looked mad. He shouted across the distance and threw his hat at his old partner. "Why you keep *burying* me?"

Feeling that he should pull the trigger, Lane struggled to understand what he was seeing. Buck was even more filthy. Drying dirt crusted in his hair, clogged his ears, and clung to his eyebrows and clothes. Drying clumps crumbled off the shirt he'd borrowed from Lane the day before. Knocked out of shape, his hat looked as if it had been stuffed down a privy. Reaching where it had come to rest, Buck snatched it up and slapped it on his head, covering the white bone of his skull so Lane wouldn't have to look at it.

At a loss for an explanation, Lane lowered the rifle. For some reason, it seemed natural to engage the walking corpse in conversation. "Well, I thought you died for good again at sunset. You went limp and dropped to the ground. You weren't breathing, but hell, you didn't breathe all day long in the first place. I just figured that Death got lost somewhere along the way and finally caught up with you."

"I done told you I ain't dead, dammit! This time it wasn't like the first. I knew what was going on from the minute my knees buckled, but my eyes wouldn't work and I couldn't so much as move my tongue, but I *heard* you. I did. I heard my head slap the ground and you sniffling while you dug the hole. You were crying over me."

"No I wasn't. There was something in the air and it got to me a little bit and made my nose run."

"Liar." Buck finally grinned. "Well, I was trapped inside with nothing but my brain and ears working. While I was laying there under the ground, I remembered that damned deformed Comanch' putting a curse on me for killing his boy. He won't let me die, and I'm not to get any rest, so when I'm out, it's not asleep. I'm just paralyzed.

"If it happens again, *please* don't bury me, I can't hardly stand the feeling of dirt falling in my face. You don't know how aggravatin' it is to have to dig your way out of a grave every morning." He rubbed at one eye with a knuckle. "I still got dirt in my eyes."

Shaking his head, Lane rested the rifle across the crook of his arm. "This is the damndest thing I've ever seen."

Buck stopped and slapped dirt from his sleeve. "You ain't a-woofin'." Looking down, he unbuckled his gun belt. "Look at this. Dirt in my holster, and the belt loops. And where'n hell is my pistol?"

"It's mine, I just loaned it to you yesterday, it and them shells. It's in my saddlebags. It's too good a firearm to bury."

"You didn't mind burying *me*." Buck unbuckled the belt and shook dirt from it.

"What else was I gonna do, leave you for the wolves?"

"Maybe they'll leave me alone. But don't bury me no more."

"You're a corpse, or would be if you'd act decent and lay down like you're supposed to. And by the way, that's my only spare shirt you're wearing too. Now look at it. I had more time to think about it last night. I figured you wouldn't need it anymore, but I dislike the idea of wearing a shirt a dead man's walked around in all day."

"Well." Buck grunted and shook the gun belt again to dislodge the last of the dirt. He buckled it back on, then dug a pebble out of his ear. "I'm gonna want that pistol back. I don't walk right without that weight on one hip. And I need my knife too. Now, what happened last night? I remember talking to you and the next thing I know, I drop like a sack of taters and that's an odd sensation. What'd you see?"

"We were talking, just like now and then I shot you and you grew a finger back and then fell dead."

"Yeah, I remember that. When'd I drop?"

"Soon as the sun went down. Then I dug a hole for you, again, said some words, and rode on this way."

"I heard the words, though they were kinda muffled through five feet of dirt. This is gettin' to be a bad habit."

"One I don't like even a little bit." Lane knelt and opened the saddlebag. He withdrew the pistol and knife.

Buck dropped the spare handgun into the holster and slid the Bowie knife into its sheath. "I meant to ask you yesterday. Where's my rifle?"

"Indians took it after they killed you." He paused, thinking about what'd he'd just said. "*That* don't sound right."

"Oh, I figured you'd have it wrapped up there in your blanket." Buck's eyes narrowed. "You could have wrapped *me* in that. At least I wouldn't have dirt in my ears."

"Take off your hat."

"Huh? What for?"

"I want to get a good look at the top of your head."

Buck reached for his hat, paused as if considering the request, then took it off to reveal the horrendous wound that hadn't filled in. The skull was white in the morning sun, the edges of his scalp raw and damp.

"Well, that didn't grow back, but everything else closes up and heals." Satisfied by what he saw, Lane waved his hand. "Put it back. I don't think you want to let anyone else see your skull." He noticed that Buck's ear looked perfect, and his trigger finger was where it belonged. "Wonder why your scalp don't close up."

"Beats me."

"Does it hurt?"

Buck gingerly felt around the top of his head, then shivered and replaced the hat. "Naw, but it don't feel natural neither. It's a queersome feeling to touch your own skull plate. Come to think of it, I don't feel much of nothing anymore."

"Wait a minute." Lane had a thought. "Take your hat off again."

"What for? I just put it back on."

Lane flicked his fingers, and Buck removed it with a scowl. Lane came closer. "Lean forward."

"What for?"

"I need to see something." Buck obliged him by making a small bow and Lane reached out to gingerly rub both sides of his forehead near the hairline.

"What are you feeling for?"

"Horns."

Startled, Buck straightened and slapped the hat back on his head. "You think I'm the Devil, now?"

"Nope. No horns. Not even buds or buttons."

"I can't believe you'd think that of me . . ." Buck trailed off, noticing that Lane was looking past his shoulder. He whirled.

Mounted warriors appeared on the horizon with the rising sun at their backs. Behind them, the plains glowed in the light. Seeing the two Rangers and one horse, the painted warriors charged forward, their war hoops shrill and full of excitement.

"Comanches!" Buck shouted. "Here they come!"

Lane grabbed his horse's reins and yanked the Henry from its scabbard. The shouts and drumming hooves frightened the animal. Humping its back, the buckskin crow-hopped sideways, nearly knocking Lane down. Cursing, he dug his heels in.

Buck plucked the rifle from Lane's hand and knelt, resting his left elbow on a knee to steady his aim. It was hard to see, staring almost directly into the sun. He squeezed the trigger and the lead horse pitched forward, throwing the rider. The man landed hard, rolled, and staggered to his feet. Buck levered another round into the chamber and squeezed the trigger again. The bullet caught the warrior square in the chest, his trademark shot. The brave sprawled backward.

Seeing their friend fall, the others shouted louder and charged forward.

"Damn!" Using the horse for cover, Lane drew his pistol and waited until they got closer. Buck would shoot long. He'd fire when they got within range.

A bullet whistled between them. Another fell short, plowing into the ground and throwing up a spray of dirt. Lane finally fired, and a

Comanche dropped his rifle and grabbed a badly wounded shoulder. He turned his horse, colliding with another warrior's mount. The horse stumbled, and he swept to their right.

Shooting fast, Buck killed two more horses, leaving their riders to drop behind the animals for cover. A Comanche near the rear reined up suddenly and threw up one arm, waving with frantic energy. His other rested in his lap, flopping with a strange motion. He shouted at the others, apparently urging them to break off the charge and gather around him out of rifle shot.

Reluctant to give up the element of surprise, one muscular Quahadi with exceptionally long hair rode in a wide circle, shouting and gesturing in fury. Kicking his horse, he charged toward one of their men hiding behind his dying horse. When he came close, the Comanche rose, grabbed his arm, and swung up behind the brave, who rode back to the others.

Two more Comanche rushed forward and picked up stranded men the same way. A third loped up to a wounded warrior struggling to regain his feet, but when he stood, Buck put a round in the man's chest, leaving his would-be rescuer to retreat alone.

Lane stood. "That's Twisted Root waving his arm back there. He's their medicine man."

"How do you know that?" Buck squinted into the harsh sun and shucked another round into the rifle's chamber.

"Look how he rides. I heard his left side's dead. Some say it's from apoplexy. Others vow he was shot in the head and it paralyzed that side. Someone else told me he was kicked in the head by a mad stallion and crushed his skull. I don't know which to believe, though it's bad medicine all around, no matter how it happened."

Buck rose and squinted in their direction. Pulling his hat brim down low to shade his eyes, he finally nodded. "I know that son of a bitch."

"Of course you do. He's Twisted Root, like I said."

The band of warriors milled around the misshapen medicine man with a large head and broad face, their excited horses throwing their heads in agitation. They shouted, flailing their arms and gesturing toward the two Rangers who waited to see what would happen next.

"No. What I mean is, it was him did this to me."

Lane cut his eyes at Buck's profile. His face was a shade grayer than two days earlier. Unable to help himself, Lane leaned in a couple of inches and sniffed.

"Dammit. Stop *smelling* me. That's starting to get annoyin', and this ain't the time."

"Wasn't no more'n a sniff. I keep expecting you to smell ripe."

"I doubt that's gonna happen." Buck stared at the milling warriors.

"I can't wait to hear you explain that one."

"I remember everything now that I see that crazy old medicine man over there. I was shot, fading in and out while we rode to get away. Something slammed into my back like I was hit with a sledgehammer. My horse went out from under me and I rolled. I recall my head cracked against that hard ground, and I was laying there, knowing you were there beside me, but I couldn't move a muscle."

"I'm sorry I ran." Taking his eyes off the gathering of warriors who continued to argue, Lane scanned the ground around them, just in case an enterprising buck was creeping up on them through the grass. "Your eyes looked empty and they had dirt on 'em."

A sick feeling pinched his stomach from guilt.

"They mostly were. I was going, and there was still enough light in me to know you were hightailing it out of there. I came to and got my wits about me, and then the fight was on. Somehow, I pulled myself up behind my horse and went to work with my guns. Brother, let me tell you, it was something for a while and I was doing all right against them rascals until I felt somebody behind me. I tried to turn, but this old body was about give out and the next thing I knew I heard what sounded like a shotgun and everything went numb.

"I was laying there paralyzed, when that twisted up sorry excuse for a human being out there straddled my chest. He was mad, and hol-lering, but I had no idea what he said. I believe he was about to cut my throat when he saw there was still a spark or two left in my eyes and had me hauled over to those trees and staked out."

"I really don't want to hear the rest of that."

Still out of rifle range from both rifle and pistol fire, the Rangers watched as the war party mounted on fine horses shouted and gestured around Twisted Root. Better armed than Lane expected, they brandished a variety of rifles. Those that didn't have firearms carried lances adorned with feathers and fresh scalps, backed by heavy shields of thick buffalo hide painted with yellow, ochre, and vermilion.

A muscular, long-haired Comanche out front of the band rode back and forth as the others conferred behind him. Bright feathers and sparkling ornaments dangled from his hair. He waved a lance at the Rangers and pointed at himself.

Buck glanced over his shoulder to scan the grass behind them, then turned back to face the threat. "Anyway, they worked on me with knives for a lot longer than I can remember, but like I said, I couldn't feel a thing from the neck down. They figured it out pretty quick and had a grand old time carving on me like a Christmas goose."

Lane swallowed his rising stomach. "You can stop now."

"I will at the end. Anyway, the next thing I know, they drug a dead feller over and held him up so I could get a good look. I was fading in and out, but I figured they were going to make me pay for killing him."

"Look, they're thinking about backing off, I think." Lane refused to look at Buck as he talked. "But that big bastard with the long hair's starting to annoy me."

Buck kept going as if he hadn't heard. "And, brother, I paid. I think I died after a while, but that medicine man blew some kind of powder in my face and reached out and caught my soul as it rose up through that fine dust. He rassled with it like a woman shaking out a blanket, then the next thing I knew he pried my mouth open and stuffed it back down my throat and I could feel again."

"Think I can reach that long-haired son of a bitch with my rifle. I bet I can."

"Goddlemighty, did I hurt *then*. Partly because that man stuck his whole fist down my throat. Since I was staked out, I couldn't move much, but my soul wasn't attached anymore, though I knew it was back in there. That's hard to explain, I know."

"I'd like for you to explain how I might be able to hit one of them. The wind's at our backs. I bet I can do it, though it'll be a long shot. Gimme my rifle."

Buck passed it over. "Well, do it then. I'd aim high, if it was me. Anyhow, my soul was flopping around in my chest like a bird in a cage. You see, I think our souls are somehow sewn into us like a sock within a sock, but once it's tore loose to go on to the next life, it don't stick no more."

"I'm gonna try a shot now. Don't talk while I do it." Lane tried to close his ears and concentrate on the situation at hand. Using a thumb, he flicked the adjustable rear sights upright to compensate for the distance and settled his cheek against the stock.

"I can feel it in me now." Buck could have been talking to himself. "It's not fluttering as hard, but it's there. It's kinda like a shirt hanging on a line, and every now and then the wind catches it. That's the only way I can explain how it feels. Anyhow, Twisted Root knows enough English to make me understand that I'd killed his only son, and he was mad about it. Since I couldn't move my head, I got a sense of him working on his son somehow, out of my sight, and the next thing I knew, he held up that feller's bloody heart. I could see the hole I put in it, and I didn't expect things to get any better after that."

Lane sighed. "I'm gonna shoot that biggest one there. If I hit him, it might break their spirit. You reckon?"

"Might."

"Quit talking while I do it. I need to concentrate."

"Back to what I was saying, Twisted Root cut a slice of his boy's heart pump and stuffed that piece of heart so far down my throat that I should've gagged it up, but it wriggled for a second and slid down like a red worm into a hole."

Lane's stomach spasmed at the thought. "Please don't talk for a second so I can concentrate."

"Here's the part that might turn your stomach."

"*Might?* It's already flipped a couple of times. I'm shooting now so be quiet for a minute. They're standing pretty still." Kneeling, Lane shouldered the rifle and paused when Buck continued.

"The second that piece of heart slid down my goozle, it woke up and wriggled around in there like it was looking for something. The next thing I knew, he used a butcher knife to cut a stuffed bluebird out of his boy's hair and held it up for me to see. Said it was his son's medicine. Did I tell you his son's name was Blue Bird?"

"No. Hush up." Lane paused. "Wait a minute. When did you learn Comanche enough to understand him?"

"Well, I don't rightly know. Must've happened when that piece of heart went down my goozle."

Lane took his cheek from the stock and closed his eyes for a moment to calm himself. "That's enough. Maybe I'll just empty this rifle at 'em. The noise'll drown you out."

Still staring at the medicine man, Buck continued as if they were discussing how to cook supper. "He told me the bird would keep both of our souls trapped inside me, and then he jammed that blade between my teeth. Chipped a tooth that time."

He revealed his teeth in a grotesque smile. "See?"

Lane cut his eyes to the side. "It's not chipped anymore."

Using the tip of his tongue, Buck explored his teeth. "Well, I'll be damned."

"I'm thinking I might shoot *you.*"

"Judging by this ear and what's happened in the last day or so, all you'd do is waste a bullet."

"All this talking is more annoying than them Comanches out there."

"You're the one complaining. You have the rifle. Shoot if you're going to. I don't know what you're waiting for."

Lane cut his eyes at Buck's profile. "Are you finished with your story?"

"No. When he'd forced my mouth open that second time, he stuffed that dried bird down on top of that sliver of heart. It wasn't the bird that would've made me gag, but a hair went in with it and you know I can't stand a hair in my mouth. I swallowed, and that damned hair trailed down my throat and stopped there, half in my mouth and the rest of it down my throat. Can't think of anything worse than swallowing a long Comanche hair that gets hung up and won't go up or down."

"All this and it was a hair that bothered you?"

"It was a long one, and it wasn't mine. Belonged to that ugly Indian. Anyway, the bird shuddered, and then everything faded to gray and I smelled smoke and cooking meat and then I was gone until you pulled that bird out. I was somewhere between this world and the other, but I was groggy, like when you wake up the morning after a bender, still about half drunk." He paused. "You know, I gagged a lot right there at the end."

Lane's stomach lurched, and he swallowed it down and tilted the Henry at a ridiculously high angle. It roared when he pulled the trigger. They watched and could actually see the big slug rise into the air and then disappear into the distance. The long-haired Comanche's horse humped in the middle, bucked once, and threw the man off. The horse humped again and ran for a hundred yards before falling.

"Gut shot." Buck stood as the band fell farther back. "Just like when you shoot a deer too far back. You missed that aggravating son of a bitch too. See him there showing you his bare ass? I didn't think you'd make that shot. You kept worrying about it too much."

"Are you finished with that damned story?"

"I am now."

A shout from behind caused them to turn. Two dozen mounted buffalo hunters raced toward their position, weapons at the ready and aching for a fight. The Comanche vanished like smoke.

Buck rose and grunted. "I'm gonna have to get used to that, I reckon."

"Get used to what?"

"Didn't I tell you. I do believe that hair I swallowed, and that piece of heart got together and turned into a snake in my belly that sometimes talks to me."

Lane turned and puked up nothing but bile.

"I doubt we need to explain all this to those boys when they get here." Buck threw up a hand in greeting when the hunters came close. "I don't think they'd take the news as well as you have, and I doubt they'd appreciate talking to a dead man."

NINE

THE BUFFALO HUNTERS THAT GATHERED around the two relieved Rangers on the open prairie were full of excitement at the sight of the retreating Comanche. Other men of varying professions were also there. One, James Hanrahan, owned a sod saloon and made good money selling liquor to the hide men who came in tired, hungry, and extremely thirsty.

"You boys had Lady Luck on your side. I guess she made sure we were close."

Buck Dallas shrugged. "Things haven't been very lucky for *me* lately."

A young, smooth-faced man with a high forehead held a big Sharps in the crook of his arm. "You'da been goners if they'd charged. Having just one rifle, I doubt y'all would have taken more'n one or two before they swarmed you."

Lane was annoyed by the young man's confidence. "You're an experienced Indian fighter, I reckon."

"I've taken a crack at one or two."

"I'll remember that, if we need an extra Ranger." His tone was cool and dry, but the apprentice hunter didn't recognize it. "What's your name?"

"Masterson." He smoothed his wide mustache with a finger. "Everyone calls me Bat."

Buck flinched. "You know, for some reason, I don't like the thought of bats anymore." He covered his outburst with a wave in the direction the Indians disappeared. "I wonder if I saw some kind of bat medicine on one of those Comanches out there."

"Your eyes ain't no better'n mine, and I didn't see nothing of the kind." Lane scanned the men who'd come to their rescue. "At least they weren't two days ago."

The men gathered around them missed the look between the two Rangers.

Hanrahan shaded his eyes, peering into the sun to see if the Indians had left, or if they were gathering for another attack. Finally satisfied, he turned back to the Rangers. "Well, y'all come on back to the saloon and I'll give you a drink. Man needs a drink of whiskey after an Indian fight." He paused to give Buck the once-over. "Damn, son. You're filthy. You been rolling around in the mud? I 'spect that'd be a good trick so's you'd blend in with the ground. Never thought of that myself."

"You could say that. Trying to survive is tough these days." Buck paused as Lane sniffed.

His partner threw an accusing look at Buck. "There's something dead close by."

One of the hide hunters grunted. "There is. About a million dead buffaler, I reckon." He slapped a man on the shoulder, ain't that right, Rath?"

The man pointed. "We're the Mooar brothers." He grinned through a thick beard that hadn't been untangled in months, if not years. "His name's Myers, and we've killed a passel of them beasts you're smelling."

The others laughed, bleeding off the energy and disappointment from not getting to fight. Lane extended a hand. "We're Texas Rangers, on the trail of a girl taken by Comanches. I'm Lane Newsome and this here's Buck Dallas."

Inclined not to shake hands, Buck nodded and swung up into the saddle, surprising Lane. He stuck out a hand and Lane took it, jumping up behind him.

Hanrahan bit off a chew of tobacco and tucked the remainder back in his shirt. "Lost your horse, huh?"

"One of them Comanches shot it out from under me. Lost our other rifle back there too." Buck looked down at Lane's saddle horn under his hand. "We been dealing with it ever since."

Another pair of brothers led the way. The Shadlers were in high spirits, whooping and slapping each other on the back as if they'd done something more than simply ride out on the plains to run a few Comanches off.

Once settled, they moved on down toward the little handful of buildings and Lane leaned in to sniff at the back of Buck's neck again. Buck rolled his shoulder to force him back. "Stop trying to *smell* me." His voice was low.

"You heard what Hanrahan said, and the truth is, your hand's pretty damn cold."

"He was smelling all those other men. I doubt there's been a bath among any of them in six months and out here away from all those stinking hides stacked up down there and drying, they likely smell worse. I can't believe the man's smeller can recognize anything at all."

"First thing I'm gonna do is buy you a damned horse so I can have mine back." Lane adjusted his position to get more comfortable. "Man ought not to have to ride double in this country behind something he don't understand."

"That's a hurtful statement." Buck whispered over his shoulder. "I can't help what happened."

Lane hissed right back. "You might ought to lay down like you're supposed to, instead of bringing me misery."

"Is that any way to talk to your old partner?"

"I've done said words twice and come to grips with going on without you, but you keep popping up like an old turtle in a pond."

The Mooar brothers closed in too close for the Rangers to continue their conversation and they quit arguing. The rough men with stained clothing, long hair, and beards bristled with rifles, pistols, and razor-sharp knives big enough to skin a full-grown buffalo, walked their horses back to the Walls.

Billy Dixon kneed his horse closer to the Rangers. "You boys are lucky. Just a few days ago I ran across two of my friends named Dudley and Williams. Found 'em out on the plains. If them Comanches had got hold of y'all, you'da wound up the same as them."

Buck cut his eyes at the young hide hunter. "How so?"

"Why, they staked them boys out and propped their heads up so they could see what was happening to them. Them savages cut their ears and tongues off and stuffed their testicles into their mouths before they sliced 'em into ribbons. I can't imagine a more horrible death."

Buck threw a glance over his shoulder at Lane. "I can. I know somebody who went through something similar."

Instead of answering, Lane flushed in embarrassment, hoping Dixon wouldn't notice and start asking questions. His mind was so full, he doubted he could come up with a good enough story to satisfy more than a surface question or two.

As they grew nearer, Lane took in the single 700-foot street with all the adobe and picket-pole buildings lining one side, their doors open to the east. The simple store, a split wood corral, Hanrahan's sod saloon, a blacksmith shop, and another sod store with a crude sign reading *Rath's*.

Lane figured Rath sold highly inflated supplies in addition to purchasing buffalo hides as evidenced by the tall stacks that stretched out back, proving the settlement was there only for the convenience of hunters.

Masterson rode close by, and Lane caught his attention. "Hey, Bat, why're so many men here? I'd expect y'all to be out hunting."

"Quite a few of the boys are drifting in because there's been a lot of Indian trouble hereabouts." The young man looked much too young to be a hide hunter. "Two hunters were killed about twenty-five miles that way, on Chicken Creek.

"Two others went under down on the Salt Fork of the Red, and a family that didn't have good sense built a soddy ten miles south of here. A war party following some deformed Comanche medicine man named Twisted Root led that one and they massacred 'em all. Killed a baby by slamming its head against a corral post."

He paused and shook his head at the image. "Hard times all around."

At the mention of Twisted Root's name, Buck shuddered and Masterson noticed. "I can't abide the killing of a child neither. I'm about done with this." Bat pointed. "I think I'm gonna team up with Billy Dixon there and drift on back east after this season's hunt is over to find me a job in a town somewhere there ain't no Indians other than them wooden ones standing in front of a cigar store."

Lane thought about it a minute. "A town job."

"Yep." Bat straightened in his saddle. "I was thinking either a newspaperman or a lawman. Which do you reckon would be the best?"

"A newspaperman, I reckon. That sounds safer."

THE INSIDE OF THE ADOBE AND SOD saloon on the single street was dim and cool, a luxury provided by two-foot-thick walls. Lit by the yellow glow of a single lamp at that time of the day, the dirty glass windows provided even more light, though they were something of an extravagance in that part of the country. Loud and full of excitement, more than a dozen hide hunters led the way inside the surprisingly large interior and scattered to the rude tables and chairs. Three headed for the bar.

Lane glanced up to see the ridgepole stretching the length of the crude building. Smaller poles placed perpendicular to the room rested on the outside walls and the sagging ridgepole. "That pole's cottonwood and too thin to support the roof of this place much longer." He shook his head. "Cottonwood's brittle and I wouldn't put much trust in it, especially with all that heavy sod on top."

Buck followed his point and spoke barely loud enough for Lane to hear. "Hope it don't snap while we're in here. I'd dislike being buried a third time in as many days."

"You'd just get right back up again."

"That ain't the point I was making."

Hanrahan rounded the plank bar and plucked a plain whiskey bottle from the shelf carefully placed out of the reach of those lubricated patrons with a mind to serve themselves. "First one's on me, boys, and after that, you're on your own." He sat two tin cups on the bar and splashed a couple of ounces into each one. "These are for the Rangers."

Lane sniffed the warm brown liquid with caution. Plains whiskey was often pure alcohol with a little tobacco for coloring. But the liquor in his cup was legitimate. It smelled wonderful, rich, and with a hint of oak. Taking a cautious sip, he smacked his lips and tilted the rest into his mouth. "Didn't think I'd ever get to drink whiskey again."

Hanrahan noticed that Buck hadn't yet touched his. "Something wrong, Captain Dallas?"

Buck's stomach spasmed enough for both Hanrahan and Lane to notice. It was obvious he was trying to control the urge to vomit on the saloon floor.

Misreading what he saw, Hanrahan laughed. "I reckon that scare them Indians put into you filled your belly up with bile. I've seen it before." He reached out, picked up the glass, and drained it in one long swallow. "No need to waste good whiskey that'll likely come back up on you in a few minutes. Your belly'll settle down in a little bit."

A stout white woman came from the shadows in the back. "I'm Missus Olds. I manage what we call the restaurant out back over yonder for Charlie Rath. In my opinion, you need food instead of whiskey, young man. When did you boys last eat?"

Lane answered when he saw Buck swallow hard. "It's been a few days since we had a decent meal, ma'am. Until then, it's been a bite of jerky and some water every now and then."

"You boys sit down there, and I'll bring you some stew. Will that do? Or maybe you'd like a slice of roasted buffalo tongue instead."

"Stew will be fine." Lane answered for the both of them and nodded toward a table in the darkest corner of the saloon. "We'd sit over there, if it's all right with you."

"Light wherever you want." She gave Buck's arm a pat. "Honey, you look as pale as any man I've ever seen."

"I've been sick."

TEN

THE SUN WAS FINALLY STARTING to fall that afternoon when two smelly buffalo hunters came into the saloon, along with a shy Kiowa woman who stopped just inside the door. They paused to let their eyes become accustomed to the dim interior after being in the bright sunshine all day.

Sitting with his back against the wall, Lane noticed them first and tapped the table with a forefinger to get Buck's attention. "Look. That little gal's as wide as she is tall."

Buck was staring at the tabletop, as if trying to make sense of all the letters and lines carved into the surface. "This summer must have been good for the hunters in her village."

Hanrahan looked up from pouring the remains of one bottle into the other and waved a swarm of flies away from his face. Hide camps were filled with flies and lice which reproduced at astounding rates in such a rancid environment. "You boys know we don't allow no Indians in here."

"Of course we know that." The tallest of the pair waved a hand in the air to shoo a fly out of his face. He had long blond hair that reached beyond a pair of broad shoulders. "She has some information. Said she wanted to tell it to someone important."

"I don't believe she thinks we got good sense." The shorter of the two barked a laugh that erupted from a filthy beard. "She's been telling us that it's not smart to kill all the buffalo 'cause they hold the earth down."

"What makes y'all think I savvy Kiowa?" Hanrahan placed both palms on the rough plank bar. "And besides, I ain't important, unless you consider providing good whiskey is a noble endeavor. Who are y'all, anyway?"

The tallest jerked a thumb toward his partner. "This is Henry Henderson. He's my skinner. I'm Big Bill Almquist. This gal speaks a few words of English. Says her name's Tall Grass Blows in the Wind. We just call her Windy 'cause she has some kind of problem that makes her fart all the time. Probably because she eats so much. I swear, never saw anyone eat so much in my life."

Buck slumped over the table, poking with a fork at the remains of cold buffalo stew with enough congealed fat on top to look like thick cream. Flies covered the table, just out of reach from the Ranger.

To cover up for Buck's lack of appetite, Lane worked on both meals whenever Mrs. Olds wasn't watching, along with four huge chunks of coarse bread. He felt he'd consumed a good number of flies in the process too.

Hanrahan crooked a finger at Windy. "All right, come over here and say your piece." She was halfway across the room when one of the hunters who hadn't been in on the rescue party rose in a rage. "What'n hell are you doing, Hanrahan! There ain't no redskins supposed to be in here, not even a woman."

"It's my place, and I don't intend to walk all the way over there for some Indian to talk to me. She can come here if she has news."

The bearded man with fire in his eyes pulled a long skinning knife from his belt. "I won't allow it."

At the outburst, the two buffalo hunters who brought her in held up their hands. "The tallest shook his head. "We ain't getting into no fight with white men over an Indian squaw. We've done our do." They backed out the door.

Hanrahan threw a glare toward the antagonistic hide hunters. "You'll do as I say! Sit down, Alfred!"

"She won't have no ears on her head by the time she gets there, then." Alfred kicked his chair back to clear the way.

The distinct clicks of two thumb-cocked revolvers stopped him in his tracks. He turned to see the Rangers with six-shooters pointed at his midsection.

Still seated, Buck waved his pistol. "Mister, I've had a bad couple of days, so bad no sane man would believe it, and I'm settled in here as comfortable as I can be to work things out. You're bothering me and Captain Lane Newsome. We have the authority to maintain order here by the state of Texas, and by *God* we'll shoot you down if you continue to threaten that woman."

Albert paused, the knife held edge upward. "You won't shoot me over no Kiowa squaw. Besides, my skinner there'll back my play so we're even, two to two. There ain't nothing you can do about it, and if you don't put that hogleg away, I'm gonna notch *your* ears."

"Your skinner there won't be getting involved." Bat Masterson's voice floated through the tense air. "I have my pistol on him and if he moves, I'll kill him for you, Captain Dallas."

"I'll do it myself, then!"

At that news, Buck shot Alfred in the leg and the man collapsed with a groan. At the report, Lane swung the muzzle of his .44 over to cover Albert's skinner, who sat with both hands palm down on the table. He needn't have worried because true to his word, Masterson had his own weapon pointed directly at the man's skull.

Albert howled, rolling around on the floor.

"That was for failing to follow a legal order from a lawman." Buck paused, thinking. "And for threatening my witness right there to boot."

"You." Lane motioned toward the skinner with his pistol. "Drag your buddy there out of here and get him patched up. That bullet went through the meat of his leg. He'll be right as rain in a week or two if y'all get gone."

The skinner stood, hands out from his sides. "You're gonna make us leave this camp? Them Comanches are out there, just waitin'."

"Well then, find somewhere else around here to light, but if I see you, we'll finish this dance."

Keeping one eye on Masterson and Buck Dallas, Albert's skinner helped him up and they shoved past the Kiowa woman, blistering her with looks of fury as they passed.

Unfazed by the shooting and the trail of blood on the hard-packed dirt floor, Hanrahan crooked his finger at the woman. "Well, come on over here and say what you have to say. That Ranger's already paid for you to have the opportunity."

Her doeskin dress made a soft rustling sound as she hurried to the bar. Hanrahan looked over her head. "Anybody in here savvy Kiowa?"

Eyes downcast, she shook her head and answered in almost perfect English. "I'm white. I still remember the language."

Surprised by her soft, melodic voice, Hanrahan squared his shoulders. "Good lord. With that black hair and skin dress, I thought for sure you were Kiowa. Now I know why you wanted to talk to me. Tell me your American name, and we'll get you back to your family. I expect you were stole by them savages somewhere in the past."

"Years ago, but I do not want to leave my people now. I have a husband and children, and that is why I am here. He allowed me to travel with these hunters because I want to tell you that my husband traded four horses to the Comanches for a young girl about a week ago, out on the Arkansas River. Times are changing, and he thinks she should go back to her family."

Buck was in the process of reloading the fired chamber of his pistol when he heard what she said. He and Lane leaned forward, listening.

Lane had one eye on the door, just in case Albert's skinner came rushing back in with a pistol to avenge his friend. "Tall Grass, what's the girl's name?"

"River, and thank you for not calling me that vile name they were using. It was that littlest man, the skinner, who kept fouling the air around us, not me."

Unable to believe their luck, Lane turned to grin at Buck who still hadn't changed expression. He wondered if his partner's ability to show emotion was emptying out like water from a leaky vessel. "That's just the girl we're up here looking for. I'm Captain Lane Newsome and this here's Captain Buck Dallas. We're Texas Rangers."

"I know about Rangers. We've heard about your fight against the Comanches."

"Among others." Buck threw one arm over the back of his chair and studied Tall Grass. He drew an unnaturally hard breath to speak again. "How far from here is she?"

"Three or four days, depending on how fast we can travel."

"I'm surprised your husband let you come here with those other men."

"He didn't like it, but I told him how hard it was for me when they first took me captive. I learned to live with the Kiowa, and now my heart is there. But I live in my own world between two kinds of people. Some might want to take me, as they took another white woman from the Comanche a few years ago. I hear she died of a broken heart because she was neither Indian nor white. I do not want to die that way, and the world has changed so much that I think River will not have time to become Kiowa. She should go back to her people in peace, so soldiers can't come to our camp to make us pay for something my people didn't do."

Buck snorted. "Caught between two worlds is hard all right. I know exactly how you feel."

Before he could continue with that observation, Lane cut him off. "You'll take us there?"

"Yes. My people have moved the camp. Our medicine man is sick, and he says that only the waters of Boiling Springs can heal him. The springs are protected by an old white woman who lives close, and he thinks she can make the Comanches leave us alone until we can all drink the water and it heals him. I know where these springs are, so I can lead you to Boiling Springs and my husband, but I ask only one thing."

"What's that?"

"You don't harm any of my people. Just take the child and go."

Leaning back and crossing both his arms and ankles, Buck studied the woman. "We'll go, if no one harms Lane, here."

She frowned. "Are you not included?"

"Probably not in anything, anymore." He perked up for the first time since the Comanche killed him. "We need to reoutfit. We'll leave in the morning."

She nodded and stepped to the door. Seeing no one out there waiting for her except the two hide men who'd brought her in, she disappeared from view.

Bat, who'd been listening to the whole exchange, spoke from his table. "The blacksmith over there has a Henry rifle he picked up when a supply train went through here a week or so ago. He'll sell it, but I imagine at a dear price."

"The state will pay him." Buck's voice was flat. "I suspect he'll have a saddle too."

"He does, and a horse to go under it." Bat sipped at his whiskey and waved at a fly that kept trying to light on his face. "I can't wait to get back east to get some good scotch, and away from these damned flies."

Lane tilted his head and spoke softly to his partner. "There aren't any flies on you, Buck. They're worrying the piss out of me, but not a one has landed anywhere near you."

"Let's not talk about that here." Buck leaned over to Lane. "This might work out for all of us."

"How so?"

"If those springs have healing powers in 'em, maybe they'll make me right again."

"I hope it does. Watching you draw in air to talk is like watching one of them traveling snake-oil men pull and push on them squeeze-boxes to make music."

Buck shook his head. "I never knew you'd be so spiteful to a dead man."

ELEVEN

Buck and Lane sat on straight-backed wooden chairs with hand-carved bottoms in front of Tom O'Keefe's blacksmith shop. A slight breeze kept most of the flies away as the steady ring of the blacksmith's hammer made music. The sound echoed throughout the settlement created solely from the death of a million animals that only wanted to eat, drink, pee, and reproduce.

Buck needed a horse, but he wasn't in the mood to negotiate with the blacksmith, so Lane took the initiative and bought a black gelding that needed new shoes, along with the Henry rifle. O'Keefe didn't like parting with either at the price Lane settled on, but the look in the Ranger's eye told him further arguments weren't healthy.

The steady ring of hammer against iron was driven by the man with huge muscles and a thin mustache that looked like what a woman would find under a chiffonier if she wasn't much good at sweeping. He'd promised to put shoes on the gelding so they could leave at daybreak.

Lane kept an eye on Tall Grass Blows in the Wind, who rested around the corner in the building's shade. The round Kiowa woman's former escorts were finished with her and were at that exact moment drinking themselves blind on Hanrahan's whiskey.

Buck turned his head left, then right, and then back again. Lane watched him do it several times without explanation. "What are you doing?"

"Listening to the broken bones in my neck rub together. It sounds like someone grinding corn in my ears. I'm surprised you can't hear it."

"Keep that to yourself. It almost gives me a rigor." Lane cut his eyes at Buck. "I have a ringing in my ears that maintains the same pitch day and night. It started after that gunfight down around Big Bend, when we tangled with that little band of Apaches and you cut loose with that old Greener about three inches from my head, but I don't go through any gesticulations to enjoy the malady."

Buck leaned back with a pleasant look on his face, the first since Lane found him staked out. "I liked that little shotgun. Too bad we had to leave it behind."

"Well, it was a pleasure to see how it mowed down three of 'em at one time. Broke the back of that attack for sure." Lane paused, feeling bad that they were talking about pleasant things while such a burden lay on Buck's shoulders. "How are you feeling by the way? You're not going to drop on me again, are you?"

"I feel like a dead man walking the earth. The truth is I don't experience anything pleasant or otherwise." Buck sighed. "It was like after Twisted Root broke my neck. There's no real feeling from the neck down."

"I don't understand how you can draw that pistol, then. Or move around. Hell, you have to have some feeling to climb into a saddle."

"You're asking me to explain something I don't understand myself." Buck said it out loud. "I am a dead man walking the earth." He kind of rolled the words around in his mouth.

"I'm afraid I'm getting used to that thought."

"Well good for *you*." Buck paused, thinking. "I am, too, and that's a concern as well. My mind is clear, though. I'm thinking like I always did, but there's that uncomfortable *snake* squirming around inside my chest and stomach. Sometimes it itches like a sunburn several days after your skin turns red and flakes off. Other times I don't notice it unless I get still, which is hard to do with you around."

Ignoring the jab, Lane pursued the line of questioning. "What does *that* feel like?"

Buck thought for a moment. "I done told you. I think there's a big old snake inside me and it's squirming around."

"So you *can* feel something?"

"I can feel I'm getting irritated at you. It's not in the way you're talking about. It's like I recognize a presence inside me. I guess that's the way to put it. There's an old Fox Indian legend about a witch who dies and comes back by attaching itself on another witch's back, like a tick, and then takes root there until he's fully growed like a pregnant woman's belly. They call it a *Manitou*. When he's ready, he drops off like a full tick and becomes a person full of evil. I guess that's how it is."

Lane shivered. "Good lord. What did that man do to you?"

"I've been thinking about it." Buck absently pulled his knife from the scabbard and drew a long line down his arm, a cut so deep that muscle fibers recoiled. He hissed and then watched as the bloodless wound knitted back together, leaving nothing but a faint white line. "I killed his son, and though it was in honorable battle, Twisted Root cursed me in the worst way. I can't really be hurt or killed.

"The whole thing's coming back to me in bits and pieces. I can hear his words now in my head while he worked on me, though they were in Comanche. Somehow my mind's digested those sounds and translated them into something I can understand. Twisted Root said my sentence is to walk this earth a dead man until the sun no longer shows its face, and no live water once again allows my touch.

"I have to see the sun until then but can't rest when it gets dark. I can't drink or eat, nor anything else we take for granted. He's a mean, spiteful son of a bitch, that's for sure."

Buck made sure no one was close by, listening. "Hell, you done shot me twice, and buried me the same amount of times. After you holstered your pistol, I either healed up, or crawled out of the ground to walk the earth again."

"I don't like that."

"Well, thanks a lot. Neither do I."

Lane's eyes sparkled. "It takes the option away from me if I want to shoot you myself." They chuckled, as folks do at funerals when recollecting the deceased. It was a healthy way to deal with the grief. Lane's smile faded. "One thing I'm afraid of is what will happen if folks find out about you, hoss. There's no telling what they might do."

Buck nodded, looking past Lane. "That could be a problem." He dug grave dirt out from under a fingernail with the knife. "I don't know what I'm supposed to do. Am I some kind of monster who might hurt good folks without a thought?"

"We've spent our whole adult lives enforcing the law, being Rangers and bringing outlaws in or stringing 'em up." Lane flicked a finger at nothing. "Here I am, still running around with you, sitting in the shade like old folks, and saving an Indian gal in a saloon. I believe that even though you're this way, the good Lord has a plan for you."

Buck broke wind, low and long, like a horse that had been eating oats. "That's been happening all day, and I can't do anything about it. It'll be embarrassing around womenfolk. I'd say it was something I ate, but we both know what's going on with that."

Despite himself, Lane felt his stomach roll again. "I'd stay away from proper women, if I was you." Lane wrinkled his nose.

A skinny dog trotted by and froze when it saw Buck. The animal's demeanor immediately changed. Hackles raised, it crouched, growling and showing its white fangs. Keeping one wary eye on the Ranger, the dog crept past as if expecting Buck to leap forward and attack.

His hand on the butt of his revolver, Lane kept an eye on the mangy animal until it was several yards away. Apparently feeling safe with plenty of distance between itself and whatever it saw in Buck, the dog tucked its tail and ran squalling through the corral.

To their surprise, it didn't stop there but shot out the other side and raced away from the settlement. Lane stood to see the animal disappear over the ridge.

From nowhere, a pack of wolves materialized and chased the poor animal over the rise. Seconds later, a high-pitched squeal of an animal in pain and terror reached their ears.

Lane raised an eyebrow at the sound. "What'n hell was that all about?"

"It's me."

"Wonder where those wolves came from."

"Likely been slinking around, drawn by these hides stacked up back there."

"He didn't like one thing about you." Lane resisted the urge to sniff his partner again. "Do you feel like . . . what am I trying to say? Do you feel evil or mean?"

"What're you asking?"

"I mean, like that book I read here while back by that woman writer, Shelly something or other. Remember?"

"Mary Shelley. She wrote *The Modern Prometheus* that year it was so damned cold."

"That's right. It was a strange damned book." Lane couldn't help but correct Buck. It was a pleasure he'd explored for years. "I believe it was titled *Frankenstein,* by the way."

Buck raised an eyebrow. "I'd never heard of anything like that. Most folks read Shakespeare or even Homer. You plowed through some pages written by a flighty woman who probably needed a good plowing herself."

"The point I'm trying to say is it was made out of dead bodies and then it got up and walked around. They got to calling that thing a monster."

Buck squinted at the horizon. "Like me. I'm that Frankenstein thing."

"You're something, all right, but I don't know what it is other than revenge from a crazy Comanche medicine man." Lane looked to his left, in the direction to see what caught Buck's attention. "What?"

"Four riders coming."

"More buffalo hunters, I reckon."

"No. I didn't tell you, but my eyes are a helluva lot sharper than they were. I can see the balls on a gnat half a mile away. Three men. One woman. I believe she's expecting."

"Settlers then." Lane squinted.

"Strange settlers. One of those fellers an Indian, though I suspect he's a Cheyenne, 'cause he's so pretty to look at. The others are black and white. The white's a disreputable person, I suspect."

Shadows lengthened as the travelers approached.

Lane turned his attention back to his partner. "I've been thinking. We have to decide what to do when the sun goes down. Yesterday, you dropped like someone shot you. We need to be ready when it gets dark."

"I told you. It's not like sleep." Buck shrugged. "One minute I'm here, and the next thing I know, I'm just . . . *not* . . . until I wake up."

"Well, I didn't ask for another explanation, but my point is that we have to do something about you before sundown." Lane pointed to an empty wagon used to haul hides. "I say we go over there in a little while and lay down. Nobody'll know what's going on if it happens again. They'll just think we've gone to sleep."

"I'll think on it."

"I'll be damned." Lane pointed toward the nearby ridge. "Look at those wolves. They're lined up and sitting there, just watching us."

Buck pondered the sight for several seconds. "They ain't afraid, that's a sure thing."

"I've never seen a wolf act like that. Must be used to people. If they take a notion to come for us, I'll use my pistol, and that'll take the starch out of 'em."

"They're full."

"Huh?"

"Their muzzles are red with fresh blood. That dog. Now they're watching *us*."

"Maybe they have hydrophobia."

"Naw, not all of 'em at the same time, and they aren't acting sick. They're watching *me*. I can feel it."

"So you *can* feel something. You keep changing your mind faster than a schoolgirl over a boy."

"Forget it. I'm tired of arguing with you."

The riders finally reached the Walls where the narrow track widened into a street. Buck was right. The Indian who had maybe six decades behind him rode point, head high and shoulders back. He was a Cheyenne, all right—fine featured and full of himself despite the fact that he had only one eye. The uncovered left one gaped open to the elements. He carried a good lever action rifle, along with two pistols and a knife. Eagle feathers braided into his hair flipped in the wind.

He was followed by a mule bearing the stern-looking man in a dark, dusty suit. He sported a well-groomed beard, something of a rarity in those parts. A two-shoot gun rested across the pommel of his saddle and like the Cheyenne, he carried two pistols. A long knife with a bone handle jutted out of his right boot. When they got closer, it was easy to see a ragged Bible resting on some kind of leather and wood device hanging around his neck, allowing him to read and ride at the same time.

Behind *him* was the extremely pregnant Mexican woman. Face tired from a long trip, she sat slumped forward, as if a great weight was on her shoulders, instead of her belly. Straddling a Mexican saddle in a most unladylike fashion, her dress rose above her knees on either side. Her grimy dress and black, oily hair told the story of many days away from water.

Bringing up the rear was a wide-shouldered black man with long hair and thick beard, riding a scarred mule that looked as if it had seen a hundred fights with other animals. He watched the Rangers from under a battered hat that was likely made during the War Between the States. Suspenders held up pants that were unusually baggy. There were so many weapons protruding from various holsters and scabbards that he resembled a porcupine. An odd-looking sword hung on his back, the wrapped haft rising above one shoulder. Like the preacher in front, he carried a long gun resting on the pommel. It was a Sharps that had also seen much action.

His appearance and demeanor told the Rangers that he wasn't someone to trifle with.

The shirtless Cheyenne, in britches likely chewed soft by women, reined up when they were even with the Rangers. He wore a low-crown black Victorian top hat that was faded by the sun. His dark eyes bored holes in Buck. "You have no spirit."

"I *am* feeling kind of tired, and a little peevish, so I don't need some one-eyed Cheyenne to tell me my business."

"No. Your spirit is *gone.* It has left your body. Did you know this?"

"What're you? A medicine man?"

"Yes. I work for the Great Spirit who has given me the gift of Inside Sight. Your dark wind that you pass tells me that a bad old witch has put its hand in you."

Lane felt a shiver run down his spine. This man saw something most did not, and it made him wonder if the Cheyenne could also read his own soul.

"Didn't feel it, if he did." Buck looked relaxed, but anyone who knew him could tell he was swelling up for a fight. "Went to sleep and woke up this way, so I've just been doing what I want up to this point, and sorry you got your feelings hurt by looking at me."

Lane planted his feet, prepared to rise if the conversation became threatening. "Hey, Chief. You got a name?"

"Wolf." The Cheyenne smiled, revealing two unusually long canines and fingered a necklace made of wolf canine teeth. "My mother was bitten by a wolf when I was inside her womb. She killed it with a stick, and some of its spirit got in through her breath to give me these."

"Well, they're nice'n white. What makes you say those things about my friend?"

"His soul has burned away, leaving nothing but bad-smelling ashes." Wolf fluttered his hands like a bird taking flight. He fixed his gaze on Buck. "How do you not know this? I would climb down and dismember your body if I had the time, to show you a decent way to leave this earth, but I am charged with delivering this pregnant woman to an old Spirit Lady who lives in a hole in the ground east of here in Boiling Springs. Doing it right would take several days. Maybe I can do it when I come back this way. You'll have to wait for me to free your spirit. I believe all I need is a sharp knife and the faith of one old man. Do you have any around here?"

The bearded man in the dusty suit eased his horse up beside Wolf. "For the first time since I met this hairy savage, I'm thinking that our journey is not what we expected. Maybe we have been led to you because, like Mike here, I see something too. I just can't explain it right now. Maybe a drink or two of whiskey might reveal the answer in my mind, if you would buy me one."

"Mike?" Lane frowned. "Said his name is Wolf. I've never known an Indian named Mike, and by the way, I ain't giving you no money to drink the whiskey I'd like to have myself."

"I can't pronounce his heathen name, and through the limitations of his language he can't give me a clear translation even though he is a very wise man. I tried to translate it in Comanche, which I am fluent in, but it came out to Wolf Vulva, so instead of enabling him to carry on with his blasphemous charade and be called Wolf, I call him Mike. He isn't saved by the Holy Spirit, therefore it is my duty to civilize him by a good, Christian name and it works. He comes to hand when I call and doesn't complain about the name like some self-centered prisoners I've attended to."

Buck ignored the conversation, as if finished with the whole thing. Maybe he was studying the scattered ring of buffalo hunters who were drawn to the riders and their conversation, but Lane wasn't sure. It might have been the wolves who were still watching him from afar.

Wolf spat upon the ground. "Dead Man, you are cursing that spot where you sit for generations. Once, when my favorite cousin had been murdered by the white cavalry, I followed them and waited until midnight to kill six of their men while they argued about silly subjects such as additional names. They slept. The one they left on guard also went to sleep. I killed them all. Where those dead men lay when I was finished, their souls melted into the ground because of a curse I put on them. Nothing grows there today. I understand such things, which is why I know what you are."

A short, squatty buffalo hunter named Sweat Henderson because he was forever perspiring, called from several yards away. "Hey, Buck. All that sounds like a threat to me. I think he means to kill you."

"He's no threat. There's no man in this world who can kill me."

The collection of hairy lice-and-flea-ridden men loafing in the shade burst into laughter.

Lane tilted his head, studying the woman who seemed to have a dim light around her. He'd heard other women say that pregnant women glow with health, and maybe they were right. Despite the dust on the men's clothes she wore and the dirty hair that needed soap, she was attractive in a way that gave him a pleasant flutter in his stomach.

He stood and stepped close to her. A familiar but undefined scent washed over him on the warm breeze, sharpening his mind and igniting a heat that traveled throughout his body. He blushed at the thought of such happening with a pregnant lady whose oversized shirt barely buttoned over her belly. She obviously had a man, likely the one in a suit, so he looked away.

"I apologize for being rude, ma'am. I'm Lane Newsome. Texas Ranger." He looked for something else to say and noticed the black gelding in the corral. "This here's Buck Dallas who now owns that mean-looking gelding that'd just as soon bite you as to come when he's called. He's a Ranger too."

The flicker of a smile came into her tired eyes. "The horse is a Ranger?"

Lane frowned, then realized she was making fun. "Oh, an educated woman, I see. Still another rarity in this part of the world. Since you can apparently read, and have a grasp of grammar, would you care to sit with me tonight and talk about books? I'd dearly love to have a conversation about something other than Indians and outlaws." He glanced over at Buck. "Or dead people."

The bearded man shifted something in his hands and Lane saw that it was a Bible. "I'm Hezekiah Ransom." The Mexican woman ducked her head and went silent as he took over the conversation, more evidence to Lane that she belonged to the man in a suit. "I carry the Word across this country, bringing light to those in darkness. Mister Buck Dallas, there is an ink-black well a thousand feet deep behind your eyes that at this moment look to me like boiled eggs. I'd like to read you some words usually reserved for the last time a corpse enjoys the sun's warmth . . . so consider what I offer. Whatever experience you've recently endured'll fade and soon you'll be nothing but an empty shell walking the earth. That's no good for any of us because it'll be a blemish on my record, now that I've met you."

Buck shook his head. "Now I have to hear it from you too."

Suddenly afraid that he'd been missing something others hadn't, Lane examined his partner even harder but saw nothing that was obvious. It was creepy, he thought, how two complete strangers knew something was different about Buck without a single clue. Lane could tell his partner was unsettled, too, though he had a lot to be unsettled about.

"Anyway, thanks for the information." Buck came back to the conversation and tilted his hat back, but not enough to show the raw blaze of his scalped skull. "Ma'am. Welcome to Adobe Walls. You'll be safe here tonight."

She gave him a soft smile that would have made him warm inside if he'd been alive. "Thank you, sir. I am Victoria."

It was the big Negro man riding drag who interrupted to address Buck. "I'm sorry for what happened to you."

This time, it was too much. Buck stood and stepped up beside Lane, who kept a wary eye on all three. Slowly, so as not to jolt anyone into some deadly action, he hung a thumb into his gun belt, only inches from the pistol's grip.

In the way he'd always shown that things were getting dangerous with him, Buck lowered his head and watched from under his hat brim. "I don't know what you mean."

"Yes, you do." The man's voice was soft and friendly, as if coaxing a puppy to come close. "Come go with us. Go with us and we can help you. I think maybe you can also help us. You see, we've all seen the same thing in the others."

Lane felt the hair rise on the back of his neck. Who *were* these three men attending a pregnant woman on the plains, and were they dead, also? Maybe that was why they saw the emptiness in Buck. "I'm afraid we can't do that. We're leaving in the morning to rescue a girl stole by the Comanches."

The black man addressed both of the Rangers. "Evil people, the Comanch'. They do bad things simply for fun." Rising in his stirrups, he scanned the rough buildings. "Is there a place we can stay for the night? We have money to pay."

"Yours is the only name not spoke here."

The man's gaze bored into Lane for a long moment before he spoke. "Clarence. I am an archangel sent to escort these pilgrims in their travels. I fight evil, when I'm not drunk with whiskey or personal importance."

Lane grunted. "I've done the same myself, from time to time."

"No. You don't understand. I rend bad things asunder if it's required, like that man sitting beside you."

Wolf shook his head and addressed Buck. "When we rode up, I saw a gnarled root growing from your ear and another from your butthole when you were sitting on the ground. They are trying to enter our Mother, the Earth, but she won't let them. Don't you feel it?"

Buck pasted on a grin. "I'm not sure how it would feel, so I can't answer that."

"It would feel like a snake trying to leave your body."

Hezekiah's eyes rolled back until nothing but the whites showed. Tilting his face skyward so far that it appeared that the back of his head could touch his spine, he spoke in a tongue none of them understood. As his voice grew, he flipped the unseen pages of his Bible with one hand as if his fingers were looking for Braille.

Wolf ignored the voice ringing louder and louder. "He does that from time to time. I have learned to ignore it and concentrate on the light that led us here. You are not the light, Ranger Dallas, though I think we can be of service to you, or you for us."

Uncomfortable with the situation, Lane shifted his weight from side to side. "You followed a light? You must have seen a campfire here last night."

Hezekiah's voice rose even more, capturing the attention of the other buffalo hunters who joined those that gathered around.

Sweat Henderson stepped closer. "He's speaking in tongues. I haven't heard that since I was a kid. Too bad there's no one around here to translate."

"Who could translate *that?*" Lane stayed ready, just in case one of them attempted to discharge a weapon in his direction.

"Someone caught up in the spirit." Sweat grunted. "I doubt you'll find anyone who can do that in this lot, though."

Annoyed, Lane tried again. "Wolf, you said you followed a light here."

"It was one high in the sky, sometimes, then it reduced itself to the flicker of a campfire. We have to talk with the one who kindled it."

Lane nodded in understanding. "He's talking about that long streak in the night sky that we've been seeing. You know, the one that looks like a shooting star, but just hangs there with a long tail that don't go away."

Victoria pulled a strand of long, black hair behind her ear. "That's a comet."

"That's right. A comet."

"But it's not the light the four of us are following. You probably won't believe me, but we're the only ones who can see the light. It's what brought us together from El Paso, down on the Rio Bravo, and led us to this place, for now."

TWELVE

I N A NARROW CUT THROUGH the grassland, Twisted Root listlessly carved up an inattentive buffalo hunter they'd surprised on the Punta de Agua Creek, so named by the Mexicans who tried to build a settlement there. The medicine man's father was in the band that raided it one night sixty years earlier, and rubbed them all out.

The white man wasn't so lucky. The Comanche war party had been waiting in the grass by the creek all day, like cougars at a watering hole. They'd seen him in the distance and expected him to come for water late in the evening. They were right, and when the man knelt on one knee to fill his canteen, Goes Fast shot him in the rectum, a funny place to put a bullet.

Unfortunately for the hide hunter it wasn't an instantly fatal wound, and the man fell into the creek where he would have drowned if Goes Fast hadn't jumped in and yanked his head above water to scalp him. He dragged the white man out onto the bank, and that's where Twisted Root had him staked down by driving spikes through his forearms and calves to hold him still.

NINE TOES AND SHOUTS HIS NAME STAYED back from the warrior's business. Their job was to keep the spare horses together when they traveled. They held the horses as Goes Fast staked out the man.

Shouts His Name craned his neck to watch. "That man was not smart. Comanche will never let anyone sneak up on them."

"You dropped to your belly to drink yesterday and didn't look around."

"I wasn't worried. There are many of us. I meant when we are alone, like when we squat in the morning. I always make sure I'm alone when my guts move."

"Not when you make water, though." Nine Toes felt aloof, proud to be so close to becoming a warrior like those gathered around the white man. "Right now, though, no one is paying attention to anything around us. I am. No white hunters will sneak up on us right now."

"Neither do you!" Shouts His Name was incensed. "You made water as soon as we got off the horses a few minutes ago."

Nine Toes made sure the horses were grazing and watched something flicker through the grass in the distance. "Do you see that wolf?"

"Where?"

"There. Loping to the east. My eyes are better than yours too."

"They are not. I smelled him earlier."

Instead of answering, Nine Toes sighed and wished he was a full warrior so he could get close enough to watch Twisted Root work.

★ ★ ✮ ★ ★

WITHOUT MUCH INTEREST IN HIS WORK, TWISTED Root cut out his captive's tongue and threw it into the water where a turtle ate it. He suddenly stopped in his work and squatted back on his heels, looking to the east. Tilting his head like a dog hearing its master, he rose.

"It is time for us to go kill that old woman who lives near the spring. I'm tired of going around it. That water is the sweetest and coldest in the country, and she shouldn't have it all to herself."

Goes Fast shook his head in fear. "No. That old woman can put a curse on us. She put one on my cousin, and he dried up and blew away in the wind."

"I can stop her from doing that. My medicine is stronger."

"If it is stronger, why do we ride around the spring when we need water?"

"Because I did not want to take the time to eat her spirit. She is strong, but the time is right. I've been watching that tadpole in the sky each night, and it is getting brighter. I am meant to draw its power down into this withered arm. When I do that, I can cast a spell and turn her into anything I want."

"What will that be?"

"A weasel, I think. And then I will kill it and wear the skin in my hair."

The other Comanche gambling on a blanket pretended not to hear. Two Shoot, the one who owned the double-barrel shotgun, was winning, but the conversation caused his mouth to turn down at the corners. He sat back, finished with the game.

None of them wanted to even see the old woman named Hattie, let alone fight her, for they had heard of her powerful medicine that allowed the witch to live unmolested in the middle of the Comanche nation.

THIRTEEN

S TILL RATTLED BY THE FOUR strangers accompanying the pregnant woman, Lane lay foot to head beside Buck in the back of an empty wagon. The sun drew closer to the upward slope above Adobe Walls that lay in a low place like a dimple on a cheek, hemmed in by ground that gradually sloped upward on all sides.

To the east was a wide, low mesa connected to a smaller mesa by a line of trees struggling to survive alongside a small creek. A waving sea of shortgrass separated the settlement from the higher vantage points.

Shadows grew long as the sun settled closer to another ridge, bringing dusk earlier than if they were on the western side of the rise. A new group of hunters drifted in and passed Lane who raised up to see the new arrivals.

One of them, a big man with a thick beard and a shirt fit only for rags looked into the wagon bed and nodded. "You two better be glad you're here tonight."

Lane propped on one elbow. "Why's that?"

"There's more Comanche and Kiowa out there than ants on an anthill. We laid low in a creek all day long, letting one party after another pass by. Looks like they're gathering for something big about twenty miles from here."

Lane considered the information. "Thanks."

"You don't look like a buffalo man."

"We're not. Texas Rangers."

"Heard of you." He turned to the men with him. "I hear them Rangers have it so good they take a bath every week."

The herd of hunters guffawed and turned their horses toward the corral. A couple of them frowned at the Ranger's preparations for such an early bedtime, but no one asked any questions, or commented. Men often turned in at sundown so they could get up early the next morning to do chores or make several miles before it got hot up in the day.

Folks out west were an odd lot, and each man respected the other's privacy. Some were on the dodge, others were simply loners. If the Rangers wanted to lay down in a wagon at dusk instead of having a meal, or getting a drink, well, that was up to them.

Hat covering the pistol laying on his stomach, Lane propped against his saddle, watching the colorful sunset. His wool blanket on top of the horse blanket gave him some cushion.

Buck kept his own hat on to cover the bloodless scalp wound and lay flat on his back, staring straight up at the sky. Before dying, he was particular about his hat, making sure it kept its shape. Now, the back was crushed against the stained boards.

"I believe that's the prettiest sky I've ever seen, Buck. I don't know what makes it that way sometimes, but I sure do like it. Look, you can already see that comet they were talking about back in Austin."

"There's a star already out." Buck pointed. Bending his knees, he crossed one ankle over the other knee, as if resting in a chair. "I've never seen one so cl . . ."

The sun slipped below the ridge and winked out, and so did Buck. His arm dropped, and his knees twisted as gravity took hold. A joint popped with a wet, gristly sound. A long sigh filled the air, and he was still. Somehow, Buck didn't look peaceful in death at all. The arm he'd been pointing with lay at an odd, unnatural angle.

Though he'd been walking and talking to an animated corpse all day, it was all Lane could do not to crawl away like a diaper baby and crouch in the corner. It just wasn't right for a man to die more than once.

Instead, he pushed himself into a seated position and watched his partner. "Now that's damned aggravatin'. We might have drifted into an interesting conversation, but naw, you have to drop dead again."

Taking a deep breath as if put out by the whole thing, Lane straightened Buck's legs, then wondered what to do with his partner's arms. He thought about crossing them over his friend's chest, but that would make him look even more like a corpse. If he did that, and went off somewhere to make water, someone might try to do him a favor and haul the corpse off for burial before he could get back.

Finally reaching a decision, he straightened the left arm and laid the other across Buck's stomach. Still not satisfied, he pulled Buck's pistol from his holster and slipped it into his loose fist.

That looked better, but his hat still didn't look right. Lane glanced around and saw the street was fairly empty. Only the big Cheyenne, Wolf, was out down by the stable where his crew had settled in for the night after paying the blacksmith named O'Keefe twice the going rate for a stall.

Taking more liberties than Buck would have permitted had he been normal, Lane leaned forward and untied his friend's bandana. Making sure no one was watching too closely, he took a knee beside Buck, removed his hat, and tied the bandana over his mangled scalp, making him look like a pirate.

Satisfied with the effect, he laid the Ranger's hat over his gray hand and pistol just as Lane had done his own. He settled back against his saddle and pondered his ministrations. "You know, I'm beginning to get used to this."

"You are a good friend."

The sudden voice startled Lane so badly that he instinctively reached for his pistol. Recognizing Wolf by the shape of his top hat, he relaxed, wondering how he'd closed the distance so fast. "Now that was a foolish thing to do. I could have shot you for an outlaw, or a Comanche come to take my hair. How'd you get over here so quick?"

Drawing a deep breath, Wolf rested a hand on the big knife in his belt. "I can cut him up for you now. I have the time. We can take the pieces out in the prairie and bury them a long way from each other. Of course, nothing will ever grow over those places until all the white men are gone from our world, but I doubt those limbs will find each other again. It will take a couple of days to do it properly, and that might cause problems getting Victoria to that old woman, but it would be the right thing to do."

"No. I'll shoot you if you try it."

"His head will be a problem, though." Wolf continued, as if he'd been working on a solution to the dilemma for some time. He turned his head like a chicken, to use his good eye. "It might wake up at dawn and start talking. That would annoy the animals who live nearby, and they shouldn't have to deal with such madness." He paused, pondering the problem. "I think when there is nothing left but the trunk, the snake inside him will crawl out, and he will deflate like an empty water bladder. Maybe that will silence his mouth."

"Didn't you hear me? You won't be doing that to my friend, now or ever. And if he finds out what you said when he wakes tomorrow, he's liable to shoot out your good eye for just suggesting such a thing."

"And he will wake up every morning until the waters flow no more." The Cheyenne's focus moved to Lane. "What I suggest will be the best thing for him. I would want someone to do that for me, if a witch was to curse my soul."

"I doubt that. And if what you say is true, what's gonna happen if the head opens its eyes under the ground? Then you will have double cursed him forever to live inside his own mind."

"He is already doomed. Maybe we should burn him, but that would require much wood or buffalo dung, and the smoke might draw the Comanches."

"I believe there's a reason he's like this. You know so much, why don't you tell *me*."

Wolf rested both hands on the side of the wagon as he peered in. "You wouldn't understand me."

"You're probably right. Let's talk about something else. Do little chi-chi birds ever try to nest in that eye hole of yours? I believe if I was missing an eye, I'd cover up the hole."

"If I covered it up, I couldn't see the other world." He pointed at his good eye. "With this one, I see the real world around us. It is for life here and now. The other is a window into the afterlife, and what is just beyond the veil that keeps us from seeing it. The veil is thin, and this hole lets me look through into something that is greater than all of us."

"Now that's the first interesting thing you've said. How'd you lose it? In a fight?"

"No. My grandfather was a *puha*, and he told me about what is on the other side of this life. He said if I plucked this one out, I could see in there and talk to the Old People who have gone before us. I was younger and much braver. When I was thirteen and less hesitant, I popped it out and fed it to the fire. That's when I began to understand the Great Spirit."

"That's a lot to think about. Give me some time to work over that one. Tell me what the four of you are really doing out here. If you run into a band of Comanches, I doubt you'll be able to hold them off for long if they're gathering like that buffalo man said, then you'll have to worry about the woman."

"I can't explain it other than to say this began with the woman, Victoria, who set off to follow the Great Light. She was being molested by some bad men down on Calf Creek, just north of the Llano River. She says she called for help, and Clarence came and beheaded them with the steel sword he carries on his back."

"He does look like a fighting man. I'd rather have him on my side if something stirs up. Go on."

"No. I'm not a magpie to talk all night. They say you are after a stolen child, but now you have taken on the responsibility of a Kiowa woman who sleeps over there in the dirt beside the blacksmith shop."

"She came in with two other men. I reckon she's their charge, not mine."

"No. They are drunk in the saloon, along with some others who have no respect for themselves."

"Well, I have to say I've lost that kind of respect myself a time or two. She's going to lead us to that child tomorrow in her husband's camp. Then we're going back to Austin in order to return her to her mama. Nothing much more than that."

Clarence's soft voice came through the gathering twilight. "There will be more than you think."

His sudden appearance wasn't as startling as Wolf's, but it was enough to concern Lane. He didn't like people sneaking up on him in the dark. "Sounds like you've been eavesdropping. So why do you say there's more?"

"Because you're being hunted. A Comanche named Twisted Root is out there. I heard it from someone we ran across yesterday. He was heading east to meet the cavalry at White Deer Springs. Twisted Root is looking for blood now that his son is dead. The two of you won't make it there, and if you do, you won't get back down south."

"So you say we should just give up on the little girl and scoot on out of here."

"I didn't say that. You should join us. I believe something is pulling all of us in the same direction, but for the life of me I don't know what that is right now. Hezekiah says he feels a force will also draw that child to us, but it's somewhere to the northeast."

"We might, but I'm afraid Hezekiah'd start preaching at me, and I can't abide that."

"He doesn't preach." Clarence shook his head. "Not in the sense you mean. When he's overcome with religion, he speaks to the sky in another tongue."

"Well, if it's as loud as what I heard a little bit ago, the whole Comanche nation could sneak up on us before we knew they were there."

The lone street was mostly dark, though dim yellow light spilled from oil lamps through doors and windows open to catch the breeze on that warm night. Men laughed.

Hezekiah appeared. "While you two stood jawing here at the wagon, a problem arose."

"What's that?"

"Victoria is missing. Tall Grass Blows in the Wind saw it and came and told me some of those new men took her into the saloon while I was tending our horses."

Lane frowned. "Why?"

Clarence adjusted the pistol in his holster. "She was in a convent in Santa Fe, but when the nuns found out that she was pregnant, they threw her out. She went down to find her relatives. That's where we found her, right after we were called. But men smell something in her, a musk that most women don't have. Good men feel it and take no action. Those with black souls are attracted to her as a moth to a flame. Most of the time it is men of low value, such as those who have taken her. It isn't the first time this has happened since we started north."

"She's been taken before?"

"No, but they have tried."

"So these dark people want her for that . . . scent?"

Hezekiah threw a look into the open saloon door and patted his pockets, feeling for unseen weapons. "They also want the child."

"How come?"

"I can't tell you that, yet. When it happened before, I passed her in the plaza of a town with no name. She was sitting against a building and telling men to leave her alone. There were several standing around her, like wolves, and I bid them to leave. One had a knife and wanted to stick it in me, but I killed him. Clarence beheaded one of them with that sword he carries.

"There were dead men all around us when the red rage finally cleared my eyes. Victoria was unhurt, but we knew we had to leave. I led her away while Clarence stayed behind to make sure no one followed.

"Once we were free of town, Wolf was waiting in the middle of a road. I thought we would have to kill him, too, because he was attracted to the smell, but before I could shoot, he said he was sent to help protect her. I believed him, and we have been riding together ever since."

While he was talking, he and Wolf checked their weapons. Wolf spoke without looking at Lane. "My Dark Eye sees many such men converging on this point. I thought your friend was one of them. I would have chopped him into pieces had he tried."

"He wouldn't, and I'da shot you if you did." Watching them prepare for battle, Lane stood in the wagon. "Do you know which ones took her?"

"It doesn't matter." Hezekiah looked into the open door, as if expecting to see her there, holding her arms out for help. "We will lay about until we find them."

"I'd feel better if I knew what's going on, but if what you say is true and she's been stolen, a law has been broken and I won't abide that." One hand on the wagon's sideboard, Lane jumped out and landed on his feet. "This is a Ranger's work and you're in Texas now. Y'all stay out here and let me handle it."

"They were bad men," Clarence said. "There may be more than just the two."

"I've handled more than a couple by myself." The words were no more than out of Lane's mouth when a wave of emotion washed over him. Stepping inside alone would be the first time he'd enforced the law by himself since becoming a Ranger. Buck was always by his side, and in every situation, he knew the blue-eyed boy from East Texas would always say or do what was needed.

Throwing a glance at Buck's still body lying in the wagon, Lane reached over the side and picked up his Henry rifle. He paused and thought about the interior of the saloon, and how many bodies were packed inside. He left the rifle and setting his hat, Lane pushed into the saloon.

After being in the dark outside, the room was bright with detail, though thick cigar smoke hung low from the ceiling. There were more buffalo hunters inside than the first time he and Buck were there. He paused inside the door, taking in the crowd and casting about for Victoria.

The tables were full of gamblers and drinkers. A line of men leaned against the bar with barely enough elbow room to tip a glass or bottle. Though the saloon was usually loud with noise that boiled over into the cool night air by men enjoying a drink, it was replaced by a tension thick as the smoke that filled the room. Lane noted not all the customers were buffalo hunters. There were half a dozen others who could have been travelers on the road, or career outlaws who slunk around the edges of civilization.

It took a moment to find Victoria in the far corner, hemmed in by four lean men who definitely weren't hunters or innocent travelers. They had the ragged, hard look of men who lived on the dark side of the law.

Scalphunters.

That explained the uneasy atmosphere in the saloon. The murderers who made a living by killing people were dark, rough men with long greasy hair and beards. They dressed in whatever came to hand, and the garments were usually dim and worn with age. Only their weapons were clean and oiled, testament to their mission.

With a bounty on Indian scalps, the butchers were lean as hungry coyotes traveling the frontier, ranging from the Rockies down to the Rio Grande and beyond, killing without discretion men, women, and children of any race for their black hair.

Alone as usual, though they were in the company of others, they isolated themselves in the back corner, with a five-foot no-man's-land between them and the hunters. Lane found it interesting that the buffalo men were all positioned so that each could keep an eye on the murderers, no matter where they sat or stood.

The regulars saw where Lane directed his attention. A thin, wavy line parted between him and the scalphunter's corner, where a couple of them drank heavily with lust in their eyes, ignoring Lane and staring at Victoria, who sat with her chin high in anger.

Lane felt another wave of feelings tighten around his heart. Though she could use a bath and clean hair, she was the most beautiful woman he'd ever seen.

Sweat Henderson stood with several others near the door, faces red with emotion. "Hey, Ranger, you know what's happening back there?"

"I heard."

"That gang of bandits drug that woman in through the back door."

"I said I heard. Y'all stay here." Wishing Buck was watching his back, Lane crossed halfway inside the structure and stopped in the middle of the room when a thin, wiry scalphunter with a flop hat glanced up and saw him coming.

Lane had a history with those kinds of men who murdered, raped, and robbed their way from Texas to Arizona. They understood only one thing, and there was only one way to deal with them. In the past, he'd used bullets, knives, and a rope on more than one occasion, to end their bloody careers.

Skinny leaned over the plank table and said something to a hulk of a man, who ignored him for a moment, trying to force whiskey on Victoria.

She was having none of it and shook her head violently. "No!"

The hulk drew a long, thin skinning knife honed through the years until the blade was concave. "I was trying to make it easy for you but have it your own way. I'd just as soon do it like this."

He put it to her neck and paused when the others who'd been watching grew silent, turning their attention away from the pregnant woman to see Lane set his feet. From that distance, they appeared to be the scavengers they were, eyes glowing almost yellow in the lamplight.

Lane faced more evil than he'd encountered in his entire life, and he was now bracing them as a coward, alone after he left his friend for dead. "You four men. I'm Lane Newsome, Texas Ranger. I've come for that woman, and you're bound to release her to me without any trouble. You!" He pointed. "Put that knife down now and turn her a'loose."

He expected the hulk to posture or make threats against the law. Already primed and cocked by a lifetime of survival in a world that didn't care if a man lived or died, Skinny reached under a filthy coat and produced a pistol as fast as lightning.

Shocked that the man would react so quickly with a gun, Lane snatched the Colt from his holster at the same time a river of cutthroats poured through the open back door, all drawing handguns. Others rose from the tables around him.

Realizing there weren't just the four he faced, but more than thirty scalphunters scattered around the saloon, Lane was soon to be a dead man. But he intended for them to pay dearly.

"All y'all don't make no difference. If you don't let her go, I'll shoot you dead right here and now."

"Bullshit." The hulk's forearm flexed. "Kill him!"

Lane fired at the most urgent threat to Victoria, splitting the hulk's skull with a single round that hit him high in the forehead. The man's arm dropped before he could cut the woman's throat. She went down with him as Lane thumb-cocked his revolver.

The skinny scalphunter pulled the trigger on his own six-shooter, missing Lane by a hair. An innocent hide hunter standing behind him caught the bullet and his head exploded in blood and gore. All the air sucked out of the room for a moment as everyone went silent, then the saloon erupted into violence as every man there pulled a weapon for defense or attack.

Glad that he hadn't brought the Henry that would be impossible to maneuver in the crowded space, Lane thumbed back the hammer a third time and fired at the wall of rising men.

The crowd wavered and split. Lane center-shot a scalphunter who produced two guns. Not caring to aim, the thug fired them as fast as he could pull back the hammers. The others charged, thinking their numbers would overwhelm the Ranger with only one pistol.

Some of the bystanders dropped to the floor to avoid the swarm of buzzing slugs. Others drew their own weapons, whether guns or knives, and fell upon the scalphunters who had more experience at hand-to-hand killing. Screams of pain and terror rose above the gunfire.

Lane mowed down two more as a thunderous roar vibrated off the adobe walls. Scalphunters and buffalo men fired with apparent indiscrimination. The big Sharps rifles that some had leaned against the bar, tables, and walls punctuated the melee with the hard slaps of cannonade.

The angry hiss and buzz of passing bullets sounded like dry wasps passing before gunfire swelled even louder, drowning the dry sound and replacing it with thunder.

Mouth dry and heart pounding in his ears, Lane's pistol ran out, and he drew the big Bowie knife on his belt. His blood was up for only the second time in his life, and he waded into the fight without thought of personal injury.

Firearms quickly ran out of ammunition and the fight turned to edged weapons. A scalphunter slashed his way through two tough buffalo men in a determined effort to reach Lane and at the moment he prepared to engage, a giant boulder rolled past him, bellowing like a mad bull.

Clarence resembled a mythical beast, shouting and waving the long sword drawn from the scabbard on his back. Swinging the razor-sharp blade with his left hand, he slashed and jabbed with his own Bowie knife, driving through the cutthroats and fighting toward his charge huddled somewhere in the far corner.

Bodies and body parts fell before him.

Buffalo hunters recoiled to let him work, and as they did, Wolf and Hezekiah shouldered through, firing pistols with both hands. Wolf howled and pulled the trigger, shooting into the mass of churning targets with blood on their hands and souls. Lane was never able to swear to it after the mist of battle had cleared, but he was confident that Wolf leaned in to tear out one man's throat with his oversized canines.

The close quarter battle evolved as the scalphunters formed a defensive line at the back of the saloon, while the hide hunters separated themselves and leaned into the roar of battle behind Clarence's attack. He, like the others, intended to reach Victoria and no man stood in his way.

Wolf dropped his empty pistol and went to work with a big knife, slashing with his right, and shooting with his left, as Clarence drove a wedge into the thugs who fell like wheat before a scythe. Two of the filthy, bearded scalphunters leaped forward, only to engage with his bloody sword. Half of the first man stood for a moment as his upper portion fell with a spill of intestines to the floor that was already dark with blood. His legs buckled as the blade reached the second man and cut halfway through before encountering his tough pelvis.

Wolf and Hezekiah angled out, forming a skirmish line that avoided the innocent men trying to escape, and sending the remaining army of murderers to the afterlife.

The air once thick with smoke and human humidity absorbed red sprays of blood that vaporized and hung suspended, coating the walls and floor.

A sudden silence enveloped the saloon, and Hanrahan rose from behind the bar, shoving two fresh loads into a short shotgun. He emptied one barrel at a wounded scalphunter who staggered out the back door. The charge caught him fully in the back, and he fell with both feet still on the hard-packed floor.

A loud thump caused Lane to pause in his own reloading as Clarence flipped a table out of the way to reach the pregnant woman. It landed on a wounded man who ceased moving when the edge crushed his throat.

Reaching down as gentle as if picking up a baby, Clarence sheathed his sword and Lane saw a huge Walker revolver in his hand, another product from his voluminous pants. He brought Victoria to her feet. "Are you all right?" he asked, in the gentlest of voices.

Wet, red eyes cast downward, she pulled a strand of black hair behind one ear. She nodded and picked her way through bodies that virtually covered the floor. "I am now."

Stunned hunters backed against the wall, eyeing the carnage, while horses outside thundered away into the darkness, bearing murderers who had more sense than the others. Others had already escaped into the street. Another wounded scalphunter groaned and tried to rise, and Hezekiah kicked him out of the way to clear the floor, then shot him in the head. "You and your kind brought down the lightning."

Walking backward, Hezekiah and Clarence made sure their retreat was unmolested, Hezekiah praying under his breath as they passed Lane. He caught the gist of those prayers offered for the souls of those men they'd slaughtered.

As they passed the stunned Ranger, Victoria reached out and touched Lane's arm. Electricity jumped from her hand and despite the witch's brew of odors rising from blood, smoke, and entrails, a delicious musky odor came from the woman that was almost intoxicating. "You did just fine. Thank you."

She gave him a wan smile and they disappeared into the darkness. Hanrahan laid the twelve-gauge on the bar and picked up a bottle of whiskey with a shaking hand. Bubbles glugged as he swallowed three times from the neck. He handed it to Lane, who did the same.

"That was a helluva thing." Lane started to pass the bottle back, then took another, hoping the raw whiskey would overcome the stench that again filled his senses. "I've never seen anything like it."

He absently felt the arm Victoria touched as she passed, relishing the tingle that swelled and washed through his body. To be sure he hadn't been shot, he checked the sleeve and found it intact.

The saloon owner drew a deep breath and scanned his stunned clientele. "How many of you boys are hurt?"

Sweat stuck a pistol under his belt and pointed. "Caleb there's gone. And several others I barely know, though I don't know how we ain't all dead or wounded. Wishy there's carved up pretty bad."

The wounded hunter sat on a chair, his shirt off, revealing half a dozen open slashes that revealed muscle, tendons, and bone. Another hunter knelt beside Wishy, already sewing the great wounds closed with a thick needle and heavy thread. Grimacing at every stick and trembling with pain and shock, Wishy clutched a whiskey bottle in his good hand, taking great drafts every couple of stitches.

Lane scanned the sea of greasy, unwashed corpses of the scalphunters and more than a few hide hunters' bodies. "I can walk from here to the back door and not touch the ground. I swear, I bet there were over a hundred shots fired in here." He glanced down at his body, seeing no wounds but a considerable amount of blood splatter that wasn't his.

"Well, let's get them outta here." Hanrahan tucked the reloaded twelve-gauge back under the bar. "Sweat, would you and some of the boys drag these carcasses out? Pitch 'em in my wagon and we'll haul 'em out of town tomorrow. I don't aim to bury a one of 'em, so we'll burn 'em, I guess."

As the rough survivors went to work, another drink from the bottle helped steady Lane's nerves. He thought about what he'd seen. The three men he'd just met only a couple of hours earlier had saved his life, and the life of the woman in a way he couldn't explain. There was something mythical about the way they fought, and they completed the job without a wound among them.

The breeze rose, blowing through the open front door and out the back, clearing the air. Bodies disappeared, and the customers put the saloon back together. Tables rose, and as the evening progressed, the blacksmith came inside with several buckets of fresh dirt to cover the black blood congealing on the ground.

By three that morning, they were again drinking, trying to numb their minds against what they'd seen and done. For the first time in his life as a Ranger, Lane felt safe enough with men he really didn't know to let his guard down. Overwhelmed by the gunfight, and the events of the past couple of days, he gave himself over to the bottle to quell the demons and doubt that raged inside.

Hours passed, and he drank steadily through the night until dawn pushed back the darkness. Sliding a gold coin under the base of the near-empty bottle, Lane finally rested his arms and head on the table and fell into a deep, dark sleep.

FOURTEEN

BENT BY THE DECADES WEIGHING upon her thin shoulders, Miss Hattie was cleaning out her fireplace when she heard a horse outside the soddy. Unconcerned whether the animal carried a friend or stranger, she dropped the last scoop of ashes into a rusted metal bucket and carried it outside.

The animal wasn't in evidence, and she set the bucket beside the thick wooden door and returned with a metal cup half full of chicory. Shoulders so hunched by age that she resembled a turtle poking its head out of a shell, she settled slowly on a rough wooden bench against the front wall, taking care not to drop too heavily and jar her bones.

She sighed and scanned the panorama spread out before her. To her left was a stream of cold water that arose from Boiling Springs and wove in a series of rootlike trickles that separated and found themselves. They spread out through the hardwoods bordering meandering watercourses, sometimes dribbled over tiny falls and other times widened into shallow beds barely ankle deep to eventually disappear into the waving grass stretching to the horizon.

Speaking aloud, she took a sip and addressed the dominecker hen scratching her way across the yard. "This is the one cup of coffee I allow myself of a morning, Missus Hen." A handful of chicks paused to inspect her for a moment, then resumed their task of learning how to survive.

She was watching a box turtle make his slow way toward the water when a tall shadow appeared at the soddy's corner. She nodded when she recognized the shape of a colorful scarf tied over his head. "Good morning, Ashkii Dighin."

The young Navaho man whose name meant sacred child smiled when he stepped into view and flicked his fingers at her. He understood English fairly well but couldn't respond because a Chiricahua Apache named Nantan Lukan took the sixteen-year-old captive a few years earlier and used a white settler's straight razor to cut Ashkii's tongue out for fun.

Because the boy refused to scream and ask for mercy as the Apache's men held him down, Nantan Lukan admired Ashkii's bravery in the face of such abuse and said he was more man at that young age than most of the adults he'd ever tortured. Instead of cutting off any more body parts, they doctored him back to health and let the boy live.

Miss Hattie sipped the cold brew. "I knew it would be you. Felt you coming a day or so ago."

Familiar with one of her many gifts, the smiling man said he understood by stretching his neck a little higher and raising both eyebrows.

Miss Hattie met Ashkii one day when he came to see the old witch woman for himself after hearing about her from so many travelers. She wasn't the least bit scared the day she looked up from mending a garment and saw him squatting at the same corner where he stood now, watching.

It took a while for them to communicate. At first it was a rudimentary form of sign language such as pointing at his mouth and rubbing his bare, flat stomach to say he was hungry. She quickly learned that he could understand her language, and that made communication easier. After sharing her food that day, he was there often, helping carry water and sometimes bringing roots, grains, and herbs he collected as he crisscrossed the prairie. The chicory she enjoyed every morning came from his foraging.

In time, she learned more sign language, though her gnarled fingers wouldn't let her make them herself and often mixed a few simple gestures in with her words as they grew more comfortable with each other.

"I have some soft eggs cooked up for you. They're in that skillet in there by the fire. I 'magine they're still warm."

A bright smile lit his face. Chewing and swallowing was hard for him, so he enjoyed the soft foods Miss Hattie offered whenever he came around. Ashkii disappeared into the soddy and came back out with a cast iron skillet. He settled cross-legged against the front of her house and dug in with his fingers.

They sat in silence while he ate. Without a tongue, it took some doing to masticate the food. To swallow, he raised his chin to stretch his neck, much like a chicken. Miss Hattie watched with approval as he finished and set the skillet on the ground. He wiped his fingers on the legs of his britches. The dominecker hen hurried over with her babies and they circled the pan to peck at the egg remains with the soft sound of rain.

Ashkii belched in satisfaction and signed again.

His question brought a smile to her eyes. "Yes, I've had several dreams since you were here last, and many of them I can't explain."

He signed a question and raised his eyebrows for emphasis.

"Well, like I said. These have been strange of late. I dreamed of a world where people walked around all day with their heads bent toward the ground, studying small blocks of wood in their hands and not talking to those nearby. Their fingers flew over the blocks and tapped them over and over. I couldn't hear it, but I bet that tapping was some kind of music, like the drums other tribes use across great distances.

"And at night, in the heat of summer, they went into cold houses and sat on soft chairs to cover up with blankets and stare at those blocks until they glowed in the dark. It scared me because they never put them down."

Ashkii's fingers flew into the air. "It's dangerous not to look up. It allows wolves to sneak up and eat them, as they do old buffalo and fresh-born calves that are more interested in what's at their feet, than what is around them."

"That's true, hon. That's why human beings stand straight and look forward."

"They should also sleep when the sun gives way to darkness. It is our rhythm. Being out of balance is dangerous." He signed. "Did you see anything else?"

"Yes. Thin, windows like white people have in their houses stuck to the walls and that same cold light came through them. Brightly colored ghosts moved around behind those windows. Sometimes they fought and other times laughter and conversation came out of them, but worse, lies they believed floated out into the air and settled on their shoulders making them angry or sad. Many of those lies made them scared."

"Why didn't they rip those windows out?"

"I wish I knew. Many of my dreams make no sense to me either."

He pointed at the dominicker hen and signed, "Tell me about the chicken house again."

"Oh. That's another one I don't understand. People in buggies with fat black wagon wheels full of air move without horses or oxen. They circle a building and when they come out on the other side, they have bright red striped buckets of fried chicken with an old white man's face on it and clean their hands by licking their fingers."

"All of my people clean our fingers like that." Ashkii laughed silently. "You can't put air in wagon wheels!" His hands rested in his lap for a minute before fluttering back to life. "Did you dream 'bout the woman bearing the child?" His fingers flicked so fast she had to concentrate, then translate them into words. "They are coming."

Miss Hattie frowned, deepening the lines etched by age and the sun. "How do you know that she's on the way?"

He pointed at the ground and made his fingers dart.

"Now, you know I don't believe that. Lizards don't talk."

Ashkii Dighin's eyes darted around, as if looking for a reptile to validate what he said. "Yet you have visions you say will come true." He pointed at the sky, then the horizon defined where the grass met the sky. His fingers and hands darted and swooped.

"Now hold on, hon. You know I can't read sign that fast. Shoot, being out here alone for so long, I doubt I could carry on a fast conversation if somebody was to come along and stop for a talk. But I do dream about those folks that need my help. They're on the way."

He signed again. "How many did you say?"

"Five are a-comin' that I know of right now, but you say there's more?" She smiled at his joke. "Who are the others?"

His head shake was sharpened by frustration. Another sign.

"Well, honey, I don't have no idea what you're saying about now, but last night I dreamed about two more myself, and the seventh person's hard for me to pin down, but no matter, it looks to me like I'm gonna have a lot of company when they get here." She rose on creaking knees. "Lordamighty. I believe I have sand in my joints this morning." Miss Hattie flicked her arthritic fingers. "Come on, and let's see what the garden has for us today. You can carry these ashes for me to help the plants grow bigger."

Ashkii Dighin made the sign that he was thirsty.

"Well, there's a gourd right there, and the water's fresh. I dipped it out of the spring just this morning."

He took a good long drink while she stepped inside for a grass basket to gather the vegetables in preparation for the visitors to come.

FIFTEEN

LANE WOKE UP LATE THE next afternoon, the stiff upper half of his body still draped on top of the saloon table. Dust motes thick as a swarm of gnats danced on a wide shaft of sunlight coming through the open door. Outside, a wagon stacked high with buffalo hides rattled down the settlement's lone dirt street, raising even more dust that floated through the opening.

Raising his head, he squinted at the glare coming through the open door. The bolt as bright as lightning for someone who'd swallowed a bottle of whiskey cut all the way through to the back of his noggin. He groaned and pushed himself upright before plopping his hat back where it belonged.

A woman's laugh cut through the fog. Turning slowly so his head wouldn't fall off onto the floor, he saw Mrs. Olds packing the ground with her feet. "Well good morning there, Captain Newsome. Good to see you're back with us."

"Would you mind speaking a little softer, and tell me why you're dancing all alone and without music?"

"Well, if there was music playing, you wouldn't be in such a fine humor with that skull of yours about to split open, but I'm not dancing. I'm stomping this fresh dirt down so I can level it off afterwhile."

As he drank the whiskey down below the bottle's label the night before, Lane recalled seeing bucket after bucket of dirt come in to cover the blood that was spilled. It would help cut down on the odor, also. "What time of day is it?"

"Afternoon."

The news jolted Lane to his feet. "Good lord. Me and Buck was supposed to leave with the Kiowa woman to go find that girl."

"Oh, Lane." Mrs. Old's face fell. "I let you sleep so you could take the bad news after you rested. I didn't want to break it to a man with cobwebs in his mind."

"What bad news? Something happen to Victoria while I was asleep, or was it Tall Grass?"

Hanrahan's voice came from behind the bar. "No, they're fine. Victoria and her bodyguards are sitting out there by the blacksmith shop, waiting for you. And before you ask, the Kiowa woman is fine too."

Looking back and forth between the two of them, Lane waited. Finally, Mrs. Olds licked her thin lips to break the news. "It's about your partner, Buck."

At the mention of his name, the avalanche of memories returned to weigh on Lane's shoulders. They'd found out about him, what he was, or maybe Wolf had made good on his offer to quarter his partner and bury the parts where he couldn't find them.

Head spinning from the liquor's aftereffects and his recollections, Lane held on to the table and took a moment to choke down his rising stomach before answering. Maybe Wolf would tell him where he'd taken Buck's head. At least he could do something for him, but what, he didn't know. "All right. What about him?"

"Well, he was asleep in the wagon when you came in here and braced those nasty scalphunters, and let me tell you, son, you were a sight to see. You and those guards of Victoria's killed a passel of 'em, and every one deserved what he got. Not very many men have the guts to do what you did without someone backing you up . . ." She paused to catch her breath and pull a wayward strand of gray hair from her eyes. "But anyway, you remember how the bullets were flying in here. Well, one went smooth out that door and through the side of the wagon . . . and into your partner's brainpan while he was asleep."

Lane's eyes widened.

"Now take it easy. It was about as comfortable a death as you can imagine. It hit him right in the side of the head and killed him instantly. Son, he didn't move nary a muscle. Was still laying there with his arms crossed over his chest and the pistol in his hand, though it didn't do him much good."

She pulled that same strand of hair from her face again and paused. "I swanny. I don't know how that man slept through all that, unless one of the first bullets they fired killed him right off. That must have been what done it, and I'm sure sorry to tell you."

Mind reeling and unable to speak, Lane glanced out the door to see the wagon gone. He turned back to Hanrahan. "What went with the wagon, and Buck's . . . body?"

"Well, it was this way. The boys used Hanrahan's wagon to haul off them scalphunter's carcasses. You know it was dark, so they just took to throwing them over the side and going back for another. They was piled up like hides back there when the boys were done, and at dawn this morning Sweat Henderson and a bunch of others with Sharps rifles hauled 'em off a ways down close to a little creek not far from here, along with a couple of buckets of grease fat to get things started good.

"There's plenty of downed cottonwood there, so they piled all of 'em up with enough logs and such and set fire to the whole shebang."

Lane reeled and started for the door, but Hanrahan's sharp voice stopped him. "Your buddy ain't with 'em, so come on back and set down. He was on the bottom where he started out when they finally got down to him."

Lane cleared his throat. "Did they burn him? I promised what I'd do next time . . ."

Hanrahan reached down under the bar and came up with Buck's gun belt. "They didn't burn him. They buried him close by for you, and marked the grave so's you can find it. Word came in that while they were out there, they saw a big party of Comanche gathering a couple of miles farther on.

He glanced out the door, as if a raiding party was about to come whooping down the street. "We had a couple more boys come in telling about seeing big bunches of Comanches out west of town. The way they're figuring, these parties are either gonna keep scouring around to find as many hunters as they can, or they're forming up into a big war party."

"How big?"

"Sweat's thinkin' maybe five hundred warriors. I don't believe you need to go out and find his grave right now. Leave him there to rest until it's safe again." He handed the belt and pistol over the counter. "Said I'd make sure you got it."

The leather was soft and clean, the Colt itself freshly oiled by men who loved and understood such machinery.

"Thank you for this." Lane rose. "I'm going to get my horse and go out to see where they put him."

"Y'ought not do that. They put up a marker, but you might want to spend your time making a better one, with words and all, since you knowed him."

"No, sir. Thanks for your concern, but I'm going out to find my friend."

"I figured, but I had to try. Just look up and follow the smoke. You'll find him not far away. You be careful, son, and hurry back here. We don't need no more graves out there."

Nodding thanks to both Mrs. Olds and Hanrahan, Lane stepped onto the single street. The camp was buzzing with men gathered in groups in both directions. Lane felt their tension and their eyes as he walked down the so-called street to find Victoria and the others.

Lane's head was better by the time he reached the stable. Victoria, Clarence, and Hezekiah were sitting under the shade of a skinny brush arbor. Wolf and Tall Grass were a little farther away, leaning against an adobe wall that was melting back to its original form.

He paused and scanned the area around them, seeing none of their horses were yet saddled. "I'm sorry y'all had to wait on me. Have any of you heard about Buck?"

Hezekiah stood to speak. "I heard they burned those bodies but put him in the ground for you, though I doubt he'll stay there, unless that bullet was blessed or cut some spiritual nerve that anchored him to the earth."

"Well, I don't know, but I intend to find out."

Wolf approached. "I will go with you. Together we can give him peace."

"No. I don't believe I could watch you do those things you said, and if he's awake and crawled out on his own, he'll be peevish and likely to start shooting."

"I see his gun in that belt."

"You do. But Buck always has a hideout pistol close to hand, and I know that for a fact because it belongs to me. Let me go out there and get him settled down, then come out and we'll take off from there. I need to get on the road and find that little gal, River."

SIXTEEN

L EADING BUCK'S BLACK GELDING, LANE followed the distinctive line of dual wagon tracks leading from Adobe Walls and over a slight ridge toward the north. It was late afternoon, and a thin band of dark clouds grew off to the northwest.

Wagon tracks are never straight, curving around obstacles or veering slightly as one horse or mule pulls harder than the other. Lane rode in the middle, letting the gray find his way and keeping a sharp eye out for Comanche. Though he was well armed, he was in no mood to tangle with a war party that day.

An inordinate amount of lizards and horny toads appeared in the grass as he passed, and he idly wondered about their presence. Snakes slithered nearby, though none of the prairie rattlers spun up to buzz a warning at him. Dozens of box turtles rose up on their toes and stretched their necks to watch them pass.

He'd once been after an outlaw named Percy Lewis, who stole horses most of his life. Buck and Lane followed him north to the Nakonis tribal land between the Pease and Red Rivers. They made a sandy camp half a mile from the Red, and late one afternoon Lane found himself surrounded by hundreds, if not thousands, of tiny, just-born horny toads. Neither the Rangers nor their horses could walk without stepping on them. It was an uneasy sensation, and that's just how Lane felt when he saw them, lizards and snakes of all varieties underfoot.

As he neared Thomson Creek, a thin, dark column of black, greasy smoke rose in the distance, revealing where the buffalo hunters burned those bodies.

Damn smoke's an Indian magnet.

He reined up.

Every Comanche and Kiowa in the country's gonna see that.

Lane checked over his shoulder.

I oughta turn around and head back and wait a few days so they can all come and check it out. But if I do, I'm liable to lose the trail of that River girl, and she can't afford that.

Throwing one leg over the pommel of his saddle, he settled into his favorite thinking position. He could see for miles in each direction from that elevation. Meadowlarks and quail called around him, a peaceful morning if a man was sitting on his front porch staring out at a herd of cattle or fields of corn he'd planted with his own hand.

Not a man who usually favored a smoke, some things called for a cigar. He dug one from his saddlebag and fired it alight. It hardly burned at all before a speck in the distance formed inside the optical illusion of the converging wagon tracks.

He studied the speck as he smoked, knowing it couldn't be a Comanche. At first, he thought it was a wolf or buffalo calf heading in his direction, but as it neared, the shape became more distinct. The gray must have seen or sensed it coming their way because he shifted his position, rocking Lane slightly.

"Steady on, hoss." Lane drew on his cigar, watching the horse's ears prick forward. "I believe I've figured out what that is."

He had. Fifteen minutes later, he recognized Buck Dallas, following the wagon tracks back to Adobe Walls, stomping a quick pace as if mad at the whole world.

"I'm glad I have this pistol." He addressed the horse, as if it understood what he was saying. "He looks mad enough to spit nails, and I truly hope he's forgot that hideout gun of mine."

As Buck neared, a number of smaller shapes shifted behind him. Lane finally realized they were wolves following at a safe distance. Already accustomed to talking to the gelding, he spoke again. "I've given up trying to figure this world out." Realizing he hadn't checked for Indians for a while, he gave his full attention to his surroundings.

At the end of the wagon tracks leading from Adobe Wells, he saw a band of horses and the rising dust behind them. They weren't running, he could tell. After counting, Lane nodded and spoke to the gray. "Three men and two women, all mounted and leading two packhorses. That's our bunch. Wonder how they knew I'd find Buck so fast."

The cry of a hawk overhead reached Lane's ears as he turned back around to see Buck was almost there, and the late Ranger Captain was madder'n an old sore-tail tomcat. He stopped a few feet away and pointed a forefinger like a lance. "You said you wouldn't bury me no more."

"I didn't. Somebody else did it, though it looks to me like the job they did wasn't no better'n mine."

"Well, it wasn't as deep, but it was still a pain in the ass to dig my way out. You don't know what kind of trouble that is. How come you let 'em do it?"

"Well, I didn't. I got drunk last night and slept through that part. From what I heard, somebody accidentally put a bullet in your brain while I was at it and they thought you was dead at the bottom of a pile of scalphunters they burned."

"Yeah, I saw the fire. Must've been quite a massacre. I hope you got drunk *after* it was all over."

"My drinkin' came afterwards. I did for a couple of them greasy bastards, but the rest were laid out by those folks back there." Lane jerked a thumb over his shoulder. "Them dirty scalphunters stole that pregnant woman we met yesterday, and me and them fellers who was escorting her went into the saloon after them."

Buck slapped dirt from his shirt with his hat. His scalped skull was bright inside the thickness of his hair. "You did right. Get her back?"

"Yep. She's back there with 'em."

"While I was laying in that dirt, I remembered something."

"What?"

"The reason this hole in my scalp won't close up is because that medicine man wanted his Great Spirit to look down into my skull and see both me and that snake." Setting his hat just so, Buck looked down at his pants. "I'd dearly love to take a bath, but with the water acting the way it does, I might have to strip down and get one of them women to wash me."

"I doubt either of them will relish that job, Buck. They probably don't want to touch the clothes of a dead man who keeps walking around, and I for one don't want to see you nekkid while they do it."

"Well, avert your eyes, then."

"It'll be a strain on all of us with you walking around nekkid as a jaybird, even though we ain't looking. Having you up in this condition is enough to deal with for now. How about I take a broom to you and at least knock off some of the topsoil?"

"You don't have a broom in your pocket, and besides . . ." He paused, staring at the ground as if listening. "Oh." He squinted up at Lane. "That lizard says we need to light a shuck as soon as we can. With that norther heading our way, we're liable to get slowed up by the weather."

Startled by his comment, Lane inhaled more smoke than he intended. Breaking into a cough, he swung his leg back over and found the stirrup. "You said a *lizard* told you that?"

"Yep. Strange, ain't it?" He absently rubbed the side of his head that had taken the bullet. "This snake inside me's been talking ever since I woke up, and by the time I clawed myself back out of that grave for the *third goddamned time*, I came eye to eye with a horny toad and a lizard. They were arguing over a cricket they both wanted. Found out I can talk to them through this snake in my chest, though horny toads ain't near as chatty as a lizard. They just like to squint and throw small words at you because that makes it easier for 'em to talk."

Lane shivered. "My lord. Now he talks to reptiles ever'body *else* can see."

"It don't matter right now. The other thing they told me is there's about seven hundred Comanche warriors heading this way. We need to get gone, and the only safe way's there." He pointed and Lane studied that direction for a moment.

Buck drew a deep breath to keep talking. "Your friends are almost here, so hand me the reins so I can get mounted. Thanks for bringing him, by the way."

Sticking the cigar into the corner of his mouth, Lane passed the reins over. Once Buck was in the saddle, Lane took the gun belt looped over his own saddle horn and handed them over.

"Hanrahan had these, though I'm not sure why you're gonna need them. We only seem to get into trouble these days when you're dead or passed out in whatever kind of sleep that keeps taking you over."

"Thank you." Buck threaded the buckle and settled the rig on his hips. "Just try and stay close at night, would you?"

"Well, last night I didn't have much choice." Lane raised his right hand, as if before a judge in court. "I'll never bury you again and promise to try and keep others from doing it to you. How's that?"

"Fine! You don't know what it's like to wake up with dirt in your eyes. I doubt I can get killed for good, and that's the whole point. Now I worry that if you're not around and somebody finds me on the plains, they'll want to put me in a fire like them other fellers and then I'll have to start over plumb nekkid once my clothes burn off. You know, this ain't one bit funny."

"That's a fact. If somehow you *do* get killed, and right now I'm kinda wishing I could do it myself, I'll put you up on a scaffold like the Cheyenne or Sioux. That way, you can be sure that if you wake up, all you'll have to do is climb down."

Buck cheered up at the thought. "I like that."

"You know this is a burden to me."

"A burden to you? You?" He would have launched into another tirade, but Wolf finally closed the distance.

"I see those hunters did not do the job any better than you did, Lane. Not even with half his head shot off."

Buck adjusted himself in the saddle. "Don't get any ideas, featherhead. Right now my serpent says we need to get going. That child inside your woman needs to get somewhere before she drops it."

"The child will wait until we find the old woman. That will be a good thing. Maybe the old witch woman can cast a spell on you so that you will lay down like a decent corpse and be quiet. You're a bother now that you're up."

"I'm afraid there's nothing decent about me anymore."

Wolf stared hard at Buck. "I see with this Dark Eye that your serpent is growing. If it gets too big, you will have a belly like that pregnant woman and before you know it, your skull is liable to split and fall off to be replaced by the serpent's head." He turned his horse toward the east. "If it does, I hope it doesn't talk as much."

"It will, but with a forked tongue." Buck laughed as his own joke. No one else even smiled, but something had his attention. He reined the black gelding around and, inclining his head to see past his right boot, spoke toward the ground. "Howdy, Mister Lizard, how far is it to the old woman?"

Trying to see what he was talking to, Lane leaned over, causing his gray to adjust for the shifting weight.

Buck sagged in the saddle, looking disappointed. "Well, shit."

"What is it?" Lane peered at the ground also.

"Your damned horse stepped on my lizard guide and smushed it. Now I have to find another one that's in the mood to talk to me."

SEVENTEEN

WIND PICKED UP FROM THE northwest as Twisted Root and his band sat on their horses atop a rise, watching a herd of buffalo graze with their rumps turned into the coming storm. The sweet smell of aggravated grass reached their nostrils. Like a dog winding birds, he stuck his nose in the air.

An unseen wolf spoke his piece in the distance. Two others howled from different locations. Wolves were an ever-present part of a buffalo herd, taking new calves when they could, or culling the old and sick that fell behind.

Twisted Root didn't like the sound at that time of the day. "Something is coming."

"The storm." Pahayoko, or Amorous One, pointed. "Can you not see that with your old eyes? You should at least feel the wind."

"Of course I see it. I can also see into the future to when I'm in a bad mood and I put a stick through your tongue so you cannot speak irritating words any longer. It is not the storm. I smell white men on the wind."

Tabemohats, or Bright Sun, shook his lance in excitement. "Let us go kill them!"

"It would be the right thing to do." Twisted Root nodded, thinking. "But I want to go cut up that old woman at Boiling Springs first, before it gets here. She has been a thorn in my spirit since she put this scar on my face. I think she uses crows to make her spells stronger. I've seen them in the trees every time we go past there."

Twisted Root made it a point to slip up on the sod house each time they were close by. Twice he had come close to killing her, but crows gave him away. Once, he drew a bead with his rifle on the hump that was her bent back, bent like his, only for a different reason. His finger tightened on the trigger and a crow flew into the tree above his head. When the witch woman turned and stared directly at him, lightning came from her eyes and his finger went numb.

He came by a year later with a stout Osage orange bow, thinking its silence would please the great spirit and her death would be punctuated not by the sharp crack of gunfire, but the snap and hiss of a blessed arrow. Kneeling behind a fallen log, he drew the string, bending the decorated and painted wooden strip into a sharp arc, and the bow snapped in two at the same time crows lit on top of her house to caw and fuss.

Frightened by her medicine, he fled, angry and ashamed. Only when young Quanah Parker took the warpath did he feel any strength return to his spirit. The twenty-three-year-old son of a white captive woman Cynthia Ann Parker and the Comanche warrior Peta Nocona, Quanah was the spark the tribe was looking for to fight the white men.

Twisted Root flicked his fingers eastward, away from the coming storm. "I will kill that old witch and take her hair for my lance. Then we can sit in her lodge made of dirt while this cold wind blows and eat all the food she saved. I would like to roast one of those chickens of hers too."

"I think we should join Quanah on this raid they are planning." Tabemohats shook his lance again to make the scalps dance. One was brown, and the other long and blond. "The old woman will die soon on her own. I would rather have scalps taken in honorable battle than peel the thin hair from her wrinkled old head."

The comment angered Twisted Root. Raising his hands to the sky, as if trying to hasten the storm. "It's too far. We can't catch up to them. Everyone will be dead by the time we get there, and Quanah will have all the glory while we get nothing. If you want to kill white people, I will talk to the spirits and find out where these others are. We can wait this storm out in Mow-Ways's village. He is camped on the Rio Colorado."

The Comanche nation wasn't one single tribe, rather it consisted of several independent bands traveling and trading independently of the others. The Buffalo Eaters were returning to the High Plains from a successful hunt that Twisted Root had heard about.

Tabemohats and Pahayoko disagreed. Bright Sun shouted at the medicine man. "You go look for old people. Pahayoko and I will join Quanah and Isa-tai and make the Great Spirit happy with all the white men we rub out."

Twisted Root made a sign of disgust and turned his back on the departing warriors. "Go then. We will kill the witch woman by ourselves."

Yanking their ponies around, the youngest warriors kicked them into a run, filling the air with whoops of excitement. Instead of watching them go, Twisted Root and his remaining warriors urged their mounts eastward.

✯✯★✯✯

STAYING APART FROM THE ADULTS, NINE TOES shook his head.

Shouts His Name noticed. "Why do you look like that?"

"I think going after the old woman is a mistake."

"Why do you say that? Are you afraid?"

"No. But I think this is a bad thing for the People. Look, there are more Comanche gathering together than I have ever seen. We should not divide and go off like this. We should find out where the white man's chief lives and go together as one big band to show that we are strong and will protect our land. That way, they will see the strength of our people and that we will fight."

"You think too much. You are not a war chief, or a shaman."

"You should think *more*. I also think that torturing our enemies to death is no longer the right thing to do. We should make them prisoners and take them to their chief. That will show we are trying to make peace. Maybe when we give the white man back, they will appreciate it and trade more with us. We were great traders with the Mexicans and Apaches when it was necessary."

"You sound like you are afraid."

Nine Toes shook his head as Twisted Root looked toward the east. "I am not afraid. I just think there might be another way. I don't think we can kill enough white men to stop them from swarming over our land like ants."

EIGHTEEN

T HE STRANGE PROCESSION FOLLOWING THE two Rangers fanned out behind them, more to avoid the dust from the horses ahead but also to prevent attack from the rear. The ominous blue norther built, growing angrier and darker as the minutes passed. It was as if a knife carved the sky in two, leaving the eastern portion clear and cloudless in front of them. The air was still, with not a breath moving the prairie grass.

Used to seeing the ocean of grass bob and wave in the breeze, Lane was strangely uncomfortable. "We got off pretty late, and I don't know what's gonna happen to you when that storm gets here. That curse you're carrying around might decide it's nighttime once the sun disappears behind the clouds, and if it does, you're gonna drop like you're shot and I'll have to get your limp ass back up across the saddle."

He twisted to look over his shoulder at the coming storm. "You know what it's like to load a body that's gone limp? We've done it plenty of times before. I sure hate to ask one of those fellers because I'd bet a dollar to a donut Wolf'll offer to put you up there one piece at a time and carry you off."

Buck's eyes widened in horror. "I was thinking the same thing, but don't ever let Wolf do that. I don't know what might happen if I'm in pieces when I wake up. Lordy, maybe new arms and legs'd grow out of the trunk, and then what would happen to my limbs? It's almost too much to think about." He shook his head and rode in silence for a minute. "Each piece could grow a whole body, and then there'd be five of me, and you're complaining about helping just the one I am now."

"You divide into five Bucks, and I'll for sure turn you over to Wolf."

"We don't have much choice about what to do." Buck also twisted in the saddle to evaluate the coming weather. "We either keep riding through it, and you can tie me on so I won't fall off. But the way that cloud's shaping up, I think we need to set up these tents and make camp in some windbreak before long."

Lane thumbed sweat from his eyebrows. "That's a good idea. I don't intend to squat in a buffalo waller to wait for something like that to pass."

"Me neither." Buck reined up. Seeing them stop, the others drifted close.

Wolf positioned his horse, making sure they were on the side with his good eye. "Why have you stopped? Is this where you would like for me to put you in the ground once and for all?"

"I'm getting a little tired of this conversation." Buck pointed. "It's coming up a cloud, and that storm's gonna be a booger when it gets here. I don't relish the idea of riding in it until dark. Lane and I've done that more'n once, through hail, sleet, and cold rain. I say we find us a few cottonwoods somewhere and set up those campaign tents we bought."

Hezekiah agreed. "Victoria don't need any of that falling weather, and neither do I. I prefer my comfort to misery. It'll give me a chance to drink a little whiskey too. I brought a bottle for my enjoyment and might share a swallow or two if I'm in the right mood."

Clarence and Victoria nodded. Tall Grass gazed toward the east, ignoring the coming clouds. Her round face was peaceful, and a small dimple in her cheek deepened at the thought of something pleasant.

Buck drew a long breath. "Fine, then. Wolf, have you ever been this way? Is there someplace we can light for a spell?"

"You've been here?" It was the first time Victoria had spoken since they left that morning, and it was directed at the big Cheyenne.

"Once or twice, as a boy. My people passed this way to flense robes and smoke buffalo meat. There is a canyon ahead, one that just opens up like the slash of a knife. Our band preferred the wood of a special tree that grows there to cure their meat.

"The walls will break the wind, and it's hard for anyone to know they are upon it until it's almost too late. One time we camped there when I was young and some of the warriors watched two wagons pass, with nothing more than their eyes above the rim. The white men never knew the canyon was there and my people followed behind and came back with many horses and scalps."

Hezekiah frowned and made a sign with his fingers. "Mike. You shouldn't tell people that, now that you are civilized."

"Who said I am civilized? And my name is not Mike."

"You're with us. It's your civilized name. Wear it with honor."

"I am with you because the Great Spirit told me to meet you in that wormhole down on the Rio Grande. After we have finished escorting Victoria, I may rejoin my band and become a warrior again, but I don't know. I haven't yet seen what will come through this Dark Eye."

Lane absorbed that information, vowing to keep a close eye on Wolf once they rescued the child and delivered Victoria to the old woman at Boiling Springs. Buck had already lost his scalp, and Lane didn't intend to follow the same path.

"I'm afraid it's gonna rain enough to wash us clean down to the Gulf of Mexico." Lane adjusted himself in the stirrups. The saddle creaked with his weight. "I can't swim good. So let's find something a flash flood can't reach."

"There are places where we can camp." Wolf took the lead, and the others fell in behind him.

Holding their horses where they were for a moment, the Rangers let the others get ahead. Buck chuckled with the dry sound of grasshopper wings. "I didn't know you couldn't swim."

"Well, first, don't ever try to laugh like that again. It makes my skin crawl, and second, I damn near drowned when I was a kid and was afraid of water for years. The truth is, I can dog-paddle a little, so's I won't sink during a river crossing."

"I don't think I have anything to worry about when it comes to water. You may have to learn to swim, but I think I can just walk on while it draws away from me. I bet the rain won't even hit me. It'll angle off or something."

Not wanting to get into that discussion at the moment, Lane ignored the comments. He felt he was getting good at it too. "Wolf didn't say how far ahead that cut was."

Before them lay a vast, silent land as still as a frozen pond. Not a breath of air moved as the clouds approached. The buzzards knew what was coming and disappeared from the sky. Birds often twittered and fluttered just above the grass as the travelers moved through the landscape, but they had vanished as well. Once, Clarence's horse stepped into a covey of quail, and instead of flushing and scattering to gather later with whistles and calls, they simply ran from under their hooves and regrouped behind them.

At the rear, Lane watched the little birds circle behind his packhorse and squeeze together, facing outward to preserve body heat. "The way our luck's running, that cut he's looking for'll be about two miles past wherever that storm catches us."

The strong north winds pushed a line of light clouds ahead, almost as a signal for those below that something was coming. Lane was almost right about their timing. After leading the procession arrow-straight toward the east for fifteen minutes, Wolf angled off to the right, as if he decided to run from the storm. Splintered bolts of lightning fractured black clouds full of rain, and soon thunder rolled across the open prairie.

Hearing it, Wolf kicked his horse into a lope and the others followed. They maintained that easy, rocking-chair pace, eating up the ground. Lane worried about the pregnant woman ahead. Victoria hadn't complained at all, but there was no way she could be comfortable, or safe, at that pace. Watching Tall Grass in the saddle, he wished Victoria knew how to ride as well as the round Kiowa woman.

Lane caught movement from the corner of his eye. The grass that had been still as the frozen sea suddenly rippled as the leading edge of the storm approached. In seconds the prairie changed. The waving grass ducked, swells developed as the wind roiled the plains, and the brunt of the norther was upon them.

The wind turned sharp and cold at the same time Wolf's muscled arm rose, followed by a shout that was snatched away by the wind. He pointed to the right. Turning his horse sharply, he waved them forward without checking to see if they were behind. Following immediately behind, Victoria's long black hair whipped around her head at the same time another clap of thunder vibrated the air.

Tall Grass kicked her horse in the ribs and tucked in tight behind Wolf just as he dropped from sight. It would have been startling if they hadn't been looking for a trail leading downward. One by one, the others dropped over the edge.

The wind immediately lessened, though the chill continued as the temperature dropped.

Buck followed, taking one last look over his shoulder at the storm that would soon blot the sun. Only a few feet behind him, Lane saw the concern on his face. "I'll keep an eye on you."

"If that sun goes and I drop, don't you leave me laying out here."

"I done told you I wouldn't. Now go!" Lane waved him forward.

This'll be interesting. I wonder if that damned curse is only for the dark of night, or the absence of sun. It's been bright and sunny during the day since he died. If we get out of this, I wonder what'll happen on a cloudy day. He's liable to drop like a shot duck.

That thought brought an entirely different set of problems. If clouds cut Buck's strings, they'd for sure have to stay away from regular people once they got back. Towns would be out of the question. Hell, they'd likely have to stay out on the trail, doing their best to avoid strangers.

Avoiding towns meant staying away from whiskey and women, and Lane knew Buck couldn't tolerate that. There were few pleasures in a man's one life, and giving up on those two would make the rest of his days a misery.

Buck doesn't have a life anymore, nor whiskey or women . . . or food.

The path leading down into the canyon was easy to follow. Despite the wide loads on their backs, the packhorses made it with ease. They came to a bend in the *barranca* before reaching bottom. A high, wide ledge dropped off down to the rocky floor, the result of a landslide eons ago. Swept flat, it was protected by the canyon wall itself and a thick growth of cottonwoods rooted below, doing their best to survive in the arid environment.

The deep cut was the perfect place to weather the storm. Clarence took in the surroundings and shouted above the rising wind. "Right there! We pitch the tents there."

While they dropped to the ground and unpacked, Lane loped around the little mesa, looking down another fifteen feet to the bottom. They couldn't have landed in a better spot. Satisfied they'd be above any flash flood, he wheeled the horse and rejoined his party.

The clouds finally ate the sun, and the canyon plunged into dim light. The others were busy putting up the tents and Lane dismounted. Reaching for the packhorse's lead rope, something dropped out of the sky and landed at his feet.

He looked down to see Buck lying face first as the first drops of icy rain slapped the dry ground. "Well, shit. Now I know, and I'm gonna have to put up this damned tent without him."

He was unrolling the canvas when Clarence appeared at his side. "It is the sun that keeps him upright. Though we cannot see, the sun has set."

"Yeah, well, that little bit of knowledge don't help us now."

The wind picked up, howling down the canyon as lightning crackled overhead, fracturing the black clouds with hard bolts of fire. Hezekiah was already tightening guy ropes on their tent. Wolf pushed Victoria into her shelter and Tall Grass drug a pack in behind her as Wolf rushed to hobble the horses.

Working quickly and fighting the wind and gathering darkness, Lane and Clarence finally got the second shelter erected. Clarence staked the lines tight while Lane threw packs and gear inside. The skies opened, but instead of rain, huge balls of hail thumped into the ground.

Frightened by the chunks of ice falling from the sky, the gray almost trampled Buck's body before Lane could grab his buddy's collar to drag him away. A hailstone big as a grapefruit caught Lane on the shoulder with a sickening thud. He shouted in pain and yanked Buck toward the tent. An even bigger hailstone pounded a dent in Buck's forehead with the wet sound of a crushed melon.

The horses instinctively huddled against the sheer canyon wall as more chunks of deadly ice dimpled the ground and bounced off the tents. Another hailstone glanced off Lane's hat brim, nearly knocking it from his head. Lane reached the flimsy shelter and fell inside, pulling Buck in after him.

Tying the flaps closed, he saw everyone else was already inside the larger shelter they would all share. Flopping to the ground in the small tent, Lane crossed his legs and struck a lucifer. He studied Buck's face and still form in the faint light. Had he been a normal person, the wound above Buck's left eye would have likely been fatal.

Another hailstone rippled the tent with a thud as if someone outside hit it with a stick of firewood. Lane rubbed his shoulder and watched the wall shudder from another impact. "Well, partner, if you can hear me like you said, I just want to say this dragging *your* dead ass around every time you drop is going to be a pain in *my* ass."

He shook the match out as the hail gave way to a torrential downpour drumming against the stiff canvas. The temperature dropped quickly and half an hour later it had fallen almost thirty degrees. Lane dug his coat out of the bedroll and slipped it on, shivering in relief. He considered putting a coat on Buck's still body, but figured he couldn't feel the cold, just as he couldn't feel pain.

Lane leaned back with his head resting on a gunnysack of provisions. "Well, at least I can talk to you for once without being interrupted or have to get involved in some argument that never makes much sense." Lightning struck somewhere nearby with a crack. Thunder vibrated the ground. "Did I ever tell you about the time my old granddaddy insisted I help him in the field out there in East Texas back when I was a kid? Well, he was planting corn, and I never wanted to be a dirt farmer because stoop labor is for someone else and not me, anyway . . . oh, wait. I remember I have told it to you." He settled back on an elbow. "I guess that don't matter now. Well, anyway . . ."

NINETEEN

THIS IS GOING TO DRIVE me insane. I can't move or see. Good God, how long have I been laying here? What in the world hit me so hard? I wonder if a horse kicked me. It didn't feel like it should, kinda like a hammer hitting spongy, rotten wood. My skull must have fractured with that one, but I guess when I finally wake up, if that's what you call it, it'll be healed up. At least I hope it will.

That gunshot wound to the side of my head was still open when I woke up this morning. Even though I got on to Lane about having to dig my way out, I'm kinda glad that I was underground because what I haven't told anyone is that it hurts pretty damn bad once I wake up, at least until everything closes up. That head wound especially. At least my screams were padded by all that dirt in my mouth.

Like to have never spit all the dirt out after I dug out. And to tell the truth, each wound hurts a little more each time, like my senses wake up just enough for me to feel it before everything goes numb again.

Damn that Indian.

Lane says the wounds are lighter than my skin once they heal. I'm gonna eventually look like someone who's scarred all to hell and gone. The rate I'm going, I'm gonna be mottled for sure and folks will start calling me Paint, after one of those paint horses. I'm not sure I can stand that kind of abuse.

At least I'm not underground again. I can hear Lane moving around in here, wherever in here is. It's good to have such a friend that'll stick with me, dead or alive. Rain. Rain is falling on something. We must be in one of those tents. At least he didn't leave me out there. Yep, he's always been a good friend.

Looks like I was right, though. Every time the sun hides its face, I'm nothin' more'n a pile of cow shit until it comes back out. Goddlemighty! I can't ever be normal again.

Well, partner, if you can hear me like you said, I just want to say this dragging your dead ass around every time you drop is going to be a pain in my ass.

Oh, now you're talking to me, Lane. You never had much to say all day long and now that I'm down and out, here you go yammering on. That's rude. I wish I could tell you what I think . . .

Hey! What is this? My mind's going a thousand miles a second. That's what the damned old medicine man wanted. No rest. No reprieve. No nothing. I'm a wandering, tortured spirit.

Is that what I am? Just a spirit in human form? The Indians say spirit animals are just like that, them that can change from . . .

Be quiet. You are annoying me.

What'n hell! That's not Lane talking. Whatever that voice is, it's in here with me.

I have always been in here with you, but you have been fairly quiet to this point. Stop talking and let me be at peace.

Who are you? Better'n that. What are you?

You have been calling me a snake, so I guess that is an appropriate name. Snake.

Please no. Please don't tell me I'm trapped in here with a damned snake. Good God! I really do have a snake inside me. That damned Comanche closed a snake up inside me!

I was not a snake in this world until you came along.

I'm not sure what you're saying. Get out of me!

You have been content with me up to this point. Now, calm your thoughts so that you no longer vex me.

Vex you!

Silence! You are maddening. I have only touched you with my mind so that you will be quiet and understand.

Understand what? Now I have to go through the rest of my life . . . days with you growing inside me. Only touched my mind, my ass! I feel you in there when I'm awake. I just didn't know you could talk. Twisted Root didn't have to do this. It was a fair fight. Hell, I was outnumbered and only did what I had to do.

So did he. It is his way.

To punish someone like this? It will drive me insane.

He is trying to protect what is his. We owned this land until you white people arrived and started pushing us off.

Hold on there, hoss. You were here all right, but who did you take the land from in the first place? I'll allow your ancestors took it from another tribe.

You speak the truth. We carved out our part of this land because it is our way.

Then you shouldn't be all twisted up about white people taking it away. Using your words, it is the way of the world.

Yes, so quit crying about what has happened to you, or the way we fight. It is the only way we know and has been like that since time began. Be quiet. I enjoyed the air, the wind, and the blue sky. That is what they called me, Blue Bird, until you set my ghost free. Let me tell you what happened. That sliver of my still-warm heart tangled with a long hair from his head and when he stuffed my spirit bird into your mouth so you could never speak again, they wound together like two snakes mating and now a part of both of them made me. It sealed me in there, and now I am trapped as you are.

I wish I could take a deep breath. Sometimes a man has to sigh. It does a world of good to relax yourself like that.

Neither of us will ever breathe properly again. Now, be quiet so I can think.

There's a lot to think about. What's going on in here with you, and the real world outside. You know what I look like now, Snake? I imagine Lane drug me in here and just left me how I fell. I might be sprawled out like a stomped-on toad frog. I sure hope he tidied me up a little before settling in. How long has it been?

Time means nothing to either of us.

Yeah, you're right. It's coming back to me now. I guess I forget a little each time I wake up. At least no one shoveled dirt in my face tonight. Those times they buried me seemed like an eternity until I woke up, if that's what I call it now. Hey, wait a minute. If I was buried five feet under the ground, how did I know when the sun was up?

I will answer that if you will stop making words come out of your mouth.

They're not coming out of my mouth. They're coming from my brain.

By this time your brain is nothing but melted fat. It lies at the bottom of your skull.

I'd puke at the thought of that if I could.

I wish you would. Then maybe you could puke me up and set me free. Be silent.

You be silent.

TWENTY

TWO CANDLES BURNED IN THE smallest of the two Sibley tents, giving Lane enough light to watch his friend lying in repose. At least that's the way he thought of it. He couldn't bring himself to blow them out because he sensed something was coming in the night and so he waited.

The storm had lessened, and the winds weren't as fierce. Alternating rain and much smaller hail rattled against the canvas, now an almost calming sound. Smoke curled from a small cigar in Lane's hand. He dug it out both for the comfort of the tobacco and because he'd been touched by his friend's lamentation that he'd never be able to enjoy such pleasures again.

Maybe in his sleep, or trance, or whatever state you'd call it, Buck might enjoy the scent of the rich tobacco.

Confident that the Indians weren't out prowling around in such weather, Lane finally relaxed, leaning comfortably against his saddle to enjoy the smoke and soothing sounds of rain on canvas. He exhaled, thinking of blowing out at least one of the candles when a small scratch on the tent brought him upright.

A soft female voice reached his ears. "Lane."

Recognizing who it was, he started to his feet and untied the strings holding the flaps closed. Pulling one side back, he made room for Victoria to slip inside. She was wrapped in a blanket, holding it closed with the inside hand, and carrying a handful of small hailstones in the other.

She flashed him a smile of thanks and popped one in her mouth and crunched it between her teeth as he retied the flap. "I've always loved eating hailstones. It's been a treat ever since I was a child. You want one?"

The soft, flickering light on her skin and black hair was almost a narcotic. He cleared his throat and swallowed. "No thanks. You'll crack a tooth like that. I had an uncle that broke a tooth cracking pecans, and he was in misery for weeks until a traveling dentist pulled it with a pair of pliers."

His mouth was moving, but his thoughts and emotions ran wild with her so close. He ached to reach out and touch her as that unidentifiable musk filled the tent, making him as randy as a buck deer on a cold fall morning.

Dimples at the corners of her mouth deepened in a smile and she offered one of the hailstones to him, not taking his initial refusal. She held it to his mouth, and he gave in, and she gently placed it on his tongue. The chip melted quickly, tasting of the air and clouds, as refreshing as a long drink from a bubbling spring.

"Is everything all right?" Heart pounding and nearly lightheaded, he pointed at her large belly.

She absently rubbed her stomach, evaluating the tent, saddles, and Buck lying against the side wall. "Do you think he really is asleep, or dead?"

"Both, in some way."

Victoria shivered. "It's strange, and yet I'm not scared."

"There's nothing to be scared of from Buck." He jerked a thumb at the tent flaps. "It's what's outside these tent walls that'll hurt you."

"It smells nice in here, with the smoke. Our tent smells of men, sweat, and horses."

"I wondered what it was like with all y'all crowded inside there. Someone could stay in here with us to make more room."

"They won't leave us, and Tall Grass wanted to stay with me instead of sleeping in here, though she trusts both of you."

"Well, I'm sorry for what you have to endure."

"It isn't as moist in here either. Too many people breathing in such a closed space. This is nice, and the candles give off just enough heat to drive away some of the chill."

"I've slept in worse places." A high hum filled his head, reminding him of how he felt the first time he kissed a girl.

"May I?"

Unsure of what she was asking, he shrugged. Victoria kept the blanket closed and lowered herself down against Lane's saddle. "That's better."

"I imagine you get tired pretty quick." He settled onto Buck's saddle blanket and crossed his legs. "It smells like horse sweat in here too."

She gave a soft laugh that sounded like music to his ears. "I like it, though."

"You just need to talk tonight?" He studied her dark eyes, for the first time noticing how long and curled her eyelashes were.

"A little more than that." She relaxed and pulled her long black hair back, letting the blanket settle midway down her arms. "Tell me what happened to Buck. I know what the others say, they've talked about him a lot. All three of them say he no longer resides in our world, but I'm not sure what that means."

Without hesitation, the story spilled out of Lane in a torrent. He told her why they were in that part of the country, then went on to the Indian attack, Buck's death, and his own guilt after running away.

He spoke in monotone, not really looking at Victoria's face, but instead at a spot somewhere on the tent wall behind her. The young woman's eyes widened at the part where Buck woke up after being buried for the first time, and he detailed their conversations, about how Buck was discovering his new abilities, and the few things they knew for sure.

"You need to have a priest see him."

"I thought the same thing, but after water refused to let him touch it, I can't imagine what will happen if he tries to enter a church. Hell, the priest might throw holy water at him. That could do any number of things."

"Like what?"

"Nothing I want to talk about anymore. Let's change the subject. I doubt those three over there in your tent were happy about you slipping out in the dark. I allow at least one of 'em's standing outside right now, listening to see if you're gonna holler help."

"They aren't, but I told them I wanted to come over and talk to you. I managed on my own before they showed up, though it was rough a couple of times."

"Okay, then, tell me about how they knew to come find you, or why."

"I've been feeling this tug for weeks. I couldn't resist it. The feeling is like something pulling my mind. The best way I can explain it is it feels like a weight in my head that leans in just one direction."

"So you followed it."

"I didn't know what else to do, and when we're going where it leads, I don't feel it anymore. Anyway, every now and then I have a dream about a smoking chimney and water bubbling out of the ground. It was Wolf who described a sod house near Boiling Springs and an old woman who lives there. I think it's her somehow pulling me in her direction. She's waiting for a baby to come to her."

They sat in silence while Lane pondered her story. It was just as fantastic as the one he'd told, and the odds of the two of them being in the same place was astounding. He felt there was nothing else that could be so strange, until Victoria spoke again.

"I know this is going to sound strange, but I have a request to make."

"What's that?"

"First, you have to promise that this stays between us. You can't tell Wolf, or Hez, or Clarence. If you do, something terrible will happen. Not just to you or me, but to others."

"That's hard to promise, not knowing what it is."

"I know. But it's best. It will be for the both of us."

He waited, silent.

She did something with her lips that sent a shiver up his spine. "You smell it, don't you?"

Face hot with embarrassment, Lane wouldn't meet her eyes.

"You do. It has been that way since I became a woman. I can't help it, and it isn't something I try to do. That's why I'm here."

Understanding dawned, and Lane looked up. "I'm sorry."

"There's nothing to be sorry about. It's simply human nature, but it has been a challenge most of my life."

"I bet it's hard being so beautiful in this world."

"I've never considered myself beautiful. I think I'm attractive."

He didn't know what else to say.

She adjusted her weight, sticking out one leg to get comfortable.

Lane reached for the cigar, then realized it was dead. Instead, he remained sitting cross-legged, holding his ankles until she pointed.

"Take off your boots." Before he could answer, she leaned over and blew one of the candles out.

"Take off my boots?"

"That's what I said. Boots off."

Without a word, he tugged off the knee-high boots and placed them at Buck's feet. He'd almost forgotten the body was laying there.

Victoria dropped the blanket to her waist and took a deep breath in the dim light. "I want you to be the one to take my virginity before we get there. I think it needs to be done by you, but I can't tell you why."

Lane's mouth fell open, and he pointed to the shirt stretched tight across her belly. "But you're—"

Her eyes crinkled at the corners, and he fell completely in love at that moment.

"I'll explain later." She held out a hand, and despite himself, he crawled over to her.

TWENTY-ONE

TWISTED ROOT SQUATTED BY A small fire built in a deep wash. The storm moved faster than he expected, and he gave up on his idea to reach Boiling Springs that day. Knowing it was going to be a bad one, he led his band to a place where he'd sought shelter before. The Comanche tribes knew the land from where it touched Apacheria, to Mexico, to the Cheyenne nation in the north, and as far east to where the pine trees grew.

They followed the buffalo, setting up their lodges at springs, or on rivers or creeks. It had been that way for generations, the knowledge passed down through the ages. They required little—good water, grass for their horses, and the wild game that filled their pots and bellies. The women knew where to find fruit, tubers, and the nuts they required to maintain good health.

It was their land, and they intended to keep it.

A large chunk of the rocky embankment where they sheltered fell long ago, and the slabs slid several feet before stopping, creating a shallow cave with entrances from two sides. The fire Two Shoot kindled against the outside wall, reflected heat back inside their rude shelter.

Two Shoot was a stocky, scarred warrior with much experience in fighting both their warring tribes and the white men. He'd grown up raiding down into Mexico, crossing the border in the big bend of the Rio Grande. He was known as Two Shoot for the short, double-barrel shotgun he'd picked up in a battle years earlier with the Texas Rangers.

Ammunition for the twelve-gauge was hard to come by, but he asked every trader they encountered, and to his luck, they sometimes had a handful of shells that cost dearly. It was a devastating weapon at close quarters and had rendered a number of scalps for his lance and pony's bridle.

Lone Coyote, Waters His Horses, Cut Hand, Ghost Tracker, and Stands Tall pulled up close to the fire where it was warm. The boys, Nine Toes and Shouts His Name, joined them, shivering in the chill air. The others had gone back to their village to recruit more men for their upcoming raids. Traveling light, they could cover the miles in a short amount of time and be back soon after the weather cleared.

Plenty of fuel was stacked up on one side of the shelter. They would replace the wood before leaving the next day, in preparation of the next time they or their people might need to stop.

The gnarled medicine man sitting slightly apart from the others sang softly to himself, an almost soothing sound until he stopped to throw different powders into the flames. When the dust landed on the coals, colors often sparked and twisted with the smoke. Other times the fire crackled and spit. The last palm full of black grains snapped and rose like lightning bugs to disappear into the rain outside.

An abrupt silence caused the warriors to study Twisted Root's countenance. As if sparked by their attention, he stiffened and fell, twitching and foaming at the mouth. His eyes were closed, but busy behind his lids. Familiar with the seizures associated with the chunks of lead in his brain, Waters His Horses turned the medicine man's head so he wouldn't choke.

Nine Toes and Shouts His Name pushed back from Twisted Root's strange behavior.

Two Shoot leaned into Lone Coyote, who towered several inches over the others. "He is calling on spirits to help find the girl who has a baby in her belly."

"He wants her more than he wants to kill white men."

"That is true, but I know why."

The others crowded closer to hear what Two Shoot had to say.

His eyes roamed over the faces of his tribal brothers. Their war paint needed freshening. Some had washed away in the rain, or by perspiration. The black palm print on Ghost Tracker's face was cracking and flaking away.

They would repaint themselves in the morning, before taking the trail to hopefully intercept the pregnant Mexican woman and her band.

"When Twisted Root was a younger man who stood straight as an arrow, he was a strong *puha*. Many said he was stronger than Isa-tai who now rides with Quanah. He and Isa-tai went far away and were gone for many moons. When they returned, they had famous healing powers and could raise the dead. One year, Twisted Root led a war party against a large *rancheria* farther in the direction where the sun sets. There were many men with guns who he knew would use them to defend themselves.

"They watched for two days, hidden in the grass or by sage. One evening the chief of that family took several of his men and left. Twisted Root said it was time to rub the rest of them out. They freshened their paint, and he blessed them all so that bullets would not find them.

"It was early morning, before the grass had dried. All of the *ranchero's* guards were lazy and not watching. Our people killed them all before anyone in the house knew they were there."

The others nodded and made soft comments of pride in their people's abilities to creep up on the whites. They made sure they weren't aggravating Twisted Root, who was no longer twitching, possibly listening to their ancestors over the howling wind and rain.

Two Shoot watched Twisted Root's face as he described something he shouldn't. Some things should not be talked about, but since the medicine man was in his trance, he felt it was all right for once. "The people in the house placed boards across the inside of their doors and shot at our warriors through little holes in the walls.

"Twisted Root had a vision right then. He saw a door in the back that wasn't closed, so he and two others circled around, and when they got to the door, they found he was correct. Though they had closed it, someone forgot to put the timber in place.

"They rushed in and surprised those inside. Our two brothers killed the men and took their scalps, but Twisted Root saw a woman run to a hole in the floor, holding a baby. She jumped down and pulled a . . ." He didn't know the word for trap door, so he signed it. The others nodded, eyes wide with excitement at a story they'd never heard.

"Twisted Root grabbed a handle and raised the door, and when he did, that woman was squatting there with a pistol in her hand. She aimed it at his face and pulled the trigger from only two feet away. Twisted Root's magic was strong, and he swallowed the bullet."

They reared back, stunned that anyone could swallow a fired bullet.

"He fell back on the floor, but it took so much of his spirit to digest the slug, that one damaged side of Twisted Root began to change even more than when the old witch woman shot him with her magic bullet.

"That new bullet joined the other one and grew to a great size, causing the left side of his body to droop even more. It soon warped into what you see now. One brother said he thought Twisted Root was going to penetrate the earth with his left arm and take root in the soil in order to turn into a tree. It would have been a great tree, to mark the place where he swallowed the bullet, and would someday penetrate the roof and find the sky."

They nodded around the fire as their *puha* fell even deeper into his trance. No longer necessary to whisper, they put more wood on the fire and straightened their backs to talk.

"Finally, instead of taking root, he rolled onto his side and coughed up a large amount of blood. With that, his body froze into what has become himself. We carried him back to our village and one of the old women put him in her lodge and tended to his wound.

"The next day, he sat up and saw what he had become. He asked for the woman, for they had not killed or scalped her. They brought her before him, bound by hand and foot, and left them alone in his lodge."

"For three days the woman who shot Twisted Root screamed, but no one dared to enter to see what was happening. Our warriors placed food and water outside, but he didn't touch any of it. On the fourth day, Twisted Root emerged, dragging what was left of the woman behind. When he heard that Hears the Wind intended to keep the baby, Twisted Root refused the idea.

"Instead, he ordered that the baby be given to the only Kiowa in the band, and he took her to raise as his own. It was a good fight."

They settled back, pondering the story's implications as the fire burned down to coals while the cold wind howled outside. Later that evening, Twisted Root came out of his trance and slept. The next morning, he rose and they rode out to intercept the band of travelers.

TWENTY-TWO

T HE NORTHER WASHED THE HIGH Plains clean, leaving the sun bright in the clear, blue sky. Once again, Wolf and Tall Grass Blows in the Wind led the band of men protecting Victoria across the northern half of what they knew as Comancheria. She rode fairly well, but unlike the little round Kiowa woman who seemed to be a part of the horse under her, Victoria was constantly wriggling around in the saddle, as if trying to get comfortable.

Directly behind Wolf, Victoria gave Lane no more attention that morning than she had during the whole trip, but he was sure that Hezekiah's eyes burned holes through his soul every time the man looked at him. Lane's mind kept drifting back to the night's unexpected activities that only ended minutes before the eastern sky began to gray.

He and Buck fell back to the left side of their group. Clarence trailed several yards behind, flanked by Hezekiah.

Buck kept touching his forehead. "Is it lighter there where that ice hit me?"

"Yep, but not by much. It stands out, though, because you're darker around your eyes."

"This right side, under my hair is probably scarred, too, from that bullet one of them hide hunters shot wide."

"I haven't looked that close. You're getting pretty vain, for a dead man."

"It's all I have left, except for my Rangerin'. I'm gonna be so mottled people will start calling me Paint, after them painted horses the Navajo ride. I don't believe I could abide that." They rode in silence for several minutes before Buck spoke again. "You want to tell me what went on last night?"

"No one buried you."

"You know how I meant it. You weren't alone. I could tell there was someone in the tent. I have this dim memory that you talked long and hard at first, then things got kinda quiet and I couldn't make anything else out."

A long moment passed. "What do you mean?"

"There was a lot going on while I was . . . out. I might have figured it out, but that damned serpent in me kept aggravating me so much that I couldn't make out who you were talking to."

"Serpent?"

"The snake inside me. Wants to be called Snake. Now, what went on in our tent?"

Lane shuddered. "Let's just say I had a visitor . . . visitors."

"What'd they want?"

"Not much. Just talking about what's ahead."

"For me?"

"There you go again. Everything's not all about you being the way you are, you know." It was Lane's turn to check their back trail. He changed the subject. "At least nobody stuck you in the ground last night."

"That's a fact, and it's the first time that's happened since I died." Buck considered his comment. "It's strange to say that."

"You have a snake inside you, and *that's* strange?"

"I'm tired of talking about this."

"Well, *you* brought it up. Tall Grass says we're getting close to her village. I hope River is still there so we can take her back to her folks. Then we can figure out what to do with *you.*"

"I don't think there's much to do at all, and another thing, I still don't believe they're gonna just let us waltz in and pick that little gal up."

"She says they want us to, but there's always the chance that some of those young bucks'll swell up at us. I never saw one that didn't want to at least count coup on a white man, and especially a Texas Ranger."

Lane watched a jackrabbit bound away. "I'm more concerned about running into Quanah Parker and that bunch of cutthroats he travels with. Remember, before we got as far as that little outpost at Punta de Agua, they were talking about that magic Comanch' Isa-tai and Quanah. Said he was making noise about killing as many *taibos* as they could. Supposedly, that medicine man has visions that show him killing every cavalryman in Texas, and I doubt he'll stop there. It'll be folks after that, settlers and likely friends of ours."

"That'll take some doin'."

"I 'spect they think they can do it because Quanah made a fair war chief and has considerable battle experience. All that'll put some fire in those young men riding with them."

"That little band we tangled with weren't no slouchers, that's for sure. I'm what I am because they were damned good at their job." Buck pointed at himself. "Look at me."

"Well, it'd be just our luck to run into *him* and if that happens, then I'm liable to wind up like you."

"That sounds like an insult to me."

"It's a statement of fact, and I don't intend to walk around all day only to fall out at night. If that happened, I don't know who'd be around to make sure we didn't get buried."

"It's not like you're doing a damned good job of it."

"That's not what you said a few minutes ago. What are you doing now?"

Buck had been riding with his hand first on his chest, then his stomach, at the same time looking down at the ground. "Seeing if I can feel that damned serpent inside me. It's being still right now, but it talked all through the night. In fact, I think it talks more than you, if that's possible."

"What are you looking for on the ground?"

"Another lizard, or horny toad that can tell us how much farther we have to go."

"It was chilly last night. I doubt there'll be any reptiles out this early. You might find a snake sunning itself on a rock later." Lane pointed ahead. "We're getting into some broken country, there'll be plenty of rocks and snakes in our future, I reckon."

"I just need one that won't sull up on me." Buck reached back to pat the blanket rolled behind him. "I'd like to smoke a cigar too. Up to tangling with that crazy medicine man, I enjoyed one ever now and then, but I'm afraid I likely lost my taste for it."

Feeling even more guilty, Lane didn't answer. Wolf reined up. The rest did the same when he held up a hand to make everyone wait. Kicking his horse into a lope, he rode a wide circle around the band, carefully examining the ground.

He came back to the Rangers a second time. "Comanche war party. Stay here until I get back."

He rode off, eventually disappearing over the horizon. Lane sat there as long as he could stand it before finally dismounting. "Y'all might want to step down too. There ain't no telling how long it'll be until Wolf gets back, if he does."

Buck joined him. "You girls keep them reins tight in your hands. If any Comanches show up, these horses'll be our only chance." He leaned into Lane. "I see a rise up there that looks rocky. If trouble comes, we head that way. A little high ground may give us just enough advantage, in the event of trouble."

Positioning themselves to take advantage of the full views all around, the rest drank from their canteens and chewed jerky and pemmican. The women from different worlds conversed quietly in English. Lane tried not to listen, but he picked up bits and pieces concerning River, the captive child, and the new baby to come. They even chuckled at one point, a strange sound in such a situation that made Lane flush.

Buck noticed. "You getting a fever?"

"Naw. Just heard some of that woman talk I shouldn't have."

"I wasn't paying attention. Here, put your hand on my chest and tell me if you feel that serpent. It keeps moving around in there, and every now and then something pops into my mind that it's thinking."

"Hell no! Don't ask me to do that again for God's sake."

Aggravated that Lane wouldn't help, Buck sat with his legs crossed, staring downward at the ground.

Two hours later, a speck appeared in the distance. Buck watched for a second. "That's Wolf."

He was right. The speck soon formed into the big Cheyenne warrior who finally joined them. Stepping down from the saddle, his face held no emotion.

To Lane, that was worse than anything. "You found something."

"War parties are close. Several of them."

Buck rose. "How many?"

Wolf scratched under his top hat. "War parties or Indians?"

"Indians, I guess. A bunch could break up into a few parties of twenty or thirty—"

"Hundreds."

Hezekiah heard the news and threw his head back unnaturally far once again and prayed in a loud voice. While Tall Grass backed away from him, pudgy fingers against her throat, Victoria moved closer as if to draw protection from his words. Clarence joined her, putting the pregnant woman between them, though there were no Comanche within sight at the moment.

"I hope he can talk a little louder." Buck flicked his fingers at Hezekiah. "Quanah's mama can't quite make out what he's saying down there in her grave in Anderson *County*."

"It don't make any difference. They'll know we're here soon enough, if they haven't already cut our sign." Wolf adjusted the pistol stuck in his belt.

Victoria held a hand to her mouth. "You said hundreds?"

"Yes. I found where they all traveled together, about three miles that way." He pointed to the south. "It is a wide trail stomped down by hundreds of horses a few days ago. They were traveling west, and I believe they were heading for Adobe Walls. That's the only camp or settlement back where we came from."

Clarence adjusted a couple of the weapons strapped around his waist. "It's a wonder we missed them, then. But it sounds to me like if they're headed that way, we're free to go."

"No. They must have already killed everyone there. I've cut several trails coming back this direction." Wolf waved all around them. "Now they've broken into small bands, and I believe they've decided to raid every settlement, house, or *rancheria* here in the High Plains."

"What makes you say that?"

"Because I saw trails leading toward different places I've been to. One is a crazy German who is trying to raise potatoes up that way. No one with any intelligence would bring a family here. I am surprised they haven't been wiped out already. Others lead toward where you might find buffalo herds, and even more point down into central Texas. Raiding parties headed for the ranch country and other small settlements down that way."

Hezekiah stopped praying and his head returned to a normal position on his shoulders. "Maybe they're looking for *us*."

"Don't that hurt your neck?" Buck rolled his own head and shrugged his shoulders. "I have a grinding in my neck all the time, and if I let mine go that far back, I doubt I could get it back on straight again."

Instead of answering, Hezekiah made what Lane recognized as the Mexican sign for an evil eye. "My neck doesn't bend down in supplication. I speak straight up to the Lord so he can hear well what I offer in praise and what we need."

"He hard of hearing? That why you need to holler at the clouds?" Buck worked his neck back and forth.

"You dare to blaspheme my faith? I suspect that comes from what you are, an abomination upon this earth. Mike, kill him so he and us alike can have peace."

Wolf ignored the order. "We have to find a place to defend ourselves. I say we check out that ridge and see if these bands miss us. They might."

"That storm may have saved our bacon." Clarence stood up in his stirrups, to gain another few inches of elevation. "It'll have washed everything away before we entered the canyon."

The hair on the back of Lane's neck prickled. "If one of those war parties finds the trail we left today, they'll catch up to us pretty quick, though. Look at that."

Their horses, and number, left a distinct trail of crushed grass that had yet to stand up. Small shapes moved in the distance and Lane studied them for a minute before noticing Buck was watching too.

"That they will." Clarence motioned for Victoria. "Let me help you get up on that horse, gal. Wolf's right. We need to make tracks to somewhere we can fight. I don't like being out here in the open like this."

She stuck one booted foot into the stirrup and Wolf grabbed a handful of her rear end and pushed. "I'm sorry for my impertinence."

Forking the saddle, Victoria looked down at him and the dimples appeared at the corners of her mouth again. "You are every bit a gentleman."

"Mike wouldn't have grabbed your bottom like that." Hez crossed himself. "You should have let one of us help her up."

Victoria grinned. "You know he prefers to be called Wolf."

Lane's fear of the Indians faded at her smile and that same feeling came over him again. There was that musk coming from nowhere and everywhere. He realized Wolf was looking elsewhere, and Clarence climbed into his own saddle, tight-lipped in a way that could be either anger or disapproval.

The distant howl of a wolf came to them. Dropping his eyes, Lane worked up some spit and swallowed. "Buck, the wolves are back."

"Big prairie wolves. They've been following us."

"Why?"

"It has something to do with me, but I can't for the life of me say what that is." He stopped and laughed. "For the life of me. Get it?"

"That's not funny, and you shouldn't be carrying on about it with Wolf this close."

Buck wasn't listening. Leaning off to the side, his body was almost perpendicular to his horse.

Tired of his friend's behavior, Lane sighed. "*Now* what are you doing?"

"This lizard I've been talking to says we should go that way. The land breaks apart a few miles away and she says there's a bunch of boulders we can use for the night. There's a little spring there too."

Wolf and Clarence studied him for several long seconds. Wolf's brow furrowed. "You can speak to lizards?"

"Well, in a way." Buck rose and faced them. "I haven't told y'all there's a snake inside me, and I hear the lizard through *him*, it seems to travel up my neck and . . . never mind. It's hard to explain. We need to get out of here now."

They took the news as if he'd said it looked to be sunny all day. Wolf swept a hand across the horizon behind them. "There are maybe sixty or more big prairie wolves just out of sight. They have been following us since Hanrahan's men buried you, Empty One. Do you know why?"

"Beats the shit out of me." He laughed again, looking at Lane's disgusted face.

Wolf and Clarence shared a glance, then Wolf put his heels to his mare and they were on the way. This time Buck and Lane moved up to lead, following the lizard's directions.

After a mile, Lane couldn't stand it any longer. "You had a bluebird in your mouth when I found you, not a lizard. Why don't you talk to birds?"

"Can't say, Lane."

"You said the lizard was a she."

"I did, and if that's all you got out of the conversation, we need to have a little talk later."

TWENTY-THREE

MISS HATTIE TIED THE STRINGS of a blue garden bonnet under her chin and sat against the chair in the sunshine to pluck her scalded chickens. The storm that night had killed two hens, and she wasn't one to waste.

The warm sun felt good on her thin arms and shoulders while the chuckling of spring water over the limestone bed made a comforting sound. "This is exactly the kind of day I asked the good Lord for. These old bones need some baking after last night."

Her words were directed at no one, a habit she'd gotten into. "I swanny, it'll take me two weeks to eat both of these big ol' hens." She glanced up, squinting into the distance. Her nose itched, and she rubbed it with the back of her gnarled hand. "Company's coming." She addressed the pink carcass in her lap. "I bet there's two of you because company's coming."

Her eyes weren't affected by age, and she soon made out the shape of a horse and rider. "That'll be Ashkii Dighin." He was far enough off that she had time to finish plucking both birds pink and clean before he arrived.

She was right. The young Navaho stopped at the spring to water his pony, then reined up in front of the soddy. His fingers fairly flew in the air between them. "Are both of those for me?"

Her face broke into a map of creases deep enough to hold water. "Only *you* would think that. Get down and gather me some wood so I can roast them. Then you might get a bite or two."

He swung down with the ease of youth and tied his pony to a crumbling wagon not far from the sod house's front wall. The paint immediately stood hipshot, dozing after their long trail. In only a few minutes the young Navaho had a smokeless blaze going in the fire pit. The dry wood burned hot, then settled into glowing coals just right for roasting meat.

Miss Hattie put the hens on a spit that he rested across braces he'd built months before. Ashkii squatted near her and signed. "It was a strong storm."

"Yes it was, but now I'm afraid that old south wind's gonna pick up soon. By tomorrow, it'll be hot and windy."

"It's always windy here on the plains. If you wanted calm, you should have kept traveling to the blue mountains. There is little wind there."

"A breeze is just fine, mind you. I just dislike a wind that won't quit."

"I like to feel it in my hair, and on my face."

Miss Hattie didn't respond. She watched a party of over two dozen riders pass in the distance. Ashkii saw her concern and signed. "Comanche."

"They are at that. They're passing by. Going on a raid, I suspect."

"You are still safe here. They fear you."

"For a little while longer, I suppose, but I feel a change coming in that wind we were talking about."

The war party faded into the distance, not giving her strong medicine the satisfaction of looking in their direction.

"I hope that woman gets here soon so I can help." Miss Hattie's voice was soft with concern. "They're taking their own sweet time about it, and I'm afraid either age or those Comanches are going to get me before long."

Ashkii signed. "Don't talk like that. It makes me sad."

"We'll both be sad if they get their hands on that poor woman. She's carrying something special."

TWENTY-FOUR

THE LIZARD WAS RIGHT. FOR two tense hours the party led by the Rangers entered rough, rocky country blasted by the sun and summer winds, broken by water and frozen hard enough to shatter during the winter. The rocky landscape was the exact opposite of the surrounding Great Plains.

It was an oddity that no one could explain. The Comanche said spirits pushed up from underground, creating the sharp ridges. Then they gathered all the boulders they could and stacked them around, creating a craggy crest that overlooked the prairie in all directions.

The spirits hadn't taken all the big boulders, leaving them scattered like a handful of gravel pitched onto the rolling terrain. A perfect place for ambush, the men closed in and formed a wide, protective circle around Victoria and Tall Grass who rode side by side, their legs almost touching.

Buck pointed toward the jumble of giant rocks atop a ridge, providing a wide field of view as far as the eye could see. Inhaling to build talking pressure, he sat straight in satisfaction. "I told you."

"I've been watching you." Lane nodded, as if confirming an observation. "That's the first breath you've taken in an hour."

"Are you going to continually point out the obvious?"

"I can't help myself. I want you to rub up in your hair for horns again." Buck shot him a look and Lane studied his gray face. "I'd also expect your eyes to be dry. You ain't taking in any moisture, but you still have tears to keep them wet."

"I don't know what to say to that." Tilting his hat back, Buck rubbed his fingertips against the front part of his skull, taking care to stay away from the huge scalp wound that always looked damp and fresh. "There. No horns. I done told you I'm not turning into some kind of devil or demon. I hope that satisfies you, now leave me alone about it" He reset his hat, looking smug.

It was nothing new to Lane, who'd seen that look many times in the past. Buck was always self-assured around both men and women, and the vast majority of the time right about whatever stance or subject he encountered. Even when he was wrong, he'd dig his heels in, sticking to his opinion or decision no matter what. It was obvious that his new incarnation vexed him to no end, though. Lane studied his profile, thinking that Buck's days of catching a woman's eye were over.

Feeling that familiar wave of guilt, Lane cleared his throat that threatened to close up in grief. "Well, how's your snake? You haven't mentioned him in the last five minutes."

"Shhh. The damn thing's asleep and I want to keep it that way." They neared the boulders. Some were shoulder high and looked as if they'd been placed there for a purpose. Buck inhaled again. "I'm not sure I want to talk about this anymore."

"I think it's going to be the subject of conversation between us for a good long time."

TWENTY-FIVE

Frustrated that they could find no sign of those he sought, Twisted Root finally gave in to instinct and headed east. "We will find them in this direction."

Two Shoot scanned the horizon. "They have vanished. Maybe the entire group traveling with the pregnant woman flew to the old woman at Boiling Springs."

Annoyed that *he* couldn't fly, Twisted Root shook his head. "I don't think they can do that. Even Isa-tai does not have that kind of magic."

"Yes, he does." Lone Coyote nodded vigorously. "I have a cousin who saw it. Isa-tai told his people to stare at the sun, and he would fly. They say he went into the air and then came back down."

Cut Hand pointed, cutting him off. "Look. Smoke. Do you think it's them?"

They stared into the distance until Twisted Root was satisfied that he had the answer. "The smoke is too black. I think our people have found some whites. Maybe a wagon train or hide hunters' wagons. It could even be a white man's lodge they cut out of the land. We should go see."

"No." Waters His Horses turned away. "There is no reason to go see where our warriors have been. We should go find some buffalo hunters or a wagon train to burn ourselves."

The idea appealed to the medicine man, but he still wanted blood. "We are near where we killed that Ranger."

Two Shoot shook his head. "No. We left our dead there and I am ashamed of it. The place will be full of spirits, and one is Blue Bird. You should not see your son like that. I think it was wrong to leave them on the ground. They should have been buried properly."

"I wanted that *other* Ranger." Twisted Root frowned, recalling his decision. Traditionally, the Comanche wrapped their dead in skins or blankets, and took them to a crevice in a canyon, or better, a cave. "It would have taken too long to load them up and find a good place to leave them."

"He got *away*. So it would not have made any difference. We should not have let those buffalo hunters run us off near that settlement either. We almost had them on the tips of our spears."

"Their guns shoot far." Twisted Root didn't like to think about that day. In addition to his son, they lost several warriors and the redheaded Comanchero with the big rifle the day they killed the Ranger. Though he smelled, the man was a great shot with the buffalo gun and had great value because he could kill from a distance.

Twisted Root also had mixed emotions about seeing the Ranger he'd tortured and killed, riding alongside the other not far from the adobe buildings. Though confident his medicine was strong, it was a shock to see him alive again, talking with the one who got away.

It was an odd feeling. It was a good way to make the Ranger suffer for killing his last son. Blue Bird was destined to be a great war chief, and he shouldn't have died like that. It wasn't fair for him to have been shot by a dying man, but with the magic Twisted Root pulled out of the air, Blue Bird would never be completely gone. He would always be part of the man who killed him, and the revenge would be his son deviling the Ranger for eternity.

On the other hand, it seemed a good idea at the time to curse the Ranger to forever walk the earth without rest, but now he wasn't so sure. The Ranger couldn't be killed by anyone or anything, and the whole idea may have been a mistake.

One thing was for sure, he didn't want to face the man's guns, for if he'd already figured out the truth to his curse, there was nothing they could do to stop him.

A shrill yell brought him back to the present. Ghost Tracker had been out scouting for sign. He rode up to the band in excitement, his horse's hooves throwing dirt and dust when he pulled up sharp. "Buffalo hunters. Two of them over there."

"Did they see you?"

"No. They were more concerned with a herd that was moving toward them. I crawled up close, intending to kill them myself and take their scalps, until they rose to find a shooting position. I lay there until they were gone, then came back."

Waters His Horses shook his lance, making the scalps flutter and dance. "Let us go kill them!"

"We will." Twisted Root mounted. "We will pluck them off the prairie as a woman plucks berries for her basket. It will be that easy."

Once again Nine Toes and Shouts His Name were near the horses, but they heard the discussion. Nine Toes looked immensely sad, but Shouts His Name threw both hands in the air and shouted at the sky in excitement.

★★✪★★

TWO HOURS LATER, THE BOOMING OF THE hide hunter's big guns led them to where the white men fired from their shooting stand. Leaving their horses behind, the warriors proceeded on foot until they felt they were close enough, then lowered themselves to the ground and crawled through the grass like tortoises until they could peer over a slight swell.

With only their foreheads and eyes showing, they noted the hunter's positions with their backs to the war party. The Comanche dropped back to confer. Twisted Root studied his men's fresh paint. "We will wait until they have killed all they want. Then we will take their scalps."

"I want to shoot them now." Cut Hand was impatient. "They are wasting meat, and there are not enough buffalo left as it is."

"You know how far their guns shoot, and how accurate. We wait until they are finished and lay the big guns down to start skinning. Their attention will be on their work."

"We have the Comanchero's big rifle."

"We should save the bullets and none of us are as good as the hunter with red hair."

Two Shoot considered the argument. "Ghost Tracker crept up on them, so we can too. Their attention will be on the buffalo they are killing. I say we crawl up and cut their throats while they're shooting. It will be a great joke on them that we can tell around the fires."

The others agreed and for once Twisted Root gave in. "It is good."

Broad smiles swept their faces as they readied themselves. Minutes later, they moved through the grass like snakes, their passage only marked by the slight movement of grass that would be hard to tell from what the wind stirred.

Since Ghost Tracker was the one who found them. The first kill would be his. Each time the rifle fired, they moved up an entire body length, knowing the men's attention would be on the shot, and the herd.

★ ★ ✯ ★ ★

ONE HUNTER WITH LONG GRAY HAIR LAUGHED after his shot. "Damn things are as stupid as cattle. I still don't know why they stand there while the others fall dead around them."

"They won't if you miss." The second man was the skinner, and though he had his own Sharps, he didn't fire. "I think you hit that last one a little farther back. He didn't go down as fast as I'd like."

"He went down, though, didn't he?" Gray Hair shucked the lever and reloaded with another thumb-size bullet.

"He did."

"Then shut up and let me concentrate." Gray Hair closed the breach, settled the barrel onto the shooting sticks in front of him and aimed at a cow at the outer edge of the herd. "Have you checked around us for Indians?"

Instead of waiting for an answer, he fired. The recoil jolted his shoulder, and he squinted to watch the big animal fall. He ejected the spent shell. "I said, have you checked for Indians?"

When his skinner didn't answer the second time, Gray Hair stiffened. With an empty and useless rifle in his hand, the man was at his most vulnerable. Whirling, he snatched a pistol stuck under his belt and cocked the hammer with his thumb.

The first thing he saw was Skinner on his knees, held upright by a tall Comanche with his fingers tangled in his hair. Blood pumped in a stream from the white man's severed carotid at the same time his wide, terror-filled eyes realized the horror that was happening to him.

There was no time to think. Three other painted warriors rose from the grass and charged across the remaining few feet, screaming victorious war whoops and raising war axes and clubs. Gray Hair fired the revolver. The shot was accurate and one of the men collapsed on rubber knees.

Skinner's blood splattered Gray Hair's chest, and the next thing the soon-to-be corpse registered was the warrior slicing a circle around Skinner's scalp in preparation of popping his hair off.

Gray Hair cocked and fired again at the same time an explosion rocked the world. A full charge of buckshot caught him full in the left side of his chest, and he went sideways, crashing against the shooting sticks and empty rifle, coming to a rest with one knee in the air.

The man had enough fight in him to try and raise the pistol again, but a brave slammed his war axe down with a whoop of joy, severing Gray Hair's right arm at the elbow. His dying breath rattled into the air as the Comanche celebrated their victory.

★★✯★★

WATCHING FROM SEVERAL YARDS AWAY, TWISTED ROOT stood as straight as he could, proud of his men. Goes Fast's body lay at his feet, but he died well. Two Shoot waved Gray Hair's scalp in his hand, dancing in glory. The others collected the men's possessions and weapons. It was a fine day.

Now sure that he had the Great Spirit's approval it was time to rub out the old witch and find that woman with child.

TWENTY-SIX

PRAIRIE RATTLERS BUZZED AT THE troop of travelers entering the scattered pile of boulders. To a person, they ignored them, relegating the poisonous reptiles to a position of nothing more than gnats. They continued to warn the newcomers until the moment Buck Dallas arrived, at which the snakes ceased rattling and disappeared into their holes.

Sitting atop his gray, Lane evaluated their position, then turned his attention to the panorama surrounding their craggy hill. Nothing but waving grass spread in three directions. To the east, the land became rough, filled with rolling slopes, ravines, and deep breaks.

They stopped amid a natural fortress at the crest. Boulders formed a crude circle with only a couple of entrances wide enough to admit the horses. Castle-like, it was a perfect defensive position.

While Lane remained on horseback to see over the jumble, Clarence collected the horses and hobbled them close by. To make sure they didn't bolt in the event of an attack, or if an especially talented Comanche managed to sneak in and try to steal them, they were also cross-sidelined by tying the last horse's left front leg to the right back. Finished, he returned.

He joined the others gathered around a small fire. "This will be an easy place to defend."

"It is that, but it's a little crowded in here," Buck said. "We don't need the tents up and in the way."

Wolf crossed his arms. "It will not make any difference to you in any way. Once it is dark, all you do is lay still."

"All right then, they'll be in *your* way if something happens. I'm more concerned about my friend here, and those women."

"Your concern is not necessary. We took care of them long before we ran across you."

"Until that girl was stole from you back in Adobe Wells. Look at it this way, blanket-head, you three were drawn to that girl for some reason you can't explain. The truth is, you don't know why you're traveling with them. For all you know, they could be taking care of *you.*

"Now, if we think this through, then Lane and I have been drawn to our *own* destinies. I think mine started a few days before you showed up. So here we are, two more pilgrims to see this thing through. Therefore, we have a job and both of us intend to do it."

Victoria spoke for the first time. "He is right, Wolf." She rested a hand on his arm to take away the sting. "I believe these two Texans have a role in this. Please let them alone. If nothing else, we're going to need their guns if we run into trouble."

Scowling, he dropped to the ground and rested his back against a large stone. "If that is what you want. But once we reach Boiling Springs, I may hold the Empty One under the water until he stops moving."

"Bring your dinner with you." Buck grunted. "Water won't allow me to touch it, or it, me."

Hezekiah paused in unpacking his gear for the night. "You *are* a demon."

Buck finally had enough. "All right. I'm going to tell you what happened, and then let that be the end of it."

While Lane surveyed the prairie below them as a lookout, Buck told them everything he could remember, from the time the Comanche first shot him, until the night before, carefully leaving out the part where Lane had a nighttime visitor.

WHEN HE FINISHED, THERE WAS SILENCE AMONG them all,

broken only by the crackle of the dry wood fire. Buck watched them absorb the details in awkward silence. "So it's through no fault of my own that I'm this way."

Having learned nothing new, Lane dismounted with the Henry cradled in the crook of his arm. He spoke as if it were a normal day without threat of Indians, or another discourse with a dead man. "Clarence, would you hobble my horse with the rest of them."

Still speechless, the big man scratched his thick black beard and led the gray to join the others.

Lane saw Hezekiah's head start backward and stopped him. "Hezekiah, I'd appreciate it if you'd hold off on that prayer that's forming in your gullet and take the first watch in that direction. We don't need you hollering across the country and drawing every Comanche within ten miles of us."

Before he could answer, Lane continued to issue soft orders and pointed to the south. "Wolf, I'd thank you to watch that direction. Me and Clarence will switch with you guys in a couple of hours." He jerked a thumb at Buck, who was staring toward the direction of travel. "Buck, it'll be dark in a little bit. Let's you and me scratch up some grub for everyone while you're still upright."

Victoria was already ahead of him. She was unpacking supplies. "I'm tired of chewing jerky. We're going to make some beans and bacon and coffee too. Tall Grass knows how to make it strong and black."

With one simple sentence, she'd taken some of the starch out of Lane's orders. To ease his sensibilities, she flashed him a quick grin, once again revealing those two dimples buried in the corners of her mouth. That was enough to satisfy him.

"Good idea. We could all use a hot meal."

Buck grumbled under his breath. "Speak for yourself."

That task removed, Lane checked his weapons and placed them near to hand.

Already primed to talk, Buck rested on a rock and watched Victoria and Tall Grass work. "Victoria, I know how me'n Lane came to be here, but what about these guys. How'd they come to travel with you."

It was his old, easy way of getting women to open up and be friendly with him. It worked again, but there was something missing. Lane figured it was the spark that was once in Buck's eyes, which were now dark and flat.

Despite those empty eyes, Victoria shrugged and frowned in thought. "I don't know what they went through to find me, or what it was that told them to come, but I know a little about each one of them. Hezekiah was a traveling preacher. He moved from town to settlement, spreading what he calls the Word. Before he did that, though, he fought in the war, though I haven't asked him what side, for it doesn't matter.

"Clarence was a freed slave from New York. He left when he was young and drifted down to Texas. He rode with the cavalry for a couple of years, then hunted buffalo for a while, but the work sickened him. After that, he hired out to guard wagon trains, and tiring of that, joined the cavalry for a year.

"Wolf, though. He doesn't say much. He just looks at you with that one eye while the empty socket sees deep into your soul. I don't think he has much allegiance to anyone, other than me."

Finished with the horses, Clarence joined them and watched Tall Grass move quickly around the camp, preparing their meal. She squatted with ease to add small sticks to a tiny blaze. She glanced up at the big man and gave him a soft nod. "I have something to say."

"Go ahead on," Buck said.

"I have not used my English much, until I met you all." She spoke slowly to gather the strange words together. "You are all good men, who have been chosen by the Great One to do an important job, just as He has chosen Quanah Parker to lead his people to do what they must."

She tightened the headband to hold her long, black hair in place.

"Fighting and killing has always been the way of our world. I learned how my adopted family felt about war, and I understand it from their thoughts. I also am a victim of this difference in our cultures. My mother and father were killed when I was taken by the Comanche and given to my Kiowa people. This is why I wish to help the child named

River. Maybe her name was given so we would understand her because rivers are life, and we also give beautiful names to describe who we are."

She added larger sticks and heat rose from the clean, yellow blaze. "The Comanche have always been a warring tribe because that is their way. To most of us, it is not right or wrong. It just is. They pushed out the old people who lived here when the earth was young, just as those pushed out the Old Ones before them. It is the way of the world and the way it will always be.

"I hope the old woman will make you all understand that this must cease. This is a wide country. We can all live together in peace and stop taking land and lives away from each other. The child Victoria carries, I believe, is a special child that will make everyone see that we are all the same. It is not the color of our skin, or the tribe we belong to, or the beliefs we have taken as our own. It will be the words of understanding and the true way of life we share."

A coyote howled in the distance, heralding the setting sun. Buck looked at the darkening sky and sighed. "I'm sure everything you said is true, but there are people like the medicine man who made me the way I am who won't agree with you because they—"

He collapsed in a heap, sending his hat rolling toward Tall Grass's fire. Clarence caught it and rose. "I will help you place him somewhere for the night."

"We have got to pay more attention to sunset these days." With a sigh, Lane rose. "And just when the conversation was getting good." He considered their campsite. "Let's put him over there, where the horses won't step on him, and he'll be out of the way."

Victoria picked up a blanket. "We should at least cover him. Wrap him in this."

"He doesn't feel a thing. He told me that."

Clarence stepped up. "It is the right thing to do." Lane took Buck's feet, and Clarence lifted the heavy end. "He has no body heat."

"Yep." Lane adjusted his grip on Buck's ankles. "But he isn't cold like a dead man neither."

A voice came from behind them. It was Wolf keeping his good eye on the surrounding countryside, and the hole in his skull angled toward what was going on near the campfire. "It is the snake inside him."

"Snakes are cold," Clarence answered.

"Not that one that's coiled in his stomach. The Empty One is somewhere in between life and death, and that's what keeps him the way he is. When the snake is dead, or gone, so Buck will be. That is why I think he needs me to help him pass on to the other side."

"Not till either he or I agree." Lane helped them lay Buck's body against a broken slab of rock. "And you better be careful. He's getting a little tired of you wanting to chop him into pieces. Don't aggravate him too much."

They gently laid him out of the way, but within sight of the camp and the fire. Lane looked down at his partner. "But don't you be getting any ideas about killing him. When Buck's ready to go, he'll let you know."

Hezekiah spoke up, still keeping his eyes on the surrounding area, despite the failing light. "He can't tell us to kill him, though. That will be tantamount to the sin of suicide. It must come as natural as possible, without forethought."

Lane watched Tall Grass cover the still form with a blanket. Despite her bulk, she moved with surprising ease. She covered Buck's face with his hat. "He won't ask anyone for anything. It isn't his way. Buck's days will end the way they're supposed to, and that's that."

They made their way back to the fire. A kettle of water was already boiling, softening several chunks of jerky to season the dry beans. Tall Grass's round hands skillfully erected racks from strong, sun-bleached sticks and hung saddle blankets on them to act as a screen and block the fire to prevent anyone from seeing the flicker of light in the dark night.

So hungry they couldn't wait until the beans softened properly, they then dug in. As soon as everyone had eaten, Victoria smothered the fire so its glow couldn't be seen through the rocks. Lane watched her and Tall Grass use the horse blankets as makeshift beds to smooth the rocky ground.

The stars glittered in the night sky like distant sparks from the fire by the time Wolf and Hezekiah came in from their posts. The moon soon chased away the stars and was bright enough for them to move around without difficulty. Wolf studied Buck's dark form in repose. Lane watched for a minute, his hand near the pistol on his belt just in case the big Cheyenne decided the time was right to send his partner along, but he finally turned.

"There are wolves out there." Wolf waved beyond the rocks. "Many. They accompany this man. Maybe they were his spirit animal, but I can't see that for the truth. Don't be afraid when you see them. They are just sitting out there, waiting."

"Thanks for the information." Lane picked up his Henry and tried not to look at Victoria and her great belly. "Come get me in a couple of hours."

"Don't be asleep when I do." Wolf showed his oversized canines. "If you are, I will cut your throat for the Comanches and save them the trouble."

"I got here by staying awake, Rusty Guts. You won't get the opportunity."

He and Clarence took their posts as the silver moon rose higher over Buck, a man who once loved to lay on his bedroll and admire the heavens but now couldn't even be there after dusk.

It was a cruel world that was about to get worse.

TWENTY-SEVEN

DAWN WAS A THIN, DIM promise on the eastern horizon. The air was clear and cool over the land that was cold in the light of the moon. Lane stood with his back to a large boulder, the Henry rifle in hand.

The light crunch of stones under a moccasin behind him made Lane tense for a second, until the casual next step told him it wasn't a Comanche putting the sneak on his outlook post. He spoke softly over his shoulder. "I heard you coming."

"It is a good thing." Wolf's voice was barely discernable. "I am surprised you are not like most white men who sleep when they should be watching." Wolf stopped beside him, rifle resting in the crook of his arm.

"Those wolves are still out there. I see them moving around from time to time, like they're waiting for something . . . or watching for it."

"Animals have patience. Humans do not."

Talking so quietly made Lane hoarse. He wanted to clear his throat, but the sound would carry like a rifle shot in the still, early morning air. "I have plenty of patience when it comes to certain things, like keeping awake to stay alive."

"You can go sleep now. I will watch the sunrise."

"Naw, I'm wide awake. Can you see pretty good with just that one eye?"

"Most people cannot see with two eyes. I miss little, on this side." He touched his left cheek.

Their conversation paused at a sound so slight, Lane couldn't identify it. He turned an ear to one side, then the other, listening. His whisper was soft as a baby's breath. "Did you hear that?"

"Yes."

Remaining motionless, Lane stared at one spot in the distance, letting his peripheral vision work in the night. He'd learned long ago never to look directly at something if he wanted to see it in the darkness. Finding nothing, he realized he'd been holding his breath. Exhaling as soft as possible, he turned to Wolf and whispered. "I'm going to check the horses. Something is out there, and I don't like it."

"White man, something is always out there. Ready the others."

Lane faded back toward camp to find Hezekiah leaning over a large boulder, keeping it between him and the downslope. Lane made a hissing noise with his teeth to gain the man's attention. "Hez, it's me."

"I see you. There is movement around us. I believe it's Comanches."

"Don't start praying loud."

"I've been praying to myself."

"Watch over the women."

"There is no need to give that order."

Lane knelt beside Victoria and put a hand on her shoulder. She awoke in an instant, and he looked over at Tall Grass whose eyes were already open. "Something's about to happen. You two crawl up under Hez over there. I'm going to check the horses and Clarence."

Not waiting to see if they followed his orders, he took stock of the camp. There was no wind and Lane could hear only the constant ringing in his ears from too many gunshots and past gunfights. He couldn't see Clarence and wasn't sure where he might be. Conflicted, and afraid the heavily armed man might take him for an Indian and shoot him in the dark, Lane moved through the camp with caution.

"Clarence." His voice carried in the night air.

It was several seconds without an answer, and Lane's nerves jangled, thinking the man could either be asleep, or dead, his throat cut by a talented Comanche. He was about to move forward again and try a little louder when a familiar shape rose against the few remaining stars resting on the horizon.

Clarence raised an arm and pointed outward. It was obvious he was telling Lane that indeed, someone was near. One of the horses snorted. Leaving Clarence on guard, Lane crouched so as not to silhouette if a Comanche was crawling up on him. He crept slowly toward their mounts, placing his feet with great care.

Another horse shifted its weight. They'd been quiet all night, and now someone, or some*thing*, was agitating them. Taking a knee, he tucked the Henry's stock against his shoulder and waited. A sound came, so slight that Lane thought it was his imagination. It could have been the brush of buckskin against the ground, the creak of the leather hobbles, or a shifting hoof.

He again chose a single focus point on a gray boulder, letting his peripheral vision go to work. Still as that big rock, he listened. There it was again, and at that same moment, a tiny flicker in the shadows.

He shifted the muzzle and watched the shadows. More movement, and he identified a shape that soon defined itself. A man was on his stomach beside the horses. The knife in his hand glinted as he reached to cut the hobbles. Lane sighted on the thick of the Comanche's trunk, closed both eyes to preserve his vision, and squeezed the trigger. A lance of fire shot from the muzzle and the quiet night shattered.

A shout of pain followed, and the horses tried to bolt. Unable to run, they shifted and jumped, whinnying in fear. He jacked the lever at the same time guns from several directions opened fire, the flashes filling the darkness and briefly illuminating men and rocks.

"They're among us!" Hezekiah's voice rose. "Defend yourselves!" From his position, pistols belched fire in two directions.

A shrill, terrible shriek filled the air. Lane whirled as something plucked his collar. A hot lance of pain raked across his ribs. He caught a figure rushing toward him and drew his pistol without thinking and shot into the middle of the shape, then again as it collapsed only three feet away.

The rattle of gunshots was fast and intense rising to a crescendo before it faded. Then it was over.

He remained on one knee, waiting. When he twisted to check over his shoulder, something was caught on his shirt collar and Lane reached up. His fingertips felt the fletching of an arrow stripped off halfway through the material. He pulled it free at the same time a single gunshot split the night from Wolf's position, followed by the crisp sound of him levering another round into the magazine.

"Everyone all right?" Lane stayed where he was.

Victoria's trembling voice came first. "Hez is hurt."

"How bad?"

"Lots of blood. Tall Grass is with me."

Knowing the Kiowa woman could handle any wound, Lane checked his burning side to feel a shallow channel seeping blood. Relieved that it wasn't a dangerous injury, he knelt beside the second man he shot. There was enough light in the sky to tell for sure it was a Comanche. A bow lay beside him, as well as a butcher knife he'd dropped. Both of Lane's pistol shots took him in the chest, the big .44-caliber slugs punching through the animal-bone breastplate that did little to turn them. He made sure the man was truly dead by tapping his eyeball with the muzzle of his pistol. Nothing alive could tolerate that type of personal invasion and still play possum.

Maintaining caution, he approached the horses, talking softly. Recognizing his gray, he slipped his fingers under the bridle and calmed him down. Sensing it was over, the others settled down.

Another Comanche lay at their feet, shot side to side through both lungs. The slugs would have been fatal, but the hooves that caved in the man's head did much of the work. The hobbles on Buck's new mount were cut and the black apparently took issue with the attempted theft.

Holstering the pistol, Lane drug the body away from the horses and checked the surrounding area to be sure they'd all fled or weren't hiding in wait for another opportunity. Satisfied it was truly over for the moment, he returned to where the girls were working on Hez.

Clarence was already there, blowing on a small blaze to start a fire.

The odor of woodsmoke covered the coppery smell of fresh-spilled blood. Hez lay on his back, a deep slash through his shirt seeping blood. A gunshot wound in his upper chest leaked even more of the precious fluid.

Face composed and lips moving quietly, he kept still as Tall Grass cut the remainder of his shirt away. Her fingers were gentle as she checked the deep slash across the upper part of his abdomen but frowned at the bullet wound.

"I can sew this one, but the hole is not good. Victoria, hand me that bag."

Leaving them to their ministrations, Lane joined Clarence. "You hurt?"

"No. I did for three of those savages, and would have killed more, but let them go when I saw Hezekiah."

"Let's go check on Wolf." They made their way around the rock and boulders. Wolf was there, as stoic as ever, maintaining a lookout for a second attack. Four bodies lay sprawled nearby. Two slash wounds in his left arm and a third in his upper chest told of the savagery of his fight.

He pointed. "They are on that ridge. Sitting there and watching. They are Yamparika."

"You know that how?"

"There." Wolf nudged one of the bodies with his toe. The light was better, and Lane saw that each man's throat was cut, in addition to the wounds that killed them. "The fletching on his arrows, the paint on his face, and the beading on his moccasins."

"I thought sure it was Quanah Parker, or that crazy medicine man who left Buck the way he is."

"Quanah *could* be there, but I did not see him. The Comanche nation is made up of many bands who live separately but often blend together for raids or ceremonies. It was our misadventure that they came upon us."

The sun sought escape from the horizon as they watched more

than a dozen mounted warriors mill around beyond rifle distance. "You think they're planning another go at us?"

"I do not think so. The ones shaking their lances and rifles are young men, full of fire and anger. They want to charge, maybe count coup. The others are older, more experienced warriors who see they lost many men."

A yellow sliver of light peeked over the horizon, throwing long morning shadows across the ground. One of the agitated warriors pointed at the sun, jerked the reins toward the jumble of boulders and charged.

"See? That one is young. He is full of himself and wants to show his bravery." Wolf calmly watched the mounted horseman eat up the distance between them. "Do you want to shoot that one?"

Lane shook his head. "I don't want to shoot anyone."

The big Cheyenne grinned, revealing his large canines. "Then I will do it."

The horse pounded toward them, and when he was only fifty yards away, Wolf shouldered the rifle and fired. The brave went limp and fell off the side. He landed on his neck, obviously dead.

The sound of the shot faded away, to be replaced by angry whoops from the watching Comanche.

"Did I miss everything?"

Buck's voice caused Lane to whirl. He'd forgotten his partner for the time being and now beheld an astonishing sight. Buck stood there with four arrows protruding from his chest and abdomen. Shot at close range by one of those Comanche laying in camp, there was little more than fletching sticking out of his shirt.

Even though he'd come to grips with what was happening with Buck, Lane couldn't help but gape and point.

"What?"

Buck looked down, surprised by what he saw. "Well, *damn.*" He touched the notched end of one arrow with a finger, then grasped it. "This is gonna *sting!*" He yanked on the emphasis, and the arrow pulled free. "Whew."

Wolf and Lane watched as Buck pulled two others out with quick gasps. The third refused to budge. After the third attempt, Buck lowered his hands. "Uh, Lane. This one's stuck. You're gonna have to help me."

Swallowing hard, he stepped forward, opening and closing his fists. "Turn around."

The arrow tip made from a piece of tin had deformed going through the shoulder blade. Pulling on it from the front had lodged the tip back against the shoulder. Dark fluid leaked out of the hole in his shirt.

"Buck, push it on through. There's not enough of it for me to get a good hold."

With a grunt, the Ranger pushed the arrow back through his body and suddenly Lane felt swimmy-headed. He held on to his partner's shoulder for a moment to steady himself. Wondering what was going on behind him, Buck turned his head. "You all right?"

"Hell no, I ain't all right. You should see the nasty stuff on this arrow." He swallowed and took a deep breath. Without hesitation, he grabbed the shaft with both hands and yanked. Buck hissed, then relaxed. "Glad that's over with."

The hole immediately quit seeping. Lane dropped the arrow and wiped his hands on a nearby rock before kneeling to pick up two handfuls of sand, which he used to absorb the black liquid.

Buck was already joining Wolf. "Now, don't get any ideas against me. You had your chance last night. Why don't you pop a shot at those fellers and run 'em off?"

"The distance is too great."

"Not for this." Clarence joined them, holding his Sharps. Taking a wide stance, he leaned over a boulder, adjusted his sights, and pulled the trigger.

They waited as the big slug arced toward his target. It finally struck a horse in the chest. It collapsed, throwing the rider off. Most of the band turned their mounts and charged away. The last warrior shouted in their direction, then offered his hand to the horseless rider who swung up behind and they disappeared over the horizon.

"Good shot." Buck slapped Clarence on the shoulder. "Now, tell me all about what just happened."

Lane sighed. "You're gonna owe me for that shirt."

Buck gave him that signature grin of his and waited for the story.

TWENTY-EIGHT

Twisted Root watched dark wings circling the sky ahead as his band of warriors rode across the prairie. He studied the omens of danger. To his people, a buzzard was a troublemaker who lies and cheats, using its size to bully other birds. His late son, Blue Bird, despised buzzards.

"I hope they are feasting on white people."

Two Shoot shivered. "Maybe they are over *tasiwoo*. If they smell buffalo on the ground, there could be more hunters nearby that we can kill. I would like to add more scalps to this gray one."

"Maybe, but we need to join the others at Mow-Ways's village. I should rest and make medicine with the others before we go kill the old woman."

"You say you want to kill her, but we keep finding different trails and reasons not to go there."

"You should be glad I am not Apache. I would cut your tongue out so you couldn't talk so much."

"You would find reasons not to do that too." Two Shoot chuckled.

The boys, Nine Toes and Shouts His Name, hid grins behind their hands, lest they draw the wrath of Twisted Root.

The raiders walked their ponies in silence for a while as Twisted Root frowned into the distance. "There is much dust in front of us. I think it is a war party driving stolen horses."

The distance to the band crossing their path was far. Waters His Horses kicked his pony to join them. "Are they some of our people?"

"I can't tell," said Twisted Root. "My left eye is blurry today. What do you see, Two Shoot?"

"They could be. Maybe Cheyenne going back to their lodges after a raid? Maybe Arapaho."

Ghost Tracker whooped. "If they are, we can catch them and maybe count coup! It would be a good thing."

The distant band suddenly reined up and Twisted Root was able to focus with both eyes. "They see us. They are not running. Some are pumping their weapons in the air."

The others responded in the same way, and both parties closed the distance. Waters His Horses yelped. "I know them. They are Yamparika! One of my cousins lives with them. Maybe he is here."

One of the five major bands of Comanche, the Yamparika, or Yap Eaters, were the ones who lived farthest north. Twisted Root's men were Kotsoteka, the Buffalo Eaters, who claimed the Canadian River valley.

Driving nearly a hundred horses, the war party three times the size of theirs grew near and circled the herd to a stop. The two groups quickly met, and the air filled with cries of joy. Their leader, Iron Tip, was painted for war with two dark streaks running from his forehead, through his eyes, and down each side of his mouth. They symbolized aggression and power. The horizontal white streak across his nose told he'd lost someone.

Twisted Root's paint was similar with the white strip across his nose. Symbolizing his own power, a black handprint across his mouth and face told Iron Tip he'd survived hand-to-hand combat.

Noting the same stripe across the bridge of Twisted Root's nose, Iron Tip raised his hand. "Twisted Root, it is good to see you." He glanced around, then frowned. "I see you have lost someone, as have I. Where are your warriors? There are not too many of you."

The words cut deep, and he didn't want to tell Iron Tip that part of his band had splintered off to join Quanah Parker. Twisted Root had no interest in discussing the death of his son, for that would be bad medicine. "We have killed many hide hunters and even a Texas Ranger." He sat straight as he could at the pronouncement.

A murmur of excitement and respect came from the newcomers. To kill hide hunters was a common occurrence, much like slaughtering settlers on their land, but to actually kill and count coup on a Ranger was worthy of admiration.

Iron Tip slapped a fist into his chest. "It is good. Let us camp here and smoke."

"It is early. We are going to find a band of white men traveling with two women. I want their scalps to hang from my lodgepole, and then we are going to Boiling Springs to wipe out that old witch woman."

Twisted Root saw expression on the two boys that oversaw their horses. Their eyes widened at the number of mounts the other band stole. He felt he needed to add even more excitement to his story, to save face with the youngsters. The Yamparika's herd of stolen horses was impressive, but his own band had yet to acquire any new mounts, and in fact, had lost several to the dead Ranger's accuracy and way of fighting.

"Three of our men went to join up with Quanah. They will tell him where we are going and maybe he will join us."

The light in Iron Tip's eyes went out. "You do not know what happened at the place the whites call Adobe Walls."

"No. I spoke to him and they were going to rub out the hide hunters there. They wanted us to join them, but I have my own path to ride. Was he killed?"

"No. Quanah and Isa-tai gathered hundreds of our people, and they took the war trail together. But the hide hunters there had medicine to tell them our people were coming. They were ready and there was a great battle. Many of our warriors died, and Isa-tai was shot off his horse, but he survived. One was even struck by a magic bullet that traveled farther than any ever has. It flew beyond that ridge." Iron Tip pointed at the distant horizon and Twisted Root's men murmured in wonder. "It killed one of his people."

"Isa-tai wove a spell to turn bullets. How could his warriors die? How could one hit *him*?"

"It wasn't strong enough. Quanah's warriors killed several whites, but they finally gave up." Iron Tip cast his gaze over Twisted Root's band. "They have all taken the war trail. Mow-Ways's village now has over a thousand lodges. There are even Cheyenne. Many bands scatter from this village to kill all the white men who have moved onto our land. That is what we will do. Join us. We can go back that way and kill some white people who are camped over there."

"Why did you leave them alive?" Twisted Root's people listened for the answer as Iron Tip considered the question.

"They are heavily armed. I lost many men to their bullets and knives. It is the same as Adobe Walls. They are warriors that we cannot kill at this time." Iron Tip considered the rifles the Kotsoteka carried. "Where did you get all the rifles? We have only a few and have to rely on our bows and lances."

Twisted Root considered the weight of what he heard. "We had a Comanchero with us. He was a great warrior and hated his own people. He provided the weapons in exchange for traveling with us to kill whites. He is dead now."

He didn't use the man's Comanche name, for it was bad luck to speak the names of the dead.

"We have two of the big guns from the buffalo hunters we killed. You can have them."

He gestured back for Lone Coyote to hand over the weapons. Two Yamparika warriors pushed forward to accept the gifts with great joy, whooping and admiring the weapons.

Twisted Root had a thought. "Were there crows about? Maybe it was them who told the white travelers you were coming."

"No, but we saw many wolves. I think they are white men who changed, then slipped through the grass to tell the others about us. I think they gathered to feast on the bodies they expected us to leave behind." He grew quiet for a moment. "We had to leave some of them behind, but if you will join us, maybe we can take the white men's scalps to make our warriors rest better."

Twisted Root grunted in confirmation and made a sign. "Then will you go with us to kill the old woman?"

"Where is she?"

"Boiling Springs."

"I know about her. She's a witch."

"Yes, but *my* medicine is stronger."

"That is what Isa-tai said, but he was wrong."

"I am not."

Iron Tip grinned, cracking some of the paint on his face. "Then we will ride with you."

The prairie echoed with the sounds of their celebration.

Nine Toes remained solemn, but Shouts His Name joined with his own shouts of joy.

Twisted Root couldn't help but look past the Yamparika warriors to admire the horse herd they could now draw from. He heard one shout for joy. They were not old enough to be warriors yet, but they would likely be persuaded to cut out some of the newcomers' horses when the parties separated.

He studied them and they noticed the bent warrior looking in their direction. Shouts His Name, the more muscular of the two, smiled and waved then lowered his hands when Twisted Root didn't respond.

The other boy sat astride his pony, face impassive, and that worried the shaman.

TWENTY-NINE

THE SUN WAS HIGH AS Wolf led the band northeast, until they came to a creek fringed with hardwoods. Trees lined both banks, but Wolf continued through the muddy, belly deep water and up the opposite side.

Experienced Indian fighters, Lane and Buck simultaneously nodded approval for the move. What they sought was beyond the creek and it made good sense to cross when they could. A sudden thunderstorm could turn the slow-moving current into a torrent in minutes. And second, if they were trailed by a war party, the strip of water was a perfect barricade to slow a charge.

In addition, the trees were slightly thicker on the north side of the creek, providing plenty of shade for Hezekiah to rest. In pain and weak from the loss of blood, he'd ridden without complaint, only murmuring a constant stream of prayers as the horses' hooves ate up the distance.

Lane and Clarence lowered the wounded man onto a pallet in the shade of a tall cottonwood. Victoria and Tall Grass made him as comfortable as they could. Digging through one of the bags she carried on one of the packhorses, Tall Grass indicated with her head. "Sitting in the Saddle's village is close. It is where my husband is, and the girl, River."

Staying out of the way while the women worked, Buck leaned against a tree. "How far?"

"A day."

"That's good news. Then we can get that little gal and take her back to her parents, if she's still of sound mind."

Lane raised an eyebrow. They'd heard of captives who'd gone insane from torture or the trauma of being taken from their families. Buck noticed and responded the same way. Tilting his head as a sign for Lane to follow, he moved away from camp.

While Wolf watered their mounts, Buck and Lane walked out of earshot. Buck had been unusually quiet all morning and it worried Lane.

"What's going on?"

"Not much going on with a dead man."

"You're too damn quiet. I feel better when you're rattling on like you do."

"Nothing seems to matter anymore. I'm just going through the motions, pretending to be alive, but I'm afraid I'll get you killed too." He absently dug at the dirt under his nails with one thumbnail. "I always figured one of us would get it, and my luck ran out on that ridge, but I thought once I was gone, somebody'd lower me in a hole in the ground with the worms and I'd be in for the long sleep.

"This is a helluva way to die. Now I'm aggravated all night long by this damned snake that was once an Indian." He dug under another nail. "And I feel like I oughta be mad, mad enough to bust something up, but at the same time there's nothing there. Does that make any sense?"

"It does." Lane watched his old friend, wondering just what of his humanity was left inside that cursed shell.

"Now that the shock is over, and the new's worn off all this, I wonder what I'm supposed to do. I don't intend to just wander around and be miserable until the sun winks out forever."

Clarence's voice startled both of them. "Maybe there is something you have to do." He settled some of the armament hanging and tucked around his waist and adjusted a weapon or two in his pants. "Look around us. We're all here for a reason. Us to escort Miss Victoria to the old woman, but y'all might have a destiny too."

"I don't intend to get into a discussion about religion." Buck scowled. "And if I was, I'd figure that'd be Hezekiah's territory."

"Wasn't talking about religion. My mama always said everyone has a duty here on earth, no matter who they think's put us here. Hers was to raise us kids at the same time she served the massa, least till the Emancipation. From then on it was to keep us safe, until I left home. She told each one of us to find what we're supposed to do, and then do it."

Clarence absently fingered the outline of a pistol in his pocket. "I thought it was to be a good cavalryman, least till I mustered out, then I thought it was other things until I had a dream one night about Miss Victoria wanderin' out here in the plains, and an old woman beckoning me to come her way. Hez and Wolf had the same dream too. Wolf said it felt like something was *pulling* him inside his head, pulling him up to a big spring boiling with water.

"That's the best way to describe it. Like there's a knot tied around the front of our brains, and the rope leads that way." He pointed to the northeast. "So here we are, and then you two show up. 'Course, Mister Buck, Wolf still keeps an eye on you. I always thought that once you're dead, you're dead, no matter how it happens. Now I see there's a different world I never knew about."

Buck snorted a weak blat, then inhaled and did it better the second time. "I got to remember to keep a little air inside. I didn't know about any of this either. Truth be told, my brain might be scrambled mush right now, but something's keeping me going, and that's a fact."

Wolf appeared and Buck gave both of them a disgusted look. "When me and Lane got off away from everybody, that meant we wanted to talk alone."

"None of us are alone in this journey." Wolf angled his head to see Buck with his Dark Eye. "At first I wanted to help you into the spirit world, but now I see that you might be of some use to us."

Lane couldn't help himself. "In the light."

"Yes, but in the night also." Clarence rested his rifle over one shoulder. "You laying there asleep last night made a good target. That brave who snuck into camp and shot into you with his arrows was distracted because you didn't move after the first one. I believe he expected you to jump at the very least, but because you didn't, he felt obliged to shoot the others. His attention was full on you when I shot him. If he hadn't took so long, he may have turned to kill Miss Victoria or Tall Grass next.

"That *may* have been your purpose," Wolf said, studying him with the empty socket. His other eye moved constantly, looking for any danger around them. "If so, you may have already served it, and if that is the only reason you are with us now, then I will gladly help you cross over to see the Great Spirit.

"But no matter, I have been thinking about it, and I need to kill that snake inside of you. That done, you will no longer be forced to walk the earth any longer."

Looking disgusted, Buck met Lane's eyes. "He'll be the one who makes that decision when the time comes."

"There you go again, dragging me into a mess behind you." Lane sighed. "Now you're putting me up against Wolf if something happens to you. I swear."

Buck saw Wolf's nose flare. "Are you trying to smell me *too?*"

"I just realized that you should smell like carrion now. This is puzzling."

"Well, I'm glad I can give y'all so much to think about to occupy your time, but right now we need to get back over there to the girls and the horses."

"Why is that?" Wolf wanted to know.

"Because the rattler laying over there under that log just told me a whole passel of Comanches are heading this way." Buck shook his head in disgust. "I bet it's the ones y'all tangled with last night, and now they have some help."

Despite himself, Lane jumped at the thought of a prairie rattler so close. Keeping an eye on the log, they rushed to the horses and hobbled them. They had another fight on their hands, and this time there was no good cover.

THIRTY

"Ashkii, I need you to get us a deer, or an antelope, maybe two." Miss Hattie stood in the door of her sod house, staring to the southeast. "Some greens too. We're about to have visitors, and I smell trouble in the wind."

The young Navaho raised his nose like a coyote sniffing rabbits. He signed. "We will need water."

"I've thought of that. If Indians lay in a siege, we'll need water in the worst way. Even though that spring's so close, I don't have but a couple of bladders and the water bucket. I swanny, I don't know how we're gonna store any more'n that."

"I have an idea." His fingers flew as he waved toward Boiling Springs. "How long before they get here?"

"A day or two. Three at most."

His face broke into a smile. He pantomimed the act of using a shovel.

"I do. Some travelers left it so I could dig a new privy. Just haven't gotten around to it yet." She disappeared inside and returned with it.

Ashkii leaned it against the side of the house and signed. "Going hunting."

Minutes later, he was astride his paint horse.

✳✳✰✳✳

That evening, as the sun settled and the air cooled somewhat, the young man had finished cleaning two fat does and one antelope. He'd already given her a sack full of wild onions, prairie turnips, groundnuts, and Jerusalem artichokes. Miss Hattie was preparing the vegetables, watching Ashkii dig under the edge of the soddy.

"These turnips are a little early, but they'll help make a right nice stew." The deep ravines in the corners of her eyes deepened. "I don't have any idee what you're doing, digging there."

Instead of dropping the shovel to answer, he nodded that he understood and kept working. An hour later, near dusk, he'd dug a ten-foot trench leading toward one of the small streams running off from Boiling Springs. To show her his idea, he gathered small stones and gravel to fill the trench three-quarters to the top. Once that was done, he laid wide, smooth rocks on top and covered it all with coarse dirt.

By the time she lit the lamp, Miss Hattie understood that he was digging what amounted to a sluice box leading from the stream to the house and under the wall where he'd already excavated a washtub-size hole in the dirt floor. Lined with clay, the water that trickled inside would be available any time they needed it. Those inside could start and stop the flow by removing a section of barrel stave that served as a small dam.

"Why, aren't you *smart?*"

Holding up his hands and building an excessive frown, he indicated that he didn't understand. To clarify, she tapped the side of her head with a bent forefinger.

Breaking into a wide smile, Ashkii nodded with enthusiasm. He signed again. "It will be finished in the morning, and then I will go for more food."

She gave him a soft pat on the shoulder and brought out two bowls of venison and turnip stew. They ate as the even pinkish glow in the west faded to black.

THIRTY-ONE

OWL EYES, ONE OF IRON Tip's warriors, rode up with excitement. Despite the paint on his face, his unnaturally wide dark eyes gave the man a perpetually surprised look. He gestured back where he came from. "I found a trail. Nine horses with iron on their feet."

Twisted Root felt a shiver of excitement. These were the people he'd seen in a dream. The announcement was all it took for the war party to kick their ponies into a lope. An hour later, they came across grass bent from the passage of several large animals. Some of the long stalks had already raised up, telling the Comanche how long it had been.

It was easy to follow the tracks, and while the sun blazed overhead, they maintained a steady pace until Owl Eyes circled his pony back around. "Blood. One of them is wounded."

Iron Tip laughed. "I hope he still has some in him when we get there. I want to make him pay."

"It will be fun to put hot coals in his eyes." Cut Hand's eyes glittered with anticipation. "After we beat them with heavy sticks. That is my favorite because I like the sounds of their bones snapping, and their grunts."

Appreciating his thoughts, the others chimed in with their own preferences of torture until Twisted Root had enough. "We will not catch them standing here talking like women around a fire." He kicked his pony's ribs and led off.

Irritated that he was no longer in the lead, Owl Eyes slapped his mount on the rear and raced ahead. The others, thinking he intended to run their prey down within the next few minutes, urged their horses into a run and the entire band and horse herd thundered across the plains.

THIRTY-TWO

WOLF STRAIGHTENED FROM THE COTTONWOOD he leaned against and walked a few feet toward the open grassland and stopped. "Dust."

Lane and Buck joined him. Listless after their discussion, Buck was suddenly energized and reverted to his old self. "Comanches. Lots of them. Check your guns, boys. We're in for a fight."

"You know this how?" Clarence squinted into the distance. "They're too far away to see."

"His vision is better than ours now." Lane checked the loads in his Henry. "I believe what he says."

"Then I trust you." Clarence picked up his rifle. "You don't have to tell us to check our weapons."

Wolf didn't even glance down at the rifle in his hands. "We tend to them just fine."

Still watching the dust cloud, Buck wouldn't give an inch. "I 'magine you know how to clean a gun, but that has nothing to do with having enough shells in your pockets when trouble comes."

"He's used to giving orders, not that I always followed them." Lane set his hat and loosened the pistol in his holster. "What he meant was make sure you have plenty of bullets nearby. Buck and I saw too many Rangers run out of ammunition in dangerous altercations. Like down on the Rio Grande that time we ran into that bunch of Mexican bandits and horse thieves. Remember, Captain McNelly sent us down after them that kept coming across the river."

Buck absently rubbed his abdomen, and Lane was startled to see it bulge slightly, as a pregnant woman's abdomen when a baby's elbow or foot pushes for more room.

"That was a rough fight all right." Buck looked into the past. "There was more of them than us, and those boys had better guns too. We thought we had 'em hemmed up against the river that was running pretty strong, but they'd set a trap for us.

"Those desperados opened up on us the minute we closed in. Bullets were thick in the air, and we had to take cover in just such an area as this. We no more'n dismounted than here they come. I snatched my saddlebags the minute I got down, but some of the others just hit the ground running.

"After two hours, some of the boys were running low on ammunition. The horse thieves didn't know that, though, and shot their way free. We killed half a dozen of them, but every one of us learned our lesson."

"For a dead man, you talk a lot." Wolf turned his Dark Eye back toward Buck. "When I am dead, I will just lay there for the worms to eat me and will not annoy people with my stories."

Clarence chuckled, patting his pockets. "It's a good cautionary account, though."

"How's Hez?" Lane moved to a downed log where he'd placed ammunition. He intended to begin the fight there but had no intention of staying in that one spot if the tide of battle changed. "We need to make sure his arms are close by."

"He is resting, but in pain." Clarence swiveled to look back at Hezekiah. "He will rally when we need him."

Lane opened his saddlebag and took out a box of bullets and held them aloft. "Clarence, I suspect your pockets are full of pistols. Would you spare a .44 for Victoria?"

Reaching behind and under his vest, the former buffalo soldier withdrew an 1860 Colt Richards-Mason with a short barrel. "They'll fit this one just fine."

"Lordy. This thing'll break her hand."

"When she's frightened and fighting for her life, she won't notice." He also produced an oft sharpened butcher knife with a wooden handle and a razor-edge. "Give this to Tall Grass. I can promise she knows how to use it."

The women were beside Hezekiah, who lay on his back, clutching his Bible. Both eyes were closed, but he breathed easy. Lane stopped beside them. "How's he doing?"

Victoria glanced up. Dimples formed at the corners of her mouth and Lane felt the newly forged ache. She stood. "He is resting easy now. Somehow those bullets didn't do the damage I thought, or else the herbs Tall Grass has in that bag are strong."

"I think he'd say it's because of those words in that book he's holding." Lane handed her the Colt. "Use Hezekiah's shotgun if they get past us. It's not going to be much use at a distance, but up close, it'll be a cannon." He swallowed, looking down into her dark eyes. "Then if it comes to us, use this pistol. Save the last round for yourself. Do not let them take you alive."

She bit her bottom lip. "All right."

"No. You hesitated. You don't know what they can do." He intended to drive the point home. He'd seen Comanche barbarity more than once when they arrived too late to save a settler's family or encountered an attack on a supply train when everyone was killed. "They'll rape you over and over, maybe for days. If you're still alive after that, they'll take you to their camp, and the women there will torture you every day. I saw a woman when we were younger with a burned-out nose that was nothing but a seeping hole in her face. Both ears were gone too.

"Some of their women are also like warriors and can hold their own with any man. If they have a woman riding with them when they get here, and don't believe that's not possible, she'll start in on you right then. You understand?"

Victoria nodded, her eyes wide.

Lane handed the butcher knife to Tall Grass. She took it and used the blade to point. "I told you my village is close by. After he rests for a few minutes, we should make a run for it."

"We would if Hez was in a little better shape. But he'd fall off. Even if we tied him on, the ride would start the bleeding again and I 'magine that would kill him. This is a good place to fight."

"Then let *me* go. I can find my husband, Santee, and he will come with many warriors. His father gave him that name when he once killed three Sioux in a battle."

"Do you think he'd come?" He hadn't considered that idea. Thinking, Lane turned his attention to the approaching dust cloud and noted it was bigger than he thought. "I hear the Kiowa are allying with Comanches."

"Some are, but Santee says there are too many white people to fight. He just wants to be left alone."

"How far away do you think they are?"

She shrugged her round shoulders. "They are close, but I do not know. They were moving the village when I left and told me where they planned to camp. But either way, they can help."

Coming to a decision, Lane nodded. "No one's keeping you here. Take your horse and hightail it out of here. At least one of us might make it, and it may as well be you."

Tall Grass reached out and touched him on the shoulder, then Victoria. "I will be back before the sun goes down, I think."

"You better be because by then, we'll be down at least one man . . . gun, and can use the help."

She rushed to the horses and removed the hobbles from the one she'd been riding. Clarence saw what was happening and came over. "What is she doing?"

"Going to get help. Says her village is close and she's going to get her husband and some of his men."

"That is good."

Crawling slowly onto her pony's back, Tall Grass leaned over his neck and slapped the horse's rear with the flat of her hand. Buck joined them as it thundered away. "Running sounds like a great idea."

"She's going for help."

"We're going to need it. A lot of that dust comes from a big herd of horses, but I believe there may be over a hundred fighters."

"Any *good* news?"

Buck's glassy eyes met Lane's. "No."

THIRTY-THREE

AS THEIR PONIES' HOOVES THUNDERED across the prairie, Twisted Root was ecstatic. They met still another larger band that was looking for scalps and the raiders joined them, swelling their ranks to well over a hundred warriors. He felt they allied with his and Iron Tip's band because of his own strong power.

It was a good war party. Twisted Root's chest swelled with pride. The impressive size brought back memories of his younger days when everyone Indian, Mexican, or white ran in fear. Back then they cut a bloody swath from the Northern Plains to Apacheria and all the way down to the coastal lowlands—killing, burning, and stealing horses.

The trail beaten into the grass led directly to a ribbon of green he knew to be a creek. The rolling plains in that area were crisscrossed with creeks and streams that provided habitat for humans and animals both. There was a good chance that the group they were trailing had stopped to water their horses. They might be there now, a rabbit waiting in a snare.

Unable to contain himself, an excited whoop of joy erupted from Twisted Root's mouth, followed by a chorus of excited men intent on killing everyone in their path. He shouted again, and a glorious feeling washed over him, making it feel like they were charging a settler's house to burn, murder, and rape.

One of the younger men shouted and pointed. "There they are!"

The band spread out into a wide skirmish line. Long hair and feathers flew in the air as the new chief, Kot-sa-tay, drifted left while Iron Tip and Twisted Root charged straight ahead.

Behind them, the two young boys turned the horse herd aside to wait until the white men were all dead. Together they stood on a rise and watched.

His eyes weren't what they used to be, and the left was once again blurry, but Twisted Root saw movement in the trees. "They are across the creek!" Irritated that the water was between them, he wondered if it was a trap. Glancing left and right, he didn't see any other figures moving around, but they could have been well hidden.

He let his horse drift back slightly. In his excitement, Iron Tip didn't notice that he was now the point of a wide, shallow arrowhead of fighters rushing across the prairie. Twisted Root knew the charge could easily break through whatever line the whites had cooked up, but the problem was going to be crossing the creek.

"We have to be fast!" Iron Tip shouted. He'd recognized the danger also.

"Wash over them like a flash flood!" Twisted Root pointed his rifle forward, as if it were a lance. The distance closed rapidly, and the trees came into sharp relief. Flecks of sweat flew up from his pony's neck, and he tasted the saltiness on his lips. It felt like the last time he attacked with Blue Bird. His heart swelled in his chest. It would be a great victory to avenge his son.

A bee buzzed past, followed by the quick slap of a rifle report. The war whoops and rumble of hooves were punctuated by more gunfire, some from the Comanche braves around him.

He shouted at the near miss. "Save your bullets until we are closer!"

Beside him, a horse went down, rolling forward. The brave on its back kicked sideways as the dying animal slid to a stop. The man slammed into the ground and lay there as the remainder of the band charged past.

A jolt of fear went through Twisted Root when another horse went down, throwing his rider face first onto the hard ground. Were these men aiming at their horses, like the Ranger he'd tortured? That was the first time they'd ever faced an enemy that intentionally killed the horses. It seemed cowardly somehow.

Now he was close enough to see the defenders. Rifle stocks against their shoulders, the men's faces were hidden by the big hats they wore. One crouched behind a fallen log, and another off to the side fired from behind the trunk of a cottonwood log. A third flash revealed a large black man kneeling and firing. A fourth flash to the right was where another man fought.

Ghost Tracker's horse pulled up beside Twisted Root at a dead run. The warrior guided the pony with his knees and notched an arrow. It was good to see him fight this way. Ghost Tracker was an excellent shot with a bow and had killed many men that way.

With the wind in his ears and noise of battle, Twisted Root couldn't hear the bowstring snap, but the arrow arced away and buried itself in the log shielding one of the white men.

Twisted Root hadn't noticed until that moment that he was once again at the front of the pack. Guns roared across the creek and another horse went down. A warrior shot an arrow, but it was impossible to see where it went.

Iron Tip shouted something, but the words went unheard in the melee. The crackle of rifle fire coming from the creek was deadly. In front of him, a slug caught a warrior in the forehead. The back of his head exploded in a red and gray mist of blood and brains that filled Twisted Root's good eye. Unable to see, he wiped at the matter.

Though hazy, his right eye was clear enough to see still another horse go down. It was Lone Coyote, and he kicked free, then regained his feet to notch another arrow. A bullet punched through his chest, staggering him back. Another snapped a braid off, and a third caught him in the abdomen, blowing a large exit hole in his back. His knees buckled and Lone Coyote dropped to a squat, then fell sideways and was still.

Kot-sa-tay waved his lance. "Back away!"

The others withdrew to regroup for another charge.

THIRTY-FOUR

"HERE THEY COME." BUCK'S VOICE was soft and calm. He'd been through a dozen or more engagements and knew *they* shouldn't get excited, but he couldn't generate much of anything at all. Half hidden by the cottonwood trunk, he checked on Lane, then peered up through the leaves above at the clear blue sky.

Lane saw him looking upward. "Don't think you're gonna climb that tree and fight from there."

"Just seeing where the sun was."

"We're a far piece from dark. You're finally gonna do me some good."

That familiar grin that swooned the ladies appeared. "I've always done you some good. Just stick with me for some more." The light went out of his eyes and Lane felt it too. His good humor was always there at the beginning of a fight, but this time it was gone because neither of them was sure what the future might bring, the way Buck was.

The air was crystal clear, marred only by the dirt kicked up by the charging horses running full out. Buck carefully shouldered his rifle. Lane had seen that many times before and waited for the inevitable outcome. Many of the Indians had guns, and a scattering of bullets rattled through the trees.

One cut the grass in front of Lane and buried in his log. Shooting from running horses and across a creek wasn't accurate at all, but he'd seen men buried from wild, supposedly inaccurate shots before.

Buck fired and a second later a horse rolled head over heels, throwing his rider to the ground. So many of the warriors were packed together, Lane took a bead on one of the lead riders and fired, figuring that even if he missed, the bullet had a good chance of striking someone.

The Henry roared, but the shot must have missed. Things were happening too fast to see if it had any effect on man or horse behind his intended target. He jacked the lever and fired twice more in quick succession.

Clarence and Wolf fired. Men and ponies fell, and Lane was confident that it was Buck doing most of the horse killing. One went down, and the rider somehow landed upright and maintained his feet. Buck shot him, then shot him a second time before he toppled sideways.

Clarence's big Sharps boomed, the distinctive sound of the heavy round punctuated the battle. One warrior beyond the range of Lane's rifle threw up his hands and went down, evidence the buffalo gun's reach was always deadly.

The charge turned. Six or seven warriors split off and headed upstream. Another bunch did the same going downstream. The remainder of the war party retreated beyond the range of the Sharps and milled around. Some of them dismounted, standing behind their horses.

"They've been shot at from a distance before," Clarence said, thumbing a round into his rifle.

"Anyone hurt?" Ears ringing from all the shooting, Lane looked around to be sure everyone was all right. Wolf left the tree he was using for a shield and disappeared downstream.

Buck saw it and reloaded. "Clarence, slip over to your right. They've split up and I imagine they'll cross a little ways down and try to surround us."

"They won't like what they find." He rose and ducked through the underbrush.

A tangled drift of logs and limbs offered a breastwork of sorts. Victoria and Hez were behind them. Keeping one eye on the warriors, Lane craned his neck. "Victoria. Are y'all right?"

"Hezekiah is still the same. A couple of bullets went over us, but we're just fine."

"Stay down."

"I can fight."

"You will if they try to come around behind us. In fact, keep that shotgun close and an eye on the rear."

"Lane's right." Buck stood in the open, as casual as if in a churchyard. "There's more cover around us than I'd like. Victoria, if things get too hot, see if you can rouse Hezekiah and get him to a horse. We'll be right along behind you and try to outrun 'em again, if we can."

Buck was unnaturally calm. "Lane, I believe there's too many of them. If this all goes to pieces, I'm going to stay back with a rifle or two and cover for y'all. You light out for that village Tall Grass told us about."

"Hell no. I'm not leaving you again."

"It won't matter this time. They can't do no worse to me than they already have." He lowered his voice. "And this snake inside me's been twisting and turning since this fight started. The damn thing's excited. I don't know what's gonna happen next, but I'm afraid it's gonna try to find a way out, and I can only think of a couple of ways it can do it. Y'all don't need to be around when it happens."

Wide-eyed, Lane shuddered at the thought. "Maybe they can all get away and I can stay here with you. I can kill that thing for you if it comes out."

"I don't know if you can . . . here they come again."

At the same time, bird cries came from up and down the river, birds that shouldn't be calling in the middle of a gun battle.

THIRTY-FIVE

SOME OF THE YOUNGER HOTHEADS insisted on another charge, but the three, more experienced chiefs had other ideas. Still mounted, Iron Tip kept his voice low, but authoritative. "We will stay right here so they can see us. Give the others time to work their way around them."

"I can hit them with this rifle you took from the hide hunters," Owl Eyes said.

"You can shoot at them, but you have not practiced with it. Don't waste your bullets." Twisted Root was standing behind his horse, using the animal's thick neck and chest as a shield. "Let Cut Hand creep up on them. He will kill many with his arrows."

"That is right." Kot-sa-tay unconsciously signed with his hands as he spoke. "My braves are coming around on the other side as well. They will circle around like wolves closing in on a wounded buffalo. When they are distracted, we can ride in and kill them all with our hand weapons." He grasped the head of a stained war club in a leather belt around his waist.

A lance of pain went through Twisted Root's head, so severe he thought he'd been shot. He would have staggered back had he not been holding on to his horse. Two Shoot saw it and reached out to steady the medicine man. "Are the bullets in your head rubbing against each other again?"

"No. A ghost came in through my ear."

Frightened, men from the other band backed away, but Twisted Root's men moved closer. "What kind of ghost?"

Blinking his eyes clear, the damaged medicine man held on to a leather loop tied in his horse's mane. "I feel the shape of a bent old woman. She is trying to use my eyes to see what is around us."

Kot-sa-tay frowned, studying the man who let go of the loop and dropped to one knee. "This is bad medicine at this time. If there is a witch here, we need to leave."

"No!" Twisted Root gagged and held out a palm, as if it would shield him from the other chief's reluctance to fight. "A cloud in my mind shows the reflection of a woman with child across the river there. She is what the old woman wants to see."

To a man, the warriors looked toward the creek, as if they could see what Twisted Root was talking about. One of the newcomers turned to look back toward the horse herd, in case something was going on behind them. He gasped. "Look. Wolves."

A line of prairie wolves approached in a wide, ragged line. Nine Toes and Shouts His Name saw them and moved the horses away. Several of the men raised their weapons, preparing to kill them, but Twisted Root, now sitting on the ground, held up both hands.

"Stop. There is too much going on around me. I need to fight this old woman."

They waited as his face changed expressions half a dozen times. One moment he looked to be in great pain, and the next, frowned as if in deep concentration. From there it was a constipated grimace, a smirk, then miraculously, his twisted face relaxed into what was normal years earlier. That one lasted for several seconds before it wrinkled back into the features they recognized.

He jerked upright and turned his head toward the creek. His eyes widened, whether in amazement or fear, they couldn't tell. "It is him."

"Who?" Waters His Horses studied the tree line.

"The one I killed and cursed for taking the life of Blue Bird. The one we saw near the hide hunters' camp. It is the dead man who walks this earth."

Murmurs of fear swept through the band. Stealing, raping, and murder raids, they all understood, but evil spirits were something else. Two men threw up their hands and walked back toward the horse herd, leading their mounts. They wanted no truck with spirits.

"She is afraid for the child." Twisted Root wiped cold sweat from his face.

Kot-sa-tay tilted his head as he watched the medicine man on the ground. "Who?"

"The old woman in my head. She wants to see the woman over there across the creek. We have found them. These are the ones we want."

A raised eyebrow was Kot-sa-tay's question. Two Shoot answered. "He says a pregnant woman is traveling with these white men. He had a vision about them, and about the old woman who lives at Boiling Springs."

"Crows." Twisted Root's voice went flat. Dead.

Two Shoot knelt and put a hand on his shoulder. He looked around them, but no birds were in evidence. "There are no crows here."

"No. They sit upon the old woman's dirt house. She is using them to get inside my head. Fire your two-shoot gun and run them off."

The warrior immediately slung the double-barrel off his shoulder and fired twice in the air without aiming. The deep reports jolted Twisted Root back to life. He opened his eyes and looked around. "They flew away."

Iron Tip frowned and shook his head. "There were no crows here to begin with."

Twisted Root made his forefinger sweep around. "And no wolves now either."

The startled warriors looked, but the medicine man was right. The wolves were gone as quickly as smoke in the wind.

Suddenly deflated, most of them were uneasy. They couldn't take their eyes off Twisted Root, still sitting on the ground. The fresh crackle of gunfire down on the creek startled them, and they all turned to see what was happening.

THIRTY-SIX

"WHAT'N HELL ARE THEY DOING out there?" Lane squinted into the distance. "I'd give your left nut for a pair of field glasses."

"How kind of you." Buck stared too. "They're arguing about something. I figure the younger men want to charge again. They like that style of fighting for some reason. Quite a few of them are behind their horses."

He watched intently, reporting what he was seeing.

"One of them is half hidden by his horse, but it looks like he's been wounded. I can see his legs every now and then when his horse moves. He's going down."

"I wish I could see that far."

"You don't need to as long as I'm around."

"Yeah, well you're not something I can rely on."

The boom of the big Sharps came from Clarence's position.

SQUATTING AGAINST THE WAIST-HIGH CREEK BANK, CLARENCE chose a position that allowed him to both see downstream and through the underbrush. He leaned one elbow on the dirt and peered through the willows and shrubs.

He waited.

It didn't take long before a tiny limb moved in the completely still air. Tucking the buffalo gun against his shoulder, he waited. A pair of legs appeared, the owner moving at a glacial speed.

Holding his fire, Clarence searched for more signs of approaching warriors.

The trunk of another person several feet from the first advanced toward their camp. Still another closer to the water came into view. Clarence's problem was which target to shoot first. He decided to aim at the farthest brave, then shoot the next nearest with his pistol. With those two down, the man closest to him on the creek would hopefully come within reach, and he could empty the pistol into him.

The whole plan went to pieces when a figure suddenly loomed only feet away. This one was talented and had crawled like a lizard through the shorter grass. He raised up to see if an enemy was close and stopped. Totally unexpected, they were both surprised when he and Clarence saw each other at the same time.

He shifted his aim, dropping the barrel of the rifle to almost ground level and cut loose. The grass between them shredded and dust and chaff billowed from the ground from the muzzle blast. The man dropped back to the ground with a thump.

Clarence drew his belt gun with a move smooth as grease. He thumb-cocked the hammer and shot the next closest man, opposite of what he intended. The .44 slug took him square in the chest, and he went down with a groan.

Guns opened up around Clarence, and a second pistol appeared in his hand. The two revolvers belched a rhythm of fire, answering their shots. A Comanche charged with a whoop, brandishing a war club. He was swinging it at Clarence when he shot him twice with the pistol in his right hand. Something stung him on top of his shoulder, and he thumb-cocked the left-hand pistol at the same time aiming and shooting with the other one. Several warriors rushed his position, and he shot one at point blank range, taking off the side of the man's head in a spray of gore.

Two braves threw themselves through the air. He registered war paint and shrill cries of victory as they slammed into his upper body.

He desperately wanted to draw the sword strapped across his back, but there was no time. He fell back with them on top. Clarence threw up his left hand to block a knife thrust and stuck the barrel against the other Comanche's side and pulled the trigger. The report was muffled, and the man twisted away from him to fall half in the water.

The other warrior bent him backward into the creek. Clarence dropped both pistols and grappled with the man intent on killing him. Water had never been Clarence's friend, and the fear of drowning lent extra fire to his response. A knife flashed, and he grabbed at the man's hand. They thrashed into deeper water and Clarence's feet went out from under him as the sand melted away in the current.

Taking a deep breath, he let the warrior push him deeper at the same time pulling his own knife from the sheath on his belt. Clarence twisted to get the warrior off to his left side and plunged the sharp blade into the man's abdomen.

It slid in with such ease he thought he'd missed and stabbed again, this time slashing to the side. The cool water around his hand immediately warmed by a torrent of blood and the Comanche let go to hold his insides where they belonged.

Clarence pushed him away, then drug himself back to shallow water to emerge, shaking his head like a dog to clear his vision. Gutted, the warrior weakly pushed himself back into the shallows with his feet.

A walking armory, Clarence reached into another pocket and withdrew a small pistol. He pointed at the back of the man's head and pulled the trigger, but the snap on a dead cap told him that likely every bullet he had was wet. Dropping it, he pulled the curved sword from the sheath hanging between his shoulders and decapitated him. Twin geysers shot from the stump and the body sank.

Another who'd fallen half into the water was dragging himself back up. Two strides, and Clarence ran the sword between the man's shoulders.

Stepping back onto the bank, he made his way back to the hobbled packhorses where he had even more guns, with dry powder that would fire.

WOLF HEARD THE BATTLE UPSTREAM. IT WAS only a matter of time before the other small band appeared. He settled behind a bush and waited. A minute later, the snap of a twig told him someone was closing in.

He waited as still as the bushes around him, knife in his left hand and pistol in his right. A Comanche drew near and when he came close, Wolf shot without aiming. The man fell and two others rushed toward his position, firing.

Wolf dropped to the ground, rolled sideways, and came up against a downed log. A bullet plucked the decaying wood and another cut through the grass beside him. He fired twice at a figure, spinning him around, and then rose and did the unexpected.

He charged.

Momentum was behind the others, and they didn't have time to set their feet. The knife in his left plunged at the nearest Comanche. The blade cut through his diaphragm with a fibrous sound. The dying man rose on his toes, as if to lift himself off the blade, but Wolf released the handle, leaving it buried to the hilt and plucked a hatchet from his belt.

The pistol in his other hand roared and still another painted enemy fell sideways, thrashing in the soft green grass. A gun went off nearby and pain seared along his forearm as the bullet cut a long, bloody channel down the length to his elbow.

Wolf closed with a warrior wearing black-and-red paint on his face. They grappled, and Wolf roared in fury. At the sight of his frightening canines, the Comanche recoiled in horror and Wolf leaned in and buried his teeth in his throat. With a great yank, he tore out the man's jugular and pushed him away as a fountain of pressurized blood sprayed across Wolf's face and body.

"YOUNG MEN." BUCK WAITED AS A HANDFUL of mounted warriors charged the creek.

"Don't surprise me none." Lane's heart was beating out of his chest from the two gunfights going on up and down the creek. "I hope they're able to hold them off."

"They will." Buck didn't seem bothered at all. "You know, being dead takes some of the fear out of an Indian attack."

"I don't intend to find out." Lane snorted, the sound harsh. "Thanks for the information, though."

Instead of answering, Buck shouldered his rifle, aimed, and fired. The rider's horse humped, bucked, and crow-hopped to the side. "Bad shot." He jacked the lever and fired again. The Comanche went backward with a shout of pain the same time the horse bucked again and fell. The man flipped off, rising high in the air before coming down on his shoulder. The body folded in two, then flopped back to lie still.

A warrior bearing down on them turned away, the horse cutting to Lane's left, and launched an arrow. Lane missed with the Henry. Keeping the stock to his shoulder, he reloaded the chamber and shot a second time. The brave fired another arrow in the same amount of time and the air was suddenly filled with a rain of arrows that arced up and down toward the two Rangers.

More warriors rose up from the grass where they'd crawled close and remained hidden until the charge. They notched a second round of arrows that rattled through the trees. It was a fine coordinated attack but they were close and still, giving the two experienced lawmen virtually stationary targets.

A third rifle joined in, and Lane took his eyes off the Henry's sights long enough to see Hezekiah lying on his stomach, firing slowly.

The extra rifle broke the attack, and the Comanche retreated.

"Well, shit."

Lane turned to see Buck standing in the open. Two arrows protruded from his body. He pulled one out and threw it in the direction of the retreating warriors.

"That stings, dammit!"

"Well, you should have been hiding behind that tree like anyone with good sense."

"I decided that I don't need to hide anymore." He plucked out the second arrow from his stomach and paused, his hand on his abdomen. A strange look came into his eye as he doubled over.

"What's the matter?"

"That one hit the snake." Before Lane could respond, Buck leaned over and gagged, in such a way that only a dead man can gag. His mouth opened, and he gasped and gagged again.

"Holy hell!" Lane said, and backed away as Buck tried to yak up what had been torturing him for days.

THIRTY-SEVEN

"O H, LORDY." MISS HATTIE ALMOST fell from her chair in front of the soddy's door.

The tongueless Navajo, Ashkii Dighin, grasped her shoulder and held the old woman in the rickety chair. He wanted to ask her what was wrong but couldn't let go to sign. Instead, he patted her on the shoulder, as he would pat his grandmother when she wasn't feeling good.

Miss Hattie's head rolled on her shoulders, and her hands rose like weak birds, fingers fluttering. She appeared to ward something off before they went limp and fell back into her lap. The whites of her eyes showed until her lids closed and she relaxed.

When Ashkii was sure she wouldn't fall out of the rickety homemade chair, he stepped inside and filled a dipper of water from the pool he'd finished the day before and covered with large, flat stones. It looked like a pathway laid to the spring, and he figured no one would notice.

When he came back outside, he saw she was unable to drink, so he dipped his fingers and flicked droplets onto her face. That done, he wiped her face with his wet palm, spreading the water and cooling her skin.

She finally awoke and glanced around, disoriented. He grasped her thin, bony hand and leaned in to raise his eyebrows in question. She finally focused on his face and patted his hand. "I'm all right, hon. Now, anyway."

He offered the dipper again, and this time she drained it. "Yes, Lord.

That tastes as sweet as sugar. I believe them Indians are right. There's something special about this water."

Ashkii laid the dipper in her lap and signed. "What happened?"

"I don't know for sure. I's sittin' here wondering where that pregnant woman was and all of a sudden it felt like something reached into the top of my head and pulled my brain. Just plucked it out like a chicken egg from a nest.

"The next thing I knew, I saw people down below me, some hiding in trees, and another bunch out on the prairie. They was all fighting and ever one of 'em had long, skinny strings of smoke coming out of the tops of their heads and stretching up into the sky, where the smoke spread out into what I guess you'd call a big, floppy cloud the size of that door there.

"Most were the same color, like clean cedar smoke, but one was dark, sick-looking, like it had pus in it." She closed her eyes and shuddered. "I don't know what happened, but whatever had hold of me drew me toward that sick cloud. I saw the pregnant woman at a long distance. Her cloud was the prettiest blue you ever saw, and I wanted to fly down and wrap myself in it."

She saw his wide eyes as he listened and grinned, breaking her face in a map of wrinkles. "Hon, if I'da done that, I think it would have felt like Heaven, and this old face would have turned smooth as a baby's bottom." She cackled. "But that bad ol' cloud pulled me down and the next thing I knew, I was in a dangerous brain that squirmed like a toad in a dark, wet cave.

"I surely didn't want to be in there. That cave in his mind was barely tall enough for me to stand up, and it grew more shallow out toward the edges, and in them shallow ends where there's not enough room to stand all the way up, it was like a . . . like the bottom of the privy, you know, just full of human shit caked on the walls and the ground and a big caked drain that leads down to Hell." Her stomach clenched and she put a hand over her mouth.

Swallowing, she drew a deep breath and continued. "I was in a man called Twisted Root, and I saw everything he knew. Everything he'd seen or thought, and honey, I didn't know people could be so rotten inside.

"I knew who he was. I shot him, years ago when I first come here. It was a pure accident, but I did. That Comanche's mean as a rattler now and is after that woman and her baby. He wants it to replace his dead son, to make the pore little thing dark and dirty, and not what it's intended to be.

"I looked through his eyes and saw across the grass where that party we're a-waitin' on is forted up from him. All their . . . smokes seem healthy except for two. One of 'em's hurt. There's streaks of red in his, but the other'n is skinny, and it don't spread out up top. It's like a loose string flying in the wind. Does that make any sense?"

Ashkii nodded and signed. "Was this another one of your dreams, like before?"

"No. It's happenin' right now, this very minute."

"I like your dreams better."

"So do I, but now I know why they ain't here yet, but they're close. They're coming, and we need to be ready."

THIRTY-EIGHT

LANE WATCHED IN HORROR AS Buck dropped to his knees and retched as if trying to throw up his toenails. Each gag arched his back like a frightened cat, raising him up on his fingertips to gain more pressure on whatever it was in his stomach.

With his Dark Eye on Buck, and his good one on the Comanche across the creek who were still sitting just out of gunshot range, Wolf studied Buck's actions as if he were watching red harvester ants on their mound.

"This has my interest. I thought when the time came, the snake would come out his butthole, not his mouth. It only makes sense to me, but then again, I am Cheyenne, and not white."

More shouts came from the Comanche, as the young men suffering from the confidence and stupidity of youth postured in front of what truly scared them, the defender's guns. Periodically, one would break from the pack and charge a short distance, whooping and blustering before turning his pony in a cloud of dust and returning to the band.

"Buck, fight it. Right now ain't the time to go through something like this." Lane paced back and forth. "Hell, if you can do this later, I'll hold your head and wash it with a wet rag until that thing comes up, but we need you right now."

Not hearing him, Buck hunched up and retched again.

Eyes glassy with fever, Hezekiah leaned against a tree. "Take my Bible and put it on his back."

Victoria took it from his hand. There was blood on the cover. "Whatever for?"

"I don't have the strength to pray for him, let alone read it, but just having it touch him might help."

"The demon in him wasn't put there by your god." Wolf squatted, to get a better view of what was happening. "It was put there by a bad medicine man. Your talking papers won't work."

Hezekiah tried to lean his head back in that unnaturally far position to pray, but the trunk prevented such a maneuver. Instead, he prayed quietly. Victoria returned the Bible, and he clutched it to his chest again.

"It is a welcome relief for you to pray like normal people." Clarence's back was to Buck and the others, intent on their rear, just in case another band swam the creek and tried to flank them again. "Wolf, my sword was made by a Japanese artisan, and I feel it is pure enough to cut that thing's head off when it emerges."

Ignoring him, Lane matched Wolf's position and knelt on Buck's opposite side. "Son, what can I do to help?" He cast a fearful look back toward the Comanche war party.

Buck's lower jaw elongated as he opened his mouth wide, it cracked as if the cartilage and tendons holding it together finally gave up with the strain. His stomach heaved again, and black fluid ran from his nose to puddle on the ground. The toes of his boots dug into the dirt and his whole body quivered with the effort to force the snake out.

The war party took that moment to charge again. This time it wasn't as many as before, but they crossed the distance at a dead run. Lane caught them from the corner of his eye and stood. "Here they come. They're determined to punch through this time."

Wolf stood, reluctantly. "That thing is going to enter our world while we are forced to defend ourselves. Lane, you are lucky he is a friend and has fought with us, otherwise I would allow Clarence to disjoint this thing so I can kill them both when we're finished with these annoying Comanches. Then I can sleep better tonight."

"Thanks for your consideration." Lane hurried to Hezekiah's side. "Push with your feet, Hez, you need to get back undercover and stay low." Victoria helped them and they maneuvered the wounded man behind their little fort. "Just like the last time. Y'all stay here. You keep low too, girl."

THIRTY-NINE

THIS TIME THE CHIEFS STAYED back when the younger men, who were filled with spirit, wanted to take scalps. A Comanche chief advised his people, but he did not speak for them or deign to stop anyone from doing what they wanted. The young men had their own minds and opinions and could do as they wished.

Iron Tip and Kot-sa-tay stood apart from Twisted Root who leaned weakly against his mount. He still held the loop tied in its mane to steady his weak knees. The old woman was gone, but there was a strange feeling inside his mind, as if cold water had flowed through and numbed the tissue.

It was late afternoon when the young men charged to within range and at the sound of the defender's gunshots, split in the middle and returned fire. Both groups continued in a large curve left and right to meet back in the middle and repeat the process. The maneuver was to test the white men's ammunition stores, and to possibly get in a lucky shot.

It was also to show their bravery, and once even the young horse handler, Shouts His Name, rode out to within the defender's range to prove his manhood. The other warriors shouted encouragement and charged even closer, spurred on by the young man's courage.

Agitated, Iron Tip and Kot-sa-tay swung onto their horses' backs, angry and unsettled. Waters His Horses stepped up beside Twisted Root. The chief saw the dead Comanchero's Sharps in his hands.

A wide grin split his face and the medicine man's mind cleared even more. "They will be surprised when you kill one of them with that. Now is the time to use it."

"It will be a fine day in a moment." Waters His Horses walked a few feet closer to the battle to put the horses behind him. He took a knee and brought the stock to his shoulder. Aiming carefully, he raised the muzzle and pulled the trigger. The big rifle roared, shoving his shoulder back so hard he had to release the forepiece and steady himself against the ground.

The white men's rifles continued to crackle, and a warrior fell from his horse. The others increased their war whoops, and the two opposite circles moved closer to the creek where the defenders huddled.

Waters His Horses reached into a beaded bag hanging over his shoulder and selected another bullet. Reloading the buffalo rifle, he aimed again, higher this time, and pulled the trigger. This time he was prepared for the recoil and was able to watch for the results.

He turned and threw up his right hand. "This bullet is so slow I can watch it fly through the air. This next one will kill one of those white devils."

A big slug impacted the ground twenty yards in front of the chiefs, throwing up a plume of dirt and rocks. Someone else with a buffalo rifle was searching for flesh. The heavy boom followed seconds later, clearly defined over the smaller calibers the others were using.

Ignoring the round, Waters His Horses reached again into the bag, his hand closed on another round at the same time his upper body seemed to explode. The impact of a .50-caliber chunk of lead deformed his chest and snapped the man's spine. He slammed back against the grass, dead before the shot's report reached them.

FORTY

CLARENCE LOWERED THE SHARPS AND grunted. "That'll take the starch out of them for a little while."

The sound of his voice jolted Lane back into the world around them. Until then, his entire focus was on the warriors across the creek. Now that the gunfire had ended, at least for the moment, he could tend to Buck.

When he turned, his partner lay face down on the ground, deflated and still. Lane crossed the short distance. His cheek was in the black fluid that puddled on the ground. Fighting back nausea, Lane rolled him over. "Buck. You all right?"

His eyes fluttered. "Hell no. I've been trying to puke up a snake."

Lane's eyes widened, and he checked around. "I don't see it."

"It never came up."

"The head came out for a second." Wolf's face was impassive. "I saw it. It had human eyes and I think ears. One of the eyes was a bloody hole where the arrow hit. The other one blinked at the sun, then it went back inside, and he swallowed it again."

Always weak-stomached about certain things, Lane gagged, eyes watering. Half a second later, a whistling sound came from overhead.

Clarence shouted. "Get under cover!"

A shower of arrows cut through the trees, some burying in the ground. Others stuck into logs and living trees. Luckily, no one was injured in the coordinated volley, but then a steady rain of death dropped from the sky. A skilled Comanche could loose twenty arrows in as little as forty-five seconds, providing a deadly stream of projectiles, and they rattled among the defenders.

"They moved in while we were shooting at those others." Wolf whirled and disappeared downstream. He was gone for only a few seconds and then emerged on the run. "Too many for me to handle alone! They're coming. Get ready!"

Another cloud of arrows whickered from the opposite direction, thudding all around them. Victoria screamed. A sharp lance of pain burned through Lane's calf. Grabbing his leg, he saw an arrow had punched through the back quarter shaft of his knee-high boot.

The arrow tip poked out the front. He broke it off near the fletching and pushed the polished dogwood shaft on through. He couldn't see but felt it had only gone through under the skin. That done, he limped to where Victoria and Hezekiah were half under the log. An arrow caught her through the upper arm, but the velocity was so great it went all the way through.

Hezekiah was awake, and mobile enough to grab her arm and put pressure on the wound. "It isn't bad, Miss Victoria." His eyes were bright with fever. "Better tie something around it. I don't have the strength to hold on much longer."

Wolf's rifle barked three times before he shouted. "Down!"

Lane heard another swarm of arrows arcing through the air. He pushed Victoria back against the log and draped over her body. She grunted at the weight and Lane was full into that musky smell of hers that both excited and terrified him. It wrapped around him like a cloak and for half a second, he forgot the danger that threatened them.

The next thing he knew, Buck rushed up and threw himself over both of them.

Arrows thudded all around and Hez shrieked. Buck grunted twice and spoke to the back of Lane's neck. "No matter how I try to get used to it, that still stings!"

Clarence's voice rose above Wolf's rifle reports. "They're on us!"

Buck rolled off of Lane, who registered two more arrow shafts sticking out of his partner's back as he snatched the pistol from his holster.

He caught a glimpse of Clarence firing a pistol with his left hand as he reached back with his right and drew the Japanese sword.

While the Comanche archers kept them pinned down with their bows, a party crossed the creek and rushed from the brush. A warrior charged Clarence—a war axe raised. The black man didn't see that one. His attention was on a man racing toward him with a butcher knife in his hand.

Lane saw him and fired. The .44-caliber bullet caught him in the side of the chest and his heavy club fell from nerveless fingers as the warrior crumpled. Lane swung around, putting himself between Victoria and the next attacker he was sure to come.

Clarence dropped the empty revolver and grasped the sword with both hands. He swung, and the blade took off the adversary's arm holding the butcher knife. He reversed the swing, decapitating the warrior.

Wolf charged into the fray with his own battle cry, canine's flashing and a wild look in his eye. Two young men with painted faces and upper bodies charged the tall Cheyenne, but before they could reach him, Hezekiah's shotgun boomed, then boomed again.

In his peripheral vision, Lane saw them drop like wheat under a scythe amid falling leaves and twigs as the spreading buckshot shredded everything around them. A figure, bare from the waist up rushed at him, and he fired. The man dropped with a groan, and in the next second, it was chaos as the white men did the unthinkable.

They attacked.

Clarence switched the sword to his left hand and produced another pistol from his belt. Five shots belched flame in one long roll of thunder as Lane and Wolf charged past them. It was a slaughterhouse as they fought for their lives and the pregnant woman who was reloading Hezekiah's shotgun.

Two more deep booms punctuated the shrill whoops of both Indians and white men. Hezekiah was far enough away that the shot had time to fan out even more, destroying everything in its path.

With the last of that threat eliminated, Lane whirled to see Buck on one knee, aiming and firing across the river as fast as he could jack the Henry's lever.

"The horses!" Lane shouted at Wolf and Clarence. They charged past Buck and Hezekiah, and pulled reins free, vaulting in their saddles. Lane kicked his gray in the flanks and the horse leaped toward their camp.

Buck rose at the sound of approaching horses. "Follow me!" He raced to the water, hesitating only a moment before stepping in, or rather, stepping where the water used to be. Just as it had the first time he tried to wash up, the water retreated, leaving a muddy bottom and flopping catfish.

He paused, shouldered the rifle and fired again, and walked out toward the middle of the creek that divided around him. Halfway across, the water closed in behind. Lane, Wolf, and Clarence separated and hit the creek on either side of Buck. Water splashed, dimpling the surface around them, but not one drop landed on the Ranger.

Terrified by a man who could walk through a creek that physically recoiled from his body, the Comanche warriors leaped to their feet and raced away from the attacking horsemen back toward their band. The three mounted men thundered behind them. Lane fired at their retreating backs with his pistols, while Clarence rode them down, his sword flashing in the sunlight. Arms flailed as bodies fell under the guns. Each time Clarence swung the Japanese sword, blood sprayed in a red mist. Wolf shouted and whooped, riding close and clubbing down the retreating warriors to count coup.

Realizing they were getting too close to the Comanche band waiting and watching, Lane reined in. "That's enough! We don't need to get any farther from Victoria and Hez!"

Dust flew as their horses dug in. Wolf stood in his stirrups and shouted in Cheyenne at the Comanche, shaking a fresh scalp he'd somehow acquired in the melee.

The surviving Comanche responded with shouts and shrieks before they turned their ponies and disappeared over a low rise.

FORTY-ONE

T WISTED ROOT WAS FURIOUS. SAVAGELY jerking on his mount's war bridle that was tied around the horse's lower jaw, he shouted at both the men around him. Uncertain what her rider wanted to do, the mare danced and shuffled, trying to understand.

They'd been beaten back over and over again, and just when his attack plan looked successful, the whites rose up and slaughtered every one of the young men who'd crossed the creek.

It was Twisted Root who had the idea of sending some of their men to circle around the defenders' camp while Kot-sa-tay's best bowmen crawled through the grass like ants. It almost worked, too, pinning down the white men with arrows while Iron Tip's young men, the ones who couldn't wait to get their knives bloody, came in from the west.

He saw Iron Tip's face and realized that now the war chief was angry at *him*. There was no way Twisted Root could have anticipated the deadly response the defenders dealt his men. His medicine was good and there were no crows about, as far as he knew.

"They crossed the creek!" Two Shoot's face was pale and frightened.

From his position, Twisted Root saw the Cheyenne waving a fresh scalp, and his fury increased even more.

It was Iron Tip who waved everyone back, and they retreated several miles, until Kot-sa-tay was sure no one was following. Once safe in a deep ravine, they posted people to watch while the two shaken boys took the stolen horse herd to graze.

Now, squatting in the early evening shade of the high walls, each man had his say.

"There will be much grief in our village." Kot-sa-tay slashed at his arms with the edge of his hand. "Many women will cut themselves when they hear their sons and husbands have fallen. Many will cut off fingers in their sorrow."

Comanche women showed their grief with screams and wails, slashing their arms, faces, and breasts. Others demonstrated their heartache and anguish by cutting off fingers. Some women had done this so many times their hands were horribly mutilated.

"It will be like that in all our villages." Twisted Root shrugged, unmoved. "Men will also cut off their hair and roll on the ground. Waters His Horses's wife will have his great herd killed. It is the way."

Iron Tip was angry and didn't speak for a long time. When Twisted Root shrugged, his eyes widened and his hand went to the knife on his belt. "Our war party was strong before you came! We had many horses we'd stolen from the whites. Our scalps were still dripping red, and we would have more, but we joined you instead to kill a few whites who were running. You should have taken them yourself, except your medicine is foul, like rotting meat in the sun."

"I will still kill them!" Twisted Root's eyes flashed. "And if you keep accusing me of bad medicine, I may kill you with a spell." He patted a pouch hanging over his shoulder. "Or I will blow powder in your face, and you will turn the color of clay and die."

"Enough!" Kot-sa-tay chopped the air with his hand. "Our young men are dead because they wanted to fight. They wanted scalps, but none of us expected to see the whites fight with such fury. They are usually cowards who cry and run. I don't know how they did this, but they won't stay where they are for too long. They surely know Quanah's band is coming this way too."

Twisted Root nodded, calming. "Yes. They will stay here this night. We need to circle around and wait for them out on the prairie. They won't be so hard to kill out in the open. We can hit them over and over again as they travel to the boiling spring. This will reduce their numbers and then we can kill them and the old woman at the same time. I had a vision, and the witch is waiting for them to get there."

Kot-sa-tay stared at the ground in front of him. "I have a better idea. Let us go around and beat them to the spring and kill those who are there. Then we can lay in wait, and when they get close, shoot them with our arrows and bullets. They will fall like the rain, and then we can have our spring back."

Twisted Root didn't mention that he'd suggested that to his own men earlier. Now he wished they'd done just that. "I would like to soak in those healing waters. They will take some of the twist out of this arm." He ran a finger down his left chin. "And maybe this side will return to normal."

"There is nothing normal in this world now that the white men have come." Kot-sa-tay spat on the ground. "We all saw the water move away from Black Hat, so that it would not touch him. Twisted Root, your medicine made him that way. He walks the earth again, though we've killed him more than once. Your magic is rotten. You may be right, soaking in the spring might wash away the evil that wraps you like a blanket filled with lice."

"You should not speak to me like that. I cursed the Ranger for killing my son, but this was not part of it. He should have laid there until he rotted away!"

Another voice added his opinion to the disagreement, annoying Twisted Root even more.

"Did you think he would vanish into thin air? That he would take wing and fly away, so that you would not have to look at him anymore?"

"Two Shoot. You are a good warrior and a good man, but if you keep speaking to me this way, you will soon go see your ancestors."

Instead of answering, Two Shoot adjusted the shotgun across his lap and glowered into the fire. Some of Iron Tip's men shook their heads. He watched them and lowered his head. "I think we need more men. Let me send Owl Eyes and another back to find Quanah. Then we will be several hundred strong. The Quahadi are fierce. The best warriors."

"We are strong now." Twisted Root didn't want Isa-Tai anywhere around. It would be easy for that medicine man to make a suggestion and have it followed. Then, if his idea worked out and they could murder some white people, or take scalps, or steal horses or plunder, then Isa-tai would be the favorite.

It was Twisted Root's idea to kill the pregnant woman, then the old witch at the spring. He didn't want anyone to steal his glory.

"I do not want to wait for Quanah, now. I sent Pahayoko and Tabe-mohats to find him, and he hasn't returned. Maybe he doesn't want to come." He'd wondered why Amorous One and Bright Sun hadn't come back yet. He thought maybe they'd tried to build a war party of their own and went somewhere else. Or maybe they'd run into travelers or buffalo hunters and tried to kill them, only to be killed themselves. It was always a possibility they lived with.

"We don't have to wait." Iron Tip flipped a hand to the northwest. "We all know where the sacred spring is. He can meet us there."

Nods all around told Twisted Root that there was no use in arguing any longer. He decided it was a good idea. They'd get there first and do everything he wanted. It would be big medicine if he was already soaking in the spring when Quanah and Isa-tai showed up.

"All right. But I think . . ." His eyes rolled back in his head, showing only the whites before his lids closed and the medicine man fell backward. This seizure was worse than the last. Foam ran from his mouth, and his muscles twitched and jerked.

Iron Tip and Kot-sa-tay looked at Twisted Root's men with raised eyebrows. Two Shoot made a sign at his head. "He is having another vision. It will probably be one that will let him see where everyone is, or what the old woman is doing. Maybe he is inside her head." He shrugged. "Who knows."

Neither responded and Two Shoot hated silence between others. "I think it did something to his mind the time he went with his father on a war party that went far to the south. They raided across into Mexico and then kept going. They went so far that the land changed, and great trees rose from the ground. It became a world of water that dripped from thick, rich green plants. There was fruit everywhere, and the rain fell often.

"He told me of tall leaves that reached so high they blotted out the sun. They kept going and came to a river so wide it was impossible to cross. There were many he'd never heard about, but I think it started making him this way was when they looked up in the tall trees and saw the hairy little people who lived there. They were only this tall." He bent his arm and pointed from fingertip to elbow. "Twisted Root tried to talk to them, but the little men wouldn't answer. They threw fruit and their own shit at him and then climbed even higher to shout at him and the others.

"It was then that his father, Buffalo Chaser, had seen enough. They turned around at the great river and came back home. Maybe one of their mean little spirits attached itself to him and has clung to his back like a tick until that old woman shot him. Maybe it entered through that hole in his jaw and took over." Two Shoot paused, then shrugged. "I think it was those little people who threw their shit at him and opened up this whole thing. It would make me angry too."

He rose and went to check on the horses while others made camp, leaving Twisted Root writhing on the ground.

FORTY-TWO

BUCK, LANE, AND WOLF RETURNED across the creek to find Victoria again tending to Hezekiah. His part in the fight drained most of his energy, and she was holding a canteen for Hez to drink. In addition to his previous two wounds, one of the arrows found his hip, glancing off the big bone and emerging near his right buttock. With Wolf's help, she pushed it on through, just as she had with her own arm, and bandaged the hole as best as she could.

"You better take care of that arm." Buck walked past on his way to their saddlebags to get more ammunition. "It'll fester if you don't." He stopped when he saw Lane's bloody boot. "Is it bad?"

He glanced down. "Well, I can feel blood squishing around my foot."

Buck didn't turn toward the carnage lying forty yards away. Flies already swarmed the blood and gore left behind by the defenders. "Take it off and let's look at it."

Lane lowered himself onto the log. Gritting his teeth, he pulled the boot off and tilted it. Blood splashed onto the ground. Watching Buck's expression, he frowned. "That doesn't look good to you in any way, does it?"

"What do you mean by that?"

"I'm not sure. I just wonder what interests you these days."

"It ain't a dirty sock, that's for sure. You'll have to bandage that hole, but it don't look too bad."

Lane crossed the ankle over his other knee and looked at the hole that was already black with bruising. Most of the bleeding had stopped, though the puckered, ragged wound still seeped. "I'm not sure what you'd consider bad."

"Don't worry unless it starts to stink."

Buck looked past Lane. "Someone's coming. Two people."

They waited, not really concerned, because the two were loping their mounts easily through the grass from their side of the creek. Buck finally grunted in affirmation to something only he could hear. "It's Tall Grass and a big Kiowa."

The next thing Lane knew, Tall Grass was there with her bag. A tall, wide-shouldered Kiowa was behind her, and he figured that was her husband. Ignoring the bodies scattered around their camp, she dropped to the ground. Victoria rushed forward and they embraced for a moment before Tall Grass saw her arm.

"Is it bad?"

"It went through. It's bandaged well enough right now. I think you should check on Lane and Hezekiah first."

"If that is what you want." Tall Grass swept a hand toward the Kiowa who had dismounted and was standing apart, holding both horses. "This is my husband, Santee. He is the only one who would come. The rest said they are still allied to the Comanche." She dropped to her knees and tended the wound, cleaning it with water from a deer bladder before putting a poultice of leaves on both sides of his calf. "It looks as if you did not need them after all."

"We did all right," Clarence said, watching Santee simply drop the horses' reins, expecting them to remain ground tied where they were. Resting on a rotten log, Clarence was busy reloading his many weapons that disappeared into his clothes.

Santee asked a question, and Tall Grass answered without looking up. He grunted a single word and walked over to the bodies, studying each one in turn, clearly ignoring Wolf who did the same.

"Do you have more socks?" Tall Grass pitched the bloody remnant into the fire. Buck handed Lane his saddlebag, and he dug around before finding his only extra pair.

The damp sock sizzled for a moment, producing thick, noxious smoke before the blood dried and the material burst into flame. Crossing between it and Lane, Buck stepped into the smoke and clutched his stomach. He gasped and tensed just as the breeze changed direction, taking the smoke away from him.

He staggered over to lean against a tree, head down and still. Watching him, Lane grimaced as Tall Grass pulled one of the fresh socks up over the wound to hold the poultice in place and returned the other.

"Save this one for later."

"Hez roused for a while and fought hard. You might need to check on him next."

Santee asked her a question in Kiowa. She answered the same way, then spoke to Lane in English. "He wanted to know if you were giving me orders." She gave him a quick smile, hidden from Santee by her hair.

"I don't think he likes me." Lane barely took his eyes off Buck who remained as still as the tree trunk he was holding on to.

"He doesn't." She rose and crossed to the downed log that had protected both Victoria and Hezekiah. Using her bag, she swept away several arrows that snapped off and fell to the ground. Several minutes later, she came back to Lane.

"And yes, I tended their wounds, also. Hezekiah is better than I expected. He will be fine once we get back to my village."

Finally finding relief from whatever struck him, Buck was still against the tree. He'd been watching from several feet away, keeping an eye on Santee and Wolf, who continued to ignore each other. Finished with his reloading, Clarence joined Wolf and they talked quietly.

After working out the battle, Santee came close to the women and asked another question. Tall Grass's eyebrows rose, and she turned to Buck. "He says there are many wolf prints. They tore those men's throats out. He wants to know how we train wolves to do that, and where they are."

He straightened and filled his lungs to talk. "Why does he think I know?"

"He sees something in you. He says there are too many holes in your shirt, but he sees no blood. He's been watching you for the past several minutes, and wonders what is wrong."

"What is it that you people can see things others can't?"

"If you're talking about Indians and white people, most of you don't see what is in front of you."

"You're white."

"No. My mother was Mexican mix. My father was white, but now I am Kiowa. It is not the color of your skin. It is what you believe that counts."

"I see things, now. I believe a lot more than I did."

"You didn't before. You always have something else on your mind or are always focused on the wrong things. My people are closer to the earth, and that is why we have different sight."

"Where *you* should be." The comment was directed at Buck, and Wolf's voice was firm. For the first time Santee admitted to his presence, and their eyes met and held.

And held.

And held, until Lane noticed and broke the tension. "Wolf."

At his name, the big Cheyenne finally looked away. "Yes."

"Thanks for the help."

He made the sign for "it is all good."

Watching Buck, Santee asked Tall Grass a question. She answered and translated again. "He still wants to know what is wrong with Buck. Is he sick? He asks about all those holes in his shirt again, but with no blood, he doesn't understand."

"I see those holes too." Lane tried to change the subject. He pulled his boot back on, grunting when it thumped against his heel. "That was my spare shirt and now look at it. You owe me another one, when we get to a town."

Buck let out a stale breath, then reinflated his lungs to talk. "You worry about material things." He turned to Santee. "I'm dead. Been dead a while. This is what you look like when they put you in the ground over and over again, and then when you get to the light of day, other aggravatin' Indians shoot you with arrows every time you turn around, and if you don't quit looking at me from under your eyebrows, I'm gonna make you just like me."

Tall Grass gasped. "Buck!"

"Tell him."

She swallowed and spoke for nearly a minute. Santee's glower melted, and after a moment, he smiled. He pointed at Buck, then spoke to Tall Grass again. They had a good laugh.

Lane thought it was all over until Santee stepped closer to Buck and took a deep, long sniff, then laughed again. He both signed and spoke to Tall Grass at length.

Finally, Lane couldn't stand it. "What'd you say? What'd *he* say?"

"Exactly what Buck told me. He thinks he's joking." She put a hand over her mouth to hide a smile. "He says you can't be dead. You don't smell like someone who has been dead for days. He says you're a big jokester, and he'd like to hear more."

Buck's chin lowered, a sure sign that he was mad. "On top of all this, I'm damn tired of people *smelling* me."

Lane held up both hands to him. "Don't say another thing, and for God's sake don't take your hat off. We're in a good place now with this guy, and I don't want to screw it up."

Santee asked Tall Grass another question and waited for the answer. "He wants to leave, so you can get River. He's tired of having her and all of you around. We'll make a travois for Hezekiah, and then we can go."

Lane surveyed the creek and the bodies that were already drawing flies. "I think that's a good idea."

Minutes later, they rode toward the Kiowa camp with Victoria surrounded by the men who vowed to protect her.

FORTY-THREE

MISS HATTIE WAS SITTING ON a rock, her tired, aching feet ankle deep in the chilly waters of Boiling Springs. Her eyes were closed, enjoying the current that caressed her skin. The sudden fragrance of prairie grass under the hot sun came to her, along with a similar feeling of wind caressing her face. She opened her eyes, but the wind was still, with not a blade of grass or leaf moving anywhere within her range.

"Praise the Lord, they're moving again."

Ashkii signed. He was sitting close by in the shade of a willow. "Did you have another vision?"

"No, hon. I can feel them now. They're moving this way and will be here tomorrow."

"Good. I am tired of getting ready for someone who never comes." Ashkii dipped a hand into the water to drink. Water flew from his fingers as he asked a question. "What will happen when they get here?"

"Why, I 'spect they'll stay and rest a bit. That woman's baby won't be far behind. That's why they're coming, so I can help deliver it. She'll stay awhile because she shouldn't travel, and I need to look after the little thing for her."

"When a village is moving, Navajo women have babies and dry them off and keep walking."

"I know, and they shouldn't have to. Men should understand what it takes to push a little human being out of their bodies. A woman ought to have time to rest."

He ignored her observation. "There are many women in this world that can help deliver a baby. Why do they come to you from so far away? Can't they do it in a white man's town?"

"You need to slow down on your signings, and can't answer that question. I just know that at first, I watched everyone come together in my dreams, and in those dreams, I knew I was supposed to help. Things changed when two white men joined them. I say white men. One is somehow dark, a shade more than anything else. When I saw that dark cloud of his, I took a peek for just a second. It wasn't scary in there like that nasty man, it was just gray deadness and that's all.

"But back to what I was saying, I get a feeling they're from Texas. That's good because Texans in the right ain't mortal. They sweat pride and won't quit on a job."

Ashkii signed slower. "Did you see that in a dream?"

"No, hon, it's not like a dream at all. This is more of a feeling, like I *know* in my heart they're coming, but no one's told us yet. But the dreams are as real as you and me. I just don't understand all I know about *them* neither.

"There's a thin veil between our world and others. In fact, in one of my dreams I saw dozens of other worlds separated by thick walls of spiderwebs, and the best way I know to explain it to you, hon. Some are wonderful, and others are dark as sin. We're in between, where good and evil fight all the time."

"Like the Apache and Navajo, or the Comanche and Tonkawas."

"In a way, but there's good and evil that we don't understand, always fighting around us. I think this baby is going to help stop all that."

Ashkii laughed from the back of his throat. "Babies do nothing but suck at the tit and shit."

"I don't mean right now. I mean in the future. When it grows up, it will have the power to do more good than this world's seen in a long, long time, or more evil than we can imagine. One thing that scares me, is that if this child isn't pointed in the right direction, it will do nothing at all, and every bit of that potential will be lost. We can't have that."

"Who are these white men who have joined the band?"

"I see a star over each one of them. That's all."

"Like the star you say the band is following?"

"Well, it isn't like the three wise men following the star to Beth-lehem. That was a whole different thing." She'd read to him from the Bible a number of times, but each occasion their conversations bogged down and she found herself unable to explain the old stories to Ashkii. "They see something that I can't describe because I don't know what it is they see."

He built an exaggerated frown.

"I know. It's all mixed up. Let's put it this way, when you're travel-ing at night, you follow the stars."

He nodded.

"Just like that, they can see whatever it is they're following. They might somehow see that long string of smoke coming out of my head, like I described for you earlier with those others, and you, and Tall Grass. Even her baby."

She wanted to tell him about when she was in that crazy man's head, but she'd just gotten her spirit clean through prayer and didn't want to bring him up again. In fact, she never even wanted to think about that evil, unclean person again, but she was sure that misfortune would linger. Every night he appeared in her mind, unbidden, and she would have to force it back down again until the next time.

He'd be with her for the rest of her life, and that was a disappoint-ment to have those few years left soured by such evil.

"Do I have good smoke coming out of my head?"

"Well, I can't see it right this minute, but after what I saw with those others, I think yours is as clean and pure as sage smoke."

He smiled. "That is good."

"Yes, it is. But now when they get here, trouble is going to follow." She nodded toward the old sun-bleached wagon melting into the grass where he usually tied his horse. "Pull what's left of that skin wagon over close. They might need it for something."

"The wheels are rotten."

"I didn't say they were going to hitch a team up to it. Just pull it fairly close to the house. Then I need you to poke holes all around the house so they can shoot when the time comes, and it will be because evil always follows good, and it's always wanting to feast on it, so we have to be ready."

One hand made the sign. "How?"

From her position on the shady rock, she looked to the west, past the soddy and the trees. "That's another thing I don't know, hon."

FORTY-FOUR

IT WAS NEAR DUSK, AND they still hadn't seen any sign, smoke, or otherwise of Santee's village. Behind Santee and Tall Grass, who were leading their procession, Victoria rode next to the horse dragging Hezekiah's travois. The twin poles left long, deep gouges in the prairie and Lane couldn't help but think they were two lines leading any interested Comanche war party right to them.

Flanking both sides were Clarence and Wolf. The Rangers rode drag, a little off center behind the travois where the dust wasn't as bad.

Lane kneed his horse sideways to close the distance between him and Buck, keeping an eye on the setting sun. The sky was full of color from the mid-level clouds hanging on the horizon. A slight breeze moved the grass, filling the air with fragrance.

He pointed at the side of Buck's cheek where the black blood was dry. "You need to flake that nasty stuff off your face."

Instead of immediately answering, Buck scratched at the dried blood until most of it was gone. "You're riding with people who paint their faces for war, and you're worried about a little blood on my cheek."

"It was more'n a little blood, and I got tired of looking at it. If I get tired of looking at war paint on a Comanche, I'll just shoot it off, but I can't do that with you." Lane checked their back trail and seeing nothing but the grass that showed their passage, turned back and changed the subject. "How's your snake?"

"It ain't *my* snake, but it's quiet now, though the damn thing keeps sending thoughts to me."

Wondering how that worked, Lane rode in silence for a few minutes. "About what?"

"About its eye, for one thing. One of them arrows went through and put its eye out."

"You're telling me you can't be hurt, but that snake *can.*"

"Who says I can't be hurt? Those damned arrows felt like fire going in *and* coming out."

"You know what I mean."

"The damned thing's alive in there and growing. Look how tight this shirt's getting across my belly. I never had a belly in my life." Buck winced at the word *life* and quit talking. After a while, he noticed Lane's horse moved several inches away. "Come back over here so I don't have to holler. This thing ain't gonna get you."

"You don't know that. Why don't you get down and let it come out and all of us together can kill it?"

"I don't have any choice in the matter. It was trying to get out just before all hell broke loose, since it was hurt, but now it's just lying there."

"I have a question for you."

"What?"

"How'd it taste?"

Buck shot a look across the space between them. "You ask the damnedest things. It didn't taste like anything because I can't taste."

"I figured a snake would have some taste, not that I'd lick one to see." Lane's brow puckered at the thought. "Wolf said he saw its head. Said it had human features and eyes, and even an ear, at least on his side."

"That don't surprise me none. It's part Comanche, and I'm afraid it's part me too."

"So it just thinks and whatever comes into its brain, you see."

"If it has a brain. I haven't told you, but we kinda . . . talk . . . at night. Mostly it complains and I listen, as if I had a choice."

"You do that all night?"

"When I'm not listening to you and Victoria rasslin' around in the dark."

Lane blushed. "I didn't think about that."

"You know if it'd been a couple of weeks ago, she'd've been looking at me instead. I don't know why she took up with you."

Buck had always been the one for the ladies, and they'd usually bat their eyes at him from the first time they met. Lane was less obvious about his interest in women, and when he had an interest, it was almost always mutual.

"Who said we took up with one another?"

"What I heard that night answers your question. And her expecting a baby and all. That ain't decent."

"Look who's talking about decent, a dead man with a snake in his belly."

"I can cut it out for you." Wolf's voice carried over the sound of the travois dragging through the dirt.

"God*damn* it! There ain't no privacy *anywhere*," Buck complained. "Just once I'd like to have a conversation with my partner here without somebody butting in."

"I was just offering to help. I can borrow Clarence's sword. It is very sharp. One slash and the snake will spill out and I can cut it into pieces, and then you will heal up again."

"No."

"Buck, it might work." Lane's voice was low. "Like you've said, the pain'll pass pretty fast and you can be rid of that thing."

"I could, but the truth is, I don't know what'll happen if that snake is gone."

"So?"

"So, back there I felt something in my head, like a cool breeze that reminded me of a swimming hole where I grew up. It was green there, shaded by the trees, and the water was always cold. That's how it felt, and right then something told me I had a purpose.

"There's a reason I'm like this, and I've been at it too long to waste whatever it is. I'll know when the time is right, and maybe then we can do something about it. If that snake is out, I'm liable to die for good. It might be too early."

They rode for a few minutes, thinking. Buck reined up for a moment, looking down. Lane turned back to wait. Buck stared at the grass beneath him for a full minute before nodding and kicking his horse into motion. "That horny toad we just passed said the camp is still a good hour or more. The sun's gonna be down, so we need to do something before I go to sleep and fall off this horse."

"It sure took a long time for such a short message."

"Most horny toads have a speech impediment. This one stutters bad, and it took three tries before he could get it out. Oh, and he said leave the snake in there at least until we get River and make it to Boiling Springs with Victoria. See, I told you there was a reason for all this."

"It would have been easier if you hadn't died."

"It would have been easier if I'd stayed dead too." The look on Lane's face told Buck he was thinking the same thing. Buck held out both hands. "Tie 'em to the horn."

"I have a better idea. Give me your belt."

"What for?"

"Because I want to laugh when you step down and your pants fall off. Just give it to me."

A disgusted look on his face, Buck slipped the plain leather belt through the loops, and by the time he had it free, Lane was doing the same thing. Buck passed it over and Lane buckled them together. "Here wrap this around your waist and around the saddle horn. Pull it tight. When you pass out, you'll just fall forward on his neck."

"I don't pass out. It's just like there's a deadness to my soul, and then nothing, at least until that damned snake starts thinking in his sleep."

"Well, whatever it is that you do, when you do it, you won't fall off."

In the lead, Santee looked over his shoulder and frowned at the two white men adjusting their belts. He turned back to Tall Grass, and they talked in low voices.

"They're talking about me." Buck saw it and leaned over the horn with both hands on the pommel.

"I don't doubt it."

"This feels odd." He adjusted himself again.

"Tell me what odd means to you these days."

"You're right. You know, they're gonna think I'm dead when we ride into that Kiowa camp."

"You are."

"You know what I *mean*."

"You're an aggravatin' son of a bitch sometimes." Lane sighed. "If I let you fall off, it'll take two or three of us to get your dead ass up over the saddle, and if that happens, I'm tying you head down like we do when we're bringing in an outlaw's body, so you better let me handle it best I can." He smiled to take the edge off his words.

Lost in his own worries, Buck didn't notice. He sucked in his breath, an exaggerated sound in the evening still. "Don't let 'em do anything with me. That's a worry I'll have forever."

"I'll do my best."

"That might not be . . ." The sun winked out and Buck fell forward just as they expected. Feeling the weight's unnatural shift, the black snorted and tossed his head. Lane reached across and grabbed the back of Buck's pants to keep him from slipping off to the side. "I swear, however things are, and whatever happens in the future, I'm afraid this is the end of the line for your soul, partner."

The little band rode a while longer, accompanied by the creak of leather and the muffled thump of hooves. The eastern sky grew darker, and a light wind soughed across the prairie.

"You know, I wish a traveling minstrel troupe with a guitar would come by and see you like this." Lane spoke as if Buck were upright in the saddle next to him. "I'd tell 'em all about what's happened, and they could write a ballad about it. I already have the title. The Legend of Buck Dallas, but I figure to be in there somewheres too."

They continued northward as a long streak appeared low in the sky.

"That's a comet." Lane said to Buck, but he couldn't see it because he was dead . . . asleep.

FORTY-FIVE

THE SOFT SOUNDS OF HOOVES in the grass came to Buck after the snake woke up. He tried to figure out what was happening but couldn't make out anything else. He could have been laying down, dragged behind a horse, or even hanging upside down. At least the feeling was familiar. The first time he woke up after the Dark Sleep, he was in a grave and didn't know what had happened.

Now, he was more aware of his situation, but that frightened him even more.

At least I can hear. What if somebody puts me in a grave so deep I can't get out? Then do I lay there for all eternity, until the world cracks and I can finally get out? I'll go insane if that happens. What could be worse than an insane dead man who wants to crawl from a grave?

A slithering sensation in Buck's mind told him the snake was listening.

This feels like eternity, white man, with you talking all the time. Be still. I am trying to think.

You're the one who always wakes me up. For a while there I was able to just hear the horses, now you're yammering along in my head. Let me ask you a question, Serpent. Why didn't you go ahead and get out of me when you had the chance and be done with it? Then we'd be rid of each other once and for all.

The snake didn't answer right away. It might have been several minutes, or several hours before he responded.

It was not the time. I only tried to get out because of the pain that arrow put in my head. Now I only have one eye, like that Cheyenne you're traveling with, and that gives him a hole to see inside of me. He does not know that yet, and I want to keep it a secret.

How can you get hurt, but not me?

You will have to ask my father that question. Do that before you kill him.

Can you see the future? Will I be able to kill him?

What makes you think I have those powers? He is the witch, not me.

I want to know if I'll still be around after you're gone, Serpent.

I just told you, I do not know about anything but now. Now is all I know. Now is when you are keeping me from thinking with your constant talk.

What else am I supposed to do until the sun comes up?

You can practice being quiet. When we had children that would not shut up in our village, we would sometimes hold their heads underwater so their mouths filled and they could not speak. We usually only had to do that one time and then they would see the error of their ways and be quiet.

I can see where drowning someone would make them stop talking.

We did not drown them, only held them under. There is a difference.

Let me ask you this. If Lane draped me over the saddle like an outlaw corpse, would that put the squeeze on you?

The snake was silent again before answering. *I do not know. There is getting to be less and less room in here, so I suppose I could feel it.*

Then get out and get gone.

You white people are too impatient. Now is not the time. I will know when I am supposed to vacate this vile cave, and then I will go live beneath a rock with my new brothers and sisters.

They won't let you join them. Wolf says you have human eyes and face features. Your no-shoulders brethren will probably kill you.

It would be a relief after listening to you. Now, be quiet.

No, you be quiet.

FORTY-SIX

THE MOON, WHAT THERE WAS of it, was high in the sky when Lane and his band rode into the Kiowa camp. Dogs met them more than two hundred yards away, filling the night with their barks.

The camp was still awake, with fires burning bright. Half a dozen warriors rode out to meet them. Seeing them come, Lane rested his hand on the butt of the Colt riding on his left side for a quick cross draw. It wasn't that he didn't trust Santee and Tall Grass, but young, impetuous fighters sometimes acted before they thought, and they were allied with the Comanche.

One of the warriors pulled up short when they saw Lane. He pointed with the lance in his hand. "Santee! Are these prisoners? Did you kill any white men?"

"No. The fight was over by the time I arrived. I did not even get to count coup, but these are not my prisoners. They are great fighters. They killed many brave Comanche warriors, more than I could count while I was there. These people are my guests. Go prepare Woodsmoke's lodge for them."

Unfamiliar with their language, Lane watched the man's face. There was no anger or warning there, but he kept his hand on the pistol, just in case. Tall Grass allowed her horse to fall back. She translated the conversation for Lane and the others.

To prove he was no prisoner, Lane walked his mount up beside Santee. Tall Grass followed with an anxious look on her round face. "You should not be at the front with our chief."

Lane ignored the comment. "You don't need to put us in with your people. We can use our tents."

She shook her head, watching Santee from the corners of her eyes in case he became angry about the Ranger's impudence. He ignored Lane, staring straight ahead.

"Woodsmoke is dead, killed by your cavalry two weeks ago." She spoke softly so as not to irritate her husband.

Lane shook his head. "Not *my* cavalry. I thought it was bad luck for someone else to live in a dead man's lodge."

"We used to think that, but no more. It was our way to burn the lodges and all of a man's possessions so his spirit would be free of this world, but there are few buffalo now to make new lodges, so our medicine man purifies them with sage and prayer."

"Sounds to me like you're taking up some of our ways."

"Probably only the worst ones."

"All right. When can we see River?"

"Santee says for me to bring her to you tonight, and then tomorrow you leave."

"We'd like another day, if we can. Hez back there needs his rest."

"That will be decided tomorrow."

She ended the conversation when Santee led their band into camp. The entire village was there to watch the parade. Kids and women pointed as they passed. Wolf garnered much attention, as well as Clarence. Black men always fascinated the Indians, and with his many guns, sword, and voluminous pants, he offered much to discuss.

Warriors crowded close, as much to intimidate as to see in the dim light. Santee stopped in front of the tall conical lodge and waited for Tall Grass to dismount. The long round trip must have been hard on the heavyset girl because she slowly slid to the ground and steadied herself before smiling up at Victoria and offering to help her down.

Leaving Buck still tied to his saddle, Lane was already there, and Tall Grass stepped back. He steadied Victoria as she slid to the ground and once again found himself awash in her aura. He held her a little too long and she gave his arm a pat to let go. He stepped back, embarrassed, but she cut her eyes at him with a slight smile and followed Tall Grass, who pulled back the door flap with a long stick that was stuck through the edge. A small fire burned in the center of the floor, giving enough light for Wolf and Clarence to unload Hezekiah, who was awake and alert.

They'd barely gotten him through the door when two women showed up with a dirty white child between them. Immediately reverting to being a Texas Ranger, Lane met them and dropped to a knee. "You're River?"

The little girl nodded and threw her arms around his neck. "Have you come to take me home?"

"I have. My name's Captain Lane Newsome, and that's Captain Buck Dallas. We're here for you. Are you all right?"

She dissolved into tears, nodding against his neck. It was all Lane could do to pack down the fury rising in him, but it wasn't Santee's band that had captured her. It was Comanche. The Kiowa were the good guys here for the time being.

Still holding tight, his own eyes burned. "How old are you, River?"

Getting ahold of herself, she hiccupped into the hollow of his now wet neck. "Six."

"Then you're not too big to carry." He picked her up and turned toward the lodge. The warriors had closed in around them, but he pushed through without hesitation.

Buck was still slumped in the saddle when Lane gave River to Victoria. "This is the girl we've come for. River, this is Victoria, and I want you to stay right beside her until we get everything inside."

She held on like a snapping turtle's bite. Lane gave her another squeeze and pulled gently back. "It'll be all right. You're with us now, and we're leaving in the morning."

"Come here, baby." Victoria sat on a buffalo rug and held out her arms. River wilted into her embrace and kept her frightened eyes on Lane until he stepped back outside.

A ring of Kiowa warriors surrounded Buck and their horses. Lane made a quick count of their mounts because Kiowa were great horse thieves and most times wouldn't have thought twice about walking away with two or three unattended ponies. Santee, who was nowhere about, must have ordered them to treat them more as guests than someone dropping by.

Buck, though, was a different story. One of the warriors pointed at him, then Lane, and asked a question he couldn't understand.

Standing beside Buck as if he were one of her possessions, Tall Grass translated. "He wants to know why we put a dead man in the saddle like that."

"How does he know he's dead?"

"He felt of his hand and says he has no heat."

He pointed at Santee, standing nearby. "Let him answer."

Tall Grass directed the question to the chief who spoke without expression. The crowd listened intently, then became silent before one of the warriors said something and laughed. The rest of them joined in.

Lane looked at Tall Grass for an explanation. "Santee told them what you said about him back at the creek. Red Fox said only white people carry bodies around as if they are alive."

"Wolf. Clarence. Would y'all help me get Buck down and inside?" Lane unbuckled the belts and pulled Buck down into their arms. They carried his limp body inside, as Lane turned back to the people. "Tell them he is my friend, alive or dead, and is my responsibility until I can take him back home."

Tall Grass translated as they unloaded the packhorses and carried everything inside. When Lane finally closed the flap, most of the people were still watching and only left once they saw no one was coming back out that night.

FORTY-SEVEN

RESCUING RIVER WAS ANTICLIMACTIC. THE night passed without incident, though Lane got precious little sleep from all the snoring from Wolf, Clarence, and Hezekiah, who slept like innocent babies. River curled under Victoria's arm, at peace for the moment.

When Lane rose from his blanket just before dawn, Wolf and Clarence were gone, likely saddling their horses. Hez was still asleep, but his color was good.

Buck was already up, without a shirt and sitting cross-legged in front of the open flap door, pondering more than twenty Kiowa warriors mirroring his position in a semicircle, staring back at him. His hat was pushed all the way back to the front edge of his missing scalp.

Buck didn't turn his head when he heard movement behind him. "We need to pack up and get out of here pretty quick. Some of these boys are getting themselves worked up."

"How can you tell? They're just sitting there."

"Two or three of 'em are breathing hard, and more'n one're looking at me from under their brows."

"Maybe you should put a shirt on."

"It ain't much shirt. More of a rag than anything else."

"It's those white splotches all over you." Most men they knew were pasty white under their clothes, tanned only on their wrists and hands and from the collar to the parts of their foreheads shaded by big hats. "Those scars or whatever you call 'em are even whiter'n your regular skin. I 'magine that's what interests them so."

"If they want to see something, I can take off my hat."

"Don't you dare do that, or we're liable to have to shoot our way out of here. Buck, these people are letting us come in and take that little gal without trouble. Let's leave well enough alone and get gone."

A small voice broke in. "Can we go home now?" River stood in the middle of the lodge, looking tiny and thin.

Victoria stirred and opened her eyes that crinkled at the corners when she smiled at Lane. He returned it and put on his hat. "We sure can, Sweet Pea. Buck, get what's left of that shirt on and let's get out of here. River, stay inside until we're ready to leave. I'm afraid you could be the spark that'll start this wildfire before we get out of here."

The curious Kiowa men rose when Lane stepped outside. He was right, Wolf and Clarence had the packs loaded. Wolf inclined his head toward the crowd. "I can feel their thoughts. They do not like Buck and want us gone. It wouldn't surprise me if they're laying for us out there. The only reason they are waiting is because Santee says we are guests. They want to slaughter us all and take scalps."

"That'll be after the fight." Clarence moved around the horses, purposely shouldering too close to those glaring at him. "Some of them are painted for war, and it might be here if we don't go now."

Lane planted his feet between the lodge and the growing number of warriors. He locked eyes with the closest man wearing paint. When he was a kid, Lane could always win staring contests with his friends and cousins. He brought that old childish skill back into play and they stood there for what seemed like an eternity until the warrior blinked.

Once he did, he wouldn't meet Lane's gaze again. "Go get Hez."

Forehead damp with fever, Hezekiah immediately took stock of the situation as soon as they laid him on the travois. "Hand me my shotgun, Miss Victoria." She passed it to him and despite his weakness, laid it across his chest, hand over the triggers.

The tribe's medicine man busied himself with making signs in the air and singing songs to make the demon stay away. He approached Lane more than once, irritating the Ranger who only wanted to get on his horse and leave.

A soft murmur swept through the crowd when Buck came outside. They reacted as water, pulling away from something they knew was unnatural, but Lane figured not a one of them could put their finger on it.

Buck stepped into the saddle. His hand touched the brim of his hat and Lane's mouth went dry. Time slowed, and Buck only adjusted the set of his hat. "I think as much of a Kiowa as I do a Comanche."

"They know it."

Shoulders square and sitting straight, the big Cheyenne led. The Kiowa braves backed away, except for one who almost reached out to touch Wolf. His head snapped around and the man backed away. "You will live to see the sunset, now, but your foolishness will get you killed soon."

They left the village without speaking again to Santee or Tall Grass. Lane felt bad about that because he'd become fond of the little fleshy woman. They were followed by warriors, women, children, and yapping dogs until someone noticed what was ahead, watching from a low rise.

Frightened cries filled the air behind them as they all saw the line of prairie wolves watching the procession. Without turning his head, Wolf walked his horse past them and into the open prairie. None of them looked back at the seething Kiowa camp.

The long morning shadows were quickly growing shorter by the time the travelers stopped at a nearby ridge. Lane finally turned his horse to watch their back trail. Buck saw him stop and did the same. One by one, the others realized what was happening and reined up also.

In the short amount of time since they left, the lodges had all been struck and the entire village packed up. A long line of horses pulled travois and people snaked across the prairie, leaving Woodsmoke's lodge behind. There was wood stacked around the buffalo-skin teepee, flames licking skyward.

"Kind of interesting that a warrior named Woodsmoke left behind a tipi they burned," Buck said.

"They would have burned it anyway." Wolf's statement was matter of fact. "None of his possessions should have been used in such a way. I think that medicine man wanted to put a curse on all of us, and staying in a dead man's lodge was the way to do it."

Buck barked a ghastly laugh. "He don't know a thing about curses."

They sat there without a word for several minutes, watching greasy black smoke rise from the buffalo-skin lodge they'd slept in.

Seconds later, the pack of wolves rose and vanished.

FORTY-EIGHT

HEADING INTO THE SUN ON that cloudless morning, the travelers kept their heads low, allowing the hat brims to shade their eyes. The dry air made for a comfortable journey, though the temperature warmed rapidly. Dust rose behind the horses, and the travois's two poles dragging the ground added to the amount of dry dirt in the air.

River rode one of the packhorses in the middle of the band, close to Victoria who talked with her so softly the men couldn't understand what she was saying. The brown-haired child remained silent, mostly staring straight ahead. From time to time, she twisted around to be sure they weren't being pursued.

Once, she met Lane's gaze for a long moment, as if memorizing his features. He always gave her a grin that she never returned.

By noon, they'd covered several miles without slowing. It was Buck who broke the adults' silence. "Smoke." He pointed. "Over there."

They followed his finger to see a black column rising straight up in the still air. Lane cleared his throat. "That ain't good."

There was now an urgency in the group. In the lead, Wolf straightened. "A war party has burned something."

Buck suddenly became his old self, and he spurred his horse. "Come on, Lane. We need to check this out."

Kicking his gray into a lope, Lane caught up with his partner. "Are you sure we need to do this?"

"We're still Rangers, aren't we?"

"I am."

Cutting his eyes at Lane, he reached up and tapped the place where his badge used to be. "I still am too."

The horses' pace ate up the ground, and soon they were in a little swale, protected by the rolling landscape. From that vantage point, whatever was burning just over the next rise remained hidden, though the smoke was heavier as the fire burned hotter. Lane pulled the Henry from the saddle scabbard. There was no need to check to see if it was loaded. Their weapons were always ready for a fight.

Buck rested the butt of the rifle stock on his thigh. "I doubt they're still around, but they might be doing to some poor folks what they did to me. You ready?"

In response, Lane kicked his horse back into a lope and they crested the rise. Below, a wagon burned, surrounded by its scattered contents. The war party was gone. A trail of beaten-down grass showed they were going northeast, parallel to the Ranger's band.

Still, they rode up with caution to find four mules dead in their traces, as well as a milk cow full of arrows a short distance away. Trunks and clothing littered the ground. Buck and Lane circled the wagon, looking for any signs of life.

They found a man's blackened body on the other side, sitting on the ground and tied to the rear wagon wheel that was still burning. There was no use in getting closer. His body bristled with arrows. Thirty feet away, a woman's nude body lay sprawled in the grass. The Rangers circled the area, looking for other murdered settlers.

"I only see two." Mouth set in a grim line, Lane's eyes flicked from the body to the horizon, then back again. He dismounted and covered her with the dress she'd been wearing. "They haven't been gone long. Her eyes haven't dried out."

Showing no emotion or expression, Buck rode in a wider circle. It was a process they'd worked out years ago whenever coming upon such a hideous scene—looking for tracks, other bodies, or any clues that might be helpful in the future.

He circled three times before he stopped upwind from the fully engulfed wagon that was now throwing off a surprising amount of heat. "See anything that tells us kids were here?"

"Not a thing, thank God." Mounted again, Lane handed him an arrow. "Kiowa, I think."

"I didn't see any blood other than theirs. Poor guy didn't hit anything, if he shot at all."

"Let's get back to the others, then." Lane was worried about Victoria and River." There's nothing we can do for these folks now."

"I wonder if this was a war party from Santee's tribe. He gave us a free pass for the girl, but they're all stirred up by the Comanche. This war party's likely from that bunch that was watching us this morning."

Buck slowly spun his horse, looking in all directions. "It would have been easy for them to follow our trail. They took this way to get out in front of us. It was these folks' bad luck to be coming across here at this time."

"They'll be laying for us then, up ahead."

"That's my thought. If we had the men, I'd say run 'em down."

"But we don't."

They headed back and soon the smoke retreated into the distance. Buck finally broke their silence. "I hate these people. After what we've seen 'em do, I'd kill every male son of a bitch I could find, but you know what?"

"What?"

"In a way, I don't blame them, the Kiowa, Comanches, or any other tribe fighting us. This is their home, and they're doing what they know to protect it. I'd do the same myself, if some other bunch come to Texas and tried to take it away from us."

"We did. We fought the Mexicans for it, and now it's ours."

"That's the way of the world, Lane. But it ain't right."

"I'm not sure there's a right or wrong in any of it. It just is."

THE REST OF THEIR GROUP HAD CROSSED a creek by the time Lane and Buck caught up with them. Everyone was wet from the knees down, except for Buck. It looked odd to see a water line on the horse and his saddle's wide leather fenders, but his boots were dry and dusty.

He joined Wolf, still riding point. Wolf gave the Ranger a quick look. "Was it a house, or a wagon?"

"Wagon. All dead." Buck flicked a hand past their horses' heads, in the direction they were traveling. "Kiowa, we think. Maybe that bunch from Santee's village. The war party's going that way."

"How many?"

"Couldn't tell exactly. Right smart, though."

"I could have told you exactly how many."

"Wouldn't matter, would it?"

"No. But we would have a count."

"We have enough bullets for them all, and we don't have much choice, outnumbered or not."

Hezekiah's voice came from behind them. He was praying again, softly, but with more enthusiasm than any of them expected. A mile later, his voice became stronger and then stopped. "Rider coming."

Wolf reined up and whirled around. The four men soon formed a skirmish line at the back of the travois and dismounted. Clarence turned his mount sideways to use as cover, laying the big Sharps across the saddle. "What do you see, Buck?"

Squinting, Buck answered, his voice full of surprise. "It's Tall Grass. Ain't no one that round but her."

Everyone relaxed and waited for her to catch up. When she was close, Buck saw the Kiowa woman didn't look well. "Something's wrong with her. She's riding all hunkered up."

"Has she been beaten?" Clarence's voice was sharp, clipped. It sounded as if the answer was yes, he was going back to the village to wreak vengeance.

Before Buck could answer, she closed the distance and reined up her lathered horse. Victoria stepped up beside Lane. "What's wrong?"

Hezekiah raised up on elbow. "Are you sick?"

"No." Tall Grass shook her head. "I had to come. A war party formed up and left not long after you took the trail. Santee tried to stop them, but they would not listen. They will be up ahead, waiting for you."

"Thanks for the information, but we saw some of their work back there." Lane patted her on the shoulder. "Now, you need to get back."

She shook her head. "No. You need me. I told Santee that I had to come warn you. He hit me many times when I said it and told me that you are all going to die, and me with you if I did." She touched the side of her face. "Now I have warned you, but I have also decided that I have to accompany you to the spring. When the baby comes, it will be good for everyone to be there."

Victoria smiled and urged her mount closer. "You have been one of us from the beginning."

"I am supposed to be with you."

"You left your children behind." Victoria touched her on the arm. "What about them?"

"They are Kiowa. The tribe will take care of them until I can return."

"Well, you might not." They turned to see Buck contemplating the horizon. A light plume of dust had his attention. "I believe it's that war party, and they're coming fast." He turned to Wolf. "More'n twenty, if you want a count."

"More than that." Tall Grass shuddered in pain and held her plump stomach.

River, who never let her horse get more than a couple of feet from Victoria's mount, gasped and leaned sideways to grab Victoria around the waist and turn her face into the material of her shirt. Pulling the girl close, Victoria bent and murmured into her ear while Tall Grass wrapped her hands around them both.

Wolf whirled, looking for cover, but the only tree line within sight was back behind the Indians rushing their way. He swung onto his horse. "There!" The land around them was relatively flat, but a slight rise lay just ahead. He gestured. "That is the high ground. We will fight from there."

The position was only two hundred yards away, and they spurred the horses. It was the worst thing they could do to Hez because a travois wasn't designed to bounce behind a running horse. He was thrown violently around and could barely hang on.

Once there, Victoria and Tall Grass grabbed the reins of several horses, including the one pulling Hezekiah's travois and put their mounts between them and the charging Kiowa.

Whoops and shouts of excitement reached them at the same time Clarence knelt on one knee and raised the Sharps. It boomed, and he immediately shucked the breech open to thumb in another shell. In the distance, a Kiowa horse reared and fell sideways, throwing its rider.

The attackers stopped in a cloud of dust, hesitating long enough to give Clarence a fairly stationary target. The rifle thundered again, and this time a warrior pitched off his horse. The others spun and kicked the ponies into a run to escape the buffalo rifle that spoke a third time. The man who was thrown off his horse was reaching up for a mounted brave who rushed back to pick him up. A .50-caliber slug caught the first one in the back, throwing his lifeless body forward. The rider spun and raced out of range.

"That'll hold 'em off for a little bit." Clarence rose.

Buck shivered. Lane saw it and figured the situation reminded him of the day he died.

The band of Kiowa braves gathered well out of the buffalo gun's range. Buck watched them maneuver. "They're splitting up. Gonna hit us from both sides."

"You girls pull the horses around in a circle and get inside." Lane reached across his body to make sure his pistol was loose in the holster. "Victoria, keep that pistol of Clarence's where you can use it if they get through."

"Where's Wolf?"

Lane frowned at Buck's question. "I have no idea. He was here a minute ago."

Tall Grass held up Wolf's reins. "He handed these to me and then crawled away." She used her chin to point. "That way."

"He has a plan," Hezekiah said. "Wolf always plans ahead."

"I'm glad someone does." Buck pursed his lips. "Tall Grass, how far is Boiling Springs from here?"

She thought for a moment. "Not far. We can get there by dark."

In answer to her question, Buck quickly yanked the packs from one of the horses and before anyone could ask what he was doing, shot it behind the ear. The big animal dropped in its tracks, kicking its life away. Shouts from all around asked what he was doing, but he ignored the anxious questions and drug the packs off the second horse.

Lane threw him a glance, then turned back to watch the two bunches complete an arc and charged in a pincer movement. "Whatever it is you're doing, hurry up!"

Buck yank the second terrified horse around, positioning it near the first. His pistol cracked again. The unfortunate animal dropped a few feet from the other, muscles spasming. "You girls watch his hooves and get down between them!"

Understanding what he wanted, Tall Grass pushed Victoria and River between the two large bodies. "Get on the ground."

Lane spoke, calm and easy. "Hang tight to your horses. They'll give you more cover."

Clarence grabbed the dropped packs and stacked them on top of the carcasses for extra cover, then half carried Hezekiah to the makeshift fortification. "You keep an eye on them. That shotgun might be their last chance."

Giving Clarence a weak smile, Hez slid down with his back against one of the big bodies, shotgun at the ready. His head soon fell back, and he prayed as loud as he could.

Buck shot him a disgusted look. "*Damn* that's annoying right now."

"Here they come!" Lane rested the Henry across his mount's saddle.

Facing the opposite direction, Buck did the same. "Coming from this side too."

Sensing their tension, the horses stomped and danced. Holding the reins, the men talked softly to the spooked mounts that reluctantly settled down.

Evaluating the two charging bands, Clarence faced the direction where Buck was aiming.

Tall Grass waved a hand. "Lane!"

"What?"

"Let these get close while Buck and Clarence shoot that way."

Knitting his brow, he angled his head to speak and keep an eye on the war party charging down on them. "Why?"

"Wolf went that way."

Instead of answering, Lane licked his dry lips and nodded.

Once again, Clarence's rifle was the first to fire. The bullet kicked up the grass behind the lead warrior, and he cursed, loading another round. The Indians closed the distance, and their weapons crackled. Puffs of dirt exploded several yards away.

Waiting, Buck found a target and aimed. He started suddenly and shouted. "Lane!"

"Why the hell do y'all keep talking!"

"Shoot the horses like I do."

"If I do, those warriors will still be in the fight."

"Not with Wolf out there." Buck turned and reacquired his target. A painted brave with several feathers in his hair opened his mouth in a whoop and kicked his mount into a full run. Buck shot his horse in the chest. The big animal screamed and rolled, throwing his rider. The man slammed to the ground but jumped to his feet and juked sideways to avoid the kicking hooves. He only managed two steps before Clarence's .50 caught him in the chest.

"That's why I say always go for the boiler," Buck said in case anyone was listening, and levered another round.

LANE'S RIFLE CRACKED. A PONY REARED AND fell sideways. The other warriors thundered past, and the man stood to run. Wolf rose from the grass behind and was upon him. His knife flashed in the sun and the man's limp body fell forward. Like his namesake, Wolf raced after the band.

Lane shot again, knocking still another horse down and before the rider could stand, Wolf reached him, threw an arm around the shaken man's neck, and plunged the blade deep into his kidney from behind. The warrior arched his back in pain, and Wolf struck again, then sliced deep into his jugular. Throwing his body aside, the big Cheyenne loped ahead.

BUCK FIRED, JACKED THE HENRY'S LEVER, AND fired again. One horse fell. Wounded, the other sunfished sideways and ran off, taking the rider with it. Clarence fired, missed, and fired again.

They were now within arrow distance and the horsemen veered off, allowing their riders to shoot again and again. Bowstrings snapped. Hissing arrows searched for flesh. One stuck in the ground at Buck's feet. Another struck one of the dead horses.

An arrow came from behind Clarence, slicing through the big brim of his hat. Ignoring it, he shot again, not taking his eyes off the warriors in front of him. When they drew close, he laid the rifle down and drew his Colt .44. Firing as fast as he could thumb the hammer, he sent six rounds toward the warriors as they flowed past like water twenty yards away.

Dust rose in a cloud to mix with the defender's gunpowder. A Kiowa appeared seemingly out of nowhere, mere feet away. With a shout of joy, he streaked toward Clarence, who dropped his empty pistol and reached for the sword strapped across his back.

Hez's shotgun rose and belched fire, catching the attacker full in the chest. He fell, dead before he knew it. A second warrior appeared from nowhere, popping up behind Clarence and directly over Tall Grass.

River screamed and Victoria fumbled with Clarence's borrowed pistol. It was happening too fast, and the inexperienced woman was going to be too late in bringing the weapon to bear.

Two more Kiowa warriors rushed in. Clarence's sword flashed in the sun, cutting left, then right, then back again. Blood fountained into the air as a bois d'arc bowstring snapped. An arrow whickered past

Clarence and pierced Hez's throat all the way to the fletching, pinning him to the horse carcass.

The look on one warrior's face was pure fury as he howled and raised the war club to bring it down on Tall Grass's head. Victoria caught the movement from the corner of her eye and snatched up Hezekiah's shotgun. There was no time to aim. She tilted it with both hands up and over her shoulder and squeezed the second barrel's trigger. The full load of buckshot took a good portion of the brave's face and skull away in a spray of red mist.

The warriors charging Buck veered to the right. A shower of arrows flew in his direction. His gray squealed and kicked, jerking free. It ran away, leaving Lane without cover.

Heart pounding so hard he felt it in his eyes, Lane dropped to a knee and levered round after round through his rifle. The warriors came around on a second pass, and he shot two more horses. Furious that he was killing their ponies, the braves shouted curses in their language and increased the pressure.

Lane fired so fast he almost shot Wolf, who appeared in the dust and gun smoke to fall on a pinned rider with his bloody knife. One of the Kiowa saw what was happening and spun his pony, firing arrow after arrow at Wolf who drew his pistol and squeezed the trigger three quick times. Two of the rounds caught the brave in the chest. He went limp and loose, and when the horse rushed past, Wolf reached out and grabbed an arm, jerking him to the ground.

He shot the man and turned to walk casually back to the fortifications as the defeated war party raced away.

★ ★ ★ ★ ★

HIDDEN BY A TREE LINE AT THEIR backs, Twisted Root, Quanah Parker, Iron Tip, Isa-tai and their band of over three hundred Comanche warriors watched the Kiowa's unsuccessful attack. They'd joined up only a couple of hours earlier.

"They are few, but they are all fighters," Quanah said. "We will need all of your magic, Isa-tai."

Annoyed that he only referred to Isa-tai's skills, Twisted Root spoke up. "They are weak and tired now. Let us go finish them."

"I do not think so." Quanah reached up to adjust a feather behind his ear. "We need to sing our war songs tonight after we talk with those Kiowa that are left. There is something wrong here, and we need to ask the Great Spirit for help."

"Why?"

Quanah rested an expressionless gaze on him. "Because it is the way I want to do it."

FORTY-NINE

MISS HATTIE SAW THEM COMING long before the travelers arrived. Hand shading her eyes, she counted them. Six horses, but a child rode the one bearing a travois. "There they are! Ashkii, get us a bucket of fresh water. They're gonna be thirsty after that long trip."

He stared in their direction for a long time, shaking his head in wonder. Turning back to her, he signed with an exaggerated frown. "Will they not drink from the spring?"

"They will later, but a drink of cold water from the dipper is the next best thing, and they look plumb wore out."

She dropped two sticks on the outside fire where she tended to cook when the weather was hot. A huge, blackened pot hung suspended by a tripod over the hot coals. She stirred the thick, bubbling stew, just something to do while she waited.

Ashkii squatted in the shade thrown by the soddy and considered a big Cheyenne who stopped his mount far enough away that he wouldn't throw dust on the old woman or her cooking. Sitting straight and square on the horse that looked to be a part of him, the older man who looked to be about sixty waited.

The troop reined up behind him, watching the old woman in tired silence. They'd been traveling for weeks, pulled by something she projected, and after all the time and blood, there she stood.

Bent and worn by time, Miss Hattie came forward. "You're Wolf, the elder of this group."

His eyes showed surprise. "You know my name?"

"As well as my own, but don't ask me how." She gave his bare leg a pat and pointed a crooked finger at the others who remained mounted. "Just as I know Clarence there. The warrior angel."

He gave her a tired smile. Miss Hattie's attention went to Victoria. "I know you, hon. Victoria, but I don't know that little 'un."

Victoria answered for her. "This is River. She's been a captive of the Comanche, but these two Rangers are taking her home."

"Poor child. We'll get her fed, and she'll feel a little better." Her attention slipped over to Tall Grass. "I've been waiting for you."

She showed the same surprise as Wolf. "How?"

"Dreams, hon, dreams. But I don't know the names of those two Rangers."

Lane touched his hat brim. "Captain Lane Newsome."

Buck did the same. "Captain Buck Dallas."

Miss Hattie's eyes bored into Buck, who suddenly seemed to find something interesting on the ground. "Mister Buck Dallas, we need to talk in a little while."

"Yes, ma'am, but—"

"No buts, sir. We'll talk in due time." She paused and sniffed.

"What?" Buck's voice was sharp.

"You all smell like hide hunters. Every one of you're caked in dirt, sweat salt, and blood. Y'all need to slip into that deep hole downstream and soak awhile, but you can do it later."

She walked past Buck without another sniff or word and stopped at the figure covered by blankets on the travois. "This is Hezekiah, the protector."

Victoria spoke as tears welled. "He was killed a little while ago, by Kiowas who attacked us."

"He did his job, though, didn't he? That's why he was there." Miss Hattie placed her hand on his covered head. "You were a good man. You protected that baby like you were supposed to and the Lord heard ever word you said."

She blinked away her tears. "Y'all get down and eat. There's water in the bucket by Ashkii there. He's Navajo and my good friend, but he can't talk. Apaches cut his tongue out a few years ago. He signs good, though."

They dismounted, and once again Lane reached up for Victoria. Miss Hattie noticed and cackled. "You're worried too much about the wrong mama."

They stopped at the statement, waiting for more. Puzzled by her comment, Lane tilted his hat back. "What do you mean?"

"You know as well as I do Victoria ain't pregnant. Never was."

The men were stunned. They looked from Miss Hattie to Victoria, then to Lane, waiting for an explanation.

"You should be helping Tall Grass down. She's the one with child, and if my feelings are right, and seeing the look on her face, that baby'll be here by tomorrow."

HEZEKIAH SLEPT IN THE GROUND UNDER A tall cottonwood some distance from the house. Miss Hattie spoke the words they needed to hear, and the ones necessary to show the respect they had for the good man who would never again shout prayers toward the sky.

They returned to the soddy to find shadows stretching from the tall hardwoods surrounding Boiling Springs, providing shade for those sitting in front of her little home. Their somber mood broke when Miss Hattie came outside the sod house, her arms full of the pillows and straps Victoria used to simulate an advanced pregnancy.

She cackled with glee and dropped them on the ground beside the small cooking fire. Lane and River sat cross-legged on the ground not far from the others and neither of the adults had any inclination of meeting the questioning looks from the others.

Lane's neck and face reddened in embarrassment at Miss Hattie's good humor. Victoria came outside, her chin high. "I did what I was supposed to do." Her voice trembled slightly. "Miss Hattie kept telling me what to do in the dreams."

"Oh, hon, it wasn't me doing all that, they just came through me *to* you."

Squatting nearby, Buck started to take off his hat to scratch his head, but stopped and reset it. Instead, he scratched his temple. "I don't understand any of what's going on here, and it's almost as strange as anything else I've been through in the past week, so could one of you explain it?"

"I would like to hear." Wolf remained standing, rifle across the crook of his arm.

Clarence nodded from where he sat on a stump. "Me too. We've traveled hundreds of miles to keep Victoria from harm, but it wasn't you who needed protection and you weren't with child. This is distressing."

"It shouldn't be." Miss Hattie reached out and patted Tall Grass's leg. "Your journey was successful." The Kiowa woman sitting curled up on a blanket gave her a weak smile.

Ashkii signed, but it was too fast for the others to understand. Miss Hattie waved a hand in the air. "All right. You too. Victoria, tell 'em what you know. I'm interested in hearing it myself. I don't know *all* the details of your trip."

She took a deep breath and gathered her words. "I kept having these dreams that were so real I'd wake up, thinking I'd been talking to Miss Hattie right there in my room."

"It wasn't me, hon."

"It seemed like it to me. You kept saying I needed to come here, and you'd make sure I traveled safely." She spoke to Wolf and Clarence. "I didn't know exactly when or who I'd meet on the way up. I didn't pick you three . . . two. You know that."

"When did you start this charade?" Buck pointed at the bundle.

"The day I left the Rio Grande. I had a dream the night before that if I traveled without this, I wouldn't get very far." She took a tiny sip of water from a cracked, wooden cup. "You see, I have this . . . this . . . thing about me that attracts men. It's been this way since I turned thirteen. Men of any age won't leave me alone, and I knew if I started out any other way, I'd have trouble every day.

"So one day before I left, as the dreams kept getting stronger and stronger, I saw this woman on the street who was expecting and thought that no man would want me if I looked like a baby was on the way. I experimented for over a week, trying this and that, until I made this belly. I'm sure it didn't fool women, but not one man saw through it."

Lane looked up to see Buck watching him, head tilted like a puppy looking at some oddity. "Yeah, I found out a few nights ago." He cleared his throat. "She told me."

For a moment, Buck's grin was once again light and alive, before it faded into the now-familiar tight line he'd been carrying.

Wolf merely blinked.

"But my dreams showed you as clear as day, Victoria." Clarence struggled to understand. "You were the one who needed protection. Hezekiah told me he had the same one about you, and Wolf here did too."

Miss Hattie absently reached out to rest her hand on Tall Grass's round stomach. She took the old woman's hand and moved it around for a moment before Miss Hattie's face brightened when she felt the baby kick.

"You three were drawn to Victoria for a reason. Y'all protected her, so she could protect Tall Grass, to be there at the right time. Y'all said she shot that Indian after Hez was killed. That man would have taken the lives of Tall Grass and her baby.

"I don't speak for the Lord, heaven knows there's plenty of preachers and others who do, and they're wrong most of the time. But y'all *had* to come together before you ran into Buck and Lane. It set the wheels in motion so your paths could cross at the right time, so now it was four guardians. Victoria, you were the one who bound them all together."

"You knew that happened?" No matter that Lane had seen a man arise from the dead, he was having trouble wrapping his head around the fact that dreams had been instrumental in creating their band.

"I did, hon. I felt it from the moment all y'all met. It was a good feeling because then I knew that Tall Grass was in the right place at the right time to join up together. Her husband would never have let her leave their village to come *here* so I could help with this baby. Not for nothing. But that little girl right there with the big eyes was the spark to help you leave."

River watched and listened, taking it all in. But she didn't say a mumbling word.

Tall Grass adjusted her position to get comfortable. "Santee never offered to give up a captive before. She was the first, and I wondered why. My own dreams showed two men looking for her." She turned her head to Lane. "It was you and Buck."

"That's right. This child drew you two in to meet with Victoria's protectors. When all y'all came together is when I knew Tall Grass would get here safe and sound. Hezekiah proved it when he gave his life today."

Buck watched the lengthening shadows. "So River was captured by Comanches as part of this great plan. I don't believe any of that for one minute."

"You don't have to believe, hon. You just have to accept what has happened because there's a reason for all things. And that includes you."

His eyes darkened. "Do you know what happened to me?"

Some of the lines smoothed in Miss Hattie's sad face. "I do."

"How?"

She threw a glance at Ashkii, who nodded. "Sometimes I see things when I'm awake too." She explained how her mind sometimes flew free to find a brief resting spot inside of others. "Sometimes that is good, but yesterday I was drawn to an evil man. One I knew before. And inside his mind, I saw what he'd done to you."

"Everything?"

"Yes. And yesterday whatever guides *me* put my mind in *you* for a spell. But in there, it's a gray deadness, not like a living thing. There's little more that I picked up, other than knowing you are a good man."

"The only time I've felt normal since all this happened was for a few seconds yesterday. You were that cool, green place I felt."

"It was me in this spot." Miss Hattie flicked her fingers at the spring not far away. "Which is to say, me and the Lord. He brought you here, just like the others."

"It's the water then, that can change me back."

Miss Hattie's eyes welled. "This isn't a magic spring, no matter what the Indians say. Oh, I reckon it has certain minerals it picked up from somewhere deep down in the earth, and they're liable to help someone who's feeling poorly, but with you, what's done is done. But again hear me, you have a purpose."

Buck looked over to see Lane and Victoria's fingers intertwined. He was having trouble putting it all together. "So Hezekiah is dead, and I'm this way for a baby that has yet to be born. Why?"

"Because it is a *special* child. This baby is our hope for the future. You will know for sure about your purpose when the time comes. I know *that* for a fact."

"Why were the rest of us chosen?" It was the first time for Wolf to speak.

"Because you're all good men."

"I am not." He exposed his canines. "I was born with these. This is where I get my name because I was made for one thing. I am a killer of men."

"Only when necessary. You aren't a murderer. That's something completely different."

Ashkii signed and Miss Hattie pulled a face, for they had been working on that particular commandment for weeks. "Even though that commandment says you should not kill. I believe it means you should not commit murder. There's a difference in protecting yourself or others."

"I wish Hezekiah was here." Clarence spoke up. "He could add some wisdom to this conversation."

"The wisdom is that you were all drawn together around Victoria because alone, you may have fought the urge to protect a Kiowa woman."

"I am white, part at least." Tall Grass pulled her black hair back.

"Kiowa by circumstance." Her brow furrowed and she held her large stomach.

"That's right, hon, but this is all an intricate plan to put you here and now." Miss Hattie was interrupted when Buck fell backward.

"Dammit." Lane stood. "We weren't watching the sun again. And neither was he. I wish he'd be more responsible about that."

His comment garnered no response because Tall Grass gasped and clutched her stomach. The contractions suddenly became deep, and sharp.

Miss Hattie's face broke into a wide grin at the sight of Buck sprawled on the ground and Tall Grass's pained look. "Y'all got here just in time."

Surprised, Lane studied her smile. "That don't bother you, him falling out like that?"

"Nothing bothers me about him, hon. Remember, I was in his mind yesterday. I expected this. Now, y'all can lay him over there in that wagon, out of the way."

Lane cast a fearful look at Buck, knowing he could hear them talk. "I don't believe he'd like that, ma'am. Not after what happened the last time."

FIFTY

DAWN WAS BUT A DIM glow on the horizon as the Comanche prepared themselves to take back what was rightfully theirs. Their horses stamped and snorted as the warriors applied fresh paint to their pony's necks, cheeks, and rumps.

They'd already put on their own war paint and sharpened their knives. Twisted Root was pleased that they had more guns than he'd ever seen in one war party. His good mood vanished when one of Quanah's men, Wild Horse, passed by only to pause beside the holy man.

"This will be an easy victory. I will take the old woman's scalp if you can't."

"She has great magic." Twisted Root made a sign near his head. "And those with her have proven themselves to be warriors. These men are not cowards with guns, and I told you what happened back on the creek."

"About the one you cursed."

Twisted Root scowled and refused to answer directly. "He takes arrows without feeling them. Water refuses to touch him. He is a demon that we must kill."

"You made him!"

"I *cursed* him all right, but I did not *intentionally* make a demon that fights and kills our people. I put something in him that should have made him stay on the ground, where he could see and hear, but not ever rise up to enjoy our world. A piece of my son was in there to hold him down, but I do not know what happened to make him rise and fight."

"He will not be able to do that after I cut the tendons in his legs." Wild Horse laughed. His bravado was forced, though. He'd been with Quanah at Adobe Walls and was eager to make up for that fiasco. He had no use for medicine men, and felt it was Isa-tai's fault they'd been driven away by the buffalo hunters, just like it was Twisted Root's fault that there was a demon they had to deal with.

Their raids were successful when there were no medicine men in the back, changing and casting spells. On the way to meet Twisted Root, he and two others had left the band against Isa-tai's warnings and advice to take scalps from two settlers who did not have the sense to avoid Comanche territory. To him, it proved that he didn't need a shaman's magic to kill whites.

"The warriors we brought will kill him for you. They are not frightened children who run when they see something they do not understand." Wild Horse needled Twisted Root who glared up at him. "They are not afraid of curses and spells, and that's why they will help me get my hands on the only magic I want, and that is the special child. It will be a great prize to take back to my woman."

"The child is mine!" Twisted Root rose and shouted, his face a mask of sudden fury. The others stopped preparing themselves to listen. "I don't care if you kill all the people there and take their scalps, but the baby is mine. I need to kill it myself. It is a danger to all our tribes."

Quanah and Iron Tip joined them. For once, Iron Tip agreed with Twisted Root. "He is right. We have agreed that he needs the child to make amends for his son."

Growing angry, Wild Horse slashed the air with the edge of his hand. "You can not tell me what to do. I will fight with you, but I follow Quanah!"

The half white, half Comanche leader finally spoke up. "Twisted Root is right. This is his raid." His voice rose so the others could hear. "Kill everything that moves, but do not touch the old gray-haired woman, or the child. We will decide what to do once all the men are dead."

Wild Horse walked off, grumbling to himself.

"Twisted Root." Quanah stepped close. "This will be the last time I ride with you. Our bands are brothers, but you bring a sickness that infects everyone."

FIFTY-ONE

TALL GRASS'S FOURTH BABY INTENDED to come quickly. Clarence and Lane were barely finished with laying Buck up against the soddy's outside wall and covering his still body with a blanket when a particularly bad contraction told her the time was near.

Victoria helped Tall Grass to her feet while Miss Hattie issued orders. "Victoria, you and River go inside with her, and you men, y'all can sleep outside tonight. That'll keep you out from underfoot. Ashkii, see to their horses, hon."

None of them had any inclination to go inside.

"I'll take first watch." Clarence took up his rifle and disappeared into the darkness. He preferred the shelter of the trees and walked a short way behind the sod house, out of earshot.

Lane and Wolf finished the stew that was left in the pot and spent the next couple of hours dragging logs from the nearby line of trees behind them to create a rudimentary waist-high barricade from which to shoot.

Studying their work, Lane didn't like the results one bit, but they were better than nothing.

By the time they finished their preparations, Tall Grass's cries of pain soon drove them away from the house. Wolf found a good spot to watch the starlit prairie near from where the spring water spread out into a wide, shallow flow before contracting into several independent fingers.

Responsible for Buck, Lane spread his blanket under a willow beside the spring to break up his outline. It was impossible to sleep, so he did the next best thing by closing his eyes and resting, thankful that he didn't have some strange entity inside him to argue with.

Six hours after the contractions started, Tall Grass grew silent. Worried, Lane approached the door and gave it a soft knock. Victoria opened the door a crack. Lit by pale yellow light, the only eye he could see crinkled in a smile. "Everything's fine. The baby's here. It's a girl. A special girl. She doesn't seem inclined to cry. She's just laying there in her mama's arms, looking around."

"Good." He shifted from foot to foot, unsure what to do or say. "Just wanted to make sure."

"I'm glad you did." She opened the door just wide enough to stick her head through and give him a kiss. "Go to sleep." She closed it, and he heard a heavy wooden bar drop into place, sealing the entrance.

He turned back to the darkness, wondering how he could do that with his head full of her musk.

Wolf's voice came from the shadows. "Now I understand what happened a few nights ago when she came to your tent."

Lane felt his face flush. "You knew about that?"

"We all did, but decided it was none of our business. We heard, though."

Ears burning from embarrassment, Lane struggled for the words. "I didn't think anyone could hear."

"She is a woman full of energy. Hezekiah wanted to read you some words from his book, but Clarence and I told him you were not interested in those kinds of words right then, though she kept calling for his God. Can you explain that?"

"No." That was enough for Lane. The cool evening air chilled him, so he threw a couple of sticks on the fire.

Wolf chinned at the darkness. "They will be able to see that for miles."

"They already know we are here."

"You're right. I doubt they will bother us tonight, anyway."

"What makes you say that?"

"Look out there. See all those eyes glowing in this light? Those are Buck's wolves, and my brothers. No one is going to come up on us in the darkness."

★ ★ ✬ ★ ★

BUCK STEPPED UP TO THE FIRE JUST after daylight, brushing dirt from his clothes. Lane joined him, not watching the dust fly, but minding something in the distance. "I hope you got a good rest last night."

"I done told you it ain't rest." Buck paused and narrowed his eyes, studying something in the distance.

Lane kept on, as if Buck was listening. "I'm glad I finally dozed off because we're gonna need it."

Lane finally noticed Buck wasn't looking at him as they talked. Following his gaze, he stiffened at the sight of a line of mounted warriors watching from a slight rise well out of range. "Looks like they've learned."

Wolf appeared and Clarence came from around the sod house, his Sharps resting over one shoulder with the muzzle skyward. "I don't believe our job is over."

"It is just beginning." Lane crossed his arms, considering the number of men. "They're gonna swarm us."

"What do you want to do?" Whenever Buck asked that kind of question, it meant he was out of ideas and that any action they took was questionable.

"Run like a scared jackrabbit."

"Besides that."

"We'll just have to fight the best way we can." Lane had already been thinking about defending themselves and the house. "Let's start outside here, where we can move around. Ashkii and Victoria can fight from inside the house. I saw shooting ports in there and they'll be protected. When we're pushed back, and that will happen soon judging by the number of people I see up there, then we can hole up and wait them out."

"There's water inside and plenty of food." Clarence adjusted one of his many pistols under his belt. This one was in the small of his back. "We brought enough ammunition. They can't burn down a sod house. We can hold them off until they get tired of dying and leave."

Wolf made a slashing motion with his hand. "I will not fight from inside."

"You may have to, if it comes down to it." Lane understood how the big man felt.

"No. Once we are inside, then we have lost. A man must be able to move because when he cannot, the wolves will close in. I have seen them nip, and bite, and cut a buffalo bull until he was exhausted and bled out, all because he couldn't move."

"They'll circle us all right." Buck took stock of the house. "They might get on the roof and try to dig us out like prairie dogs, but this is all we can do."

Wolf shook his head. "I will fight *my* way, as I see fit."

"I can't tell you what to do." Lane saw Wolf's brow furrowing and wanted to calm everyone down. "None of us answers to anyone here. We'll do what we can when the time comes."

Clarence straightened and moved the Sharps to the crook of his arm. "Here they come. Prepare to defend yourselves."

FIFTY-TWO

A DARK LINE OF CLOUDS FORMED to the northwest, promising a thunderstorm later that morning. It formed a magnificent background behind the warriors lit by the cool morning glow that highlighted every aspect of their bodies and horses.

It was a splendid sight for Twisted Root, watching the warriors as they sat astride their ponies formed up in a long line atop the slight rise overlooking the sod house below. Feathers in their hair and on lances, shields, and their bridles danced in the morning breeze. Many of the warriors from both tribes had unbraided their long black hair, letting it fly in the wind.

Several wore war bonnets made from buffalo skin with the horns still attached. Older, more experienced veterans of dozens of other battles sported headdresses made from golden eagle feathers and decorated with kestrel and red-tailed hawk plumage, quills, and beadwork that flowed over their shoulders and down the back. Some were long, others shorter, because each feather represented the death of an enemy in battle, or counting coup.

As befitting his position, Quanah sat astride his favorite pony in the middle of the line stretching more than two hundred yards. The young Comanche prophet kept them there, so the white men below could behold his war party's magnificence, and to scare the shit out of them.

Twisted Root and Isa-tai paced their ponies back and forth behind the warriors, singing war songs and asking the Great Spirit to look down on them with favor. Iron Tip and the Kiowa leader, Cold Nose, sat at opposite ends of the pageant.

Holding the men back was difficult and became even harder when a young man shouted a challenge to the defenders in the distance. Another answered, this time with a war whoop. Up and down the line, the others chimed in a ragged chorus as horses felt the energy in the cool air and stamped their feet.

One of the young horse handlers, Shouts His Name, rushed out, riding parallel to the line of men and shouting toward the house. Many laughed at his antics as his young voice cracked with the effort to make the white men at the soddy tremble in fear at the sound of his name.

Satisfied that he'd shown as much daring as the elders would let him, he turned his horse and loped back to Nine Toes who solemnly sat his horse, keeping one eye on the herd that was in a low spot and sheltered from the coming fight.

Still Quanah waited, a slight smile on his face. This was the way he'd described it to others when he and Isa-tai purified themselves and danced the Sun Dance, vowing to restore the Comanche nation to its former glory.

And here it was, a splendid alliance of various Comanche tribes, Kiowa, and Arapaho, who were more than eager to sweep over the men below before taking the war trail across Comancheria in bloody, lightning raids to drive the whites forever from their land.

Quanah's pony stamped its foot and danced forward. That was enough for a young warrior to make a false start, and another horse jerked forward before the rider pulled him back. Another false start raised the volume level even more. The air filled with whoops, shouts, and screams. A couple fired their rifles into the air and then one of the older veterans kicked his horse in the flanks and the undulating line dissolved as warriors spilled forward.

They charged across the prairie, raising a cloud of dust that paced ahead of them in the rising breeze and became thicker as they ran. Soon hidden by the man-made dust storm, they became invisible to Twisted Root. Confident Quanah would reserve the old woman and child for him, he walked his pony along the wide trail churned up only moments before.

His good mood evaporated at the sight of crows circling the house to land in the nearby trees. Stomach clenched in dread, he raised both arms to the sky, beseeching the Great Spirit to blow them away so his men could be victorious and deliver the newborn to him.

He had plans for that thing.

FIFTY-THREE

AT CLARENCE'S WARNING, LANE WATCHED the line of warriors melt and spill off the ridge. All of a sudden, the low breastworks they'd built in the night seemed as fragile as a lace curtain. "Y'all help me push this wagon over."

It was easy for the four of them to lift it and push. The dry-rotted wheels opposite from them collapsed with a crack and the wagon heeled over. It wasn't much, but it was something.

Lane shouted toward the soddy. "Victoria! Miss Hattie! They're coming! Get ready!"

Clarence moved a few paces over and knelt on one knee behind the stacked logs. Wolf disappeared like a puff of smoke around the side of the house while Buck and Lane grabbed their saddlebags full of ammunition and dropped them behind the wagon.

Buck levered a shell into the Henry's chamber and shoved another round in to fill the carrier tube. "This is the best idea you could come up with?"

"At the moment." He watched the charge. "Not much to work with here."

A cloud of dust rose behind the charge as battle cries and thundering hooves reached them. "They'll try to sweep over us this first charge." Buck sighted on a warrior wearing a long eagle bonnet. "Concentrate on the middle."

"Think that'll work?"

"Hell no, but it might break 'em up a little."

Once again, Clarence opened the ball with his Sharps before they got in range of the .44-caliber rifles. Taking a rest with his elbow on the log, he squeezed the set trigger, then gave the forward trigger a gentle pull. A second after the big rifle boomed, a warrior flipped off his horse. He opened the breech, pulled out the spent cartridge, and thumbed in another. Like a slow, well-oiled machine he picked off two more charging braves as they closed the distance to within range of the Henry rifles the Rangers used.

For once, Buck ignored his own advice and aimed for the riders racing straight for them. The first one slumped over his pony's neck before he fell. Not moving his elbow from the side of the wagon, the Ranger repeated the shot.

Nerves jangling and trembling, Lane matched Buck's expertise. They'd fought Indians before, and in close engagements, but had never faced such numbers. He wanted to run for the soddy and block the door behind him, but there was no way he was going to move if the others didn't.

A loose volley of rifle fire crackled from the charging men and lead whined overhead. Here and there, slugs slammed into the ground. More than one plucked splinters from Clarence's log. A round ricocheted off a hard surface to whine away through the trees and rifles opened up to their right. It was Wolf, lying in tall, green grass spreading out from the grove behind them.

Concentrating on the men directly in front of them, few of the attacking warriors saw the additional threat. Frightened riderless horses broke up the formation, veering right and left, cutting off many who were storming ahead. One mounted warrior running full out collided with a terrified horse and they both went down.

Chaos ruled as their rifle barrels grew hot. There was no way to stem the tide and the line folded into the middle like the wagon was a magnet. Every warrior there wanted to be the one to kill as many men as possible, to touch the living men and count coup.

Throwing all caution away, the arms of the attack closed in on the three who were taking a terrible toll on the Indians.

Lane's hat went flying after an arrow punched through, cutting a long groove in his scalp. Hot blood flowed down the side of his face and the back of his neck. A bullet plucked at his sleeve, and another his collar.

A long gash appeared on Buck's cheek, stretching along the side of his head, punching a hole through his ear. The arrow that caused the wound dropped to the ground behind him. Barely conscious of the sting, Buck killed another warrior as the wound closed up.

They were too close for the Sharps now. Clarence dropped it and plucked a Colt from the holster on his right hip at the same time the other hand pulled a revolver from inside his belt. He fired as fast as he could thumb the Colt's hammer, picking out one target after the other. When that pistol clicked empty, he dropped it, switched the other revolver to his right hand, and drew another from behind his belt.

Several warriors finally saw smoke from Wolf's rifle. They split off and charged his position, but he again did the unthinkable. Rising, he charged the horsemen, firing the pistol that appeared in his hand. Unnerved by the unfamiliar tactic, the horses fought their riders. One of the Comanche launched an arrow that narrowly missed. Wolf shot the nearest horse and when it reacted from the pain, leaped up to grab the startled brave by the neck. They went off the side and when Wolf rose, the man's neck spurted blood. Wolf spat out a mouthful of flesh and whirled to face the next threat.

The horses and men were yards away from the wagon when Clarence dropped two empty pistols to join the others at his feet. He plucked Hezekiah's shotgun from where it leaned nearby and cut down three men with two shots.

The cloud of dust churned up by the horses' hooves caught up with the fight and wrapped them all in a thick, gritty cloud. Lane couldn't see much beyond a few yards. When his Henry ran dry, he drew his pistol and went to work until it snapped on a spent shell. He snatched a Colt from the small of his back and went back to work.

A rifle opened up from the house, and Buck went down under the weight of two Kiowa who leaped from their horses and over the wagon.

Lane was in his own fight and couldn't help, but Buck's Bowie knife slashed over and over. As two rifles from the soddy belched smoke and fire, he rose, covered in blood and snatched up his Henry.

A voice rose from the melee and the charge fell apart. The mounted horde disappeared in the dust. Realizing the attack was over, Lane quickly thumbed fresh shells into his six-guns. Beside him, Buck did the same. Blood soaked Clarence's left side and an arrow protruded from the big trapezius muscle above his collarbone.

"Let me help you get that out." Wolf stepped out of the dust and smoke. There was so much blood on his bare upper body, it was impossible to tell who it belonged to.

Gritting his teeth, Clarence nodded. "Make it quick, please."

Most of the shaft had exited, so Wolf grabbed the longest part in back and snapped the arrowhead off. "Ready?"

Before Clarence could answer, he yanked it back through. Blood flowed from the bruised and puckered holes. Untying the scarf from around his neck, Clarence stuck one end into the entrance hole and draped the remainder over his shoulder. "Push that end in for me, please."

Wolf did as he asked and threw a look back toward where the war party had retreated to regroup. The dust was already settling. Putting one hand on Clarence's barricade, he vaulted over the top and walked to a wounded warrior who was trying to crawl away. He knelt and his knife came up bloody in one hand. A scalp dangled from the other. He raised it and gave his own blood-curdling whoop so they could see his trophy.

With a shriek of rage, one of the Comanche kicked his horse in the flanks and charged. A boom came from behind Wolf as Clarence blew him off the pony with his Sharps. "That's for the arrow!"

The soddy's door cracked open and Lane spun. "Shut the door and stay inside!"

"Are you all right?" It was Victoria's voice, shaky but full of life.

Buck snorted. "Why do people keep asking that when folks are shooting at each other?"

Lane found himself grinning, despite the sharp pain in his skull and a new one he hadn't felt up until then. "We're as well as can be expected. Get back inside."

Raising his left arm, he saw a neat hole in his shirt sleeve. Feeling with his finger, he found a hole through the meat of his arm.

Seeing Buck's eyebrows raised in question, he answered. "Went plumb through. Missed the bone."

"Tie it off with this." Buck handed him the scarf he'd borrowed from Lane on that first morning after he was killed.

The metallic sounds of men reloading firearms filled the air. Ashkii came outside with the leaky bucket full of water, going from one to the next, allowing them to drink from the gourd dipper while they could.

Lane slapped the young Navajo on the arm. "Thanks for the water. That tasted damn good. Was that you and Victoria shooting from inside?"

He nodded and signed yes.

"Good shooting. Both of you."

Ashkii's eyes widened, looking past Lane who immediately knew what that meant. "Get back inside."

The door closed as the warriors charged again. Hooves thundered from behind the soddy. Clarence grabbed his rifle. "They coming from everywhere this time."

Lane watched him run around the side, knowing he intended to use a corner of the house for cover. When he turned back around, Buck was writhing and gurgling on the ground. "Oh, hell!"

The Ranger's distended throat bulged and once again his jaw widened, appearing to unhinge. Despite what he'd been through, a numbing fresh horror swept through Lane. His head spun at the sight of Buck's snake entering the world through his mouth with a gush of black blood.

And then the damned thing looked at him with its one human eye.

FIFTY-FOUR

TWISTED ROOT WALKED HIS HORSE through the strip of trees behind the earthen one-room building that housed the old witch woman. Accompanied by Two Shoot, the shaman sang softly to himself as warriors gathered for a second assault. It was cool there in the shade and would have been peaceful if not for the gunfire and wounded horses that screamed their lives away from several directions.

He'd passed Quanah and Isa-tai who flung their arms about, arguing in a red rage. The massacre of the white men hadn't happened, and Isa-tai's medicine still wasn't working. Quanah's face was contorted in rage when he shouted. "We lost too many men! Your medicine didn't turn bullets here *either*. Just like those hide men's camp!"

"The bullet that struck me was weak. It didn't kill me, so what you say is wrong, but here it might be that old woman is stronger than I thought. We should go back and smoke and pray."

"No! You do what you said!"

More than a dozen men surrounded them, waiting for the outcome of their disagreement. Twisted Root surprised them by suddenly walking his horse away. Despite the falling-out, the warriors out for blood charged once again.

FIFTY-FIVE

A LINE OF CLOUDS WAS ALMOST on them, towering high above and threatening to blot the morning sun's rays. Lane couldn't believe how little time had passed since the first shafts of light washed over the prairie.

Any other time, he would have watched the clouds build in anticipation of a storm, especially if he had a nice, dry house to turn the water once it began to fall. There was no time to enjoy nature's beauty, though, because a man-made fury was upon them.

Mounted warriors closed in from all sides as Buck lay writhing on the ground. There was nothing Lane could do for him, and hell was about to descend once again on their position, so he left his partner to fight his own battle and faced the next assault.

Crouching beside the overturned wagon, he pumped round after round into the charging band as fast as he could jack the lever and find a target down the length of the barrel. Too soon they were upon him, and he resorted once again to his revolver.

Warriors came in from behind them. Clarence managed only two shots from the Sharps before they were swarmed. He switched back to the short twelve-gauge and laid down a wall of buckshot pellets. The devastating weapon took time to reload and like Lane, he produced reloaded pistols from his holster, belt, and pockets.

Leaping off their ponies, the attackers dashed forward and the fight went hand to hand. They were so close none of the warriors could use a firearm or bow. Knives, war clubs, war axes, and lances came into play.

The defenders resorted to razor-edged belt weapons as dust and smoke once again enveloped them all.

A stone club glanced off Clarence's skull, staggering him. His hands reached back and the long, curved sword hissed through the air laying flesh open to tendons, entrails, and bone. Blood sprayed, and a red mist surrounded them. Rifles spoke from the slots in the sod walls behind them. Backing toward the house, Clarence grunted with the pain of a knife thrust. He slashed at a warrior who'd thrust a cold blade deep into his side.

"We have to get inside!" Lane blocked a knife thrust with the useless rifle. He jammed the revolver into the man's side and pulled the trigger. "Where's Wolf!"

"Can't see through the dust. Come on!"

Lane reversed the Henry, swinging it by the barrel like a club. A thought flashed through his head. *This is how I heard Crockett died at the Alamo, swinging an empty rifle.*

A bullet cracked past Lane's ear as he and Clarence headed for the door. A figure rose from the ground, crawling on his hands and knees. He almost shot Buck before he realized who it was. Pistol in hand, dark-eyed, weak, and haggard, Buck had two arrows in him.

The shaft of an arrow appeared in Clarence's side as if by magic, and he grunted from the impact.

Lane ducked his shoulder and threw his partner on his shoulder. Staggering from the weight, he charged toward the house and safety. "Open up!"

Buck straightened his back and fired twice as Lane lunged for the door that cracked wide enough for a rifle barrel to protrude. Fire belched from the muzzle and the blast seared Lane's ear. The boys fell inside as a second rifle fired overhead. Warriors poured toward them. Clarence slid to a stop beside the entrance and pitched his sword inside. He whirled, drawing a pistol with each hand and twelve shots echoed off the hard ground, sounding like a Gatling gun.

Having gained enough time to get inside, he spun and took two steps toward safety when the familiar boom of a twelve-gauge split the air. Clarence staggered sideways from the charge of buckshot, teeth clenched with pain. Still not down, his hand dipped into a pocket, but the pistol never appeared.

A second barrel of buckshot took him full in the chest. He fell as a Comanche warrior stepped around the soddy's corner and into view, holding an empty shotgun in his left hand and a butcher knife in the right. Victoria stuck her rifle through the open door and shot the man full in the chest, and he fell across Clarence's body.

The door slammed and the bar fell into place. They were safe, for the moment.

FIFTY-SIX

WOLF LAY ON TOP OF the sod house, where he'd picked off one brave after another with his rifle after being forced to retreat from the advancing Comanche. Concentrating on the men fighting at ground level and rendered almost invisible by the cloud of dust and smoke, he'd killed several attackers before his friends fought their way into the house.

He had no intention of locking himself inside of a box, preferring to die in the open. He also had another reason for being up there. Once the survivors barricaded themselves inside, the first thing someone would do was climb up and dig their way through the roof.

The shrill cry of an infant came up through the chimney.

Blood flowed from two wounds, adding to the spreading pool beneath him. As long as his heart still beat, Wolf had no intention of letting them get to that baby down below.

He'd been called by the Great Spirit to protect it, and he intended to honor that call.

FIFTY-SEVEN

STUNNED THAT TWO SHOOT WAS dead, Twisted Root stood beside his still body. All warriors expected death, even spread their arms to honor and welcome it, but they'd been together since childhood. He always expected Two Shoot to be there, and now he was dead at the hands of the woman he'd seen in his visions.

No one approached him to take the scalp, assuming the black man was Twisted Root's kill. Warriors drug Two Shoot away from the house, and the others fell back. The shaman reached into a pouch and withdrew a handful of ground material which he blew toward the door.

A blast from one of the rifle ports made him jump. A Kiowa fell. Ducking under the port, he strode across the yard littered with bodies and empty shell casings. The rifle fired again, but he ignored it.

"Come with me and I will bless you all! Then we will come back and kill those within!"

The storm was finally upon them, and the warriors faded back as a bolt of lightning fractured the clouds overhead. Thunder crashed half a second later. Almost immediately, another jagged bolt lanced down and struck a nearby tree that momentarily burned like a candle until a deluge of rain put it out.

The rain washed the sky clean of gun smoke and dust. Twisted Root turned his face into the rain, feeling that it was a refreshing sign that they were on the verge of killing all of those inside.

FIFTY-EIGHT

DARK AS SIN INSIDE, LANE'S eyes hadn't yet adjusted to the single oil lamp burning on a small table in the middle of the sod house. The hot, humid air was thick with fear, tension, cries, and acrid gun smoke. Lane stumbled over Buck's prone body and thumbed shells from his belt loops into the Colt.

Despite Tall Grass's attempts to calm River's hysterical sobs, another fresh wave rose to match the fresh baby's shrill cries. The occasional shot from outside was muffled by the thick walls, and the shouts of the war party weren't nearly as shrill as what came from the baby.

The interior was full of moving bodies, the copper odor of blood, and the metallic sounds of people reloading firearms. Lane's pupils dilated, and he made out Ashkii standing between two shooting ports and holding a rifle.

"Victoria!"

"Right here." Her voice came from his left, opposite Ashkii, and he made out her shape backlit by the dim light streaming in. One hand over her mouth, she was weeping and Lane figured she saw what happened to Clarence.

"Stay out from in front of the holes, unless you're shooting. They can stick a barrel through them and shoot just as well as you can from the inside."

In the rear, a much larger table was overturned in front of the stone fireplace. Tall Grass huddled behind it with her baby. River pressed as close as humanly possible. Miss Hattie shuffled back and forth, passing out more ammunition.

Now that his eyes had adjusted to the dim light, Lane evaluated their position. Whoever built the sod house knew more about construction than most. The walls twice as thick as any he'd ever seen told him it would be difficult for the Comanche to break through. Strong beams overhead looked as if they could hold up a herd of buffalo. Smaller timbers running the opposite direction held up more than three feet of sod and grass.

"This place looks solid enough."

Miss Hattie finished passing out ammunition and knelt beside Buck. "It is. That's why it was still standing when I got here."

"They'll get in before long."

"They won't." She leaned Clarence's sword against the wall and dropped to her knees beside Buck who'd pulled himself against the wall and out of the way. "Hon, can you hear me?"

"Yes, ma'am."

Lane's head snapped around at the sound of Buck's weak, sluggish voice. "It's dark and the sun's behind those clouds. How can you be awake?"

"I can't say." Buck moved as if his limbs were weighted down. "It's as much a mystery to me as it is to you."

"Y'all hush." Miss Hattie examined Buck. "We can worry about that later. Lane, pull these arrows out of him and help me sit him up."

Keeping watch on the ports, Lane did as he was told. The first arrow came out easily, as if it was stuck in soft mud. The second was anchored in Buck's hip bone. Bracing his feet, Lane wrapped both hands around the shaft and tugged. It came free with a pop, and he dropped it on the ground.

Buck grunted and held up a hand. "Y'all don't need to lift me up, Miss Hattie." His voice sounded stronger. Digging his heels into the packed dirt floor, he elbowed and shoved himself up against the wall. "Just give me a minute and I'll have my strength back. This is the same way I feel every time somebody buries me, so I know I'll get over it."

River's sobs settled down to steady hiccupping, but the baby's tiny cries seemed to increase.

Ashkii was peeking through his port when he heard Buck's statement. He jerked upright, staring. One hand flashed signs that Miss Hattie ignored. "Ashkii, hon. I can't answer questions right now. You get back to looking and I'll explain it all later. Hand me that bucket of water."

"Buck."

"What, Lane?"

"I saw that thing come out of you."

"You're lucky. I had to *feel* it happen."

"Maybe that's why you're awake right now."

"Yeah. I'm surprised about that too."

"Where'd it go? The snake?"

"I have no clue, but I'm glad it's gone. I feel different now."

"That's 'cause there's no more evil inside you." Miss Hattie offered a dipper of water. "Drink this."

"Water won't let me touch it. Can't drink it neither."

"'Cause it's pure, I reckon." She handed it to Lane instead.

"So that means the spell's not all gone."

"I don't know what it means, hon." She took the dipper back from Lane and grunted herself erect. She took it over to Victoria, who was watching through the loophole.

"Lane, I see men moving out there again."

"Still raining?"

"Yes. Hard."

"Works in our favor for now." He crouched to peer outside. "Clarence is dead, and I don't know where Wolf is."

A soft voice came down the chimney. "I am here."

Lane rushed to the fireplace and knelt to peer upward. Raindrops fell into the ashes. The coals were banked against the back, providing very little heat. "Wolf. Glad to hear your voice."

"They are coming back."

"Get down from there."

"I told you I was not coming inside."

"They'll kill you this time."

"I am already dead. I have a mortal wound."

"Come inside. We can patch you up."

"No. I will have barely enough strength to kill only one or two more, so I will stay here and save it." There was a pause, and his voice came back. "Give this to Buck. Tell him to wear it when the time comes."

"What is it? What time is coming?" An object dropped from above and Lane plucked a necklace from the ashes.

"My father gave me that when I became a man. That is made from the teeth of many wolves. It will protect him."

Lane shot a disgusted look into the dark chimney. "He's *already* dead."

"Listen to my words. You have to take the battle to them. Do not try and defend this place. My spirit is growing light and trying to float away. I now understand the need for Buck's darkness. I am glad I did not separate his body like I wanted to at first. Miss Hattie will tell him what he needs to know."

Lane took off his hat and ran fingers through hair wet with sweat. "I don't understand any of this."

"You will . . . prepare yourselves. They are coming to take that baby, and this time I do not think they will stop."

"Wolf." Finally upright, Buck took the necklace from Lane's hand and tied it around his neck without question. He leaned down to speak into the fireplace. "What do you see with your Dark Eye."

"What you are about to do, and it is good. That is why the Great Spirit told me to spare you." He chuckled, his laugh sounding wet. "I saw the snake come out of your mouth. I did not have time to kill it, and that is a regret, but I wish it had come out your butthole instead. That would have been a fine thing to watch."

A shrill war whoop came to them, followed by dozens more. A rattle of gunfire sent bullets into the sod wall like hail. One slug snapped through a loophole beside Victoria and buried itself in the opposite wall.

Shouldering her rifle, she fired, jacked the lever, and fired again. Ashkii picked up the same tune.

Lane shouted and rushed toward her. "Victoria! Get back!" A lance thrust inside, just missing her. Lane grabbed it and stuck the barrel of his pistol around the shaft and fired twice. The tension on the other end went away, and he pulled the seven-foot lance inside.

In an instant, the room was filled with flame from muzzle blasts as the Comanche shoved weapons through every port and fired at the same time. Ashkii fell backward, dropping his rifle.

Victoria screamed and clutched her shoulder. Another bullet spun her around and she went to the floor. A terrible pounding thudded against their chests as warriors drove something big and heavy against the door that immediately cracked. Only the thick cottonwood bar held it closed.

One whole side of the sod house shuddered as they tried to force their way through.

Return fire from Lane and Buck's pistols drove some of the guns away from the ports. An arrow came in and flew across the room. Those outside continued to pound the door with deafening thuds.

Buck's pistol ran dry. He dropped it into the holster and pulled Ashkii away from the center of the room. "He's still alive."

Jerking Victoria from the floor with one hand, Lane saw a shape outside the loophole. His pistol barked, and the shadow dropped. "Get back there with Tall Grass!"

The door vibrated with another massive thud.

Dried mud fell from the wall as the pounding there increased as well. Despite its thickness, it was only a matter of time before the wall collapsed from the onslaught.

FIFTY-NINE

RAIN POURED FROM THE SKIES as half a dozen warriors manhandled the huge trunk of a tree in the rainstorm, battering at the door. Others crowded around, determined to keep the defenders from firing on them through the nearest ports on the front side. Around the corner, men used their knives and lances to dig at the soddy.

Quanah waited patiently, sitting on his pony fifty yards away where he could see the door. "Isa-tai, we are losing too many of our warriors. If we do not get in this time, I am leaving."

"They will get inside."

A warrior fell back from one wall, blood spurting from a hole in his head.

SIXTY

SITTING CROSS-LEGGED IN THE RAIN, Twisted Root leaned against the overturned wagon near the pitiful pile of logs stacked by the white men. He watched the warriors batter the door with a broken cottonwood trunk.

At the same time others were using a smaller log against the sod wall on one side.

It wouldn't be long now. Once inside, the interior would become a slaughterhouse. He couldn't wait to get his hands on that old woman and the baby.

His mouth watered, and he wiped away the spit with the back of a hand.

One side of his face creased in a smile at the thought of what he would do to both of them. A slight sound and movement from the breastworks broke his concentration. Thinking it was one of his men, he turned the smile in that direction.

Cold terror ran up the shaman's back. It wasn't a brave at all, but an enormous, coiled prairie rattler the size of a man's bicep. The black-eyed reptile was bigger than any he'd ever seen.

Then the unthinkable happened.

The thing's misshapen head turned toward him, and a cold wash of terror paralyzed Twisted Root's body. His heart almost exploded from horror as the serpent's features somehow melded with the mutated face of his son, Blue Bird.

Only two feet away, the monstrosity continued to rise until it was eye level with the stricken medicine man. The serpent's hideous mouth actually had a *chin.* A forked tongue flicked out, tasting the fear flowing from the shaman.

Paralyzed, he saw the creature's tongue retreat. Its mouth widened with a hiss and a set of curved fangs lowered from the roof of Blue Bird's mouth.

Twisted Root's mind couldn't comprehend what he was seeing. He'd never been so terrified in his life. The impossible reptile sent a gust of fetid breath into the medicine man's open mouth and the snake's voice filled his mind.

Father.

Twisted Root gaped as a single drop of venom formed at the end of each fang.

Do you not recognize me?

Not a sound came from the medicine man's mouth, but somehow he answered the snake. "No."

Yes, you do. You know exactly who I am. Say it!

You are of the dead Ranger and my dead son.

No! I am your son, and far from dead. This is what you did to me.

I did not intend for this to happen.

But it did. I am reborn of your magic and the rotting insides of a white man's corpse. What was it that you intended to do, if not make me like this?

He killed you. I wanted for your soul to punish his spirit for eternity.

You wanted. You dared to speak for the Great Spirit, and in doing so, cursed me for eternity.

That was not the intent of my magic. I do not understand what went wrong!

I do. There was one of your hairs wrapped around that piece of my heart that you placed in his throat. That is why there is such poison in both of us. A piece of your rotten spirit became part of us.

I'm sorry.

That is not enough.

The enormous snake struck, sinking its fangs deep into the undamaged side of Twisted Root's face.

SIXTY-ONE

INSIDE THE SOD HOUSE UNDER assault, Miss Hattie knew she had only seconds to act. She stepped in front of Buck and put both hands on his arms. "Hon, now is the time."

"For what?"

"For your purpose." Another heavy thud came from the door, but she ignored it. "That's why you're awake. It's why you're here, and why you're the way you are. Those boys, Clarence and Hezekiah, they knew their roles and did them well. They've met their glory, and I fear Wolf will very soon."

He looked down on her, understanding dawning in his eyes.

"Yes. Think about everything that has happened since you . . . became what you are. There are reasons for all things and now it is time to fulfill your purpose, and that is to save that baby over there. The rest of us don't matter. We'll go to Glory on our own and I'll go a-shoutin' hallelujah, but little White Buffalo Calf has to survive. She has to!"

"White Buffalo Calf?"

"Yes. Tall Grass, show him your daughter."

Uncomprehending, he watched the Kiowa woman rise from behind the table, with River holding on to the tail of her dress. Tall Grass peeled back a scrap of blanket and held the crying baby out for him to see.

A tiny albino child opened her light blue eyes for a moment, then twisted her face back up to cry some more.

Miss Hattie gripped his arm. "You know how Indians feel about a white buffalo?"

"They're a sign of hope and coming good times."

"That's right, they are the most sacred thing on this earth, and this child is the new hope for all of us. She is going to unite us all sometime in the new future. She will put an end to all this killing, and that's why that evil medicine man wants her. If he gets her, he will destroy this purity and turn it to the dark side. You cannot let that happen. This is simply a battle for good and evil, and you have the power to end it right here."

She reached over to the table and handed him a dark object. He took it without comprehension. "You have Wolf's necklace. Here's Hezekiah's Bible, and Clarence's sword is leaning against the wall right there. Take them now and save this baby, and the rest of us."

SIXTY-TWO

QUANAH FINALLY NOTICED TWISTED ROOT sitting between the wagon and logs piled up nearby. Of all the things he expected to see that day, it was not the medicine man and an enormous prairie rattler staring eye to eye at each other from only two feet away.

It was the largest rattler he'd ever seen. Easily ten feet long and as big around as a man's upper arm, the monster was poised to strike. He watched the rain-soaked shaman's terrified face.

What was a rattlesnake doing out in cold rain? It didn't make any sense.

It seemed that a strange bubble surrounded them that prevented the others from seeing the adversaries who stared at each other so long they could have been made of stone.

Maybe I should go kill it.

That thought disappeared when a bullet from the house snapped past him. At that same moment, the makeshift battering ram punched through the door and the warriors dropped it with shouts of victory and pushed forward.

But the sod house's door exploded *outward*—

—and a dark man wearing a black hat emerged with a pistol in one hand and a sword in the other and—

—a shape fell from the roof and on top of those who were fighting to get inside—

—when the snake struck as fast as one of the lightning bolts ripping the sky apart overhead.

Twisted Root recoiled with a scream that was drowned by the boom of thunder he felt to his very core.

Unable to believe his eyes, Quanah found he was unable to function. It felt as if something soft wrapped itself around him, preventing the Comanche chief from moving, or even comprehending what was happening.

It was too much. His head spun.

A huge Cheyenne warrior had a man's throat in his jaws while he held another to the ground and repeatedly stabbed him with a knife so fast his hand was a blur.

As Quanah struggled to comprehend what he was seeing, shouts of triumph changed to cries of fear. Prairie wolves shot through the rain, coming from all directions. They flashed toward the stunned warriors, pulling them down by arms and legs, or knocking them off their mounts.

The wraith in a black hat slashed with his sword and pushed through the clot of fighting men as arrows and bullets impacted his body from all directions. Walking with slow determination, he ignored those around him and went straight for Twisted Root, who clutched the snake whose fangs were still buried in his cheek.

Ten strides. More arrows buried themselves in the man's body, legs, and neck. Bullets plucked at his clothing, and a lance staggered him. Still he came on, ignoring wounds that should have been fatal. Behind him, the Cheyenne went down under a writhing mass of warriors. From inside the sod house, a steady torrent of gunfire mowed others down before they could get inside.

Between Quanah and the house, the remaining warriors fled, screaming in terror. Around them, wolves tore at those on the ground.

Twenty strides and the wraith reached Twisted Root. A Comanche charged, and he emptied the pistol into the man's body. As the warrior fell, the dark wraith swung the sword. The blade hissed through the air and cut through the shaman's neck with the sound of an ax in wet, rotten wood.

The razor-edge continued on through the snake that was still pumping poison into the medicine man's cheek that swelled black and glossy, severing the abomination gripped in his hands. The remainder of the snake's body fell away, twisting and writhing in death. Twisted Root's torso toppled over with a wet thud.

The wraith in the black hat that should have succumbed to his wounds turned from the bodies and saw Quanah. His mouth widened in a smile and he yanked a lance from his side, then charged the mounted warrior as fleet as a deer. Strangely enough, it wasn't any of those apparitions that finally launched Quanah into action, but rather, the fact that the falling rain refused to touch the black-eyed being.

A woman's shriek of terror erupted from the young chief's chest, and he shouted for his men to flee. Wheeling his pony, he dug both heels into its flanks. Muscles bunched and the war-horse dug in with his hooves and bolted, running at breakneck speed.

And the skies darkened even more as the bottom of the black clouds fell out and the rain descended in a torrent, washing gallons of blood into the earth.

SIXTY-THREE

NINE TOES AND SHOUTS HIS Name followed the stunned Comanche war party that rode slowly toward the southwest. To prove they weren't afraid, the warriors led by Quanah and Isa-Tai walked their horses away from Boiling Springs and the frightening shell of what once was a man.

The band was silent.

Bringing up the rear, Nine Toes and Shouts His Name kept the horses together without talking. Even after he'd proven his fearlessness, Shouts His Name was slumped, head down as if suffering from a grievous wound.

Nine Toes watched Quanah riding ramrod straight, and he considered the Comanche leader's demeanor. The young man knew Quanah wouldn't give up because their war chief had too much faith in his people. Nine Toes closed his eyes, visualizing what their lives would be like in the next few years as more and more of their warriors died in battle.

In his self-imposed darkness, the pungent odor of crushed grass that rose from under the horses' hooves acted as an intoxicant, further adding to Nine Toe's visions.

The youngster drifted away, back to the safety of his mother's lodge and the words of wisdom from his father who'd died only months earlier. Nerves that had been vibrating as taut as a bowstring relaxed. Exhausted and drained of energy, he dozed.

He was jolted awake when his horse stopped to graze. The boy opened his eyes to see he was alone on the prairie, unaware of how long he'd been asleep. Fear leaped into his chest, and he glanced around to see the war party's beaten-down trail leading over a low rise. He almost kicked the pony into a lope, then stopped. It would be easy to follow and catch up to the band, but he hesitated.

With the wind in his face, and long hair brushing his shoulders, he stared upward at the blue sky. It would be blue again tomorrow, even if he were dead. It would be blue if the Comanche continued to fight, and it would be blue if they surrendered and allowed white men to take their land.

Quail called. A meadowlark added his own tune.

At peace for the first time in weeks, he considered the path of warfare. Though the Comanche were a warring tribe and had spread terror for hundreds of miles in all directions, it was obvious they were outnumbered by the white men and that would never change. White men were like ants from a disturbed hill, swarming and stinging and no matter how brave or strong a warrior might be, they would eventually overwhelm him, and he would retreat.

It was the way of his world now. Nine Toes turned his pony toward the south and considered what lay in that direction. His people would never be strong again. If they continued to fight, they would be wiped from the face of the earth, and him along with the rest.

SIXTY-FOUR

THE SUN ROSE ON A cool, calm morning. Lane stood in front of the sod house two days after the attack. The ground was free of any reminders of that day. He glanced over to a copse of trees and three fresh graves.

It took an entire day to haul the Comanche bodies to a wash half a mile away. They disappeared after dark that night, and he figured the defeated warriors must have slipped in to honor their dead. Black wings circled the prairie some distance away over the bodies of more than two dozen horses.

Ashkii and Tall Grass were sitting outside, soaking up the warm sunshine. White Buffalo Calf was asleep in her thick arms. A bandage around Ashkii's head covered the deep scalp wound that was already healing. Other than a headache, he signed he was fine.

Their saddled mounts snorted and shifted, sensing their trip.

Lane tilted his hat back. "How long are y'all gonna stay here?"

Tall Grass shrugged. "Miss Hattie will know. This is a safe place for us. It may be months, or years."

"What about the rest of your family?"

"They will come soon. Santee will want to see me."

"Does he know about the baby?"

"No. He did not know I was expecting. It will be difficult for him, until I explain her importance and then he will be proud. He will understand how important his daughter is to our people, and others."

Ashkii signed. Lane frowned. "I don't . . ."

Miss Hattie and Victoria came outside with River in tow. Miss Hattie saw Ashkii's question. "He says he'll take care of us until then, and once Santee's faithful Kiowas show up, they'll take over."

"I'm sure he will." Lane laughed, not taking his eyes off the beautiful woman who had captured his heart.

Victoria pulled the little girl up close to her leg. "We're ready."

Lane knelt. "You want to ride with me, or Victoria?"

River pulled a strand of freshly washed hair behind one ear and pointed. "With her. Will my daddy be waiting for us?"

"I'm sure he is. We'll send them word when we get to a telegraph office."

"Are those Comanches going to bother us anymore?"

"Not now, honey. We have a talisman, and they'll remember tangling with us for the rest of their lives. Now, give Miss Hattie a hug."

The old woman's face creased and fractured with a wide smile. She pulled the little girl close. "You be a good gal, hon."

"I want to come back to see you."

"That'll be just fine."

The horses pricked their ears forward. Lane looked up to see Buck walk around the sod house. The ragged shirt and pants he wore were a patchwork of repairs, but at least he was decently covered until they could get some new clothes.

Eyebrows went up all around at the sight of Buck's clean face and hands. Lane leaned forward and sniffed. "You've *washed*."

"I am. I went down to the spring for a quick look around and spooked a covey of quail that was getting a drink. They went all directions, and one of those crazy fools flew straight over my head. I felt a drop of water hit my hand." He held up the hand, as if the drop was still there. "It didn't miss me. I stuck a finger down there and it got wet, so I had a bath."

Lane choked down his enthusiasm until he heard more. "So the curse is over?"

"I don't know. Maybe. It could be because that damned medicine man's corpse is burned up along with his snake spawn."

"No, hon. It guess it really is a magic spring," Miss Hattie cackled. "That's why I'm here, and still kickin'."

"Must be." Lane let his gaze slip up to Buck's hat. "How's your scalp?"

"Still gone. Nothing else's changed."

Lane nodded, remembering that after the battle, Buck returned for what seemed normal for him. The sun came out that afternoon as they cleared the bodies away, but when it went down that night, Buck dropped as limp as one of the corpses they'd handled. He awoke the next morning and they were back to where they were to start with.

"Well then." Lane cocked his head, studying his friend.

"So don't you be sniffing at me anymore."

"Not for a while, until you get ripe or dusty enough to grow corn. It's gonna be a challenge if we have to come all the way up here to scrub you down from time to time."

"That'll be a long way for a bath."

"Ain't that the truth."

Tall Grass hugged them both, interrupting their exchange. "I can't thank you enough."

Lane flicked a finger toward the cottonwoods. "Just make sure that baby turns out right, to honor those three good men sleeping over there."

Eyes filled with tears, she nodded and stepped away as Miss Hattie hugged them both. Lane lifted River up in front of Victoria. She touched his hand, and he got swimmy-headed from the contact. Her scent washed over him again, and he had to concentrate on tightening his saddle before he embarrassed himself.

Miss Hattie held on to Buck a little longer. "Be patient." She reached up to touch Wolf's tooth necklace around his neck. "I don't believe you're done yet."

"You think there's more, then."

"A lot more, hon." Her old eyes crinkled again. "You got your Bible that Hezekiah carried?"

"Yes, ma'am." He slipped the wolf tooth necklace under his shirt. "Everything else too."

"Good. Then come back and see me."

"Yes, ma'am." Buck swung up into the saddle, one leg over his Henry rifle in the scabbard, and the other over Clarence's sword strapped to the left side.

Lane watched him and grinned. "You know you're still dead, right?"

"Yeah, who can forget with you reminding me every other day." Buck laced the reins through his fingers. "But I don't feel empty like before, not like I did when that snake was in me."

"That don't make no sense. Empty when the snake was *in* you."

"It does to me."

"Don't forget you owe me a new shirt and pants. We look like scarecrows. These I'm wearing are about worn out too."

"All right, but we still need to be careful when we get around people. You go buy 'em and I'll take care of the rest."

Miss Hattie cackled. "You two are like an old married couple. Y'all get out of here so me and Ashkii can get back to fixin' this place back up."

"Let's get this little gal home." Buck led, headed southward without looking back.

Lane and Victoria followed, riding side by side as a murder of crows flew from the trees and disappeared behind the house. Seconds later, a pack of wolves loped around the soddy and spread out behind the Rangers who never noticed.

Miss Hattie watched until they were near the horizon. "They'll be back for sure one of these days. Buck might be dead, but they still have a lot of Rangering to do. It's their destiny."

Ashkii signed. "We'll see them again, dead or alive."

Miss Hattie concentrated on the little band of travelers and soon saw those long, mysterious strands emerge from the tops of their heads and spread into small clouds. The colors were all healthy and clean, and she smiled when those belonging to Lane and Victoria met and intertwined.

Movement at the edge of her vision caught her attention. She turned to see a tiny figure on horseback approaching the soddy. Even from a distance, she could tell he was Indian, and likely a Comanche. The thin line of a cloud attached to the rider continually changed colors as he rode closer, each bright and pure in their own turn.

She turned to tell Ashkii when she saw White Buffalo Calf in her mother's arms. The cloud above the baby's head was also full of swirling colors that told her all would be well . . . eventually.

THE END

ABOUT THE AUTHOR

NEW YORK TIMES BESTSELLING AUTHOR and multiple Spur Award winner Reavis Z. Wortham retired in 2011 and now works harder than before as the author of several series. He is also the recipient of six Will Rogers Medallion Awards, most recently taking the Gold for The Texas Job, a historical novel set in the 1930s East Texas oilfields.

Kirkus Reviews listed his first novel, The Rock Hole, as one of their Top 12 Mysteries of 2011, and compared it to To Kill a Mockingbird. TrueWest Magazine included Dark Places as one of 2015's Top 12 Modern Westerns. The Providence Journal writes, "This year's Unraveled is a hidden gem of a book that reads like Craig Johnson's Longmire on steroids."

When he isn't writing, he travels as a guest speaker for numerous organizations and clubs, and teaches writing in a variety of venues.

The author of 20 novels released in the last fourteen years, Wortham's new upcoming series, starting with Comancheria in the fall of 2025, is a new venture into the world of weird westerns. The Sound of a Dead Man's Voice and What We Owe the Dead are scheduled to follow soon after.